CAUGHT IN CROSS SEAS

Sharleen Scott

Out West Press
Yakima, Washington

Sharleen Scott/Out West Press
PO Box 185
Naches, Wa/98908
www.sharleenscott.com

Publisher's Note: This is a work of fiction. Names, characters, places, and incidents are a product of the author's imagination. Locales and public names are sometimes used for atmospheric purposes. Any resemblance to actual people, living or dead, or to businesses, companies, events, institutions, or locales is completely coincidental.

Cover design by Cheryl Sosebee @ CCR Book Cover Design
Editing by Dori Harrell – doriharrell@gmail.com

Caught in Cross Seas/ Sharleen Scott. -- 1st ed.
ISBN 978-0-9915890-0-5

to Brett, Dana, and Kyle
for believing in me

"These things I warmly wish for you: someone to love, some work to do, a bit o' sun, a bit o' cheer, and a guardian angel always near."

-*Irish blessing*

1

Harlie Cates scanned the beach from the cliff's edge, squinting into the midday sun for a glimpse of a well-worn cowboy hat and a long-legged stride. Her fingernails pressed crescents into her palms.

"Be here you ol' coot," she said. "Please, please, please, be here." She inhaled, trying to calm her rising alarm; the air was salty and crisp with a brief whiff of cigarette smoke. She released the held breath, only to catch it again when a shadow and a cry overhead startled her. She ducked, grabbing her Mariners cap in time to avoid a low-flying seagull.

"Stupid thing," she said with irritation aimed more at the cop who'd forced her on this search than the bird. Or was Buck the target of her annoyance? If he'd been where expected today, this worry knot wouldn't have lodged in her stomach like an indigestible potluck casserole.

She'd been at the Angel Beach Center, spooning pistachio pudding into chipped bowls, when the latest representative from the local PD cornered her and executed his version of a seagull bombing raid. Another death, he'd said. The second in a week. Not surprisingly, the next guy in the serving line declined the green pudding. Whether his appetite was spoiled by the cop's presence or the death of a friend, Harlie couldn't say for sure. Both made her queasy.

The cop refused to reveal particulars within earshot of the lunch crowd but pulled Harlie aside and asked her to ID the deceased for next-of-kin notification. If the unfortunate person inhabited Harlie's flock of dispossessed, there wasn't a family to inform—not one willing to admit sharing the dearly departed's gene pool anyway. She agreed to make the identification if she could, but first she needed to calm the troublesome thought barreling through her brain.

Was it Buck?

She'd delegated the pudding job to a volunteer and jumped in her car to check his favorite haunts: the bench in front of her bakery, his tool shed, and now, the Angel Viewpoint and Picnic Area. She refused to visit the morgue until she knew it wouldn't be Buck's lifeless eyes staring at her when the coroner lifted the sheet.

"Come on, Buck. Be here," she said, sniffing the air again.

Buck's seat at the Wednesday lunch was vacant today, but that wasn't unusual. In fair weather, he might skip the hot meal for a dose of sunshine and seagulls. He had a fondness for the pair, reveling in wide-open spaces and creatures with flight capability. Buck never parked anywhere long and Harlie knew he'd fly away someday. She hoped he wasn't presented with the opportunity last night.

Harlie frowned into the Oregon coast glare, relieved when movement pulled her gaze. "There you are," she said, smiling at the sight of the man sitting on a volcanic outcropping near the Angel, a rock spire shaped by many millennia of storm waves that, when the light was right, resembled a praying angel.

Harlie grabbed two insulated cups from her car, bumped the door closed with her hip, and navigated the steep path to the beach below. A handful of minutes later, her squeaky trudge across the sand ended. Except for the gray ponytail snaking halfway down his back, Buck resembled a John Wayne movie extra with his weathered Stetson scrunched to shade his eyes. He must have been a looker in his youth. For his age, he still was, despite the gray mustache and beard he hid behind. He glanced her way and took a drag from his cigarette before crushing it on the rock with his boot heel.

"Those things will kill you," she said, knocking the sand from her plaid Converse All Stars.

His laugh ended in a rasping cough. "I already died once. Might as well enjoy life before I go the next time." He reached for the coffee cup she held. "Afternoon, Angel Girl."

She smiled at him and the nickname. In Buck's opinion, Harlie was the angel of Angel Beach, not that worn-out rock. He settled back on his perch and shifted a small green duffle bag to rest between his feet. After a significant inhalation of java steam, he sighed and sipped the hot brew.

"You brought the good stuff from the bakery. Lordy that is a fine cup of coffee. Not like that swill at The Center."

"Hey, watch yourself, mister." Harlie found a foothold, grabbed a protruding rock, and pulled herself up to sit next to Buck. "I make that swill, too. Our budget is hurting right now and I have to stretch supplies further."

"Just teasing. Don't get yourself in an uproar." Buck's chuckle was low and rough. "What brought you out here? Done feeding the masses already?"

"I left it to the volunteers." She sipped her herbal tea, staring into the steam. The ocean breeze tipped her cap back. She tugged it down and adjusted her braid. "A cop came to The Center and said there was another death last night. When you didn't come in for lunch, I thought..." She looked at him and shrugged.

"You thought it was me?" He shook his head. "Not my time yet so don't be worrying over this old cuss. Most will tell you I'm not worth the trouble and I'd be one of them."

"And I'll argue with you or anyone else who says it." Harlie laid her hand over his and squeezed. His was warm and calloused.

He glanced at her hand and raised an eyebrow. "You sure you want to do that? You might catch something. I'm dirty and uncouth." His mouth lifted into a smile. "I'm unfit to associate with good people like you. In fact, it may be dangerous for you out here alone with a foil-hat-wearing crazy man like me."

"I know crazy and you aren't it."

"That's not what they say."

"Who?" she said with a scowl.

"Well, I can't say I've felt a lot of love from those retirees in the spendy condos down the highway, and your town council doesn't like guys like me calling Angel Beach home either." He shrugged. "Did you know they're planning to pass a panhandling ordinance in my honor? They're gonna legislate me out of town."

"I don't feel that way," Harlie said.

"No. Not you. You care about ol' rascals like me and all those broken folks, too."

She squeezed his hand and studied his comforting profile. "I've been where they are."

He snorted. "Get out of here. A sweet bit of refinement like you? No way. The streets harden people, Angel. It'd show."

She smiled. "I'll make a deal with you, Buck. Someday when we are both in the mood for it, we'll swap secrets."

He pulled his hand away. "I'm not prone to mood swings."

"So," she said, ignoring his rebuff, "the cops want me to ID the deceased. They say natural causes, but it sure seems odd. Two of my guys in a week."

"They live a hard life. Don't be surprised when they give up on it."

He spoke of them as if he was different. Maybe he was. He worked when he could as a day laborer. Other days, he played his guitar and sang country songs on the bench in front of Harlie's bakery. If someone tossed a dollar his way, he took it as flattery, not charity. Service provided. Money paid. The difference between him and the rest of Harlie's people, in Buck's opinion, was that he chose the drifter's life. It suited him. The others ended up there by circumstance.

"But two of them..." She blew out a breath. "I was wondering if you'd go along again. You know everybody better than I do."

"It's a little late for introductions."

Harlie rolled her eyes and laughed. "You know what I mean. He may not be one of my lunch regulars and you might recognize him better than I will."

He seemed uncomfortable with the thought but nodded. "Yeah, I'll go. George would appreciate it."

"George?"

"Professor George, our dearly departed."

"How do you know that?"

"That he was a professor?" He shrugged. "He liked to talk. Get a little booze in him and he liked to talk a lot."

"No, not that he was a professor. That he's the deceased. The baby-faced cop wouldn't tell me anything."

"Word gets around." He shifted the bag between his feet. "Let's get to it. Waiting won't make it any easier." He grabbed his duffle and jumped to the sand. Harlie followed and they fell into companionable silence broken by Buck's exclamation when he saw her red Smart Car in the parking lot.

"Oh, good lord. You expect me to ride in that?" He turned and headed back to the trail. "Come back when you have something I'll fit in."

"Come on, Buck. I'm five ten and I fit fine." She unlocked the door of her beloved escape pod.

He turned back, his face a mask of sourness. "I'm six two. I'll have to wrap my knees around my neck and I'm not as flexible as I used to be."

"That's not what Emily Johnson says." Harlie laughed when his eyes went wide. "Oh, get in."

He stared at the petite car. With a grumble, he pulled open the door, folded his large body into the Smart Car, and tucked the duffle between his knees. He turned to her, his lips pursed with disgust. "Well? What are you waiting for? Get going."

Harlie suppressed a smile and hit the gas.

It was Professor George, all right. If his stories were true, he'd been an Ivy League professor in his old life, but no one knew what sent him down this craggy path to his death. He talked literature and poetry, not personal downfall. The obvious cause of death was heart attack. They'd know more after the coroner was done but for now, natural causes seemed likely. The toxicology report would probably confirm large amounts of alcohol in George's system and little else. Harlie and Buck couldn't provide personal information, such as last name and hometown. They signed the form proclaiming him "Professor George." At least he wouldn't be buried as John Doe.

Her duty done, Harlie couldn't leave fast enough. The second trip to the morgue in a week left her jittery. She opened the outside door and inhaled fresh air. Buck lit a cigarette. When Harlie lifted a questioning brow, he said, "You purify your lungs your way, I'll do it mine."

"It's not that," she said. "Your signature in there." She tilted her head toward the morgue door.

He chuckled. "What about it?"

"Buck Owens?"

"Yeah? What's your point?"

"Last week, it was Buck Skinner. What is your last name anyway?"

"You really want to know?"

"Yeah."

He paused and glanced from side to side. "Aru," he whispered. He winked and took one last drag before crushing the cigarette on the blacktop.

"Buck Aru?" She groaned and punched his arm.

"Gotcha." He chuckled again and glanced at the Smart Car, his expression changing to wariness. "Maybe I'll walk."

"It's ten miles. Riding with me is easier on your boot leather." She climbed in and started the engine.

Buck opened the door, slid into his seat, and settled the green duffle in his lap. "But tough on my image. Take the back roads. I don't want anyone seeing me in this thing. It might confirm that crazy theory about me."

"Oh hush," she said. "There's plenty of room in this car and I don't have time to argue."

"You always have time to argue."

She shook her head. "Not today. There's an ABC meeting tonight and I don't want to be late. Actually, it may be a party." She accelerated from the parking lot and turned onto Highway 101.

"A party? For what? Celebrating George's demise, are you?"

She slapped his leg. The car swerved and Buck grabbed the door handle.

"Noah is making the offer on the property today. The Angel Beach Center Committee will soon own the Angel View Motel and Cabins." The 1950's vintage motel was perfect for her needs. A little paint and cleanup and she'd be in business. "If things go as planned, I should have the new shelter and food bank open and operating by winter. That's my goal—indoors before the storms hit."

"Nice for some," he said.

"Do you want to move in?"

He shook his head. "Too crowded. I got a place."

"What you've got is a tool shed."

"It's a workshop and garage, not a tool shed, and yes, I like it fine. A man needs his privacy and freedom to come and go. Too much confinement makes me itchy." He shifted his weight in the little car and grimaced. "Besides, I like tools. They don't make any noise unless you want them to."

"Is that why you refused Emily's offer to use the garage apartment? Too confining for the wild man?"

He smiled. "Wild man. Where do you get this stuff? The smaller place is fine. I have my woodstove, some furniture, and a bathroom. Emily lets me use the washer and dryer. My rent is cheap and she can rent the bigger apartment to someone else." He shrugged. "It works out fine."

"I'll bet the rent is cheap." She gave him a sly smile. "It doesn't hurt that you're boinking the landlady. I imagine that gets you a few perks."

He looked at her. "I'm what?"

"Boinking the landlady. You and Emily. You know..." She raised her eyebrows suggestively. "Boink, boink." She grinned. "Word gets around."

His eyes went wide. "Good grief. You shouldn't talk to a man about such things. It's not right."

"Oh come on, Buck. People talk about everything today. Consider yourself lucky you're getting the good stuff. Not everybody is." She frowned.

Buck looked like a gray-bearded goldfish gasping for its life on the living room floor. "What I'm having or not having is none of your business, little girl. And I

don't need to know what you're missing out on either."
He shifted and stared straight ahead.

"I'm far from being a little girl. And Emily says—"

"Stop!"

"Oh come on—"

"Look out! A dog! There's a dog in the road!" He pointed and waved. "Damned thing is bigger than the car! Stop!"

She swerved and missed the dog. What sent them off the road was a gust of panic slapping Harlie like a bat whacking a ball. Smack, home run, and the Smart Car's front bumper was kissing a shore pine on the edge of the highway. Harlie pressed her forehead against the steering wheel. Her breath escaped in shocked gasps and her hands trembled. Buck clasped his duffle to his chest and blinked. His cowboy hat drifted at an odd angle.

"And they say I'm crazy," he muttered. "The girl drives like a maniac."

Harlie couldn't catch her breath. "One...two...three," she counted, seeking calm. A shadow fell across the windshield. The possibility of a solar eclipse was non-existent, so she assumed a Good Samaritan was already on the scene. The shadow moved away but came right back.

"Four...five...six..." Breathe in. Breathe out.

"Are you okay, Angel?" Buck pushed her hat back from her forehead with shaking fingers and made his

SHARLEEN SCOTT

inspection. "No bruises yet. You okay?" He rubbed his chest under the seatbelt and frowned.

A face peered in the window, his brow furrowed. He rapped hairy knuckles against the glass and cupped his hand around his eyes. "Hello?" he yelled, his voice muffled by the glass. "Can you hear me?"

Harlie continued counting. "Seven...eight...nine..." Breathe. Breathe. "Ten." She gasped and took a gulp of fresh air as she rolled down the window, her hand shaking like a bent wheel.

"Are you hurt?" the man asked. "Should I call 9-1-1?"

"I'm fine. I think he's okay." She gestured toward Buck and took another deep breath. "I managed to stop before I hit the tree. I only bumped it. Really," she added when he frowned. "Is the dog okay?"

The man squinted against the late afternoon sun and glanced around. Harlie thought he looked familiar with his Buddy Holly glasses and silver hair. It didn't register how she knew him until he stuck a pastry in his mouth, leaving a crumb trail down the front of his Sea Lion Caves T-shirt. Well, she should take that as a compliment. One of her bakery customers enjoyed her apple turnover well enough he couldn't put it aside to check on an accident victim. Luckily, she wasn't bleeding or she might spoil the man's appetite.

"What dog? I didn't see one," he said, swallowing the last bite. "Did you?" He turned his attention to a second man Harlie hadn't noticed. A peek in the side

CAUGHT IN CROSS SEAS

mirror revealed another vehicle, a black Jeep Wrangler with tinted windows. The new arrival was much younger than the pastry eater: tall, blond, and wearing dark glasses.

"No," he said. "I just came on the accident a second ago. Are they okay?" He pulled a cell phone from his jeans pocket. "I could call—"

"I already offered. She says they're fine."

"It's not an accident," Harlie said with a shrug. "Just a minor detour. The airbag didn't even deploy. And I am fine—"

"I'm not so sure," the older man said. "She was weaving back and forth." He made a swishing motion with his hands as if giving a Monday Night Football play-by-play. "Then she drove off the road and hit the tree." He clapped his hands.

Harlie wondered if he'd do a fan wave for a finale, but instead, he leaned in her car window and sniffed.

"Are you sure you aren't hurt...or something?"

She supposed inebriation was a valid assumption. As the car interior warmed, it was obvious Buck had enjoyed a high-octane lunch. The car smelled like happy hour in the Swordfish Room at Captain Bob's Seafood Grill. The wonderful lummox probably began his day with a beer buzz, and from the look on his face, wished to revisit the condition soon. Harlie couldn't help but love him, warts and all. If she ever met her father, she hoped he was just like Buck.

"She looks okay to me," the blond man said.

"I still think we should call someone," the older man insisted.

Harlie let out an exasperated huff. "Stop talking about me as if I'm unconscious. I'm fine. Great, even."

Her customer moved aside and the younger man took his place, resting his forearm on the vehicle roof and leaning in. He tilted his sunglasses down and Harlie found herself staring into the most intriguing eyes she'd ever encountered. If she hadn't already established her positive health status, she might pretend to faint so this outstanding representative of the male gender could give her mouth-to-mouth resuscitation.

"Are you sure you're okay, darlin'?" he said. "Maybe we should call someone to drive you two home?"

She was shell shocked and it had nothing to do with the tree. His intense blue eyes coupled with a bone-penetrating voice had her wishing she needed assistance. A gust of ocean breeze tousled his sandy-blond hair and she restrained her hand from brushing a wayward strand from his forehead or touching the bicep straining against his T-shirt sleeve. She considered counting again to catch her breath. Instead, she slapped Buck on the back when he gasped and launched into a coughing fit. He rolled his window down and stuck his head out, his cough more violent.

"Buck? Are you okay? Buck?"

"I'm fine. Just a cough."

"You aren't hurt?" She'd seen him grimace when he touched his chest earlier.

He shook his head and tried to respond when another cough took hold. "Home. Let's...go...home."

Harlie turned back to the man in her driver's side window. "He has emphysema. He coughs all the time." Buck pulled his jacket collar around his face. "I don't have emphysema. It's the flu."

She looked at him. "It isn't flu season. As much as you smoke, of course it's emphysema. If you would go to the clinic, Dr. Tipton would tell you so."

"No doctors. Home. Now."

The attractive man in her window let out an impatient sigh. "So, you don't need help?"

Harlie took one last appreciative look at him and ended her trip to fantasyland. "No, thank you," she said, shaking her head. "That's unnecessary." She held up her hand. "See? Steady as a rock. I appreciate the offer, but we're okay. And I really should get going."

He gave her a considering gaze and shrugged. "Fine. I'll take off." He returned to his Jeep and drove onto the highway. The older man remained, uncertainty lingering in his eyes. A dog had darted across the road and she'd swerved to avoid it. Buck saw it, and if he would come out of his coat-collar hideaway, he could confirm her story.

"If you'll move aside," Harlie said to the remaining half of her rescue team, "I'll back up and see if there's any damage." She checked her watch and gave him a strained smile. The man finally moved, allowing her space to park on the shoulder. After a walk around the vehicle, with only one slip in the loose gravel, Harlie determined the car was in good shape. She waved thanks to her customer as he retreated down the coastal highway.

There was a dog. Buck acted like it was a Mastiff on steroids, but she leaned toward a lab mix. If she'd paid closer attention to the road, and teased Buck less, she'd have driven around it without incident. She shivered when she looked beyond the tree to the vast expanse of ocean—two hundred feet straight down. If she and the shore pine hadn't shared their intimate moment, her impromptu detour would've sent them over the side. Back in the driver's seat, she took another deep breath. When her pulse slowed, she glanced in the rearview mirror and accelerated onto the highway.

Minutes later, she stopped her car in front of a pale blue Victorian. Buck's tool shed deluxe was in back. He hadn't spoken since the accident and his face was pale. He clutched the duffle tight to his chest. The way he coughed earlier, she worried he'd been injured and played tough guy for her sake.

"Should I run you by the clinic? Dr. Tipton could x-ray your chest."

He shook his head slowly and when he spoke, his voice was a quiet rasp. "No, Angel. I'm fine. Just too much excitement in one day for this old cuss. You go on to your meeting and don't worry about me." He climbed from the car, duffle in hand.

Her last view of Buck wrenched her heart. He stood on the sidewalk, shoulders hunched and brow furrowed, insisting he was okay when she suspected otherwise. But she was running late and had to tuck aside her worry.

At home, a quick punch of the security code and Harlie made her way along the shrubbery-lined driveway to her beach cottage. She groaned at the sight of a vehicle near the larger house next door. A glance at her watch made her sigh: 5:30. The meeting began at 6:30 and she'd hoped for a soak in the tub before leaving. Her new neighbor's arrival demoted the bath to the back burner. Harlie needed to introduce herself and find out who shared the security code to the gated property. Considering today's bad-luck marathon, she was sure he'd be a drug dealer or a binocular-wielding pervert who would stare down the driveway waiting for a flash of skin. She knew he was single—the landlord gossiped—and Harlie couldn't figure out why a single guy would rent a secluded beach house.

She parked near her neighbor's garage, scraped a bit of pistachio pudding from her jeans, and took a step in the direction of the house. Motion on the cliff drew her attention to a man standing near the edge, staring toward the horizon.

He looked familiar. Very familiar.

Tall, sandy-blond, and dressed in faded jeans, T-shirt, and cowboy boots. If he tipped down his sunglasses, she knew his eyes would be blue. His vehicle confirmed his identity: black Jeep, tinted windows. As she neared him, he turned.

She approached with her hand outstretched. "Hi, I'm—"

"Leaving."

She pulled back her hand. "Excuse me?"

"I said you're leaving. Now. I don't know how you opened that gate, but this is private property and honey, I'm not interested."

"Not interested in what? I just—"

"You know, you've got a lot of nerve following me here." He shook his head and scowled. "I knew stopping was a mistake. I knew it and did it anyway."

Harlie wondered if the man was delusional. "Followed you? I didn't follow you, I'm—"

He held up his hand. "I don't care who you are. I'm not interested in you or whatever you're offering. Get out of here before I call the cops and have you arrested." He brushed by her and headed to the larger house, pulling his cell phone from his pocket—the same one he'd offered to use to assist her earlier.

"Who do you think you are?"

He turned back. "I'm the guy paying a fortune to rent a beach house with a crappy security system."

"There's nothing wrong with the security system."

"It let you in."

She narrowed her eyes. Most men who saw the look knew to duck and cover important body parts. "For your information, I didn't follow you. I live in the guesthouse and am not going anywhere." She turned, stomped to her car, and threw herself in the driver's seat. Leaning out the door, she yelled, "And I'd bungee jump nude into a cactus before I'd be interested in you either!" She slammed the door and accelerated down the driveway.

On the car radio: an advertisement for Mick's Rodent Extermination Service. Harlie wondered if he handled large ones.

2

"Shit." Clay Masterson frowned and rubbed the back of his neck as he watched the Smart Car's departure. The landlord said someone lived in the cottage next door, but this woman wasn't the doddering caretaker he'd envisioned. He'd sure misjudged that.

His cell phone rang. Caller ID: Harv Stockton, Stockton Management Nashville. The last person he wanted to talk to. Harv would have a thousand fits over Clay's disappearing act that morning and he wasn't in the mood to hear it. He stuffed the phone in his pocket and wandered to the deck.

A breeze drifted in and he inhaled. The air was salty and fresh. The late afternoon sun reflected off the waves, turning them into a shimmering mass stretching into forever. It was a perfect day for a walk on the beach if a guy was so inclined.

Clay wasn't.

He hadn't traveled across the country for leisurely beach strolls or to dip his toes in the Pacific. If the last hour was anything to go by, peace and quiet wasn't something he should expect either. He turned to the house and gazed upward. The sign marking the property's driveway declared the place "Beach Haven" in faded blue letters. The two-story cedar-sided house he'd rented sat on a cliff with a wall of windows facing west and a huge deck laid wide across the ocean side.

Steep stairs led to the beach. A scattering of wind-blown shore pines, their trunks contorted, gave an air of privacy but didn't detract from the view. It would do.

To the south of the main house, a couple hundred feet or so, sat the smaller guesthouse snuggled into the trees like a fairy tale woodsman's cottage. He considered walking over and offering an apology but his phone rang again. Caller ID: Tom Black. The best friend a guy could ask for. He'd take the call and worry about righting wrongs later.

"What?" Hello was unnecessary. Tom was more brother than friend.

"Where are you?" said a male voice every bit as furious as his charming new neighbor's had been moments before.

"Home." In the panoramic windows he saw a recliner, sofa, and stone fireplace. It looked like home to him.

"I was up to your place and didn't see a sign of you. Sally said you disappeared this morning with a pile of suitcases and gig bags. Harv's been having hysterics all day. Says he tried to reach you at least ten times and can't get an answer," Tom said. "So, where are you? Don't give me that home bullshit. I know you aren't there."

Clay smiled. The posse was in search mode, like he knew they'd be. Sally, his housekeeper, worried over him like he was one of her own kids. He'd intended to call her as soon as he arrived. No need now. Tom would take care of it for him. "I am home. My home away from home. At least for the next few weeks anyway."

"Weeks?"

"Yeah. If that's what it takes."

"Without saying a word?"

"Yeah."

"What's going on with you, Clay? You've been acting strange lately and now you disappear."

"I didn't exactly disappear. I told Harv a few weeks ago I was thinking about taking a break. Today was the day." So he didn't say goodbye to everyone. Big deal. Clay left the deck and walked to the Jeep. The back end was jammed with gear he needed to unload.

"Well, Harv is convinced you're unbalanced and planning something extreme."

"Hardly. What about you? You think I'm planning to off myself, too?"

"No, and it doesn't matter to me if you take off or not. You're gone more than you're here at the ranch anyway. I'm just getting tired of Harv bugging me. He's an old nursemaid where you're concerned. Did you take Stu and Phil along?"

Stu and Phil: bodyguards extraordinaire. Not such great poker players but decent guys to have around when the crowds got out of hand. But not this time. "No." Clay tensed at the implication. "I'm not some helpless wuss, Tom. I can take care of myself." He dug the keys from his pocket, unlocked the vehicle, and moved a gig bag and an amp to the ground, ready to haul inside.

"Under normal circumstances, I'd agree with you. But you don't live in normal circumstances anymore. How long has it been since you traveled without a bodyguard?"

"A while," Clay admitted. More like years since those ridiculous "sexiest man" photos started plaguing him. Every year he landed on one list or another, and now he had difficulty going out in public alone. They'd even dissected him down to body parts a few times: best hair, eyes, and the worst of the lot, sexiest butt. It wasn't the recognition a serious musician desired, and he'd considered tying a jacket around his waist when that proclamation came out.

"You need to take your security more seriously," Tom said, insistent.

"Now who's the old nursemaid?"

"I'm not kidding. You're worth a lot of money, and someone might want to take a stab at you to get it." He exhaled. "Will you at least tell me where you are so I'll know where to look for your body if you disappear? It might be nice to have all your parts for the memorial service."

"You can call my cell if you need to." Clay grabbed a suitcase and set it on the ground.

"Not good enough. Can't call you if you're dead, can I? Tell me where you are or Harv says he'll book that photo shoot with *Playgirl.*"

"He wouldn't dare."

"That's what he told me. If you don't check in soon, he's telling that *Playgirl* editor you'd love to be, no, you're honored to be the country music representative. It's a special section on cowboys and she thought you'd be perfect."

"Harv can book whatever he wants. I'm not doing it. I've told them over and over I'm not baring my ass in any magazine. He knows that."

"So, where are you?"

Clay knew Tom was serious. They'd gone a lot of rounds over the years and he knew the guy wouldn't give up. Today the threat was a *Playgirl* photo; tomorrow it could be a commercial with him dressed as a wiener and singing a ballad to a bologna sandwich. Or worse, a participant in one of those TV reality shows. But Tom's perseverance and dedication were the reasons he handled Clay's security. No one gained access to Clay's Nashville ranch without Tom knowing it. He also rode roughshod over Clay's life if he thought Clay was doing something stupid. Like today. Clay laughed and shook his head. Unless he wanted to be the next centerfold or wearing a wiener costume, he'd better cooperate. When Harv and Tom ganged up on him, it was usually best to go along. "Oregon," he said, tempted to toss the phone in the ocean and end the conversation right there.

"Details, not just the state."

Clay hesitated.

"Now, that editor did say she'd give you a fig leaf or something. Maybe a Stetson since you're so modest."

"What, no spurs?" Clay said with a laugh. "Oh, all right. I'm in Angel Beach, Oregon. Why don't you come and keep me out of trouble since I'm so irresponsible, helpless, and God knows what else."

"Thanks, but I have enough to keep me busy here," Tom said, at ease now he had the information he wanted. "So...how's the scenery?"

Clay glanced in the direction of the cedar cottage tucked in the trees. "Tall, dark brown hair, and legs that go on forever," he said with a hint of admiration.

Tom laughed. "Sounds like you've got all the bases covered."

"Nothing like that. Not with this one anyway. I screwed things up before there was a chance of it."

"How so?"

"Long story. Short version: I was rude." Clay saw a shadow in a window and knew it was her. "I'll talk to her. Apologize and all that."

"Turn on that famous Masterson charm..."

"Yeah, right. If I ever had any, it ran out on the way here."

"It'll come back. Now," Tom said, "tell me what this is really about. A vacation isn't enough to send you off the radar like this. What's up?"

Clay blew out a breath. No point in dragging out the inevitable. "Somebody saw him."

Tom was silent a moment. "Ah, shit," he said. "Don't tell me you're tracking him again."

"Okay. I won't tell you."

"You are. Damn it, Clay, you gotta stop this. Every time somebody mentions Hunt Masterson you go flying off. He's dead. They confirmed it eighteen years ago. It's like all those Elvis sightings at 7-Eleven. People are yanking your chain and you're buying into it."

Clay leaned against the Jeep. This was why he hadn't mentioned the trip. "It's different this time, Tom. One of Dad's old friends says his cousin saw him performing in a bar on the Oregon coast. He didn't know where for sure, but it doesn't sound like he's dead."

"Oh great— you're trusting the old telephone game. A friend of a friend of a friend. You know how stories get mixed up every time they're retold. No telling how many details get changed."

"I have to look. Maybe I got here fast enough this time and he hasn't taken off."

"What do you plan to do if you find him?"

"I thought we'd have a nice little reunion and talk over old times. Maybe I'll buy him a steak dinner and a beer to thank him for being an exemplary father for the five or ten minutes he spent at it." Clay focused on a large wave crashing on the beach. "And then I'm going to kick his sorry butt back to Montana. I'm sure that detective would still love to get his hands on him."

"If he is alive and he did murder that woman, he won't be happy to see you."

"No doubt. But I have to see it through. All the evidence pointed right at him and I know he did it." Clay was also sure dear ol' dad was alive enough to blackmail him. Somebody was and that somebody knew details the sheriff's department didn't release to the press. Now it was a potential public relations nightmare and he needed to find the person responsible for the notes.

"I can't believe you're doing this again," Tom said. "Maybe I should come out there—"

"I can handle it. If I can't, you'll be the first person I call."

"I'd better be. You'll be careful, right? And you'll check in with Harv?"

"Yeah, sure. Careful. Check in. Got it." The call disconnected, Clay gave the neighbor's cottage another look. No, not yet. He'd let her cool off first. In her present mood she might shove him off the cliff.

And he wouldn't blame her if she did.

3

Captain Bob's was a recurrent madhouse on all-you-can-eat Wednesdays. Harlie wound her way through the tables, dodging platter-wielding diners returning from the shrimp buffet, careful not to bump elbows and send crustaceans to the floor. She saw her group seated at a corner table near the windows and waved. On closer inspection, her group was only Dr. Wayne Tipton at a table set for three. He stood as she reached the table, pulling a chair for her.

He was in his mid thirties, tall and lean, dressed in khakis and a pale blue shirt. The evening sun streamed in the windows, highlighting his light brown hair and white-toothed smile. Dr. Tipton ran a clinic in town and was a member of The Angel Beach Center board. A real catch if a woman was interested.

"I thought this was a committee meeting," Harlie said, hoping she hadn't misunderstood the message. Had she accepted a date by accident? Wayne was nice but... "Is everyone late?" She slid onto the chair, wishing she'd changed from her jeans and Converse tennis shoes. Even if this wasn't a date, it wasn't an ego booster to have the guy acing her in the personal cleanup department.

"Noah's uncle dropped by unexpectedly, so he won't make it, and Emily is running a little late."

A waiter appeared at Harlie's elbow and she ordered herbal tea and grilled salmon. Wayne did the same for himself and Emily, substituting coffee for tea. "So, no meeting?"

"We'll discuss it when Emily arrives. Would you like to order a drink?" he asked. "You may want one."

"I don't drink." She frowned and considered his tone. "Why would I want one?"

"After we eat."

She narrowed her eyes. "Why do I need a drink? What happened?" The waiter flipped Wayne's coffee cup and filled it.

"After—"

"Now!" The waiter jumped and nearby diners looked her way. She lowered her voice. "Tell me now, Wayne."

He blew out his breath and frowned. "There is another party interested in the motel. They topped our offer."

"What? That old motel has been on the market forever and no one was interested before. There must be a mistake." She leaned back in her chair, shaking her head.

"The real estate agent says we can counter the offer if we want to."

"Counter it? But we don't have enough money. We barely had enough to start with." Harlie gritted her teeth and controlled her despair. They'd worked so hard to raise the money. Corporate sponsors, grants, fundraisers, and now Wayne was telling her it was for nothing.

"I'm sorry to be the bearer of bad news, Harlie."

"Yeah, well, someone had to risk it, I guess." Harlie drummed her fingers on the table until an idea struck her. "We need a private philanthropist, someone to champion our cause and donate the rest of the money. Like Bill Gates or someone like that." And once they found him, she knew how to get him onboard.

Wayne shrugged. "And you know such a person? I'm afraid I'm fresh out of generous billionaires."

She shook her head. "No, I don't." She puffed her cheeks and blew out a breath. "I guess we have to re-group. At least we can continue using the room at the Senior Center for the food bank, and they don't seem to mind if we have the lunch there as long as we in-clude the low-income seniors in the mix."

"Well..." Wayne began but was interrupted by Emi-ly Johnson's arrival. He waved as she made her way across the restaurant. Harlie pegged Emily at sixty-five-ish. Her dyed blonde hair made it difficult to tell. She skirted around a beverage-serving waiter and dropped into a chair at the table.

"Did you tell her?" Emily said, directing her atten-tion to Wayne.

"Yes, he told me. We'll have to find a new source for donations."

Emily nodded. "Yes, that, and a new location."

Harlie narrowed her eyes at Wayne. "A what?"

"A new location," Emily said. "The Senior Center wants us out by next month. They're expanding their programs and can't have us taking up space."

Harlie glared at Wayne. "Oh, really?"

He shrugged. "I was trying to tell you. And don't look at me as a solution. My office is small. I barely have room for the clinic."

"I doubt the health board would approve of a food bank and rescue mission running out of a doctor's office." Harlie buried her face in her hands and groaned. "It's okay. We'll deal with it." She looked up, determined to take control of the situation. "We need money. If we can't come up with more, we need to scout a new location. If we close The Center operation, I'll have people coming to the bakery again, and the council had a fit about that already. For some reason they frown on me running a soup kitchen out the back door."

Emily nodded. "Did you hear they're passing a panhandling law? That obnoxious city hall twit almost plastered the notice on Buck's forehead."

"I know. I'm already on top of it. I'm moving the corner table out of the bakery and setting up a small stage. Buck can play his guitar there. Maybe we can do some poetry readings. Something to class the place up for the tourists. I think it will be good for business and it gets Buck off the sidewalk."

The waiter edged around Harlie and placed her entree in front of her and a teapot and cup near the plate.

"So, Harlie," Emily said, surveying her own dinner, "how's your new neighbor? He arrived today, didn't he?"

Harlie nearly choked on her first bite. She'd forgotten about Mr. Personality. She wrinkled her nose and relayed the story of her roadside detour that afternoon. "You won't believe this, but my new neighbor is the guy who stopped to help us. He's a major goober though. Good-looking, but he has a serious personality disorder. He threatened to have me arrested. Can you believe it?"

Wayne's mouth hung open in shock. "You? What for?"

Harlie shrugged. "Who knows? All I can say is I won't go near him again. Ever. That bridge caught fire and I won't extinguish it. Let's eat before I lose my appetite."

Highway 101 was calm as Harlie drove home, allowing her thoughts to wander. Much to her dismay, she discovered her brain was the most traitorous lump of gray matter on the planet. Mr. Gorgeous, with the rattlesnake personality, repeatedly dropped in for mental visits since Emily mentioned him. She wished a dog would run out in front of her car so she could redirect her thoughts. What was going on? The guy was a jerk.

CAUGHT IN CROSS SEAS

With effort, she maneuvered her thoughts elsewhere. The Center was a problem but she couldn't
solve it tonight. Buck needed to see a doctor but she
couldn't force him to go. No one forced Buck to do
anything. Her cell phone sat in the passenger seat, a
message indicator flashing. She pulled into her driveway and retrieved her messages, hoping for some good
news.

"Voicemail. Terrific," the unfamiliar male voice
said. "I'm Skip Hyatt, *Seattle Times.* I don't know if
you've heard the news, but Glen Carson has been nominated for the American Humanitarian Award and I'm
doing an exposé on him." He laughed, but it was a rue-
ful chuckle. "His official bio is as full of holes as my
Uncle Paul's undershirt and I'm trying to dig deeper.
One glaring omission in the thing is you. As far as he's
concerned, you don't even exist anymore. I've inter-
viewed him but he won't discuss you. He'll agree to
talk about a million other subjects but not you. Off the
record, his personal assistant told me you are a lying
little thief and your vanishing act proves your guilt. I
figure, anyone who inspires that sort of animosity is
worth exploring further. So, I want to talk with you
and get your side. Call me."

She disconnected the call. "Yeah right," she said
with a disgusted snort. "I'll talk to you when hell hosts
the Ice Capades." But if Glen Carson was nominated
for a prestigious humanitarian award, maybe hell was

SHARLEEN SCOTT

experiencing an unexpected ice age. All it proved to
Harlie was Glen's wealth could buy anything.

She pressed the code into the security pad at her
gate, thankful for her foresight in renting the protected
cottage. If reporters were tracking her, the chain-link
fence and gate would protect her. If Glen Carson discovered her location, the fence wouldn't be enough.
She couldn't allow this reporter to expose her. Her
friends in Angel Beach didn't know about her connection to the famous heir to the Carson lumber fortune
and she planned to keep it that way. If they knew,
she'd be compromised and Glen would find her. She,
for one, didn't share the public opinion that Glen was
Washington State's golden boy. So far, Skip Hyatt had
her cell number. Nothing more. How he got it bothered
the heck out of her. A leak had sprung somewhere in
her circle of former friends.

She parked her car near the cottage and killed the
engine. Before going in, she grabbed the cell phone and
hit redial. Voicemail. Perfect.

"This is Skip Hyatt. Leave a message..."

"Mr. Hyatt," she said, "this is the person you called
about Glen Carson. I'm sorry to say, you have a wrong
number. I have no personal connection with him and I
believe you've been misinformed. Don't call again." She
disconnected the call. Problem solved.

4

As far as search locations went, Clay had experienced worse. The problem this time was lack of a definite starting point. The info he'd received was vague: a bar on the Oregon Coast in this general vicinity. Angel Beach itself didn't offer much in the way of bars and the one it had wasn't open early. But he was here. He circled several times to get a feel for the place before parking in front of The Dolphin Gift Shop. The salesperson, a grandmotherly woman wearing a dolphin T-shirt and large, floppy dolphin earrings, gave a double take as he walked in the door. The shop was filled to bursting with everything dolphin. Statues, posters, ashtrays, collector plates, wind socks, flip flops, sweatshirts, and beach towels. She probably had lingerie and steak knives in here somewhere.

At the counter, Clay produced a picture from his shirt pocket. "Excuse me, ma'am, but I'm looking for someone and am hoping you might know him," he said as he laid an old photo on the counter.

She tilted her glasses and screwed up her face. "Well, I don't know. The picture is kind of old and not too clear." She looked at him and smiled. "I feel the same way, now and then."

Clay gave her a tight smile. "It was taken twenty years ago. His name is Hunt Masterson and he was forty-two."

Her smile widened. "And you're Clay, right? I thought I recognized you. So tell me, why are you looking for this man in Angel Beach? Maybe that would help me place him."

He explained the bar sighting and she shook her head.

"No. I don't go to the bars and I can't say I recognize him." She stared at it a moment longer, motioned him closer and whispered, "If you could do me a small favor I might be able to help you though."

"What kind of favor?" Great. She recognized him and now he'd have to buy the information. He'd been there before.

"Well, Clay. I can call you Clay, can't I?"

He shrugged. "Sure. Everybody does."

"Well, Clay, maybe you could autograph a few of these for me? It would increase the value substantially." She pointed to a shelf containing dozens of dolphins of various sizes and colors. The pink and purple ones were fantasy dolphins, according to the sign. The bejeweled set was from the royalty series. Some had Mariners, Seahawks, and Trailblazers logos and others wore visors and sunglasses. Several had cowboy hats. He'd lay money on which dolphins she'd pick.

"Just a couple." She grinned and pointed. "Those right there."

Clay resigned himself to the task. At least she didn't want money. He debated how to autograph a figurine but Dolphin Lady was way ahead of him. She stuck a black Sharpie in his hand and nudged him to the shelf. He picked one up, frowned at it, and scribbled his name on the hat brim. What the heck. He'd signed worse.

When finished, he returned the pen. "Okay. What can you tell me? Do you know where he is?" Her face fell. "Oh no, sweetie, I can't tell you that. But, um," she canvassed the area and whispered, "what I can tell you is that Joann Sweeny at the photo shop has a drinking problem. A big one. I hear she spends a lot of time in the bars." She nodded. "She might know him."

Clay gave her another tight-lipped smile. He'd been duped by a grandma in dolphin earrings. Doing this alone was more difficult than he'd anticipated. "Thanks. I'll check in with her. Maybe buy her a six-pack to loosen her up."

The clerk giggled. "Oh, you're as funny in person as you are on stage."

Yup. He was a laugh a minute. Clay thanked her, tucked the photo back in his shirt pocket, and started for the door. Before he turned the knob, Dolphin Lady cleared her throat. He turned back.

She grinned and snapped his photo with her phone. "Bye."

Before she coerced him into autographing additional sea life or posing in different light, he moved on to the next shop. Ten doors and a lot of disappointment later, a heavenly cookie scent tempted him to duck into the

Sweet Stuff Bakery and Cafe. Chances were good no one here would know his dad either, but he could grab some coffee and a snack. He walked in, inhaling.

The bakery was located in the heart of Angel Beach, nestled between The Talbot Gallery and Beach Bum T-Shirts. Its façade was typical beach-town wood siding, grayed by saltwater mist. A sign in the window read: "Old-fashioned coffee—NO ESPRESSO—don't even ask." Espresso? He wouldn't bother. A jingling bell announced his arrival. Inside, a hodgepodge of secondhand tables and chairs, painted soft blues and greens. Large display cases presented cookies, cakes, and desserts. Shelves of baked goods lined the walls and the unmanned deli counter was loaded with meats and cheeses. On the radio, moderate volume: Trace Adkins' "Ladies Love Country Boys." Clay bent to get a better look at the muffins on the bottom shelf and heard a female voice.

"It's him, isn't it? Grandma said we'd catch up if we hurried."

Another voice giggled. "Oh yeah. I'd know him any-where."

Considering she recognized his backside, he didn't take it as a positive thing. "Oh crap," he muttered when he saw the cluster of excited young women re-flected in the glass case. Unfortunately, some women loved country guys too much. He aimed for noncha-lance, hoping they'd go away and leave him alone. No such luck. A finger tapped his shoulder; he turned and a woman screamed, "It's him, it's him!" Chaos exploded and Clay was forced against the bakery case by a wild pack of autograph-seeking fans. Before he could react, quick hands stole his glasses and baseball cap; both would probably sell on eBay by evening.

"Ladies! I can't breathe! I'll sign some autographs if you'll back up some!" He felt a tug and heard a rip. Shocked, he realized they had hold of his blue chambray shirt and were tearing it into souvenir-sized pieces.

"Hey! This is a new shirt!" He sidestepped left and right as eager hands assaulted him from all directions like Thanksgiving diners pulling apart the turkey. "Let go, ouch! Come on, don't do that!" He hissed when he heard the tear of fabric again and was worried he'd be standing there naked if he didn't get away soon.

He tried to slide along the case toward the counter entrance, but women blocked his path. He could easily shove his way through but was afraid of hurting someone. Without resorting to violence, he wondered how he would get out of this before they tore him to pieces. For the first time since leaving Nashville, he sure missed Stuart. Good ol' Stu would know what to do. Actually, Stuart wouldn't have let him get into this mess in the first place. Stuart thought ahead.

"What's going on out here?" a female voice yelled over the noise. The owner of the voice disappeared through the kitchen door. The radio went silent and the woman returned with two baking sheets she banged together like cymbals, finally getting the mob's attention.

"If you're paying customers, line up single file and we'll take your orders. If not, get out!" She shoved her way through the horde of women and pulled Clay behind the bakery case into the kitchen, locking the door behind her.

"Sam! Call 9-1-1. I don't know what's going on, but those women are going to tear the place apart." She looked back at Clay and stunned recognition crossed her face. "You," she said with disgust. "What did you do to cause the riot?" She looked him over and pushed him to a stool. "Sit. You look green and it's not a good color for you."

Clay took a deep breath and wondered, of the millions of women in the world who liked him, why did it have to be his neighbor who saved him? The one woman he'd alienated. And now he was at her mercy. She'd probably throw him back out there just for the fun of watching the lunatics dismember him. "I don't have to do anything to cause this," he said. "It just happens."

She looked at him with raised brows. "Oh, right. You're so darned irresistible women tear your clothes off? Maybe you threatened to have them arrested, too. Heaven forbid someone tries being neighborly around you."

The petite redhead his neighbor called Sam stepped closer. "This is the guy who called the cops on you?"

"Hey," Clay said. "I didn't call them—"

His neighbor interrupted, "You threatened to—"

"And you told her to call 9-1-1 on a bunch of people who could be your customers," he countered, pointing at the redhead holding the phone.

Sam tsk tsked and shook her head. "Harlie is a jewel. How dare you treat her that way?"

Nice. They were ganging up on him. Maybe he was better off out front. At least if the mob tore him apart, there might be pieces left to send back to Nashville. These two would probably kill him and bury him in the woods. "Ladies, I didn't say a thing to any of them. I don't have to say a word and this happens." A draft crossed his stomach and he reached around to inspect the damage to his shirt, looking under his arm. Torn from side seam to front on one side and shredded on the other, the shirt was ruined and left his stomach partially bare.

"You had to have said or done something. People don't go bananas without a reason. Confession time, pal. What did you do?" Harlie asked again, arms crossed tight across her middle.

"It's not anything I do. It's who I am and I guess what I do. For a living, I mean."

"Really?"

"You don't know who I am?"

He shook her head. "Sorry to burst your self-importance bubble, but no, I don't have a clue who you are. Enlighten me, please."

"I'm Clay Masterson."

Sam took a better look at him, holding the phone but not dialing. She knew who he was now. Harlie stared at him, appearing to digest what he said and decide what to do. She knew who he was, too, but was clearly unimpressed.

She huffed out her breath with resignation. "Clay Masterson, huh?"

He nodded.

"Wonderful. Those women won't leave voluntarily, will they?"

He shrugged. They were maniacs. Who knew what they'd do?

"Samantha, stop gawking. Did you get the cops on the phone yet?" Harlie took the phone and placed the call while pacing.

"This is Harlie at the Sweet Stuff Bakery and Cafe. We have a problem. You won't believe this, but I have a guy here who claims he's Clay Masterson, you know, that country singer, and some women want pieces of him. Can you send someone to break this mess up and get him out of here? Come down the alley. Maybe we can get him out the back unnoticed...Thanks." She hung up. "They're sending someone over," she said to Clay.

"Thanks." Clay rubbed the scratches on his arm and frowned at finding blood. "You said, 'Claims he's Clay Masterson.' Would you like to see my ID, neighbor?" He reached for his wallet.

"No, I don't need ID. Hold on and I'll get the first-aid kit." She walked to a cabinet and opened the door.

"Wow," Sam said, looking at him like a specimen under a microscope. "So, this is your neighbor. The jerk."

Clay winced.

Harlie turned and gave her a will-you-shut-up glare. "Yes, I mean, no. Will you find something to do with yourself? Go out front and make sure those crazies don't break anything." Red-faced, she retrieved the first-aid kit and returned to Clay. He held up his arm and she dressed the scrape with ointment.

"This can't be your neighbor, Harlie. You told me this morning he was a colossal goober," Sam said, ignoring Harlie's request she occupy herself elsewhere. Harlie turned a deeper shade of red.

Clay needed clarification on the goober thing, which sounded bad, but he was starting to enjoy this. Harlie was off-step and speechless.

"Clay Masterson couldn't be a jerk." Sam gushed, clasping her hands together and ignoring Harlie. "I drove up to Seattle once for one of your concerts and you were so amazing. You had me in tears when you sang 'Lost Love.'" She sighed. "I love the way you sing with all that emotion and passion and the cry in your voice sinks me. There is nothing better than an emotional man. Harlie said—"

Harlie swung around, grabbed Sam's arm, and pulled her into the corner. "Excuse us a moment," she said to Clay through gritted teeth. "What's the matter with you, Sam?" he heard her say.

Sam looked around Harlie and smiled at Clay. "Nothing is the matter with me. That's Clay Masterson, Harlie." Sam pointed at Clay. "I love him!"

"I caught that," Harlie said. "Would you stop telling him everything I said?"

"Do you know how many times he's been voted sexiest man?" She glanced around Harlie for another look. "Wow." She sighed with appreciation.

"Ladies?" Clay said, hoping to interrupt Sam's adoration fest. "If you're busy, I could get my own Band-Aid, or maybe we could call a truce or something? You know, for humanitarian reasons?"

Harlie walked back to him with her jaw set and put the bandage on his arm. "A truce?" she asked, looking him square in the eye.

"Yeah. A truce. I was in a bad mood yesterday. I'm sorry." A guy had a right to a bad mood when his dead father kept springing back to life. It was like a horror movie where the monster never dies. Hunt Masterson wouldn't stay dead and it would make Clay's life a lot easier if he did.

"You're apologizing?"

"I guess I am."

She stared at him. "You guess you are or you are? Which is it?"

"I am." Clay smiled. Man, she was a toughie. "I apologize for my rudeness. I'll even make it up to you."

"Make it up to me? How?"

"I'm not sure yet. I'll let you know."

Harlie frowned. "Don't worry about it."

"I'm not worried about it," he said. "I want to make it up to you."

She shrugged and appeared uncomfortable with the mellower course. Her humanitarian duty completed, Harlie turned away and filled the waiting time with kitchen chores. Clay patted his torn shirt pocket and pulled out the photo, wondering if these women knew dear old dad. When he looked at the picture, he swore. "Shit!"

Harlie looked at him wide eyed. "Excuse me?"

Clay blew out a breath. "Sorry. I wanted to show you a photo—I'm looking for someone and thought..." He stared at the picture, at least, half of it. In the brawl out front, someone tore the picture right along with his pocket. Most of the face was gone.

Harlie and Sam moved around to him, frowning as they looked. "Oh dear," Sam said. "I'll go out and see if the other half is there." She ran for the door and stopped briefly to listen. The hubbub outside had calmed, but when she opened the door the clamor resumed. "Oh, give it a rest already! Do I look like him? I'm short with red hair, for Pete's sake!" She stepped out, continuing to chastise the crowd.

Clay scowled at the torn picture. It was the best one he had with him. Luckily, he'd scanned it into his laptop and could print another copy later. But that didn't help him now.

"So," Harlie said, squinting at the half photo, closing one eye. "Who are you looking for?"

"My dad."

"How long has he been missing?"

"About eighteen years."

Harlie's mouth fell open. "Eighteen years and you're still looking for him? That's..." She blinked several times. "Heartbreaking."

She stared at him with big brown eyes. Sympathetic brown eyes surrounded by long lashes. When she stopped snapping at him, she was an attractive woman from her dark brown braid to her plaid shoes. What was he thinking? She was attractive while she snapped at him, too. He just hadn't taken the time to appreciate all the details. The concern remained in her eyes and Clay held back a smile. Apparently, his goober status was diminishing, and he might have been demoted to plain jerk. "Yeah, well, I have to look. Maybe you know him? His name is Hunt Masterson. Someone saw him performing in a bar somewhere in this general area. He was a guitarist and I'm assuming he still plays."

The kitchen door swung open and Sam rushed in with something in her hand, locking the door behind her. "Is this it?"

Clay took it and frowned, disappointed to see another small fragment. He stuck it together with the other, but a chunk was missing from the center. Harlie studied it.

"Well, it's hard to tell with his eye and nose missing." She shrugged an apology. "Can you describe him?"

"Back then, he was blond, lighter than me. He'd be in his sixties now so I'm assuming he's gray or maybe he dyes it. Blue eyes, like mine. But he doesn't really look like me. I look like my mom's family." He stuffed the photo pieces in his jeans pocket. "Heck with it. I'll have to print another picture. If you don't mind, I'll run over to your house and show it to you when I get it done."

Harlie bit her lip, obviously unsure if additional contact with him was wise. She nodded. "Sure. I'm usually home around five."

A police officer stuck his head in the door. "Ready to go, Mr. Masterson?"

"I guess so. Sorry to cause a problem."

"Not a problem at all. Stuff like this happens every once in a while in a tourist town like this," the officer said as he waited for Clay. "A while back we had one of those teenaged singers trapped in the T-shirt shop. Those girls went nuts and about killed the kid before we got him out of there. This isn't too bad compared to that." He turned to Harlie. "We have an officer out front to help with that mess."

She nodded. "Thanks."

Clay and the officer departed through the back room. Feeling like a criminal and an idiot, he wondered about the wisdom of coming to Angel Beach. The only thing saving this day from disaster was the look Harlie gave him as he walked out the door. Her earlier disgust was now replaced with something he knew how to handle: female interest. If he played it right, he might have a guest for dinner tonight.

5

Post lunch-hour traffic crawled through Angel Beach. Payton Shaw was caught at a stoplight, his fingers drumming against the steering wheel. It was an undersized town of eight thousand inhabitants and he calculated he'd be in and out in no time—if the traffic would progress. It had one bar to speak of which wouldn't be open for hours. Until then, he'd visit the shops, dropping a few well-placed questions. Days earlier, he'd checked the property listings in Angel Beach and found a choice piece of real estate withering from neglect and considered it the perfect excuse to leave the office for a few days. The price was right, so he made an offer. He wasn't sure what to do with it, but several possibilities came to mind and both would make a profit for the Carson Family Trust.

After bulldozing the old motel, the lot would be cleared. He might offer it to Clay as a location for the country music club he intended to build "someday." The way Clay dillydallied around someday would never come. With a suitable property in hand, Payton might give him a push. If Clay balked at the idea, he'd resell the property and easily triple the Trust's investment. A win-win situation.

At the change of the light, Payton waited for the pedestrians to clear and accelerated. The most difficult prospect was parking his Mercedes along the narrow highway. Since the town skirted the beach and rocky coastline, the business district parking was limited to one side. A sign reading PARKING NEXT LEFT loomed ahead. He took its advice and paid the ten-dollar fee.

The day was cool and breezy. He shed his suit coat, exchanging it for the more casual black Burberry jacket from the backseat. This was a tourist town, not downtown Seattle and he needed to blend if he hoped to find answers. He'd start with the galleries. Angel Beach boasted a handful in the literature he'd collected from the visitor's bureau and he'd begin with the Ocean Mist Gallery. His own art collection was extensive and he considered galleries his milieu.

He walked the necessary block and entered the establishment. Numerous oils lined the walls. In the center, blown glass sculpture and pottery filled the display tables. He concentrated on the oils in order to discern if a single artist was responsible or if it was a group showing. One painting nearly took his breath away. The artist captured the power of the ocean. The angel jutting from the squalling waves was simplistic and all the more alluring because of it. It gave him a sense of peace and then shattered it with equal force. With his hands clasped behind his back, he admired the artist's talent until a woman wandered over, adopted Payton's stance, and tilted her head. She was petite, well put-together, and polished. Her blonde hair was puffed into a becoming style and her mouth slanted in a smile.

"The light in this one...the Angel...she almost speaks to you, doesn't she?" she said with a sigh. "Lisa Corolla has such a gift. Don't you think?"

Payton waited a moment, pondering. "Yes. It is extraordinary. I'll need to bring my wife by later for a look. Nadine covets Oregon seascapes and this may be the thing for the dining room." He nodded and stared, mesmerized by the churning sea and the Angel rising from it. Hell with Nadine. It would adorn his office like the rest of the collection.

"Wonderful. I look forward to meeting her, Mr...." She held out her hand.

Payton pulled his attention from the painting and shook the offered hand. "Smith."

The woman smiled. "Gwen Banks. It's a pleasure, Mr. Smith."

Payton nodded. "Indeed. Yes. I will speak with my wife about this, but first, I wonder if I may trouble you for some information."

Gwen nodded. "Certainly. I own the gallery and am intimately acquainted with each piece."

Payton shook his head and smiled. "Pardon me. I must explain. I'm looking for information concerning a...relative of mine. A cousin who disappeared sometime ago. We've received word he may be in the area."

"Oh my. A missing person? I'll help if I can but the police may be a better choice."

Payton pulled an old photo from his pocket, a studio shot taken nineteen years earlier. In it, Hunt Masterson held an acoustic guitar and grinned like he had the world at his feet. He and Clay had formed a band and were planning a trip to Nashville. Clay made it to Music City. Hunt never did.

Gwen scrutinized the photo, frowning. "No, I can't say I know him."

"He's a country music musician, if that helps. My source tells me he's been spotted playing in a local bar." His source was Clay, who called him upon hearing the news. Since Payton had been Hunt's childhood best friend, Clay knew Payton would aid his search again.

She laughed. "Well, Angel Beach only has one bar, Captain Bob's, and I don't believe they have live entertainment there regularly. We do have a few wine tasting rooms featuring quartets and such." She took another look at the photo. "The closest we come to a floorshow in this town is the homeless man who plays his guitar in front of the bakery." She chuckled at her own cleverness. "I will admit he's good, but I doubt he's your cousin." She looked at Payton, taking in the expensive clothing.

A homeless person was an interesting thought. Considering Hunt's circumstances, he couldn't have a conventional music career. He'd draw too much attention to himself. A homeless street musician made perfect sense. "A homeless man, you say? I doubt it could be him, but one never knows. Can you describe him?"

"Oh yes. I walk by him every day at lunchtime. He's rather tall and his gray hair is worn in a ponytail."

"A ponytail?" Payton asked. Hunt in a ponytail? He'd like to see that. Hunt had always had that Marlboro-man aura around him. Outdoorsy and masculine. Payton smiled at the idea. If Hunt now sported a ponytail, would he wear sandals and khakis, too?

"His hair is long and in the wind a ponytail is a necessity, I would think. He does have a deep, pleasant singing voice." She smiled and blushed. "Gravelly at times."

Payton gave her a taciturn smile. The woman was enamored with the musician, confirming for Payton the homeless man could be Hunt Masterson. It had always been that way. Even as teenagers, the girls always made a big deal over Hunt with his beautiful blue eyes and musical talent. All but one. Lynette had always been Payton's. Not that Hunt hadn't tried with her. He had. Even now, Payton felt a twinge when he thought of Lynette. Her death would haunt him forever and he wouldn't stop searching until he found Hunt Masterson.

"He plays country music, mostly," Gwen went on. "I've asked him to play a few tunes for me at times. I love romantic ballads." Her blush deepened. "He needs the money, you know. It's the charitable thing to do."

"Yes. Of course. Would you happen to know this homeless person's name?"

She shook her head. "No. You might ask at the bakery. The girls there would surely know."

Payton nodded. "I'll do that next. Thank you for your assistance." He shook her hand and executed a head tilt resembling a bow.

Gwen shook the proffered hand. "It was my pleasure. Possibly I'll see you again? The painting?" she quickly added.

"Possibly." He turned to leave.

"Oh, Mr. Smith? You may want to wait on the bakery visit."

"Why is that?"

She laughed. "Well, a little earlier they had a commotion going on there and I doubt it's cleared yet. Last I knew, the police were trying to straighten out the mess."

Payton waited, his eyebrows raised.

"There was a big brouhaha concerning a celebrity, a country music singer, I understand. We seem to have an abundance of them at the moment."

Payton restrained the urge to laugh. It sounded like Clay got himself into trouble. "Oh really? What happened?"

"Well, a large group of women cornered him in the bakery and from what I heard, stripped his clothes from him." She said it with shock, but Payton could tell she wished she'd been in on it. "Then the police picked him up and took him home. It was quite a thing for this little town."

"I imagine so. I appreciate the warning. I'll delay my bakery visit. Thank you for your time." He left the gallery wearing a smile. Clay's brush with the female population made his next move much easier. Knowing Clay, he'd hole up in his house for a while and as long as he was sequestered, Payton was free to investigate this homeless man further without involving Clay.

He would need to change tactics though. On his way into town, he'd spotted a consignment shop and thought it might have what he required. He glanced in a store window reflection at his clean-shaven face. That wouldn't do. He'd need to let the whiskers grow and muss his hair some. While he contemplated other transformation necessities, he hit speed dial on his cell phone and reached voicemail.

"Clay. Payton here. It looks like I'll be delayed and may not make it to Angel Beach until next week. I'm so sorry to leave you on your own but you know how things are at the Trust these days. So much need and so little time. I'll be in touch...oh, and let me know if you find out anything about your father. See you soon."

He disconnected the call, smiling. Hunt Masterson was nearby. He could feel it.

⊙≫

The police cleared the human clutter from Clay Masterson's fan-club jamboree, but Harlie was left with the fallout. She swept the mess, grumbling irritably between broom strokes. Beach sand made up the bulk of the pile; cookie crumbs and bread scraps came a close second. During the rampage, several lunch trays were knocked to the floor, sending plates and sticky pop into the mix. When she saw a blue fabric scrap from Clay's shirt in the heap, her temper surged but fizzled. The blame for this chaos lay squarely on Clay Masterson's shoulders and she wanted to unleash her anger on him.

Damn the man, anyway. He had to tell her he was searching for his father and now she couldn't flat out dislike him.

She surveyed her progress. There was still a jumble of cockeyed chairs and tables to tackle. But the mess was only half the problem. Clay himself created a host of new complications. As if she didn't have enough already. Clay would make life miserable, maybe even dangerous. She imagined it wouldn't be long until the screaming crowd of hormonal women discovered where he lived and would hover around the beach gate hoping for glimpses of him. Now, more than ever, she needed her privacy, safely tucked behind the security fence, and she feared his fans would breach her sheltered world with their camera phones and celebrity obsession. If it happened, her life would be agony.

Harlie dumped the dustpan in the garbage can and stopped for a breather. On the radio: Lady Antebellum. The doorbell jingled. A pair of young women, beach bags thrown over their shoulders and hunger in their eyes, entered. Harlie's spirits lifted.

"Can I help you?" she asked, leaning on her broom.

"We heard Clay Masterson is here." The taller of the two glanced around as if she expected the man to be waiting for her with open arms.

Harlie frowned. "No. He isn't. And we aren't sure if it was him. Might have been a look-alike," Harlie added, hoping to kill the rumors and avoid a home invasion.

"Oh. Okay," the girl said, disappointed. "Thanks anyway." They departed empty handed.

In and out all afternoon, one star-struck female after another asked for Clay Masterson as if Harlie had him on display like a prize salmon from a fishing derby.

At 4:00 p.m., she closed for the day and departed with an armload of bread and other goodies. The afternoon was crisp, but the horizon remained clear. A few miles north of town, she drove into a private campground. As soon as she turned off the engine and opened the door, two boys ran out of a travel trailer, screaming.

"Harlie! Did you bring cookies?"

She held up a bag. "Would I visit you without cookies?" The two boys, both towheaded, bounced with excitement, waiting for their treats. "Chocolate chip or snickerdoodles?"

"Chocolate chip," they said in unison. She handed the eldest the bag.

"How is your mom today?" Harlie noticed their energy level slackened. "Is something wrong?"

The smaller boy frowned. "Mama's crying again."

The older boy nudged him and glowered. "You weren't supposed to tell. Mom said."

A knot hardened in Harlie's stomach. She rubbed her hand cross the younger boy's soft hair. "Don't worry about it. I'll talk to her." The boys wandered to the picnic table and tore into the cookie bag. Harlie grabbed other bags filled with bread and lunch meat and knocked softly on the door of the twenty-foot travel trailer Lisa and her sons called home. Not waiting for a response, she entered and heard sniffling in the dark interior. The shades were drawn and Lisa lay inert on the sofa. Streams of daylight highlighted an easel propped against the stove. Paint and brushes covered the counter. Harlie set the bags on the dinette and sat on the floor near Lisa and brushed her hand across her pale blonde hair. She was such a pretty woman, but her difficult life was beginning to show. She was too thin and always wore dark circles beneath her eyes.

"What's wrong, sweetie? Bad day?"

Lisa sniffed. "How about a bad life?" She squeezed her eyes tight and tears trickled down her cheek. "Why did Larry have to die?"

Harlie tightened her arm around Lisa and laid her cheek to her head. "I don't know." Harlie hadn't known Lisa's husband, having met her after his death when the struggling mom brought her hungry boys to The Center's Wednesday lunch. The three had appeared so forlorn Harlie sat with them while they ate and asked what she could do to help. Lisa sat straight-backed and refused to talk, but the boys held no such reserve.

"Daddy died and Mama cries all the time," the older one said. He was only nine but his eyes were old and sad.

Lisa told him to hush. "We don't need any help. I heard there was a nice lunch served at the Senior Center every week so we came to visit with people."

Harlie didn't believe that for a second. "It's a good place to hang out. Enjoy your lunch," she said and went back to work. After lunch, Harlie watched as Lisa and her boys went into the large room housing the food bank. Judging by the boys' excitement, their cupboards at home were empty as Mother Hubbard's. Harlie grabbed a cardboard box and filled it with extra goodies she had in the back: cookies and bread from the bakery, kids' cereal, and feminine products. When Lisa reached the front of the line, a food bank volunteer filled a box with staples: rice, flour, spaghetti, tomato paste, and beans. Lisa took the box with reluctance and immediately left The Center, her head hung low. With the box she'd prepared, Harlie followed Lisa to the parking lot and watched her leave in a dilapidated Chevy pickup. Harlie hopped in her car and followed Lisa to the Forest Grove Campground. When

Lisa saw her, she glared. When she saw the box Harlie carried, Lisa broke into tears.

"The boys left without their cookies," Harlie said. "We always give the kids extra cookies." Lisa invited her into the trailer and they'd been friends since.

Harlie gave her friend a reassuring squeeze. "Whatever's wrong, I'll help you any way I can. What happened?"

Lisa sat up. Her eyes were puffy and red and her hair scrunched on one side. She raked her fingers through it. "Everything is wrong and won't ever be right again." She blew out a shaky breath. "I had a meeting at the unemployment office last week and they told me this week was my last check. No extensions. When I went to pay my site rent, I told Mr. Quist I was having money trouble and asked him if he'd work something out with me. He said he'd think about it." She grabbed a piece of paper from the table and handled it to Harlie. "Today he brought me that. He says if I can't pay the rent, he wants me out of here by the end of the month. He's not running a charity for squatters." She bit her lip and shrugged. "I have no money and nowhere to go, Harlie. If I lose this spot I'll have to park the trailer in the woods somewhere, and we won't have electricity or sewer. It's not safe..." She swallowed hard. "I can't find a job and I've been looking hard. There isn't anything and people are getting tired of me asking. And my plumbing is leaking."

Harlie drummed her fingers on the sofa. What should she tackle first? "Okay. Here's what we'll do for now. I have a little in savings. I'll pay for another month—"

"No, Harlie. I won't take your money."

"Yes, you will."

"No—"

Harlie held up her hand. "Hear me out, okay? I could really use some part-time help this summer. Sam comes in around three in the morning and should be gone by eleven. She hasn't been able to do that because Annie is taking summer classes at the college and doesn't make it in until twelve thirty. So, I need help."

Tears welled in Lisa's eyes and her lip quivered. "Oh Harlie, could you really? You aren't creating a job because you feel sorry for me, are you?"

"I need the help. At least for now. June isn't too bad but July should be busy. I'm also staying open on Sunday for the summer, so I need someone. After Labor Day, I can't make any promises. We should know what's going on with the motel property soon. It has kitchenette units and I'd like to use one wing for families. If that doesn't work out fast enough, I can talk with my landlord about putting a hookup by my cottage. You won't live in the woods if I can help it."

Lisa laughed and wiped her eyes. "As much as I would love to live at your place, I doubt your landlord would agree. With the huge house next door and the oceanfront location, that place must be valued at over a million."

"Three." Harlie sighed. "You're right. I'm in pipedream-land again. You could stay with me in the cottage. It would be tight, but—"

Lisa laughed again. "Harlie, your cottage is perfect for one person. Maybe two. Four of us would burst its seams. I'll take the job."

"Good. It will help us both. Now, about the plumbing. I'll talk to Buck and see if he'll come by and take a look at it. He can fix anything. I'll do that on my way home."

"Thanks, Harlie. I don't know what I'd do without the two of you. Did you know Buck's been coming by and hanging out with the boys while I go to interviews? He tells them hunting and fishing stories and says he'll bring his guitar sometime and teach them to play. The boys call him Grandpa Buck." She laughed. "He seems to like it a lot."

"He told me once he had a couple of sons. He probably likes to spend time around your boys because of it." Buck used past tense when he spoke of his sons but he'd never explained what happened to them. "He's a good guy," Harlie said. She stood and gave Lisa a hug. "I need to get moving. Let me know when you can start working and I'll get you on the schedule."

She left the campground with a heavy heart. Her solutions were a Band-Aid on a gushing hemorrhage. Lisa needed a good job and a real home for her kids.

Harlie needed help to stem the tide of disasters. But who? She'd exhausted every avenue. Her mind churned as she pulled into Emily's driveway. Buck would help with the plumbing. The part-time job would take care of the site rental for a few months. But what happened after Labor Day? What happened when Lisa's trailer was too old to fix? She needed an apartment or house, but there was no way she'd come up with first and last month's rent. If Lisa could sell a painting it would help, but the galleries were hurting, too. Harlie was running out of answers.

She knocked on Buck's garage door. No answer.

"He's in here!" Emily called and waved from the porch of her large Victorian home.

Harlie trotted along the sidewalk, slowing to give Emily a raised brow.

Emily laughed. "What a dirty-minded thing you are. He's asleep on the couch. Obviously alone."

They walked in the kitchen. Harlie peeked through the door to the living room and saw Buck sleeping on his side, a green afghan across him. "Is he okay?"

"He's sore where the seatbelt grabbed him but that's all I can see. For some reason that little accident really stirred him up. I asked if he wanted to go out for breakfast this morning and he refused to leave the house." She shrugged. "Maybe he'll talk to you. Want some tea?"

"Herbal?"

"Would I offer you anything else?"

Several cups of peppermint tea later, Buck stirred and wandered to the kitchen and leaned on the doorframe, bleary eyed. "Hey, Angel."

"Hey, Buck. Are you okay?"

He shrugged and blinked several times. "Normal, I guess. A little sore." He rubbed his chest. "Had a headache earlier. Nothing serious."

"Good. Can I ask a favor? Lisa says her plumbing is leaking. Can you take a look?"

"Sure. I'll wander out that way. Tomorrow soon enough?" Buck grabbed a beer from the fridge and sat in a chair at the table, wrinkling his nose at Harlie's peppermint tea.

She nodded. "I don't think it's an emergency yet." She sipped her tea. "You won't believe who my new neighbor is."

"Oh, the goober has a name now, does he?" Emily said with a smile.

"Does he ever. A big one."

Buck smiled. "What does that mean? You can't pronounce the thing?"

"No. I mean he's famous. Since you're into country music you probably know who he is."

Buck shrugged. "I don't follow the new guys much. Who is he?"

"You'll know him. He's one of the super biggies— Clay Masterson. He came in the bakery today showing a picture around. Says he's looking for his dad." She leaned her elbows on the table. "Get this. His dad disappeared eighteen years ago and he's still looking for him. That's love, isn't it? Can you imagine having someone care that much? I haven't seen my mom in fourteen years and I doubt she's given me a thought."

Buck was quiet, concentrating on the beer tab as if it held the secrets of the universe. "I suppose that's one way to look at it. Has he said why he's so determined to find the guy?"

She shook her head. "No. We didn't talk much."

"Did you recognize the man in the picture?" Emily asked.

"No. A large part of the picture was missing. A bunch of women cornered him and the picture was torn into pieces. He said he'll print another one and bring it over for me to look at. Isn't that wild though? Eighteen freaking years."

"It's quite a story all right," Buck said. "You gotta wonder though. The kid is famous, right? A big-time star like him wouldn't be hard to find."

"So?"

"So, why hasn't the father gone to him? What kind of bad blood is there between the two that the father doesn't want the kid finding him?" Buck shrugged. "I don't know that I'd help him, Angel. You might be stirring a nest of spiders."

"I didn't say I planned to help him," Harlie said. "I agreed to look at his picture."

Buck laughed. "Angel Girl, you've never turned down a cry for help since I've known you. But this guy isn't one of your normal down-and-outs. He's got a whole shitload of money and could easily hire detectives to do this for him. Ask yourself, why is he doing the legwork himself? Guys like him throw their money around and get other people to do their dirty work." He pushed back from the table and tossed the beer can in the trash.

Harlie frowned. "It's more like a labor of love, not dirty work. Why wouldn't he do it himself?"

"Did he tell you that?"

She shook her head. "No, but—"

"Take my advice, Angel. Stay clear of him. He seems like bad news to me." He leaned down and kissed Emily. "I've got some things to do. See you later, honey." He wandered out the door, closing it quietly behind him.

Harlie looked at Emily, smiling. "Honey?"

Emily blushed. "Don't you be reading anything into it. Not a thing."

6

As Harlie drove along her shrubbery-lined driveway, a shiver cruised along her spine. Something wasn't right and it had a lot to do with the large man sitting on her front step. He wore a gray sweatshirt with the hood up and she couldn't see his face. How did he get in the gate? If it was the reporter, she should back up and run. If it was Glen Carson, she couldn't run fast enough. He looked up, waved, and smiled. Harlie sighed with relief.

Clay Masterson.

And as fast as her relief came, it deserted her. Why was Clay Masterson sitting on her step? Buck's warning came to mind but she waved it away. Buck had a suspicious mind honed by years of living rough. Clay wanted to show her a picture. She'd look at it and he'd go home.

Easy.

She stopped her car near the cottage and climbed out. The late afternoon air was brisk, but Clay was busy scratching her cat's stomach and didn't seem to care. Spud was about as unsociable as a cat could get, and she couldn't figure out why he was flat on his back, writhing in ecstasy, while Clay scratched his massive white belly.

"My cat has serious issues with people touching him. How'd you get him to do that?" she asked.

"What?"

"The belly exposure thing. He never does that for anyone but me."

Clay shrugged. "I didn't do anything but sit here and he flopped down next to me. I love animals. Maybe he senses it." He scratched Spud's ears, sending the cat into spasms of joy.

"Well, he certainly likes you. Did you bring the picture?"

He shook his head. "No. It's on my laptop and I don't have the printer connected yet."

"Well, okay. Let me know when—"

He looked up at her, squinting into the afternoon sun. "I was wondering if you'd have dinner with me...to make up for my poor manners. I can show you the picture after we eat."

Harlie poked at her hair, trying to assess the workday devastation. The braid was messy and loose pieces hooked around her face. "You want to take me out to dinner?"

He smiled. "Sorry. Not dinner out. I cooked spaghetti and was wondering if you'd like to come over and eat. Nothing fancy, just a casual get-to-know-the-neighbors mixer."

She glanced around. "There are only two of us."

"I noticed. What do you say?"

She couldn't think of a valid reason not to go. "Can I have time to clean up first?"

Forty-five minutes later, Harlie knocked on Clay's door with a shaking hand. This wasn't a date so why the sudden case of nerves? The matter was settled when Clay opened the door and his billion-watt smile knocked her into next week. She wished he'd quit doing that and go back to being the grump she met yesterday. This good-natured gorgeous man was almost too much for a woman's system to handle on a Thursday night.

He wore faded jeans and a striped, pale blue shirt that intensified his blue eyes. She'd bet that was calculated. Harlie wore a white blouse and purple pullover crewneck sweater and her hair was braided and tidy. It was a no-frills look that suited her. Clay took her corduroy jacket and hung it in the hall closet while she glanced around the grand house. She'd seen it before with the rental agent, for a curiosity-satisfying look-see, but hadn't seen it when occupied. Now, newspapers lay in a haphazard pile on the coffee table and guitars, amps, and sheet music were scattered around the room. His laptop sat on the end of the dining table, which had a perfect ocean view through the wall of windows. A fire burned bright in the native stone fireplace.

"Something to drink?" he asked. "Beer, wine..."

"I don't drink."

"How about tea?"

"Decaffeinated?"

He shook his head and looked a bit lost, apparently running through his list of available beverages.

"Water is fine," she said.

"It comes out of the tap. Unfiltered. Any problem with that?"

"Tap water is fine. We share a well so I know it isn't fluoridated."

He raised his eyebrows. "Fluoridated is bad?"

She shrugged. "According to some studies."

He gestured toward the kitchen. "Would you like to come in and inspect dinner to see if I produced any ecological disasters? I know the spaghetti sauce isn't organic and I can't say where the ground beef came from, but I'm reasonably sure it doesn't possess mad cow disease." He paused. "You do eat beef, right?"

"I'm not a vegan. I take care of my body, that's all. If I didn't eat beef, would you have a problem with that?"

"Hmm..." He frowned. "Are we arguing again? I thought the whole idea was to bury the hatchet somewhere other than my head. For the record, I'm a fourth-generation Montana cattleman and believe every person on the planet should consume at least one serving of beef daily. Maybe two. But then, I'd also like world peace and I doubt I'll get that one either."

Harlie resisted but a smile tugged at her mouth. "Are you ever serious?"

"Not when I'm nervous about having dinner with a beautiful woman whose attitude toward me is debatable."

"A beautiful woman, huh? Are you expecting another guest for dinner?" Harlie almost bit her tongue. He'd think she was fishing for compliments.

"Just you, darlin'. Are you ready to eat?"

Clay brought the spaghetti pots and salad from the kitchen while Harlie sat at the table. The guy could cook, even if the food came from dubious origins. She was starved and didn't care if the beef had taken a trip over the moon.

Harlie took careful bites of her spaghetti, making sure she didn't slurp and slap herself in the face with a noodle. A tense silence grew between them but eventually, Clay broke it.

"You're uncomfortable."

She looked up from her meal, unwilling to admit it was true.

"I said I was sorry. I am sorry. I acted like a jerk or a...a...what was the word you used?"

She swallowed a bite of spaghetti and dabbed her lips with a napkin. "Goober. It's a personal favorite."

He nodded and pointed at her. "That's it. A goober. It's a good one, by the way. But I apologized. I cooked you dinner. What can I say? I wasn't having a good day."

"Because of your dad?"

"That and other things."

"Like what? They didn't upgrade you to first class on the flight?"

"I don't fly commercial. No, I thought you were a stalker. You know, a whacked-out fan."

He said it as if that explained everything, like she should understand his problem. Unfortunately, she had experience with a stalker but she wouldn't call hers a fan. He was more of an obsessed lunatic whose last name she happened to share for a while. Harlie nodded, thoughtfully. "A stalker?"

"Right. It happens all the time."

"My elderly companion and I were stalking you?" Buck would kill her if he heard that loathsome word attached to him. "Hmmm... And I had a car accident, nearly plunging over a two-hundred-foot cliff into the Pacific Ocean, so you would stop and I could follow you home?"

"Well, no. I thought, maybe, you'd recognized me, and—"

"And was so filled with fan lust I followed you home so I could jump you and have wild jungle sex in the driveway?" She set her fork down when a laugh bubbled up, punctuated by a snort.

"Well, if I'd known your intention..." He looked thoughtful. "I know, it sounds pretty stupid now, but at the time it made perfect sense." He smiled. "I did say I was acting like a paranoid idiot."

Harlie nodded and wiped at her eyes with the napkin. She laughed so hard, tears filled them. "Yes, you did and you were." She finally controlled her laughing fit and saw he was grinning at her.

"What?"

"I like the way you laugh. That snorting thing is adorable."

"I don't snort."

"Yeah, you do. It's great. I like it and I'm trying to figure out how to make you laugh again."

She scrunched her brow and looked at him, trying to remain serious. "What's for dessert?"

"Tillamook Ice Cream. It's almost local and I understand their cows are quite happy and live long, meaningful lives."

She covered her mouth and laughed, trying to cover the snort she knew would pop out. When she could talk without snort-laughing, she said, "I appreciate your humor. I haven't had a great day either."

"Ice cream will fix it. Come on. I'll show you the photo and then we'll have dessert." He moved to the laptop and pulled up two chairs. When he opened the file, the full face of Hunt Masterson stared at her. Without the Picasso distortion, she could see he was an attractive man. She stared, trying to determine if she'd seen him before. Something nagged at her, but she couldn't put her finger on it.

"Like I said earlier, this was taken twenty years ago. Try to imagine him with some wrinkles and gray hair."

"I don't know. I see so many people in the bakery." She concentrated harder. There was something familiar about him. The eyes, maybe the smile. Clay looked a lot like his father whether he wanted to admit it or not. She shrugged. "Sorry. I don't think I've seen him."

"You're sure?" He let out a disappointed sigh when she shrugged. "It was worth a try. I'll get the dinner mess cleaned up."

"I'll help."

He waved her offer away. "Guests don't do dishes."

"Do you mind if I look on the Internet while you're busy?"

"Help yourself."

While Clay cleared the table, Harlie Googled Skip Hyatt and struck cyber gold when more than fifty hits appeared. He was a bear of a man, heavyset, bearded, and sharp-eyed. He'd won an amazing number of journalism awards, mostly for investigative reporting, and his articles were strewn across cyberspace. This explained his dissatisfaction with Glen Carson's standard bio. Hyatt was a junkyard dog looking for a fight. Harlie would love to see Carson's underbelly exposed but she couldn't help Skippy the Bloodhound do it. Not if she wanted to continue her present life.

When she read everything pertaining to the reporter, she closed the websites, minimized the Internet, and found an open file on the screen behind. The file contained scanned images of typed notes. The first said: "Follow the blood. He was there." The second said:

"Low E plays death's song." The file name was "NOTES," which didn't clarify anything. Harlie heard footsteps and closed the file, returning to the Internet.

"Clay, did you know you have close to four thousand e-mails?"

He walked around behind her. "Already? I had it culled down to thirty-five hundred last night."

"Don't you have secretaries or assistants for this stuff?"

"Yeah, but I like to answer some fan mail myself. It gives me something to do when I can't sleep. Let me see the mouse." He leaned over her, closing the fan mail account and opening another. "This is the personal account. Not so much here." He glanced down the list. "Huh, there's another one. I hadn't heard from him lately."

"Someone special?"

Clay sat in the chair next to her and opened the e-mail. The screen name was Countryman.

"I guess so. It's kind of funny. This person started e-mailing the fan club about three years ago. The letters were full of compliments and stuff, the normal fan mail material, but then he starting giving me guitar advice. I thought he was a real nervy crackpot or something. I mean, I have a fair concept of how to play a guitar. But when I read it again, I realized this guy really knew his stuff. He really knew my stuff, too. He told me how much he liked my new song but if I played a certain part different, the effect would be

amazing. I'm always open to new ideas, so I tried it."
Clay smiled. "He was right. I made the change and still
play it that way. I wrote back and thanked him for the
suggestion and we've been corresponding ever since. I
gave him the private e-mail a couple of years ago. I
have no idea who he is. He doesn't sign his name, just
calls himself my biggest fan." He read through the e-
mail and closed it. "I'll answer him later." He moved
around the table, grabbing the last of the dinner mess,
and returned to the kitchen.

Harlie saw an acoustic guitar leaning against a large
footstool and sat by it and strummed the strings. Clay
cringed and laughed. "You don't play, do you?"

She shook her head. "I never had the opportunity
for lessons. No, I shouldn't say that. My friend Buck
plays and offered to teach me but we haven't had time
yet."

"If you'd like to learn, I'll teach you."

"Really? You'd teach me?"

"Sure. As long as I'm here, I'll give you lessons." He
handed her the Gibson guitar from the floor and he
grabbed another from a nearby stand.

After fifteen frustrating minutes of chords and basic
guitar theory, Harlie was ready to give up. Clay
wouldn't hear of it. He crouched in front of her, offering a hands-on teaching approach. "Put your left hand
here, like this." He moved her hand and positioned her
fingers on the frets. "Then move your right hand, like

this." She did and they both cringed at the horrible sound she made.

"Ouch!" he said.

She laughed. "I'm completely inept."

"Don't say that. You need practice."

After a few more minutes of her mangled music, Clay stood and swung his leg over the foot stool, filling the space behind her. "This works better," he said. With his arms around her, he moved her fingers to the proper position and strummed the guitar with her right hand. "Like that," he said. "You try it."

Harlie was warm, like a fever moved through her body in search of a virus. She tried to strum the guitar as he'd shown her, but her mishmash attempts didn't resemble the sound he'd made. He moved her hands again, his calloused fingers positioning hers. As his long legs cradled her hips and his arms held her close, her focus strayed from the guitar lesson to the man behind her. He continued his instructions, but Harlie couldn't concentrate. His low, smooth voice in her ear was too distracting. He shifted his weight, pressing tighter. Harlie's breath caught. She could feel his body heat against her back. The bad part: she enjoyed it. Good grief, she'd known him a little over twenty-four hours and she already wanted to lean into him and never leave. He shifted again and his breath grazed her ear. She tensed.

He chuckled. "Relax, Harlie. You'll never get it if you're tensed up."

"It's tough to relax when a man I barely know wraps himself around me like a giant squid."

"It's a guitar lesson. I'm not hitting on you."

She swallowed. "I didn't think you were."

"Yeah, you did. And since you have a problem with it, I wouldn't consider it. Yet. When I'm ready to hit on you, darlin', you'll know it." He moved her fingers again. "This is E," he said.

Harlie stiffened again, remembering the computer file. "Is that low E?" Low E plays death's song... She wondered about the note but didn't dare ask. Possibly it was a morbid song lyric.

"This is. The thicker one. In standard tuning, it's low E." He picked it. "Hear the difference?"

"Yes. Clay?" she whispered.

"Hmm?"

"I need to use your bathroom."

"Sure." Clay moved the guitar so she could get up. "There's one beyond the kitchen."

Once free, she hurried to the bathroom. As she suspected, the face reflected in the mirror was flushed. "Oh, man." She closed her eyes, splashed cool water on her steaming cheeks and smoothed her hair. She returned to the living room and stopped in the shadow inside the hall to watch Clay play the guitar she'd mistreated earlier. He stopped playing and glanced over his shoulder to where Harlie stood, as though feeling her eyes on him. He smiled and her heart launched into a frenetic bongo beat. She took a deep breath and crossed the room to the couch, putting distance between them.

"What was the song you were playing?"

"Oh that." He laughed. "It's a little song my dad wrote. He called it his protest song."

"What was he protesting?"

"Anything that came to mind. He'd change words around whenever he felt like it. One day he protested taxes, another day it might be war, or maybe artificial sweeteners. It was a mood thing. Man, I haven't thought about the song in years."

"Can I ask you something?"

"Sure."

"What happened eighteen years ago? Why is your dad missing?" She might as well poke the spiders' nest.

Clay lay the guitar aside and was quiet a moment. "The official story was he was driving through Wyoming. The highway patrol thought he fell asleep at the wheel and crossed the centerline. A semi crushed the driver's side."

"But you don't believe he died?"

"For a long time I did. But I heard stories about people seeing him. My friend Tom calls them Elvis 7-Eleven sightings. I ignored it for a long time. Then about five years ago, I got more and more calls about it, so I began investigating the sightings."

"But how could he survive an accident like that?"

"I don't think he was driving. I heard he had a friend with him and I think it was the friend behind the wheel. My dad walked away. Maybe he was thrown out on impact or something." He shrugged. "The highway patrol said the ID matched the registration so they didn't question his identity. The body was cremated in Wyoming and the urn sent to me."

"So, he has amnesia and is wandering around the country in a fog?"

He laughed. "I doubt it. Dad left some problems behind I think he wanted to avoid. His death would take care of it."

"Problems? What could be bad enough to make a man want to disappear?"

Clay blew out a breath. "Drinking, gambling, women."

"He cheated on your mother?"

"No. She died when I was two. After that, Dad had no problem finding women to fill his time and he frequently got himself into trouble with them. His supposed death came at a bad time for him though. We'd put together a band and decided to head to Nashville and give it a try. Made demo tapes and had pictures taken." He frowned. "Next thing you know, he's dead."

"But why hasn't he contacted you? I can't imagine you'd be difficult to find." she said, repeating Buck's theory.

He shrugged. "I guess he has his reasons. I'd like to find him to confirm if he's alive. Then he can drift into the mists again if it's what he wants." He picked up the guitar and laid it in a stand. "I was wondering if you'd be willing to help me with this."

"How could I help you?"

"Go out with me tomorrow night," he said.

"And this would be the hitting on me situation you warned me about earlier?"

He grinned. "No. I need to check out some bars and clubs in the area. I usually have a friend with me but he can't make it until next week. I'd rather not go alone and I'll bet you could find these places easier than I can. What do you say? I'll buy dinner and whatever beverage you deem pure enough to put in your body."

What could she say? Buck was right; she'd never turned down a call for help. She had a hero complex or something. "Wait a sec…how can you go out to bars after what happened today? I don't want to get caught in the middle of some hormonal rampage."

"Well, I have a good idea what happened. I heard one of those gals say 'Grandma said we'd catch up to him if we hurried.' The lady at the Dolphin Shop set them on me. I think I'd have been fine otherwise. Besides, bars are different. People are wrapped up in themselves and if anyone wants to hassle me, there are usually bouncers. Will you go with me?"

She looked into those pleading blue eyes and found him hard to resist. "How tall are you?"

"Six three."

"Good. I can wear heels."

7

"You did what?" Buck sat on the same stool Clay had occupied the day before, looking at Harlie like she'd escaped a padded cell and needed a one-way ticket back. Right now, Harlie might agree with him. What possessed her to help Clay? She didn't know, but she planned to follow through. The way he'd looked at her with those beautiful blue eyes, she'd follow Clay Masterson into any skanky bar he wanted to visit.

"I said I'd help. It's not a big deal, Buck. He wants to do some bar hopping to show his dad's picture around. I'll give directions. Not much else I can do." She picked up a tray of sugar cookies for the front case. "Have you checked on Lisa's plumbing yet?"

"It's fixed and I messed up my hand doing it. Don't count on me playing out front for a while." He held his bandaged hand up like it was a war wound and he deserved a medal.

Harlie set the tray down. "Let me look at it."

"Let it be. I'm fine." He grabbed his duffle bag with his good hand and headed out the back door, stopping for the last word. "Remember what I said. You don't know what you're getting into with this. There might be a lot more to this story than he's telling you."

"I'll be careful."

"You should—"

"I know! I'll watch out!"

Buck harrumphed and pushed his way out the door, mumbling under his breath about foolish young women. "Can't tell them anything."

Harlie pushed the door to the front counter open with her hip, skirted around Samantha, who was filling a lunch order, and deposited the cookies. She couldn't stop thinking about Buck's warning because there may be some truth to it. What did low E strings have to do with death songs and who was connected to blood? It was a puzzle and she'd lain awake last night wondering if it was relevant to Clay's search. Maybe his father was hiding from more than an overactive libido and a drinking problem.

"Smile, Harlie," Sam said. "Your scowl will scare the customers. What's wrong?"

Harlie leaned her back against the counter and sighed. "Buck is giving me grief over helping Clay. I knew he would but, darn it, I have to look at the big picture."

"Which is?"

"Clay has lots of money and I need some. It's a blunt way to put it but it's the truth. If I help him, he may be willing to help me."

Sam frowned. "What is going through your crafty brain?"

Harlie grinned. "I've got a plan."

"Oh, man, that sounds dangerous."

"Hear me out, Sam. Somebody outbid us on the motel property and we need to make a counter offer. We can't because we're out of money. I'm thinking I'll drop a few hints to Clay and see if I can convince him to help a worthy cause. People like him do things like that." She smiled. "I think I'll wear my red dress."

Sam crossed her arms and frowned. "The one with the oo-la-la neckline and the slit up the side?"

"It's perfect, isn't it?"

"If you want to get yourself in trouble. Harlie, that's one nasty little dress and I'd be real careful teasing him with it."

Harlie laughed. "This is me we're talking about. On another woman, it's a nasty little dress. On me, it's a simple red dress. Don't worry. I know what I'm doing."

⁂

Payton Shaw hated his new persona. His beard itched, the fishing hat rubbed his forehead, and the jeans, plaid flannel shirt, and Carhartt jacket were more befitting a logger. As much as he detested it, the look would get him closer to the people he needed to talk with.

The owner of the art gallery said the homeless guitar player plied his trade at the bakery during lunchtime and it was nearing noon. The Sweet Stuff Bakery and Cafe was crowded when he arrived. Too crowded. He went across the street and sat at a beachside picnic table, waiting for the crowd to thin and watching those who departed.

Angel Beach proper was built in a small valley created by wooded ridges crawling to the sea. The main business district fronted the long, sandy beach that curved around cliffs to the north and south. The angel rose from the roiling ocean north of town, fully visible from the beach and his picnic table perch. Payton had stopped at the viewpoint on arrival and enjoyed the sight of her. Now, his gaze was transfixed as his mind returned to the painting. Gwen, the gallery owner, was correct. The angel spoke to him, reminding him of his past love. Lynette hadn't deserved to die. She was only thirty-eight. Too young for a grave. His hands clenched as he thought of Hunt Masterson and his part in her death. If he'd left her alone, she'd be alive now. Payton dwelled on his memories of her, so beautiful with her long brown hair. Lynette was his first love. His only true love. Nadine was an adequate wife in every way. She was a good mother to their daughter, a fine hostess, and her family connections had paved Payton's way when they moved from Montana to Seattle. The Shaws assimilated with Seattle society quickly. But he'd never loved Nadine the way he'd loved Lynette.

He watched the bakery storefront, waiting for the homeless musician to appear, but the bench next to the flowerpot remained empty. He glanced at his watch and noticed the lunch hour was disappearing, as was the crowd. Traffic was thick, forcing him to wait for an opening to cross.

Inside the bakery, several tables held diners eating sandwiches and munching chips. Behind the counter, a tall brunette and a petite redhead were engaged in conversation. As he neared the counter the brunette walked toward him. She was attractive with not much makeup to speak of. Her hair was braided and the apron tied at her waist indicated a good figure, though she wasn't too thin.

"Ready to order?" she asked.

He took a moment to scan the menu behind the counter. "A cup of chicken noodle soup and coffee, please." He'd prefer the roast turkey on ciabatta bread, but he doubted a working-class man in flannel would order such a thing and it was too early in the game to draw attention. He paid his bill and took a seat at a small table near the windows. The angel wasn't visible from this position, which disappointed him. He'd formed a serious attachment to her. Unfortunately, he'd used a false name at the gallery. To return now to buy the painting would destroy his plans. Later, he'd call and purchase the painting on behalf of Mr. Smith. He'd have it yet.

The tall brunette brought his order. "Anything else I can get you?"

"No, this looks fine. But may I ask where the guitar player is today? Someone said he was really good and I'd like to hear him."

"I'm sorry. He won't be here today. He hurt his hand and is taking a break." She smiled. "But I'll pass on the compliment. Enjoy your meal." She stepped away, stopping when Payton addressed her again.

"Miss? This guitar player...is he a professional? Maybe I've heard of him..."

"He has enough talent, but I really don't know. His name is Buck if that helps you."

He shook his head. "No. Can't say that I've heard of him. Maybe I'll come by another day." He concentrated on his soup and she returned to the counter.

Buck. It wasn't one of Hunt's stage names but it would fit him well enough. Over the years, he'd used a number of them. Payton assumed the name changing was mainly to keep Hunt out of trouble with his lady friends. When he and Clay teamed up Hunt used his own name. Clay had the talent to make it in Nashville and Hunt knew it. He wanted everyone to know Clay was his son.

And then he messed with Lynette.

Payton finished his soup, left a small tip on the table, and wandered into the afternoon sun, inhaling the fresh ocean air deep into his lungs. The streets were filled with tourists carrying shopping bags. The highway traffic crawled. He doubted the main highway would produce results, so he made his way up Starfish Lane. The people he sought were backstreet and alley dwellers, not tourists. After a few minutes, Payton came across a small park where a man sat on a picnic table, staring into space. Dressed in faded jeans and a threadbare wool coat, Payton doubted he was a tourist.

He walked to the table and asked, "May I sit here?"

The man shrugged. "Not my table."

Payton sat and stared the direction of his new companion's gaze and saw kites bouncing in the ocean breeze. "Have they been up there long?"

The guy nodded. "Yeah. They'll fly 'em all afternoon. I like to watch the one shaped like a fighter jet."

"Can I ask you something? Do you know a guy named Buck?"

The man turned and gave him an assessing gaze. "What if I do?"

"He plays guitar, right?"

He shrugged. Payton knew where they were heading and reached into his pocket for some loose bills. He handed the man a twenty.

He held it up to the sun before stuffing the bill in his pants pocket. "Yeah."

"What does he look like?"

The man shrugged. Payton gave him another twenty and was wishing he'd started with tens.

The man slid the second twenty to his pocket. "He's a big dude. Long gray hair. Wears a cowboy hat."

Payton knew he'd hit pay dirt. "Plays country music, right?"

The guy shrugged. Payton took that as a yes. "Do you know where I can find him? Where he lives?"

His recalcitrant companion remained silent. Payton took another twenty from his pocket and handed it to him.

"Nope. Can't say that I do. He comes and goes. There's a couple of places I see him. He likes the bench in front of the bakery. Usually at lunchtime. You might catch him at The Angel Beach Center. They do a lunch and food bank on Wednesdays. What do you want him for?"

Payton shrugged and adopted his companion's nonchalance. "Nothing special."

8

Voicemail: 4:00 p.m. "This is Clay. Leave a message. If I want to talk to you, you'll be the first to know."

"Smartass. This is Harv. I talked to Tom and he says you're gone for a while. Nice of you to tell me. I shuffled your schedule and can rebook most of it. Luckily, you were lightly scheduled. There is one concert you're stuck with and I'm assuming you won't bail on your own Foundation. I need to hear from you soon. If I don't, you'll want to work on getting rid of any tan lines on your backside. There could be a *Playgirl* centerfold with your name on it. CALL ME!"

Clay disconnected the call, kicked the recliner back, and hit speed dial. Tom Black answered after the second ring.

"It's about time you called."

"Nice to talk to you, too, bro. What's so urgent?" He grabbed the remote and turned on the TV. He had a few hours before he needed to shower and dress for his night out with Harlie. He wondered if she'd wear her Converse All Stars. He was kind of fond of the plaid ones she wore last night, but she said she'd wear heels. That put a different twist on it. The TV blasted out SpongeBob Squarepants and he flipped the channel.

"Are you listening, Clay?" Tom said, irritated.

"What did you say?" The next channel played a Gary Cooper western. Good enough.

"You got another note. Sally found it in the mail this morning."

Clay groaned and turned off the TV. "Shit."

"My sentiments exactly. You out there alone is looking like a real bad idea."

"What does this one say? Any requests for money yet?"

"No. It's the same as the others. I really doubt this person's intent is blackmail. More like puzzle pieces. Whoever it is knows what went down in Montana and wants you to know he knows."

Clay stared out the windows at the rolling sea. "But why? There are only a few people who know about the low E string. The sheriff announced the murder weapon was a guitar string. He didn't specify which string. If it's my dad, why would he do this?"

"I don't know either. The new one is weird, too. It says 'Beer cans don't lie.'"

"Come again?"

"Beer cans don't lie."

"You're kidding me, Tom. Beer cans don't lie? What kind of bullshit is that?" Clay laughed, sure it was a hoax.

"I know it's stupid, but it's authentic. It came in the same kind of envelope on the same paper."

"What's the postmark?"

"Spokane. I've tried to figure out a pattern but don't see one."

Clay couldn't either. The others were mailed from Miami, Houston, and New York. He hadn't searched for his dad in any of the postmark cities. He blew out a frustrated breath. What the heck did a beer can have to do with it. Unless... "I got it, Tom."

"What?"

"The beer-can connection. Beer cans don't lie. They found a beer can in Lynette's trash and it had Dad's print on it."

"And a second one they couldn't identify."

"Right. So, is it my dad and he's playing with me, or is someone else trying to tell me something?"

"Maybe it is your dad. But why?" Tom sighed. "Now you have me buying into the idea he's alive."

"Maybe someone knows where he is and wants him found. Maybe Lynette's family? Her brother swore he'd kill Dad if he ever found him. Maybe he decided to look."

"But why send the notes to you? If Buster Dalton wants to kick Hunt's ass, he'd find him and take care of it. He isn't the kind of guy to mess around this way," Tom said. "I think it's either your dad or some-one with a score to settle. I have a theory about the second note and you aren't going to like it."

"What?"

"I don't think Lynette Dalton was the only victim."

Clay tensed. "Have you found something to prove it?"

"No, but I'm wondering if, 'Follow the blood. He was there,' could mean other crimes were committed. I gave Ed Meade the list of places you've searched over the years and told him to look for unsolved murders. His law firm has a guy who does research for him. An investigator. I thought they might come up with some ideas. Ed said he'll get back to me."

"I thought the old man could be a lot of things, but I never thought he could be a serial killer."

"It's a theory based on the notes. I could be way off. But if I'm right, that makes it much more danger-ous for you out there in Oregon playing Sherlock Holmes."

Clay laughed. "With the kind of luck I've had to-day, it's more like Inspector Clouseau."

"You need to talk to the police and—"

"And tell them what? My dead father, who won't stay dead, has possibly been murdering people all over the country and is sending bizarre notes to me? I have no proof, Tom. They'll think I'm crazy like the sheriff at home did when I told him my suspicions. They all think I'm still grieving for him and can't let go." He blew out a breath. "No. I have to keep at it and see if I can track him down. Payton will be here next week."

"And you'll wander around by yourself until then?"

"No. My neighbor is going to some bars with me tonight."

Tom chuckled. "This would be the neighbor with dark brown hair and legs that go on forever?"

"That's the one," Clay said, grinning.

"She'll be a lot of help."

"She's the kind of help I need right now. She knows the area. And if push comes to shove," Clay said, "I think she could hold her own."

At seven, Clay knocked on Harlie's door. The temperature was cool and he wore a leather coat and cowboy hat in case it rained. Harlie opened the door and Clay swore his heart stopped beating.

"Hey, Clay. Come in. Spud needs food before I leave. I'll be a sec." She sauntered into the kitchen, her liquid hips swaying in a seductive rhythm.

Clay tried to remember how to breathe. He never dreamed Harlie looked like that under the jeans, T-shirts, and Converse tennis shoes. He stepped into the room to grab a clandestine peek through the kitchen door. The way her red dress fit had his nerve endings jumping like theater popcorn. When she bent to pour the cat food, the slit revealed a beautiful thigh. He groaned. Her dress would ping the radar of every guy on the Oregon coast tonight. It was already bashing him like a sledge hammer.

"Okay," she said when she returned. "I'm ready to go." She grabbed a coat from the closet. Clay jumped into action and helped her put it on. She gave him a glorious smile over her shoulder, sending his heart into hyperdrive. "Thank you." She looked at him with her brow knitted. "Are you okay, Clay? You haven't said a word. Is my hair all right?" She ran her fingers through the wild riot of curls she'd unleashed from the braid. He wanted to put his hands in it, too.

"Your hair is beautiful," he managed to say without choking on his tongue.

He kept his eyes on the road, despite the distraction in the passenger seat. She was telling him something and he needed to stop ogling her legs and listen. Something about homeless people and shelters.

"It's a huge problem and it's getting worse. These unfortunate people have no place to go."

"Right. I'll bet it is a problem."

"It is. I have a friend, Lisa, who lives in a travel trailer with her two boys." She went on to explain the husband's death and the home foreclosure. "And that's just one. Rents are so high on the coast that a lot of employed people have trouble finding affordable housing. We see a lot of them at our food bank. It's heartbreaking."

"I imagine it is." Following her instructions, Clay pulled into the parking lot of a brewery pub touting a wide selection of ales. He walked around the Jeep and opened her door, gulping when she slid her legs out. Her dress rode up and she had to shimmy it down. Unfortunately, everything shimmied when she did it. He looked away and suppressed a frustrated groan. When he looked back, he was sure a satisfied gleam lit her eyes.

The pub was classy but comfortable and Clay liked the look of it. If he ever got his club idea off the ground, this kind of place appealed to him. Inside, the air was heavy with the aroma of fermented hops. He and Harlie made their way to the bar around crowded tables and Clay noticed all male eyes followed Harlie. He took her hand and kept her close.

Clay leaned on the bar, released her hand, and signaled to the bartender. After explaining his mission, the bartender shook his head.

"Never seen him before," he said. "Our clientele is younger so we don't hire older musicians. You might try the place on the point. Their clientele is more mature."

Clay thanked him and headed toward the door. Halfway there, he noticed Harlie wasn't with him. He backtracked and found her backed up to the bar with a small group of young guys vying for her. Clay tried to get her attention and failed. She was enjoying herself.

He elbowed through the crowd and grabbed her hand. "Come on, darlin'. We need to go." To the men he said, "Sorry boys. She's with me."

At the next bar, Clay again talked with the bartender. He didn't know Hunt Masterson but corralled other employees to look at the photo. While they debated if they knew him, Clay noticed Harlie had another salivating entourage. If he didn't pay attention, they'd pilfer his date. Clay reached through the crowd, grabbed her by the hand, and pulled her to him, holding her against his side. She was warm and soft and felt good there.

The bartender handed Clay the photo. "Sorry. We haven't seen him. Try..." And they were on their way down the highway to the next town.

"Any chance we can eat soon?" Harlie asked after a voracious stomach growl at the fifth stop. "If we keep going like this, you may need to carry me."

Clay glanced at his watch and saw it was getting late. "I'm sorry. Once I get going, I lose track of time. How about dinner at the next stop?"

It was nearly nine when they were seated. The pub was smaller than the others, the atmosphere cozy and romantic. Their table had a good view of the stage. After ordering coffee and herbal tea, Clay asked the waitress to look at the picture. She studied it but shook her head.

"He doesn't look familiar to me. Can I take this and show it to the bartender?" She did and returned a few minutes later.

"He says he doesn't recognize the guy, but we have someone new performing tonight. The owner hired him and the bartender hasn't seen him yet. It's an older man with a small band and they play country music. It might be your guy."

"Thanks." Clay returned the picture to his pocket and turned to Harlie wearing his first smile of the night.

Over dinner the conversation returned to Harlie's pet project: homelessness. She seemed to have her finger on the homeless pulse of the Oregon coast and wanted him to know every microscopic detail. It wasn't that he didn't care. He did. But it had been a while since he'd sat across the table from a beautiful woman and he wanted to enjoy it. He wanted to know things about her, but she was telling him another story.

"You should meet him," she said.

Clay frowned. "Who would that be, darlin'? I was busy admiring the view across the table and missed what you said."

Her cheeks flushed. "My friend Buck. You kind of met him already. He's the older guy who was in my car the day of the accident."

"I thought you said it wasn't an accident." He leaned on his elbows and smiled. "It was some sort of detour, you said. Not sure where you planned to detour since it was a good drop down the cliff to the ocean. Do Smart Cars float?"

She smiled and laughed. "I was shook up when I said that. Poor Buck was coughing up a lung and I thought I'd killed him or something."

"He's okay though?"

She nodded. "He was fine until he messed up his hand fixing Lisa's plumbing."

"Lisa who lives in the trailer?" She smiled, so he must have remembered correctly.

"Right. His bum hand will make it tougher for you to meet him though. We'd have to go by his tool shed and try to catch him there."

"Tool shed?"

"He lives in Emily's tool shed. Well, it's her deceased husband's workshop and man cave. He'd fixed it up with a woodstove, furniture, and bathroom. So it isn't like a garden shed. More like a no-frills apartment."

"You have interesting friends, Harlie."

Her face softened. "Well, Buck is pretty wonderful. He's gruff and opinionated, but he's the best."

Clay saw a sparkle in her eyes when she talked about this guy. "He's a friend, right? You two aren't...involved...are you?" It would be his luck to be attracted to a woman who was into geriatric men.

Harlie blinked several times. "Me and Buck? Involved? You mean like a boyfriend?"

He shrugged. "Well, the way you talk about him—"

Harlie laughed. "Me and Buck? Well, I hadn't thought of that. He's real good-looking and all, but I'm usually not into boinking old guys. He's at least sixty."

"Boinking?" Maybe if he was around Harlie longer, he might figure out her vocabulary. Sometimes, it was like she spoke another language. "What exactly is boinking?" As soon as it left his lips, he knew what she meant. "Oh, that."

She laughed at him. "Yeah. That."

"Boinking...must be another of your personal favorites?" he said.

She leaned across the table and gave him a serious stare. "Well, I have to admit to a lengthy dry spell, but I have been known to enjoy it on occasion."

Clay laughed and felt heat rise up his neck. "That wasn't exactly what I meant. I was thinking about your use of the word and..." He was babbling and she was laughing at him. Well, two could play at this game. He leaned across the table. "A dry spell, huh? When you're ready to break it, let me know."

She winked. "Maybe when I know you better."

The waiter brought dessert and Harlie returned to her previous topic. "Did I mention I run a food bank and weekly lunch for the impoverished in our area? We're having a tough time of it though. With the economy in a sinkhole, there are fewer donations. We've been the recipient of several food drives over the years. This year we benefited from the mail carriers' food drive, but the need is so great it isn't enough." She took a bite of her chocolate cake. "And to add insult to injury, the senior center says we have to move in a month and we were outbid on the property we want. My challenge now is to find additional funding so I can counter the offer before the deal closes."

Clay nodded and muttered "uh huh" frequently. He admired her dedication to her cause but he also thought she had great eyes. They were big and brown and gave him the impression of gazing into chocolate heaven. And it wasn't just her eyes. Man, what a package. A great body she wasn't afraid to show off and stunning legs. She was everything a woman should be—all sexy curves and soft places. "Uh, huh," he said. "I'll bet the economic crunch makes your job harder." Now, she was telling him another story about several homeless men who died. Professor George was the most recent.

Clay perked up at the mention of a death. "What happened to him? He wasn't murdered, was he?"

Harlie frowned. "Murder? Here in Angel Beach? No. Natural causes the coroner said. It's so sad. They live such hard lives. If I get my new shelter going I can offer others a safe and dry place in the winter. Our storms are brutal. So, we're on the lookout for corporate sponsors or caring individuals who may be willing to help." She smiled and returned to her cake.

Clay relaxed. If his dad was a serial killer, he hadn't found a victim here. His attention was pulled away from Harlie by musicians entering the stage. Two guitarists, a bass player, and a drummer took their places. Clay studied them but could see there wasn't a chance of finding Hunt Masterson among them. They were too young, too short, or too heavyset. Harlie looked at him with stricken eyes.

While Clay and Harlie finished dinner, the band covered a string of country artists including Alan Jackson, Jason Aldean, and Hank Jr. When they settled into a soft Keith Whitley ballad, Harlie tilted her head toward the dance floor and asked Clay to dance. He didn't hesitate to accept. She took his hand and led him to the dance floor, now filling with other couples. She slid into his arms, not shy about the tightness of the embrace as they spun in slow circles. She felt good there, pressed against him. Too good. Thoughts drifted through his mind—spicy thoughts involving Harlie and her sexy red dress. She slipped her hand around his neck and pulled him close. She began with a nibble at the corner of his mouth, teasing and slow. She brushed her lips across his mouth, her warm breath skimming his skin. When she finally laid her lips to his, coherent thought scattered from his brain. The band could have been playing a Souza march for all he knew. He'd stopped listening. His heart's frenzied beat sent blood cascading through his system. He pressed his hand firmly against her, straying lower until his fingers caressed her lower back.

When the song ended, he released her with reluctance and led her back to the table. Harlie excused herself to the bathroom, returning a few minutes later to her seat. The band played a fast song, the volume loud. Talking was impossible.

"Want to leave?" he mouthed.

She nodded and grabbed her coat from the chair back. Clay moved behind her, assisting, taking every opportunity to touch her. She smiled over her shoulder. Hand in hand, they found the Jeep. The sun had set. Before starting the engine, he caught her eye and then her mouth with his. It was a slow, seductive kiss that left them both breathless.

"It's late," she said. "I've been up since five. Any chance we can quit looking for tonight?"

He nodded. "I'm done." His brain was scrambled and he couldn't concentrate on the search now.

Driving south on Highway 101, she again brought up her work with the homeless and her need for funding and he finally figured out what she was doing. He'd been there before and recognized the signs of manipulation. His disappointment turned into irritation at discovering he was nothing but a checkbook to her. All the flirting was priming the pump.

At her cottage, he parked the Jeep and killed the engine, retaining his ignorant façade to see how far she'd take it. He opened the vehicle door and she gave him a sexy smile, the same smile that lured him to the dance floor and into the first incredible kiss. She took his hand, led him to the door, and leaned against it. She pulled him against her and he went, stopping a breath from her lips. He wanted to kiss her again but fought the urge.

"Would you like to come in and...talk?" Her breath warmed his mouth.

"What do you want to talk about?"

"Oh, I don't know. I'm sure we could think of something."

"I know," he said. "We could talk about homeless people. Maybe homeless shelters? Funding shortfalls? Food banks?" He slid his arm around her waist, clamping her tight to him. "How far are you willing to take this, Harlie? All the way to your bedroom?"

Her dark eyes went wide. "What do you mean?"

"Don't pretend you don't know what I'm talking about. You've looked at me like I was a big fat bank account all evening." He slid his hand down her back and squeezed her butt.

She gasped and tried to push him away. "Clay, that's not exactly—"

"I'm wondering if we should even bother going inside. Maybe you want to play ATM right here against the house." He released her and stepped back, his muscles tensed and his anger growing. "You've been working me all night. Is sleeping with me part of your plan?"

"I'm not—"

He laughed. "You sure are. Every word you said tonight was designed to make me contribute to your shelter project."

"Okay, but I can explain—"

"But one thing you didn't count on, darlin'..."

She blinked and appeared confused. "What?"

"That I'd catch on so fast, that I'd figure out you were selling yourself for your project." He shook his head. "I hate to tell you this, but you're too late. I've already been worked over by the best. From the day she married me, my wife wanted money. Lots of it. You know what's funny? I'd have given her anything she wanted. Anything. The act wasn't necessary for you either." She looked at him with big eyes. He stepped further away so he wasn't tempted to grab her again. "Ever hear of the Masterson Foundation?"

She shook her head, sending her curls into a delectable bounce. Clay clenched his fist to keep from touching.

"That's me. I make more money than I can ever spend in a responsible way. I don't need multiple mansions or a garage full of sports cars. If people need money, the Foundation gives it to them. I'll give you the phone number if you want to call. I'll even give you a personal recommendation. Just don't work me, Harlie. It doesn't suit you and it cheapens what you and I could have together. If money is all you're after, stay away from me. I've been there and learned a hard lesson." He stepped into the dark and paused, rotating his tense shoulders. He sighed and turned back. "I need to know something though...that kiss on the dance floor."

"What about it?"

"Was it part of the act? The way you kissed me, I mean." She was like touching an electric fence in wet grass and he hoped she felt it, too.

Harlie shrugged. "I don't know. Maybe it was. I really don't know."

He took a deep breath. "I like you, Harlie, or at least I like the woman I thought you were earlier today. If you decide the kiss meant something to you, let me know."

The walk to the Jeep felt miles long, maybe because he wanted to kick himself for being an uptight, moral idiot. Right now, he could have Harlie in his arms. He could have Harlie in her bed. But he didn't want her on the terms she'd proposed tonight. Sex wasn't a financial transaction. He wanted her, but he wanted her to want him, too.

If she didn't, he was better off without her.

❦

Harlie gnawed her lip as she watched him leave. Chances were good the taillights disappearing into the garage were the last she'd see of him. She unlocked the door and stepped inside the cottage, leaning against the door as it latched. She rubbed her mouth, remembering the jolt when she'd touched her lips to his.

She hadn't intended to kiss him. Until that moment, the thought hadn't crossed her mind. He'd looked so dejected after seeing the band she'd wanted to cheer him up with a dance. What happened next was instinctual and beyond her control. She closed her eyes and sighed, regretting the lie she'd told him. The kiss meant something but she wouldn't admit it when he was so angry. He'd think she was playing him again.

She smacked her palm against her forehead. "He caught you red-handed, Dum Dum, and you couldn't even defend yourself because most of what he said was true. It looks like ol' country boy has more operating brain cells than you gave him credit for." A guy probably didn't rise to the top of the music business exercising stupidity. Sam warned her, but she didn't listen. "And now you got some explaining to do."

She pushed away from the door, kicking it as she did. Tomorrow was soon enough. If she went after him tonight, they'd end up in another argument or, she smiled, in bed. After the hot kisses they'd shared, she could see it happening. Not for the reason he implied but simply because she wanted him. She wanted him to hold her and whisper pretty words in her ear. She wanted to make love with a man who wanted her, for who she was, not who he thought she should be. Was that a terrible thing to want? She didn't think so.

But his temper needed to settle, and she needed to formulate her story. She'd give him the straight scoop, or at least the amount he could handle.

She kicked off her shoes as she walked through the living room filled with antique furniture and overstuffed blue plaid chairs. She loved this room, especially when a fire burned in the native stone fireplace. But fireplaces symbolized romance and she didn't feel romantic at the moment. Far from it. She felt grubby for trying to manipulate Clay. He seemed like such a decent guy now that she knew him better. How many people would search for their missing father this long? Most would write the man off. And how many people in his financial position would give their money away? Most probably gave some, but Clay donated large amounts. He had to if he kept a charitable foundation operating.

She glanced out the paned window toward Clay's dark house and wondered if what he said was true. Could he be interested in her? Would he still like her once he learned her background? Her past humiliated her and she kept it private, but for some insane reason, she wanted to tell Clay who she was and where she came from. There was something special about him and she thought he might understand and not judge her. Tomorrow, she'd drop her personal history bomb and see what he was made of. With a tired sigh, she pulled the shade closed, wandered to the bathroom, and turned on the shower.

Steam filled the bathroom as she climbed out. She put on her favorite robe and was brewing tea when her cell phone rang. The call went to voicemail before she could reach it. When she saw the name, she groaned: Skippy the Bloodhound was back on her scent. Apparently, he hadn't bought her story about not knowing Glen.

She retrieved her messages, weeding through until she found Skip Hyatt's.

"This is Skip Hyatt, *Seattle Times*, again. I don't want to play games with you, Charlotte. I don't have time for it and it isn't my way of doing business. I know who you are. A friend of yours gave me this number and confirmed your identity. I have questions and you are the only one who can answer them. I'm running into a brick wall and need your help. Please call me."

Harlie disconnected the call and stared into space, biting her lower lip. She was sure her friend Alicia was the leak. The woman had the common sense of a gerbil and would tell anyone anything. Too late, she realized her error in giving her old friend the cell number. Harlie blew out a breath. She had to call him back and settle this thing. She connected with his voicemail.

"You've reached Skip Hyatt. I can't take your call right now. Leave a message and I'll call you back..."

"Mr. Hyatt, my name is Harlie, not Charlotte. As I said before, you've been misinformed by this person. I have nothing to say to you or anyone else about Glen Carson. I don't have any personal connection to him and I have no opinion of him whatsoever. Please stop calling this number."

Harlie ended the call and tossed the phone on the counter, smiling about proving Buck wrong. She didn't answer every call for help, only those who deserved it.

"This champion of the underdog," she said to herself as she headed for bed, "is off duty tonight."

9

On normal Saturday mornings Payton Shaw logged miles on a treadmill and consumed copious glasses of fresh vegetable juice at his health club bar. After a good workout, a well-muscled masseur worked the soreness from Payton's body before he retreated to the showers. This Saturday was about as abnormal as a day could get. To avoid raising suspicion, he parked his car on the outskirts of town at the Angel View Motel parking lot and walked the necessary mile to the bakery. Hunt, or Buck as he called himself now, had an attachment to the place. As he entered the establishment, a bell jingled, alerting the brunette behind the counter. She glanced up and smiled.

"Back again?" she asked.

He nodded and refrained from scratching an itch beneath his lengthening beard. He removed his hat, baring his ill-kempt hair. "I enjoyed the soup yesterday and thought I'd try a pastry with coffee." He studied the offerings in the glass case. "I'll take one of those. The lemon-filled." He glanced around. No sign of Hunt this morning, but it was too early for the lunchtime troubadour to arrive. Knowing Hunt, and Payton knew him better than most, he was probably sleeping off a bender in some woman's bed. The brunette rang up the sale and set the white bag and coffee cup on the counter. Payton dragged some bills from his pocket and paid.

"May I ask when the guitar player will come back? Buck, I think you called him."

"Right. His name is Buck." She shrugged. "I can't say for sure. He comes and goes on his own time. Sorry."

He thanked her and found a table with a view of both the street and the bakery patrons. When no one resembling Hunt appeared, he wandered outside and began his search again. When opportunity arose, he questioned likely people. Near lunchtime, he found a woman near to Payton's sixty-two years, sitting on a bench in front of the post office. She wore a plaid flannel shirt over a sweatshirt, baggy jeans, and a crocheted hat.

"May I sit here?' he asked, pointing to the vacant portion of the bench.

"Suit yourself," she said and returned her attention to the bulk mail flyer she held, giving it more attention than a box-store advertisement deserved. Her lips moved as she read. On the bench sat what must be her mail, addressed to Myrna Snow.

After a few minutes, he leaned her way. "May I ask you something?"

She looked at him with irritation in her sharp eyes. "What? I'm reading here." The woman radiated anger like a furnace spewed heat.

"Sorry to interrupt, but I'm wondering if you might know a friend of mine. His name is Buck." No response from his bench mate. "He's tall...plays guitar...wears a ponytail."

"What? You think I'm stupid or something? I know who he is. Everybody knows him." The cool breeze grabbed her thin gray hair from under the hat. "Who are you to be asking about him?"

"A friend."

She looked him over and he had the impression he didn't fare well in her estimation. "Friend, huh?"

"Right."

"Wrong. From what I'm hearing, the guy looking for Buck is no friend of his. More like trouble."

So Hunt knew he was here. That wasn't good but not unexpected either. He'd talked with a lot of people the past twenty-four hours. Someone was bound to tell Hunt. "I assure you, I am a friend of his."

She scrutinized him again. "Well, you do look older than Buck said you'd be. Not tall enough either."

Ah. It was Clay, not himself, who Hunt expected. Good. Maybe Hunt wasn't aware Payton was on his trail, too. "So, you can tell me where to find him?" he asked, hopeful his search was coming to an end. This god-awful beard plagued him.

"Not a chance. Buck says the guy looking for him wants to give him over to the cops and he didn't do anything to deserve it."

Payton frowned. "I'm not planning to have him arrested. Buck and I are friends. I want to help him. Can you tell me—?"

"No! I'm telling you to go away. Buck doesn't want to be found. Got it?"

Payton raised his hands in mock surrender. "Fine. I'm going." He gave her a taut smile and stood to leave. "What if I told you Buck is a murderer? That people die everywhere Buck goes?"

"Buck? A murderer?" She cackled. "That's the funniest thing I ever heard. Buck has a heart of gold. Not a mean bone in his body."

"Meanness isn't a necessity where murder is concerned. Mental instability can cause a person to do horrible things."

"Well, if you think that, you're no friend of Buck's. Nothing crazy about him. The man is as normal as I am."

Payton didn't think that was a particularly good reference. "I can assure you, Buck is a sick man and if I were you, madam, I'd stay away from him or you could be his next victim. If you are a friend of his, you'll assist me in finding him so I get him the help he needs." Payton listened to her cackle as he retreated across the post office parking lot.

The fool. She might not find it amusing if his prediction came to pass.

10

Harlie grabbed her sweatshirt and a bag of saltwater taffy she'd bought at the Candy Shack. If she found Clay, it was a peace offering. If she didn't, it was a snack she'd attach to her hips one bite at a time. She stood at the top of the beach steps looking north and south. Déjà vu tickled her senses.

His house was empty; the Jeep was in the garage. Clay must be on the beach, but which way? A mental coin flip had her choosing north. Ten minutes and three pieces of taffy into her trek, she spotted him sitting on a driftwood log, eyes trained on a distant western point. The storm brewing on the horizon wouldn't arrive until later, but the storm within Clay was plain to see. If he heard her approach he gave no indication. Harlie sat next to him but he still ignored her. She scrunched the top of the candy bag down and tossed it in his lap. He flinched and grunted.

"I suppose I should be thankful that wasn't a rock," he said with a dry tone. He peeked inside the bag, selected a piece, unwrapped and ate it. He handed her a brown piece and took another for himself. "So?"

Harlie's translation: what do you want? Judging by his tense shoulders and angry glare, she had her work cut out for her. He resumed his ocean vigil, watching the seagulls and cormorants that sat on the rocks. Occasionally, one dipped into the chilly waves for a meal.

When Harlie finished chewing her taffy, she jumped in with both plaid tennis-shoe clad feet. "I'm sorry about last night. My intentions were good but my methods were...crude, inappropriate, and maybe even manipulative."

"Maybe manipulative? Let's say, absolutely manipulative." He was quiet a moment before appearing to make a decision. "Thanks," he said. "I can't say I didn't enjoy the experience and I kicked myself all the way home for not taking you up on it. Your offer was better than a cold shower." He set the bag aside and reached for his wallet, extracted a card, and handed it to her. "Masterson Foundation" it read. "I'm sorry, too." Clay said. "I shouldn't have blown up that way. I'll call my director and tell her what's what with your situation. She'll work with you. As for you and me though, I think it's best if we don't spend time together."

"Why?"

"Isn't it obvious? All we do is argue."

"Arguing has its virtues. It clears the air and gives people great opportunities for making up."

He laughed. "I suppose that's true, but this thing with my dad is getting complicated and frustrating and I need to concentrate on it. I spent the day trying to find someone who might know him and came up empty. There are other facets to the thing I need to figure out and I'm not great company right now."

If that was his get-lost line, she wasn't biting. Instead, she laid her hand on his and squeezed, giving him an understanding smile. "Which is why you need me around. I have a feeling you'll beat yourself to pulp if left to your own devices." His hand was warm under hers and he didn't pull back. "I never knew my father," she said. "I don't even know his name. My birth certificate says 'father unknown' and Mom wouldn't even take a wild guess at which guy it might be. Helping you look for your father gives me emotional satisfaction. If you really want me to get lost, okay, I'll go. But I want to help you."

"It's probably a waste of time." He stared toward the ocean. "But if you really want to, it's up to you."

"I do, so that settles it." She smiled and waved the card at him. "And thanks. I had no idea you'd do something like this or I wouldn't have—"

"Forget about it, Harlie. It's done. We apologized and it's time to move on." He looked at her hand laying on his. "I used to give money to anyone who asked. I didn't need so much and there were others who could use it." He shrugged as if it were a small thing. "But my accountants took away my checkbook. They said I was making a mess of my taxes and my security guys were tired of dealing with people."

"You have a good heart, Clay." She squeezed his hand again.

"But I don't know if my Foundation can give you everything you need. There is a more local organization you could try if it isn't enough. The Carson Family Charitable Trust in Seattle is bigger. A friend of mine runs it and I could call him for you."

A shiver traveled her spine at the mention of Glen's name. "No." She shook her head. "The Carson Family Trust won't help groups like mine. Glen Carson is into high-profile projects where he can rub shoulders with Hollywood glitterati and get humanitarian awards."

"I don't know about that—"

"I do. Glen Carson would walk by a starving child in his own city and not lift a finger to help."

Clay frowned.

"I saw him do it."

Clay turned his hand and laced his fingers with hers. "I don't know the guy so I won't argue his merits or sins with you. I'll see what I can do on my end to help you. Your dedication to your cause is amazing. Not many people would go to such lengths for another person."

Harlie steeled her nerves. It was time to confess and see if he ran. "I was one of them, Clay. I ran away from home when I was sixteen and lived on the streets for nearly two years. Now that I have the opportunity to help, I can't ignore them." She waited for his reaction, expecting shock and revulsion.

"What caused you to run away?"

"My life was a living hell."

He nodded. "That would do it."

She could tell he wanted to know more but was too nice to ask. "Mom had lots of boyfriends and they partied a lot. Things got a little wild one night and someone called the cops. I hid behind my bed and watched them cuff and arrest her for possession." She swallowed. "Her boyfriend of the moment came back from a beer run, saw Mom was gone, and decided the party should go on...with me."

"Shit," Clay muttered. "What did...did he...you know..."

"No. I kicked him in the balls and ran as fast as I could."

He gave her fingers a squeeze. "Good for you. He deserved more than that to go after a kid."

"Maybe he has gotten what he deserves by now." She shrugged. "For all I know, Mom could still be doing time, too. Maybe even life since she was close to getting her third strike."

"You didn't go back?"

"No. It's been fourteen years and I doubt she's missed me."

He looked at their entwined hands, his face difficult to read. "How does a sixteen-year-old girl survive the streets? How did you get here?" he said.

"I stayed with friends when I could, got a part-time job in a bakery, panhandled when it wasn't enough, and stayed in shelters when my friends' parents got tired of me. I never hooked or got caught up in drugs," she said, hoping he believed her. "When I was almost eighteen, I met someone who wanted to take care of me. I moved into his house. He sent me to school. When I was twenty-one, I married him and thought I was Cinderella." She chuckled ruefully.

"But you aren't married now?"

She shook her head. "No. I found out there is no such thing as happily ever after. At least, not for me. I moved here after the divorce and used what money I had to buy the bakery." She looked up at him. "Do you see why I need to help them? Why I want to help you? I would love to see you and your father reunited. It's something I can't have and I want it for you."

"It's a complicated situation, Harlie. He may not want to see me."

She smiled. "We'll convince him of what a wonderful, generous man you are."

He laughed. "I'll leave that to you. It might sound arrogant coming from me."

She leaned against him. He moved his hand to her shoulder and brushed his fingers along her neck, sending a tingle through her. She'd known him three days and was already comfortable with him, like she'd always known him. Buck inspired the same feelings of comfort and contentment, in a fatherly way. She shifted and looked into his blue eyes. "We need to settle something."

"What? I thought we'd settled everything."

"Not quite. There is still this." She turned, slid her hand behind his neck, laid her lips on his, and it happened again. One touch and she was lost. He slid his hand down her back, holding her tighter to him, his mouth moving over hers. He took control and she let him. She liked the taste of him, lemony from the taffy, and the feel of his warm body against hers. It was the type of kiss she never thought she'd experience, soul wrenching and hot. Her toes curled inside her shoes.

He broke the kiss. "So, are you saying...?"

"Yeah, I'm saying it meant something."

He caressed her cheek and smiled. "Me, too." He dipped and took her mouth again. She wanted closer and looped her leg over his, pressing tighter. Clay pulled her into his lap and took the kiss deeper. Their mingled breath came in hungry gulps. If they weren't on a public beach, she could see this situation getting complicated. She hadn't been with a man in years and, back then, she didn't want him the way she wanted Clay.

"What are those people doing, Mommy?"

Clay and Harlie pulled apart. She looked over her shoulder and saw a woman and preschool-aged boy walking on the beach.

"Nothing you need to see," the woman said as she covered the child's eyes and pulled him along. "Take it inside!" she yelled their way.

Harlie buried her face in Clay's neck and giggled. "Oh, great. We're corrupting the nation's youth."

"It isn't the first time I was accused of it." Clay trailed his fingertip down her neck and cupped her face in his hand. "What do you say, Harlie? Should we take it inside?" His voice was husky and his blue eyes were engraved invitations to paradise.

"What? You mean..."

He brushed a wayward strand of hair from her face. "I mean I want you to come home with me and stay tonight."

She shook her head. "I don't think so."

"Why not? You were willing last night." He kissed her temple, working his way to her neck. His breath warmed her skin and she fought the urge to throw her head back and let him continue. The man's mouth was magical. "And we both agreed my behavior last night was crude and inappropriate."

"That was last night. This is today. I want to take you home and..." He laid his lips to hers and kissed her gently. "...make love with you all night. You can be as crude and inappropriate as you want."

She shivered and considered it. Waking up in Clay's arms would be heavenly, yummy, and wrong.

"Please, stay with me," he said into her hair.

"I can't."

"Can't or won't?"

"Take your pick. I can't sleep with you now, Clay. You got it mixed up last night and thought I would sleep with you for money. Now you'll think I'm doing it out of gratitude for having your Foundation help me."

"Hmmm. A boink to show your appreciation. That was the word, right?" He laughed when she scowled at him.

"I would never sleep with you for that reason. If I do, it's because I want to."

He caressed her lower back and smiled when she shivered. "I really don't have a problem with it. Show your appreciation any way that suits you, darlin'."

She shook her head. "No. I won't. The message will get garbled in the delivery. Besides, I've only known you a few days and that isn't enough. I like you a lot, but I won't sleep with you after a couple of kisses." She pulled away and climbed from his lap. "I need to go home. We can discuss this again later." She nodded and licked her lips as she stepped away. "Much later."

"It was more than a couple of kisses," he said to her retreating back. "It was more like three or maybe four if you count where we came up for air as separate kisses. I'd say it counts as two when the lip lock is broken for more than a few seconds." She turned back to him and smiled at the humor in his eyes. "If you're counting, that is."

"Apparently, you are."

"And if intensity and the kissee's response ups the count, I'd say we might be up to five or six." He stood and took a step closer to her. "Are there official rules on how many kisses it takes to make love to you? If so, I need a copy of the game plan. Maybe a tally sheet."

Harlie laughed and backed up a step, looking for her escape route. Her neck burned from his touch and her body was about to make a liar of her.

"Don't look so shocked," he said. "I want to be with you."

"I caught that. Not yet though." She walked away before her overactive hormones decided to have an up-close and personal discussion with him again.

"Hey, Harlie!"

She stopped and turned back. "What?"

"Just so you know," he said with a grin, "I'm hitting on you now."

"I figured that. I'll keep you posted on your progress." She returned the smile and ran home before she changed her mind.

11

Buck had sown seeds for two days. Now it was time to assess the crop. The sun would set soon and a storm threatened to hit the coast later in the night. If he completed his recon mission quickly, he could retreat to Emily's cozy house to wait out the storm. The problem was, most of his friends were erratic types and he never knew where he'd find them. He wandered the streets of Angel Beach, coming up empty until he meandered by Myrna's house.

It was a puny thing, more cabin than house, divided into four miniscule rooms. Considering Myrna was on medication for anger issues, knocking on the door was an adventure not dared by the faint of heart.

He rapped three times. "Myrna? It's Buck." He stepped aside in case she greeted him with a butcher knife or a baseball bat. Myrna had a large arsenal under the bed and wasn't afraid to use it.

"Buck you say? You better be Buck if I open this door," Myrna said.

"It's Buck. Open up."

The door opened a crack. "Buck?"

He stepped closer so she could see him. "In the flesh. Can I talk to you?"

The door opened wide revealing Myrna in blue flannel pajamas and red furry slippers. "Why the heck are you standing out there? Get in here, you fool. I got a six-pack if you're dry."

A smile crossed Buck's lined face. "I'm always dry." He entered the small house, removing his cowboy hat before it scraped the ceiling. He made himself comfortable on the sofa, parked his duffle, and stretched his long legs across the narrow floor while Myrna scuttled to the kitchen for his beer. She returned, grinning, and took a seat in a scuffed dining room chair opposite the sofa.

"I saw a guy, Buck." She nodded and smiled. "I talked to him."

Buck popped the tab on the beer can she handed him and took a drink. "Who is that?"

"Not the big, young one you told me about, but an older, scrawny one."

Knowing Myrna, some guy probably smiled at her and set her off. It didn't take much. "What did he say?" And what did it have to do with him? Clay was his immediate problem, not some guy making google eyes at Myrna.

"He says he's your friend, but I don't believe him. Not for a second. He's got mean eyes. You wouldn't have a friend like that. But he said he was looking for you."

Buck sat up straighter. An older guy looking for him? "And you told him what I said to say, right?"

Myrna blinked several times.

"You told him you don't know me, didn't you?"

Myrna bit her lip.

Buck leaned forward, put his elbows on his knees. "Myrna? Tell me what you said." Damn. She probably blew everything. He shouldn't have said anything to her.

She swallowed and twisted her fingers together. "Well, I didn't say exactly that. You told me to say that stuff to a young guy, not an old one." She winced.

Buck took her chubby fingers in his large hand and smiled. "You're right, honey. I said he'd be young. But now, I need to know what you said to the older guy. What did he say?" He released her fingers and gave her knee a reassuring pat.

"He was talking to me like I was stupid or something. You know I don't like that."

"Right. I know that, but what—"

"I'm getting to it. He acted like I was too stupid to know my own friend, so I told him I knew you." She smiled. "Everybody knows you."

Buck inwardly cringed. "Did he ask about me by my name or any other names? What did he say?"

"He said he was looking for a tall guy with a pony-tail who plays the guitar. He didn't use any other names though. Buck was all he said. He wanted to know where to find you."

"You didn't tell him, did you?" If she did, he was screwed.

Her eyes flashed with anger. "Now don't you be treating me like I'm stupid, Buck. I didn't tell him where to find you." She looked at her hands and her lip quivered. "He said mean things about you. He says you're a crazy murderer and I should be careful around you. He says he needs to find you so he can get you help. Why is he saying those things about you? You've been so nice to me."

Buck suppressed a groan. Payton was here and he knew to call him Buck. Damn, he didn't need that. He could avoid Clay easy enough. The kid couldn't go anywhere without causing a stir. But Payton, armed with too much information, was another story. "He's lying to you, Myrna. I didn't kill anyone."

"So, he's no friend."

Buck shook his head. "He was a long time ago but not anymore." He leaned forward. "You need to listen to me, Myrna. This man is dangerous. If you see him again, walk away. Don't talk to him again. Understand?"

She nodded slowly. "I understand. You think he'll try to hurt me?"

"He wants to find me. That's all. Stay away from him and you'll be fine." He drained the beer and picked up his duffle as he stood. "I need to get moving. Remember what I said."

"I will. I'll remember." She took the empty can from his hand. "Be careful, Buck. That man looks mean. He scares me."

He smiled. "I'll be okay. Lock your door after I go."
His stomach twisted as he left Myrna's house. Payton
Shaw wasn't someone he wanted to see.

The sun had set and the night was dark. When he
reached the street, he saw a friend coming toward him,
hands stuffed in his pockets and shoulders hunched.

The man lifted his chin in greeting. "Whatcha doin',
Buck?"

"Talking to Myrna. Done now though. You?"

"The usual." For Jack, the usual meant miles of
walking every evening to wear off his frustration.

"How's the wife? Have you talked to her?"

Jack shrugged. "About as well as can be expected.
The shelter in Portland hasn't thrown them out yet
but they might soon." He blew out a breath. "I'm still
waiting for word on that casino job. The HR guy is a
retired marine and he asked about my service. I'm hoping he'll take that into consideration when he makes
his decision. I gotta have that job, Buck. Cleaning fish
isn't exactly computer science, you know?" He kicked
at a rock. "I need a place for my family. And no, we
can't crash at your place."

"You could if you need to. You know that. You use
the place more than I do already." If he and Emily
kept going the way they were, he imagined he'd move
into her house soon. Jack could take the place. But he
knew Jack wouldn't. He wanted a real house or apartment for his family. Homeless was a rough place for a
young veteran trying to maintain his pride. "Em would

cut you a deal on the apartment if I ask her. I hear the renter is moving out next month." Myrna turned off the porch light, leaving them in inky black. Buck slid his cowboy hat on his head. "I'll mention it to her." He heard a scrape, like a boot on concrete, and tensed. "Did you hear that?"

"What? I didn't hear anything."

"Shhh" Buck stood still, listening. It was probably his imagination, but he thought he heard footsteps. If so, they quickly disappeared. He took a few steps and stopped. He heard a muffled screech.

"Hear that?"

Jack laughed. "You mean that cat howling? There are a couple of them on the next block that try to kill each other every night."

Buck laughed. "Cats. You're probably right." Paranoia was getting the best of him. Myrna mentions Payton and he starts hearing noises in the bushes. He shook his head at his own silliness. "Let's head out to the beach and see if we can find Joe." This late on a Saturday night, he might find him around the picnic tables on the beach. If everyone had stories of Payton Shaw, he'd need to consider moving on.

When Clay got close to him before, he'd always moved fast. But now, he didn't want to go. He'd hoped Angel Beach was the end of this tortuous road he was on. He'd developed relationships here that he hadn't allowed himself before. Harlie was like a daughter to him and as much as he fought it, he was in love with

Emily. He hadn't let a woman into his heart since his wife died, but Em was wiggling closer every day.

For now, he'd lay low. Clay would get frustrated soon and need to get back to work. Payton would return to Seattle. He'd be cautious and stay out of sight until they left town.

Sometimes, he wished he was shorter and less conspicuous. When a guy was trying to hide, size did matter.

12

Clay lounged on the sofa, feet resting on the coffee table, guitar in hand, broken angels spinning through his mind. Kissing Harlie did wonders for his creative process and he was in the zone. When he finished the song he was writing, he might wander over her way and see if she was interested in picking up where they left off that afternoon. She'd had a few hours to think about it and Clay had never been one to procrastinate. If he wanted something, he went after it.

And he wanted Harlie.

The security buzzer shook him from his music-induced haze long enough to open the gate. Thinking it was the delivery guy he'd hired to run errands, he didn't bother to check the security camera before going back to work. More words scribbled on a pad and he smiled with satisfaction. The song was coming together.

At the knock on the door, he called for the driver to come in. The door opened and he heard footsteps in the entryway. Clay glanced at his watch and frowned. Nine thirty. "Running late, aren't you? Set the stuff in the hall and I'll take care of it." He heard a scuffling noise. "Are you ready for a nip of that scotch, Andy?" The old guy had a taste for the stuff and had brought him a bottle as a housewarming gift.

"I've never cared for scotch."

Clay looked up, surprised to find a willowy blonde staring at him and not the gray-haired Andy.

She looked different than the last time he'd seen her. Gone were the dark streaks through her sunny hair and the makeup that could have covered three women's faces. Missing also were the mini skirt and short top which had revealed her belly button ring—all affectations that appeared after their wedding. Now she looked as she had when they began dating and he'd been struck by her false illusion of sweetness. In white slacks and pale pink sweater, Crystal looked like she was on her way to church and Clay was stunned silent. She was back to the dazzling woman he thought he'd fallen in love with six years earlier.

"Are you going to say hello or anything?" she whispered.

"Hello."

"Can I come in and sit down?"

"Yeah, sure." He continued to stare, trying to connect this apparition with the woman he'd divorced. She walked in slowly, as if unsure of herself, and sat primly on the sofa, looking at him from beneath long lashes.

"Say something, Clay."

"You're looking good, Christy," he said from the fog bank he'd settled in. He frowned and mentally shook himself free from the haze when he remembered who he gazed at with such admiration. She wanted something, he was sure of it. Since his accountant made the last payment on the settlement last month, Clay had a fair idea what Crystal was after. She'd managed to blow through millions and wanted more. "What do you want?"

"I called the ranch," she said. "Tom said you were gone." She frowned and looked away. "I told him I needed to talk to you, that it was important, but he refused to tell me where you were. I looked on your website, so I knew you weren't on tour. He wouldn't tell me one way or the other."

"There isn't any reason for you to know where I am. The divorce was final three years ago and you've been taken care of. Why should Tom tell you anything?"

"I hoped he might but he always hated me. Even when we were kids he hated me." She clasped her hands in her lap and her lip quivered. "I guess I was asking too much."

Clay thought the quivering lip was a nice touch.

She looked at him with huge blue eyes. "I wanted to see you, that's all. Tom didn't need to be so mean about it."

"He isn't mean. He's doing his job. Why do you want to see me? If you are looking for your father, he isn't here yet. Next week, maybe."

"I know. Mother said he was away on business and would be stopping here to see you. But it's you I want to see."

"Why? We have nothing to say to each other anymore."

"Yes, we do because...I was wrong and I want to apologize to you. I've missed you so much."

When tears swam in her eyes and her lip quivered again, Clay laughed. Her acting ability had improved over the years. He set the guitar in its stand and leaned back. "What is this bullshit?"

"It's not bullshit. I've been thinking about how rotten I was you. I want to apologize for cheating on you."

"Is this part of a twelve-step adultery program where you have to apologize to the people you've hurt?" he said with disgust.

"I want to set things straight with you. You don't like me anymore, do you?" She looked as if she was close to spilling tears.

"What's there to like?" He shook his head. There was a time when those tears held tremendous power over him but that was before she'd shown her true character. Despite her softer appearance, he knew the viper still lurked inside her, ready to strike without hesitation. A person couldn't change that much.

"I want to apologize for hurting you."

"Which time?" he said flatly.

"It wasn't that bad. You're overly sensitive."

"It wasn't that bad?" Clay laughed. "You slept with half of my band and worked your way through the roadies. What is your definition of bad?"

"I never went near the roadies," she said with indignation.

"That's not the way I remember it—"

"And why did I need those other men, Clay? Where were you? On the road, that's where, leaving me alone for months at a time."

"Oh no, you don't. You aren't laying this on me. I invited you to go every time and you wouldn't." He scowled, remembering the times he got on his tour bus alone, leaving his wife behind—knowing she wouldn't be alone for long.

"And I begged you to stay home with me and you wouldn't."

"Why are you bringing up this crap now?" He fought to keep his voice down. "It's ancient history. You know I couldn't stay home. Too much was happening in my career for me to sit at home. You knew how it was when you married me."

"Yeah, I knew. Your career was always more important than me," she said with trembling lips.

Clay recognized it for what it was: an effort to manipulate him and he was falling into her black widow's web all over again. If he didn't jump out fast, she'd eat him alive, just like before. He stood and put some space between them. "And how do you explain the fact that a lot of your little indiscretions happened when I was home, Christy? How many ranch hands had to leave because of you? You even tried to seduce Tom, of all people."

Crystal straightened her spine. "He lied about that and you believed him."

"Tom had no reason to lie about that or anything else. I trust him. I never could trust you."

"I've changed, okay? Cut me some slack. I'm trying to apologize to you."

"Don't waste your time. I don't want or need any apologies from you." He glanced at his watch. "It's late. What do you want?"

She took a deep breath. "Let's talk about it later, after you calm down."

"I'm calm enough. Where are you staying? Maybe you'd like to go there."

She gave him that saucer-eyed look again. "With you?"

"I don't think so." The thought of having Crystal in his home overnight gave him chills. He knew what she was capable of.

"All the motels are full. I haven't anywhere else to go."

He let out a frustrated breath and thought of a few places he'd like to send her. It was so typical of her. Impulsive Crystal would never think to make a motel reservation. "You can stay in one of my extra rooms. But I want you out of here first thing in the morning."

He needed out of the house, away from her. He headed for the front door, grabbed a leather jacket and Stetson from the hall closet, and turned to find Crystal standing behind him. In a swift motion, she wrapped her arms around his neck and kissed him, nearly knocking the hat from his head. It was a long, sensuous kiss that momentarily stunned him. He let her kiss him to see if there was a chance the old flame still existed. He waited for the oomph to the stomach but there wasn't any reaction other than impatience that she took so long to finish her assault. When Harlie came to mind, he gently pushed Crystal back and frowned. There was a definite oomph when he kissed Harlie. "I'm seeing someone, so don't waste your time." He turned to the door, resisting the urge to wipe at his mouth. "I'll be back later." Even though it was risky to leave Crystal alone in the house, he walked out, relieved to get away from her. A few steps from the house, he realized she followed him. He stopped near her parked Jaguar. "Where are you going?"

"With you."

"I'm going for a walk." He glanced at Harlie's cottage and noticed the lights were off. She'd gone to bed. So much for that idea.

"In the dark? Why don't you come back and we can talk about...things." She gave him a sweet smile as she returned to the house, leaving Clay to wonder what she was up to this time. Sweet had never been Crystal's thing.

"Clay!" Crystal called from the door. "Come on. It's cold out here."

Once inside, Clay hung his coat in the closet and went into the kitchen for a pop, returning to the living room with two. He stopped, his mouth open at the unexpected sight: the TV on—Bon Jovi played loudly, "Have a nice day"— and his ex-wife lay on the sofa in a sheer pink pushup bra and matching thong. He laughed at her tenaciousness but averted his eyes. When Crystal wanted something, she held nothing back.

"What are you doing?"

She rolled up on her elbow and smiled. "I didn't bring any pajamas."

"You can't sit around here like that."

"I'm comfortable this way."

"I'm not comfortable with it." He ran upstairs, dug through his closet, and returned with a pale blue striped shirt. "Put this on." He tossed the shirt her way.

Crystal glared as she caught the shirt but slipped it on, leaving the buttons undone. "You are such a prude, Clay. We were married for two years."

"And we aren't anymore." He handed her the cold pop he'd brought from the kitchen and sat in a chair. "What do you want from me? You wouldn't have gone to this much trouble unless you want something."

"That's not nice. I just wanted to see you."

"You've said that with nauseating repetition. Why do you want to see me now? After three years?" He popped the top on the Pepsi can and took a long drink.

"Because...I've never stopped loving you," she whispered.

The pop caught in his throat and he choked. Alternating between laughing and coughing, he tried to breathe again. Clay wiped his eyes and cleared his throat. "You can't stop something you never started." He coughed again. "I know it's asking a lot from you, but can you be honest with me? What do you want? Money? I know you sold the Nashville house a few years ago. Blown through that and the settlement already?"

She was quiet a moment. "I'm in a tight spot but it isn't anything major. At least it isn't to someone in your financial bracket. If you would be willing to help, I'd appreciate it."

"I see you're still driving the Jag. Sell it," he said, referring to the car he'd bought her as a birthday gift back in his naïve days before he'd figured out her game. "That should give you enough to live on for a while. It wouldn't hurt you to drive something cheaper."

"No. That car has..." she raised her eyebrow "...sentimental value. Remember the night you gave it to me and we—"

"Don't," he said. "That's over and I don't want to think about it anymore."

"I think about it all the time. We were great together. Especially in the front seat of the Jag..." She sipped her pop and looked at him over the top of the can. "We could be great together again."

They'd been great together for a short time before he'd found out she was cheating and lying. Until he found out she'd never loved him. It was the money she wanted, always the money. He looked at her with narrowed eyes, considering.

"It's you, isn't it?"

"What are you talking about?"

"The notes in the mail. You're the blackmailer, aren't you?"

She pressed her hand to her chest and gaped. "Blackmailer? Me? Are you kidding?"

He leaned forward. "Sure you are. It isn't quite your style, but your bluntness isn't effective anymore. I caught on to you a long time ago." He laughed. "It's gotta be you. What happened? The process too time consuming so you decided to come in person?"

Crystal furrowed her brow. "What are you talking about, Clay? All this cloak and dagger garbage over your father is turning your brain into mush."

"What do you know about that?"

"All of it. Daddy told me. He's as obsessed with finding Hunt as you are."

He raised his brow. "So you do know enough to send the notes."

"Clay, I know nothing about any notes. If I want money, I'll ask you for it. I'll flirt with you, screw your brains out or whatever it takes, but blackmail isn't my thing."

He supposed that was true enough. Blackmail took time to execute. Christy had a short attention span. "Okay. But it's not a big leap between you and the idea of extortion. You know more smarmy ways of getting money out of me than there are fish in the ocean."

She grinned. "Well, I'm glad we're on the same page. I do need money."

"That doesn't surprise me. Let's make this easy." He stood. "No money and I'm going to bed. Alone. Pick a room, there are several." He stood and headed to the stairs.

"Clay, I need your help. It's serious."

He stopped at the base of the stairs. "How much?"

"Fifty thousand. It's for a..." She looked away. "A project I'm working on. A very important project."

"What kind of project?"

"It's personal," she said. "Just help me, okay? If I ever meant anything to you..."

As always, Crystal would continue to pull every heartstring until she got what she wanted. She had meant something to him once and it irritated him that he'd been such a fool where she was concerned. He couldn't believe he considered helping her. It wasn't that the money was important to him but the principle of it. In three years, she'd blown through millions of dollars and now wanted more. "I'll give you half. You'll have to figure out the rest."

"That's not enough."

"It's what I'm willing to do. Twenty-five thousand and you leave. I don't want to see you again. Ever."

"If you help me, I won't have to bother you again. I'll be set for life. But I need some things to get this thing set up."

"I said half. I meant half."

Crystal crossed her arms and glared. "I could make your life miserable. You may want to reconsider that offer."

There she was, the Crystal he'd known and despised. The façade had to crack sooner or later. "You're already making my life miserable. I doubt you could make it worse."

Crystal laughed. "Oh, I could, believe me." She made a production of inspecting her fingernails. "There is another DVD, you know."

A cold tremor rolled down his spine. "No, there isn't. I destroyed everything and smashed your camera. Tom and I searched the house and the tour bus to make sure you hadn't planted any others." And when they were done, he'd brought in a professional to look again.

She lifted her brow and smiled. "I have a copy, Clay, and an interested buyer. I'd planned to sell it for what I could get, but maybe it's more valuable to you. If that video hits the Internet, you could have a few problems with your fans." She smiled. "I've always thought it was one of your better performances."

Clay repressed the urge to throttle her. If she had a copy, she'd have used it by now. Crystal lacked the necessary patience to wait three years to ruin him with the bedroom video she'd made of them. No, he knew he'd destroyed it all. Crystal was careless in her camera placement and he found it that night. Much to her surprise, she was out of the house and on her way to divorce court by morning, her latest moneymaking scheme stopped cold. He swore he'd never forgive her and he'd kept his vow. How could he forgive her for hiding cameras in their bedroom?

He ran his hands through his hair and exhaled. "You don't have another copy and I'm not playing this game with you. Twenty-five thousand and you leave for good. Take it or leave it."

Crystal glared at him. "You're asking for trouble—"

"I'm calling your bluff, Christy. Behave yourself or I may reconsider helping you." He walked toward the stairs. "I'm going to bed. You can sleep on the couch and I want you out of here first thing in the morning. Go on your own or I'll throw you out."

And as soon as she was gone, he'd find an electronics expert to sweep the house. Just in case.

13

Harlie stood in the cottage doorway, scanning the yard and driveway. Early morning fog clung with stubborn fortitude to the tree tops and surrounding hills. She pulled her cardigan tighter around her. "Spud! Here kitty, kitty!" She considered leaving him outside for the day but the weather report wasn't great. The cat would get soaked and she'd feel guilty. Slipping on shoes and a coat over the sweater, she wandered around the yard looking under bushes. After exhausting Spud's favorite hiding places around the cottage, Harlie worked her way to Clay's house, giving the unfamiliar Jag parked in the drive an appraising glance.

She peered under the large rhododendron near Clay's deck and was startled by the glass door sliding open. A leggy blonde—wearing nothing but Clay's blue striped shirt and bedraggled hair—stared out. Harlie blinked with surprise.

"Who are you?" the woman asked, stifling a huge yawn with her hand. "If you're the cleaning lady, you can come back later. We're busy."

"I'm Clay's neighbor." She gestured toward her cottage. "I'm looking for my cat," she said, wondering what she'd stumbled into.

The woman gave Harlie an insulting once over. "I'll bet that isn't all you're looking for. You're the woman Clay hooked up with, right?"

"We've been—"

"I thought so. Look, honey, there's nothing for you here. I'm Clay's wife and whatever services you've been providing won't be necessary any longer."

"Wife? Don't you mean EX-wife?" Harlie couldn't remember if he'd used the term "ex" or not. Maybe he hadn't.

"For now, but that will be changing." She smiled. "I'm back now."

"Back?"

"Oh, I get so tired of this." She gave a bored sigh. "He's been calling me for months to come back and I finally gave in. Did you think he would keep you around?"

Harlie was shocked silent.

The blonde continued. "He can have any woman he wants and he wants me. Go away before you embarrass yourself."

Harlie jumped when the door slammed in her face and the shade dropped down. Her anger rose at the thought of Clay using her. It must be true. The woman was in his house, wearing his shirt. She located Spud near the deck and walked home, vowing to steer clear of Clay Masterson and his dishonest little games.

⊙❦

She spent the morning scrubbing the bakery spotless, or would have it spotless when she finished the pastry case. Cleaning was her usual method of dealing with stress or in this case, confusion. And Clay definitely confused her. He'd seemed interested in her, so interested he'd proposed taking her bed. But, according to his ex-wife, he wanted reconciliation with her. Was Harlie nothing more than a time-filler? Harlie was a fool for believing she could mean more to him. But it shouldn't surprise her that a guy like him wouldn't be interested for long. Not when he had a cultured beauty like that blonde keeping him busy at night. Why settle for a street rat when he could have mink?

Lost in her thoughts and her scrubbing, she was startled when a face appeared in the glass, smiling at her. She waved, indicating she would be a minute.

"Wayne, hi," she greeted as she straightened her back. "What's up?"

"Got any poppy seed muffins?" he said with a broad smile. She compared it to Clay's smile but stopped herself. Clay's wife was back. End of subject. "I have some muffins in the back. Just needing one?"

"That should do it."

She retrieved the muffin, bagged it, and rang the sale on the register. "That's a dollar twenty-five."

He dug in his wallet for a couple dollar bills and handed them to her. "I talked to Noah a while ago. He found out who we're up against on the motel deal."

Harlie leaned on the counter. "Who?"

Wayne pulled the muffin from the bag and took a bite. He held up a finger and mumbled, "Just a sec." When he finished chewing he went on. "You won't believe me when I tell you. No matter what, we're way out of our league."

"I have news for you, too. Clay Masterson says his Foundation will help us. We may not be screwed, Wayne."

Wayne frowned. "Clay Masterson? That's interesting."

"Yes, it is. Who bid against us?"

"The guy's name is Payton Shaw."

Harlie shrugged. "Never heard of him."

"You'll have heard of his boss. Payton Shaw is the director of the Carson Charitable Trust in Seattle."

Harlie was sure the floor shifted under her feet. Not Glen. Anyone but Glen.

"And there is some connection there with Clay Masterson."

"What kind of connection?" But she already knew. Clay said his friend ran Glen's Trust.

"Leave it to Noah to uncover all the details." He took another bite of his muffin and mumbled, "This is delicious."

Harlie wanted to grab the darned thing and throw it to the floor. "What details, Wayne?"

"Okay. Here's the deal." He swallowed. "Noah found out about Payton Shaw from the real estate agent. Noah said he hoped he could talk with him and explain our predicament. That's when he found out about Glen Carson. Shaw said he had several plans for the property. First, he wants to enter into a business deal with a friend of his. They want to put a club there. He says it's perfect for what his friend wants to do. If the friend bails on that deal, the Carson Trust will sell the land for a healthy profit. He says it's worth three times what he's paying for it."

"I know it is. That's why WE could afford it," Harlie said. "What does this have to do with Clay?"

Wayne laughed and shook his head. "Guess who Shaw's friend is? Clay Masterson is the guy who wants to build a club here. Can you believe it?"

"No. I can't." So what was Clay's game now? Why would he offer to help when he was the reason she was losing the property? It made no sense. Unless he thought making his generous offer of assistance would get her into his bed quicker. He'd almost gotten what he wanted from her easy enough. Turn on that cowboy charm and everyone falls into line like dominoes waiting for a shove in the right direction. "Is there anything else I can get for you, Wayne?"

"There is something I want to ask you."

"What?"

"Are you busy tonight?"

Clay crossed her mind and she shoved him away. "I don't think so."

"Will you have dinner with me?" He waited. "A new place opened in Lincoln City and I thought I'd drive up there tonight and give it a try. I heard the pasta is exceptional."

She hesitated. It was a long time to be trapped in a car with Wayne. She tapped her fingers on the counter, debating.

"We don't have to call it a date, Harlie." Wayne smiled. "I know how that word freaks you out."

"It does not—"

"Yes, it does. So, we'll just be two friends sharing a meal. Will that work for you?"

Harlie smiled. Wayne knew her better than she thought. "Dinner sounds great, my friend."

"Wonderful. I'll pick you up at six." He smiled and turned to leave.

"See you then." As Harlie watched him depart, her momentary pleasure in thwarting Clay dissolved and she wondered if she'd made a mistake. No, she hadn't. Wayne was a good guy, a friend, and dinner with him was what she needed.

Sam walked up to the counter and watched Wayne leave. She turned to Harlie. "What did you do?"

"Made plans to have dinner with Wayne." Harlie grabbed a tray of cookies from the deli counter and slid it into the clean case.

"Why would you do that? I thought you and Clay Masterson—"

"You can quit thinking that way."

"But I liked thinking that way. It gave me hope the whole Cinderella-Prince Charming fairy tale thingy could happen." She made a dreamy sigh and Harlie laughed.

Sam glanced at the clock and hung a "Be back in ten minutes" sign on the door. She grabbed two bottled apple juices from the cooler and motioned for Harlie to join her at a corner table. "Sit and tell me what's going on, Harlie. You've been acting squirrelly all morning. Moping and frowning all over the place."

Harlie did as directed but stared out the window at the pounding waves instead of spilling her story. Try as she might, she couldn't rid herself of the heaviness in the pit of her stomach. Damn the man, anyway.

Sam banged her hand on the table to get Harlie's attention.

"Well?"

Harlie shrugged. "Some people shouldn't step out of their predestined box, simple as that." Harlie frowned and nodded with conviction. "I tried and was slapped down. I should crawl back in my dingy hole and quit trying."

"Care to explain that bit of philosophical bull to me?" Sam sipped her juice and waited.

Harlie sighed and explained Wayne's disclosure to Sam, leaving out her connection to Glen Carson.

"Rich people are always investing in things. That's how they get richer. So what?"

"He's the reason we can't buy the property for the shelter."

Sam blew out her breath. "And you're giving up that easy? That isn't the Harlie Cates I know. Try to work this out before you let him go."

"Did I say I was the one letting go?"

Sam's blue eyes narrowed. "He dumped you? Forget every nice thing I said about him. The man is a freaking low-class rodent."

"Whoa." Harlie laughed at her friend's quick and brutal defense. "First off, we weren't together. I mean, we've shared a few kisses rating right up there with the best of them and made a few exploratory moves, but we haven't even been on an official date."

"You've had dinner with him twice," Sam said.

"The first was a peace offering. The second was thanks for helping look for his dad." Harlie waved her hand for silence when Sam opened her mouth to protest. "His ex-wife came back."

"No!"

"Yes. She's back and was at his house all night."

"But that doesn't necessarily mean they're getting back together," Sam said. "Maybe they have one of those friendly divorces and they get together to play poker or something."

Harlie shook her head. "Very doubtful. I was looking for Spud near his deck this morning and this stunning blonde opened the door. From the look of her, she'd just crawled out of bed. She had that I've-just-had-fabulous-sex look in her eyes and Clay is the only man in the house I know of."

"I'll bet he can do that to a woman." Sam sighed and leaned her elbows on the table. "But you're speculating. You don't know for sure."

"She made it pretty clear he wants to reconcile and she finally gave in. She implied this is fairly routine for them." Harlie sipped her juice.

"You need to fight for him. It doesn't sound like this relationship with his ex-wife is stable. There could be room for a determined woman to squeeze in there," Sam said with a nod. "I can help you with that. I've knocked aside my share of unworthy women to get the man I wanted. Unfortunately, the men proved unworthy once I got them. That's always real disappointing."

"No, I'm not fighting anyone for him," she said, resigned. "It's done. I stepped out of my box and reached for something too far out there and lost. It's better this way. I'm afraid a relationship with Clay would have been too much for me anyway. His life is too public and I don't think I could stand it." Clay would bring unwanted attention. No. It was better this way. Safer.

"But Wayne? Come on, Harlie. He's okay, but do you want to settle that way?"

"Since when is having dinner with a doctor considered settling? Wayne is a decent guy who wants to feed me pasta and that's good enough for me right now. I'm not marrying him." She frowned. "Why do you suppose every man I meet wants to feed me pasta?" She shrugged. "Oh well. It's a good way to break out of my rut, slow and easy like riding a tricycle."

"If Wayne is a tricycle, Clay is definitely a sport bike. I don't know that I'd want to go back to peddling my own ride after cruising at top speed," Sam said.

A voice called from the back room, "Are we open today or what?"

"Yeah, we're open, Lisa," Sam called back to the blonde who peeked in through the kitchen door.

"What's up?" Lisa asked when she saw the sign on the door.

"Emotional crisis," Sam said.

Harlie laughed. "You're more in crisis over it than I am."

"I know," she said with a frown. "What a bummer this is. I was looking forward to being a bridesmaid in one of those million-dollar celebrity weddings and having my picture in *People*. He probably knows Blake Shelton and Jake Owen. Now the best we'll get is Wayne at the Angel Beach Community Church and Barbara Thurston on the piano."

Harlie stood and brushed her apron with her hands. "I'm not marrying Wayne. It's not even a date. Let's get back to work. There's a man standing at the door."

Sam removed the break sign and opened the door for an elderly gentleman. "Morning, Mr. Finch," she said. Harlie stepped behind the counter and waited for him to make his selection.

Sam walked through, heading to the kitchen. "Hey, Harlie? Do you think Clay knows Eric Church? I guess it doesn't matter now."

"No, it doesn't. Get to work. Lisa can help you with that huge birthday cake." She turned her attention to her customer. "Would you like a sample of the banana bread, Mr. Finch?"

14

Clay wandered down the drive to Harlie's cottage, humming the new song he'd been working on. She wanted a couple of days to think things over. He thought twenty-four hours was long enough. She insisted he was moving too fast. Fine. He'd slow down and use a little old-fashioned courting if she was more comfortable that way. He picked daisies from beside the house and, to earn extra romance points, chilled a bottle of organic sparkling apple cider. He wore a newer pair of jeans and a dark blue shirt. A light drizzle required a jacket and hat. Rain dripped from the brim. He was soggy but presentable.

Near the cottage, he stopped short. A green Volkswagen sat in the drive and a dark-haired man knocked on Harlie's door. Before Clay could back away unnoticed, Harlie opened the door and greeted the man. Under her open raincoat, he glimpsed a tight-fitting, black dress neatly flattering her curves and revealing a tantalizing glimpse of cleavage. Sexy, spike heels finished the ensemble and screamed hot date with piercing clarity. Clay wished he was anywhere else on earth when Harlie turned and saw him holding flowers and cider, looking like a first-class dufus.

"Hey, Clay," she said, drawing the other man's attention to him.

"I didn't know you had plans tonight. I'll catch you another time." He started to back away.

"Sorry. Where's the blonde woman?"

The blonde woman? Oh, the blood-sucking parasite he called ex-wife. Clay shrugged. "She left this morning."

Harlie pursed her lips and nodded. "I suppose I should introduce you. Wayne, this is my neighbor, Clay Masterson. Clay, this is Dr. Wayne Tipton."

Clay nodded as he stepped closer. Wayne held out a hand and Clay shook it, juggling cider and flowers in the other hand. The two men eyed each other, sizing up the competition. Harlie's emphasis on doctor wasn't lost on Clay.

But why was she doing this? Clay hid his confusion behind a smile. Harlie was obviously angry. Since she knew of Crystal's visit, he assumed that was the problem. Considering she didn't invite him to stand under the dry porch roof with her and her date proved she was ticked off about something.

"I'm on the Angel Beach Center Committee with Harlie. It would be interesting to meet with you sometime," Wayne said with a taut smile matching Clay's. "We all have questions about this ill-conceived project of yours."

"What project?" Clay said. Tension built steadily between the two men and the doctor's odd comment was only a small part of it. The sight of Harlie with the other man bothered Clay. A lot. Maybe he'd missed something in the conversation. "Do you mean my offer to connect your group with my Foundation? I don't see how that is ill-conceived. I thought it was a perfect fit and I'm glad I can help."

"Harlie told me about it. Nice of you to offer to solve a problem you created. But it still doesn't make you popular around here at the moment."

Clay looked at Harlie, hoping for clarification. He didn't get it. "I'm getting that impression."

Wayne put his arm around Harlie and continued. "I'm thinking you may want to change your plans and build somewhere else—"

Harlie noticeably stiffened under Wayne's grasp and Clay tensed. "Build what?"

"We need to get going," Harlie said with a nervous laugh and a quick shrug to dislodge Wayne's arm. She stepped away and led him to the car.

Wayne gave Clay a patronizing smile. "Oh, by the way, Clay...it is Clay, right?" The smile broadened. "Harlie doesn't drink."

"I know." Clay held the bottle up, controlling the urge to throw it at the guy. "It's cider. Organic." He thought he saw Harlie's eyes soften but wasn't sure. "She doesn't like fluoride or caffeine either."

Harlie climbed in the Volkswagen, her eyes lingering on him as she fastened her seatbelt. "See you later, Clay," she said before closing the door.

"Yeah, sure. Have a nice evening." Clay turned to leave, his mood dragging to his knees. When the car cleared the gate, he turned back and set the cider and flowers on her doorstep.

Then, he stewed for hours. She was out with another man and he couldn't stand it. Another man was telling her stories, making her laugh and smile. Another man was touching her. Would she kiss him? Would she let him make love to her? Would she let him spend the night? Had he before? The thought made him crazy.

To kill time and keep his mind occupied, he worked his e-mail. Countryman hadn't responded but that wasn't unusual. They'd go months without corresponding. Tom sent a couple e-mails, mainly telling him the lawyer hadn't got back yet on the serial killer theory. He hoped Tom was wrong about that one.

Next, he opened one from Harv Stockton, his manager at Stockton Management, Nashville. From it he gleaned what he needed to know about the concert. He wouldn't dream of canceling it. Several times a year he performed solely for the benefit of the Foundation. This summer, he was heading to Seattle. He had a great fan base in the Northwest and expected a sellout crowd.

Harv arranged a limo to take him to the nearest private airport. A suite was booked.

Last, he opened an e-mail from Jana Martin, his Foundation director. She agreed with Clay on the worthiness of the Angel Beach project and wanted to meet Harlie to discuss details. Could Clay bring Harlie to Seattle?

He responded that he would invite her and let Jana know.

That business completed, he shut off his computer and went back to stewing about Harlie and her date, wondering what the guy had been talking about. Other than looking for his dad and offering to help with the shelter, he didn't have any projects in the area.

Tense and restless, he prowled his house and watched the driveway for her to come home. He finally settled in a recliner, sipping a pop and staring out the picture windows. He dozed off and was jerked awake by a sharp knock. In stocking feet, he padded to the door and opened it to find Harlie with the cider and flowers. Rain dripped from her raincoat hood and splashed on her sexy shoes. She looked angrier now than she had earlier. Not good.

"I thought I should return this considering the circumstances." She handed him the bottle and flowers and walked down the steps.

"Considering what circumstances?"

She turned back. "I don't play games like this, Clay."

"I didn't realize we were playing a game. You're a beautiful, fascinating woman and I'm interested in spending time with you. Where's the game in that?"

"Oh, don't play dumb with me," she said. "Your wife is here."

"Ex-wife and she left this morning."

"But she'll be back."

"Not if I have anything to do with it," he said. "And I do."

"That's not the way she tells it."

Ah. It all became clear to him. He blew out his breath. "You talked to Crystal. When?"

"This morning when I was looking for my cat under your deck, she came out and explained a few things to me. Some interesting things. How long did you think you could keep up this deception?" She narrowed her eyes and looked as if she wanted to smack him.

"Maybe you'd like to come in and tell me what I'm doing. I'm out of the loop on this." He stepped aside and motioned for her to enter. This whole thing was getting so complicated he needed a program guide.

"No, thanks. The gist of it is that you've been asking her to come back for months and she finally decided to give in."

He shook his head. "That's not—"

"Well, it worked and you got what you want. But don't expect me to be the intermission between acts." She took a few steps back.

"Crystal lies. There isn't an honest bone in the woman's body," he said. "Our entire marriage was based on her deceit. If you would like to come in, I'll tell you the truth."

Harlie turned back. "What's the point, Clay? There's still the rest of this mess."

"What mess?"

"What mess?" she said with exasperation. "This whole Payton Shaw, Carson Trust, country music club project fiasco. That's what."

Okay. Either Harlie was having a mental breakdown or he was. "What are you talking about? What country music club fiasco?"

"The club you are building on MY shelter property!" She turned and stomped away.

"What club? I'm not building any club," Clay said to her back. "Harlie! Come back and tell me what you're babbling about!"

"I'm not babbling!" she yelled over her shoulder.

"Well, you aren't making any sense. Wait up!" He chased after her, splashing through puddles, his wet socks stretched from his feet like scuba fins by the time he caught up with her. "I don't understand what you're talking about, Harlie. Come back and explain this to me. Please."

"You don't understand? How can you destroy everything I've worked for and not understand?"

"I don't. You lost me somewhere before Payton Shaw was mentioned." He wrapped his arms across his chest and tucked his hands in his armpits, the bouquet of flowers in one hand, the cider in the other. The earlier drizzle was now a deluge. Icy rain snaked down his face in rivulets.

Harlie finally noticed he was standing in the rain in his sweat socks, flannel boxers, and a T-shirt. "Good grief. You're in your underwear in a rainstorm? You're going to freeze to death." She let out a frustrated breath and grabbed his wrist like he was an ill-behaved toddler. "Come on. We're closer to my house than yours. I don't want your premature demise on my conscience."

Clay slipped around in sopping socks, pulling them off as he ran in her door. Harlie removed her wet coat and ran it into the bathroom. When she returned, he was holding his blackened socks and shivering by the door.

"I hope you closed your door," she said.

He nodded and tried to control his chattering teeth as he handed her the flowers and cider, which she deposited in the kitchen. She motioned for him to follow her to the sofa where he sat, dripping, until Harlie grabbed a sofa blanket from the back of a chair and tossed it at him. It didn't quite fit around his broad shoulders and left his goose bump-covered legs and wet feet exposed. Harlie went to the bedroom and returned with another blanket, which she draped across him.

"Better?"

He nodded.

"I'll make some tea and we can talk."

As soon as she left the room, he slipped off his wet T-shirt and boxers, tossing them in a pile on the floor. The teapot whistled and Harlie soon emerged from the kitchen with steaming mugs. She set them on the coffee table and raised an eyebrow at his soggy laundry. Without a word, she took the clothes and, judging by the sounds coming from the kitchen, either tossed them in the microwave or the dryer.

Harlie came back and sat in an overstuffed plaid chair. "Okay. Make your case."

Clay wrapped his hands around the steaming cup and sipped. From the look on her face, it was a safe assumption she would toss him back in the rain if he pissed her off again. "Fine. I gotta say I'm completely confused about everything you've said to me. I'll tackle my ex-wife first because it's the only thing I can attempt with confidence. For the record," he said, "marrying her is one of the stupidest things I've ever done. No, correction, it is the stupidest, and I guarantee you I'd never call the woman and ask her to come back. She arrived late last night, uninvited. I haven't seen or talked to her since the divorce was final so I knew she was after something. She tried every angle to get back on my good side, including trying to seduce me. It didn't work. She killed whatever feelings I had for her a long time ago."

"What did she want?"

"Money. With Crystal that's what it always boils down to. Believe me, I would never call her and ask her to come back. The woman thinks I'm low-class trash who happens to have something she wants."

Harlie lifted a questioning brow. Clay frowned at her insinuation.

"It's the money she wants. Not me. I told her last night I'd help her out this time, but I didn't want to see her again. Ever. She left this morning."

Harlie frowned and appeared to consider his arguments. "Okay, so I was misled," she said and relaxed into the chair. "But there is still the other problem."

"What problem? Payton Shaw is a friend of mine, the friend I mentioned who works for the Carson Family Trust. He's also my former father-in-law, but we don't let his daughter disrupt our friendship. As for the rest of it, I have no idea what you're talking about."

Harlie blew out her breath. "I'm so confused about your motives here I don't even know where to start. You are building a club on MY shelter property."

He frowned and shook his head. "No, I'm not. Where did you get that idea?"

"Wayne."

"And what does Wayne know about my private business? I'd never met the guy before tonight."

"Wayne said Noah, another member of our board, found out from the realtor that Payton Shaw is the guy who outbid us on the motel property."

"Payton won't be here until next week. There is no way he could have bought that property."

"He told Noah he did."

Clay shrugged. "Well, okay. He does purchase property for the trust so it's possible he bought it. Maybe he saw it on the Internet. But what does it have to do with me?"

"He told Noah he purchased the property for you to build a club."

Clay ran his hand through his wet hair. "Payton hasn't said a word to me about it." He leaned back, rearranging his blankets. "I've kicked around the club idea for years, but I haven't done anything about it. Payton wants in on the deal, but I haven't had time to bother with it. I'll call him in the morning and talk to him about dropping his offer."

"You will?"

"Sure. The timing is wrong for me to build something now, and I haven't done any research on the location. I mean, this is a great little tourist town, but we'd need demographic studies and other stuff to see if the area could support what I have in mind. I don't go into business deals blind. Besides, I'm here to find my dad. Period. I have no other agenda." He smiled at the confused look on her face. "Harlie, I'm not your enemy. I want to help you. In fact, I contacted my Foundation director and she wants to meet you Tuesday in Seattle."

"Seattle? I can't go to Seattle."

"Sure you can. I'm doing a benefit concert for the Foundation and she'll be there. She likes what you're doing here and wants to discuss it with you."

"In Seattle?" Harlie bit her lip and shook her head. "No way."

15

Harlie finished her tea and returned the cup to the kitchen. She couldn't go to Seattle with Clay.

Glen was in Seattle.

Skip Hyatt was in Seattle.

"Why not?" Clay called from the living room.

"I have too much to do here. Wednesday is our lunch and food bank day. I have a business to run. I can't take off like that."

"But going will help your shelter, Harlie. Can't your employees handle the bakery for a day? I'm not leaving until tomorrow night and I'll have you home by Wednesday. I could have you back before lunch if you want. The plane flies when I say so."

She looked up. Clay stood in the door, her blanket wrapped around his hips. His blond hair curled from the rain. Darn him. He was killing her arguments and looking delicious while he did it. She turned away to better resist temptation. Temptation stayed at the door, a frown creasing his brow.

"Look, Harlie. I get it. Seattle isn't the problem. I am."

"Clay—" She turned back.

He held up a hand to stop her. "It's okay. I thought we had something going here but apparently I was wrong." He shrugged. "I'm not trying to push you into something you don't want. Or at least, I didn't mean to. You're something special and I guess I got carried away hoping you might give me a chance. If I horned in on that other guy's territory you just had to say you weren't interested. Maybe Wade or Waldo or whatever his name is suits you better. I'll let Jana know you won't be in Seattle. She can set up a phone conference with you and probably accomplish the same thing. Sorry if I overstepped. As soon as my clothes are dry, I'll take off and leave you alone."

When he left the doorway, Harlie buried her face in her hands and groaned. He had it wrong but it wasn't his fault. She took a moment for a calming breath before following Clay. The living room was dimly lit, chilly, and the scent of chamomile lingered. On the sofa, Clay lay on his back, his hands behind his head, biceps taut. How could the man think she wasn't interested in him when he cornered the market on delectability? It was all she could do to stand in one place and not fling herself at him.

Harlie flipped a wall switch and the gas fireplace ignited, sending flickering trails across the room. It was a mistake and she knew it. Romantic light was not what was needed. Bright, eye-piercing fluorescents were. She crossed her arms and tried to calm her pounding heart.

"You think you're the problem?"

"It's a theory."

"You are a problem but not the way you think."

He leaned on his elbow, knocking the blanket down around his hips. She was tempted to cover him so she could think.

"You are a problem for me because I can't stop thinking about you. My brain hasn't functioned right since you stuck your head in my car window on the side of the road." She pressed her fingers to her temples and shook her head, trying to clear the image of the man on her sofa. "I've never had this problem before and I'm starting to wonder what's wrong with me. I'm pretty sure its pheromones but that doesn't make it any easier to handle."

"Pheromones?"

"Yeah. The hormonal juju that attracts people to each other and your DNA must be pre-programmed on my hormonal microchip because I can't control this."

"Pheromones, huh? I guess that could explain it." His mouth tilted into a smile. "Your pheromones have been waging biological warfare on me since we met. I'm under attack right now." He chuckled.

"It's not funny, Clay. I'm serious. I can't stop imagining what you'd be like to, you know—"

"Boink?"

"To put it crudely, yes."

"Hey, it's your word, darlin'." He grinned. "Okay. So, you're consumed with lust for me and I'm willing. What's the problem? I'm missing something here."

She let out a frustrated huff. "The problem is I've only known you since Wednesday. I do not sleep with men I've only known since Wednesday."

He frowned. "So, you're saying we wouldn't have this problem if we'd met on Tuesday? Damn. I should have got here quicker."

Harlie clenched her fist and pressed it to her forehead. It might keep her from banging it on the wall. "That's not it. It's just...I don't know you and yet I feel like I've always known you. I can talk to you about things I've never told anyone and I can't figure out why." She frowned. "I find myself wishing you'd call and ask me to help with your search again so I can be close to you. I'm hoping you'll knock on my door to borrow a cup of sugar so I can look at you. I even bought your latest CD so I can listen to your voice when you aren't around." She swallowed hard. "And then you lay on my sofa looking like that and all I want is to be close to you. But it's too soon."

Clay nodded. "So, you're saying we're like a smoked ham and need time to cure, right?"

Harlie rolled her eyes when he grinned. "Not exactly. More like a vintage wine. But then you mess me up by making this wonderful offer to take me to Seattle to meet a woman who can solve some of my troubles, and I'm torn between wanting you and wanting to stay here where I'm safe."

"Safe?"

"Emotionally safe. Not only are you an emotional minefield, but I haven't been back to Seattle since my divorce and I'm afraid to go there again. That city is loaded with bad memories of a mother who filled her body with every vile substance she could find—legal and not—and an ex-husband who represents my largest failure. The whole city is a monument to my personal dysfunction. So, no, it isn't you. Not entirely."

"Let's make some new memories," Clay said. "Come with me. Meet with Jana, get your shelter on firm ground, and Seattle can represent the start of something positive. You were a helpless kid then. You're a strong and successful woman now."

"You really know how to flatter a girl, don't you?"

"It isn't empty flattery, Harlie. I've meant every word. Considering the crap you've lived through, you're an amazing success. You're a scrapper and I find that admirable. But you don't need to fight me. I'm on your side. You can trust me."

"That's a tough one," she said. "Really tough."

"What is?" he said with a frown.

"Trust. When you've been kicked around it's hard to do. You should know that."

He nodded. "Yeah. I know. The one person I should be able to trust is playing dead. It's hard to trust when our own families treat us bad. But it might explain this mutual comfort level. I feel it, too. I get where you're coming from because I've been there, too."

"Really?"

He smiled. "It's a theory. And the rest of it? I've been feeling the same way. I watch down the driveway to catch glimpses of you. I want to borrow sugar I don't need so I can see you. I want to beat up doctors who take you out to dinner. I feel the same way, Harlie. I want to try this thing out and see where it takes us. Trust me."

Clay looked at her with those intense blue eyes and she wanted to believe him. She wanted to believe in him, too. Was he telling her the truth? Would he follow through on his promises or use her and go home to Nashville? She'd trusted a man before and regretted it.

"It's entirely up to you. Your call. Your schedule." He laid back and clasped his hands behind his head. After a moment, he started to hum and then, sing softly about angels and broken wings.

Harlie moved closer to the sofa, listening. She sat on the edge, next to him. "Why are you singing that?"

"It's just a little something I've been working on since I've been here."

"About broken wings? That sounds painful. Why write about that?"

He smiled. "It's a metaphor for a wounded heart. The woman in the song has been damaged by love. The guy singing the song is wondering if his love will heal her or drive her away. You're like the angel in the song who needs her heart mended." He sat up and leaned toward her. "If I help mend you, will you fly away?" He rubbed his finger down her arm and her skin tingled beneath his touch.

"Is that why you invited me to Seattle? To mend me?" She'd hoped it was something more.

"Will it help?" He trailed his finger from her arm to her neck, leaving his hand where he could stroke her skin.

She wanted to lean into his touch. "It's wonderful of you to offer your help with my shelter."

"Maybe. But my motives may not be as philanthropic as you think."

"Oh? How so?"

His smile was wicked and sexy. "Think about it."

She swallowed hard. "Did the angel in the song leave him?"

Clay shrugged. "I don't know. I'm not done writing it." He brushed his hand across her hair and Harlie went limp, wanting him to touch her more. "You have to help me finish it. How do you think it will end?"

Harlie bit her lip and changed the subject. "That's what Buck calls me. Angel or Angel Girl."

"You're kind of a kickass angel, but you have the basic qualifications."

He was so close; she could smell the rain on his hair. She thought he would kiss her, but he reached around and pulled the band from her braid, loosening the tight mass and mussing the released curls with his hands.

"Why'd you do that?"

"I like it that way, all wild and free. But it makes me wonder about something. When you went out with me you left it down and let your curls go natural." He let out a breath. "Man, you were so sexy, I couldn't breathe. Tonight, you go out with Dr. Waldo and it's braided tight. Does that mean something?"

She raised an eyebrow. "Is that your clever way of finding out about my evening?"

"Nothing clever about it. No point in messing around when you want to know something. You were out with one guy earlier and now you're on your sofa with a love-starved, naked man who would be on top of you in a second if you crooked your little finger. Maybe I should get a status report on the success of the competition. How many clothing articles was he allowed to remove?"

"None," she said with a laugh. "He was unsuccessful in all areas." She reached over to brush his hair back from his forehead and absently ran her fingers through it. "His name is Wayne, by the way."

"Like it matters," he said. "What's the deal with him anyway?"

"No big deal. He's a friend who has been asking me out for about a year—"

"A year?" He snickered. "Talk about pathetic. I had you on my lap in a matter of days—"

She pursed her lips at him. "He's more of a gentle-man. What can I say?"

"No seems to be the word where Waldo is concerned," he said with a chuckle.

"Anyway, he asked me out to dinner and I went."

"And?"

"It wasn't a date. We're just friends." She smiled. "He thought you were going to hit him."

"The thought crossed my mind." She continued to play with his hair. He closed his eyes and sighed. "So you won't be going out with him again, right?"

"He asked about you when he brought me home. I hesitated and he answered for me."

Clay opened his eyes and waited for her to finish.

"He said he could see there is something between you and me. I didn't say one way or the other and he said it was obvious to him I was interested in you." She blushed when he laughed. "I felt bad about the whole thing until he gave me a lecture on the recklessness of any involvement with someone like you and then...I lost my temper. It's a pretty safe bet he won't ask me out again."

"Poor Waldo," Clay said with mock sympathy.

"Why feel sorry for him?"

"Several reasons. First, I've been on the wrong end of your temper and it's not a pleasant experience. And second...poor Waldo took you out to dinner and I'm here getting real close to making out with his date. Hell of a deal for me. I get all the romantic action and didn't even pay for the meal."

"His name is Wayne. And it wasn't a date."

"Whatever." He slid his hand behind her neck. "You know what I'd like to do?"

"Make out with Waldo's date?" she whispered.

"You said it wasn't a date."

She swallowed hard. "It wasn't. I can't think straight."

"Good." He buried his fingers in her hair and pulled her into a kiss. His mouth moved over hers, slow and determined. He shifted, taking the kiss deeper. Harlie wrapped her arms around him, pulling him closer. He trailed his lips down her neck and his hand roamed her thigh, skimming hot skin, until his fingertips met lace. The blanket shifted, exposing Clay's hip.

He stopped and looked at Harlie's hand inching across his warm skin. "So, the wine is ready to decant?"

"The champagne is ready to blow its top." Harlie's laugh was sultry and she wondered where it sprang from. "This is so wrong," she blurted. "We haven't known each other—"

"Shhh...it doesn't matter," he whispered.

"But it does."

He shook his head. "Only if you make an issue of it. I don't care when I met you. I'm just glad I did."

Before she could protest, Clay kissed her again. She leaned into him and they fell back on the sofa. She'd never been this crazy before. Her blood simmered and her mind spun as she assaulted his mouth. She couldn't even remember why she'd wanted to protest this. Right now, she wanted him to do whatever he wanted, however he wanted to do it. He pushed at her dress, sliding his hand along her thigh, moving the fabric above her hips. His fingers skimmed the warm skin beneath her panties and she was breathing hard when he cursed and groaned.

"Ah, shit." His breathing was heavy and his body tense. "Shit!"

"What's wrong?"

"I don't have my wallet."

"Your wallet?" Her eyes went wide.

"Condom." He groaned and laid his head back. "I shouldn't have started this."

"I don't see the problem, Clay."

He looked at her. "You don't? I'd love to have some kids, but I don't think reckless sex is the way to go about it." He shifted and groaned.

"I don't want any kids but that's not what I mean. I have a condom."

"You do?"

"Uh huh. I bought it."

He frowned. "It? You bought one condom? Nobody buys one condom. They come in a box with other condom buddies to use at a later time."

"Well, I bought one condom. When we went out. One of the bars had a dispenser." She smiled, feeling smug at her foresight.

"So you were prepared to take your homeless cause to your bedroom?" he asked, his eyes wide with shock.

"No." She shook her head. "I was prepared for whatever might happen between us."

He groaned. "All those cold showers for nothing. I am a moron." He sighed. "So, you have one lonely condom?"

"Isn't that enough?"

"It'll have to do. Where is it?"

"In my purse. I'll get it." She untangled from Clay's arms and legs and made a quick trip to the kitchen. When she returned, he was gone. "Clay?"

"In here."

She followed his voice to the bedroom and laughed at the sight greeting her. He lay on his back across the double bed, the blanket draped decorously across his lap, and Spud stretched out on his chest—man and cat, nose to nose. She put her hand over her mouth to muffle the expected snort.

"I had it all planned," he said. "You'd come back and find me on your bed, looking irresistible, of course. You'd be overcome with lust, jump me, and we'd spend the night making that wild jungle love you mentioned before."

"But Spud got here first."

"Yeah. The hairball factory got here first and instead of you panting with lust, you laugh." He sighed. "So much for my ego."

Harlie grinned. "I think you have enough of an ego to survive the hit." She walked to the bed and picked up the large cat, which protested with a loud yowl

when she set him on the floor. Spud stretched with indignation and left the room. Clay moved to sit on the
edge of the bed, the blanket hastily pulled across his
lap with much less decorum than before. Harlie held up
the condom. "One lonely condom," she said, setting it
on the night stand. She squealed when Clay grabbed
her by the hips and pulled her to him.

"Turn around."

She did and he pulled the zipper on her black dress,
following the zipper with his mouth. When he reached
the bottom, he ran his calloused fingers along her
spine. She shivered.

"I have to tell you—" She closed her eyes and
sucked in her breath when he pushed the dress from
her shoulders.

"Tell me what?" He rubbed his hands down her
arms, pushing the dress until it pooled around her feet.

"I'm not skinny." She winced at the admission.

"Okay." He turned her toward him, pressed his face
against her skin and inhaled. "You smell great."

"But I'm not fat either."

"Okay." He kissed her breastbone. The kiss turned
into a lick. "You taste good, too."

She shivered again, the tremble lasting longer than
the previous one. "I mean, no one could ever accuse me
of being overweight."

He continued his kisses, exploring her skin with his
mouth. "I wouldn't dream of it."

"Good," she said with a satisfied nod. "It's settled. You won't be disappointed that I don't look like your ex-wife."

"What?" Clay stopped mid nibble, his brow creased into a confused frown. "Why would you want to look like her?"

"She's the type of woman you're used to and, well, I don't have the kind of body she has. I wear a twelve and she must be a six or less. I want to tell you up-front that I'm not like her. I'm normal. Not exactly sex goddess material."

Clay laughed. "Darlin', your body is damned near perfect."

Harlie recoiled and shook her head. "Don't say that. I'm not perfect and I don't want to be." She took a breath. "No one should be expected to be perfect. It isn't natural...or real."

Clay took her hand and gently guided her back to him. "Okay. Perfect was the wrong word. How about..." He paused and looked thoughtful. "Stunning...dazzling...out-of-this-world sexy...the stuff my most tormenting dreams are made of..."

Harlie blushed and laughed. "Now you're being ridiculous. I'm just me. Can that be enough for you? Plain, everyday, garden-variety Harlie Cates. I'm more like a favorite pair of shoes. A little worn in places, but comfortable. You don't find women like me in fashion magazines or country music videos."

Clay's eyes softened. "There is nothing plain about you, darlin'. You're exactly what a woman should be— soft and female."

"I don't want to disappoint you."

Clay caressed her back and hips. "Harlie, you are beautiful and real. There is nothing disappointing about you."

Harlie saw the heat in his eyes when he looked at her and debated if she should believe him. Since no one had ever looked at her that way before, she didn't have a sexual attraction yardstick to use. Glen had treated sex with her as an obligation. When she uncovered his office affairs, she understood the problem. Harlie wasn't the kind of woman who inspired passion and she'd accepted it...until now. Clay certainly appeared inspired.

"Come here," Clay said. He pulled her to him and lay back on the bed. A quick flip and Harlie found herself staring up into his beautiful blue eyes. His hand rested on her ribs and a revealing pressure against her hip told her everything she needed to know.

"I've never wanted a woman the way I want you," he said. "Every delicious, imperfect bit of you..." his breath brushed her lips. "...fits flawlessly with every imperfect bit of me."

"I like the sound of that, but just so you know—"

"Now what?" He laughed.

"I don't usually do this. I'm not into one-night stands."

Clay smiled. "This coming from a woman who buys condoms from public restroom dispensers."

Harlie huffed out her breath as well as she could, considering her breasts were squashed to his chest. "That was an impulse. I'd never bought one before and the machine was there. It was a new experience for me."

"Okay. Let me get all this straight. You aren't skinny. You aren't fat. You sure as hell aren't perfect."

She nodded.

"You're not a sex goddess, but a normal woman who buys dispenser condoms because she craves new experiences...not necessarily sex, but the thrill of buying a condom from a dispenser."

Harlie smiled sheepishly. "You're making fun of me."

"No. Just trying to keep up. For the record, I'm not into one-night stands either. If you're agreeable, I'll be back." He paused and brushed his hand across her cheek. "I get it that someone did a number on you and left you with some insecurity."

She tensed and opened her mouth to protest, but he laid his finger across her lips.

"You can trust me when I say you are an incredibly hot woman and I want you, Harlie. You. Not a woman with razorblade hipbones and a foul disposition. You." He kissed her and then looked at her with what appeared to be regret. "But not tonight."

Her lips were still warm from his kiss when his weight lifted from the bed. She opened her eyes to see Clay standing by the bedroom door, the blanket wrapped around his hips, his hand on the doorknob.

"But you just said...I thought..."

He nodded. "I know. It pains me to say it, but you're right. It is too soon and I get it now. I'll be gone for a couple of days and we'll see where we are when I get back."

Harlie reached for a pillow and covered her body. "Well. Okay then." She wanted to crawl into a ball and die. "When you get back..." She bit her lip and nodded. "Can I ask why you changed your mind so fast?" She steeled herself against the painful truth.

"Yeah." He rubbed the back of his neck and laughed. "See, here's the deal." He blew out a breath and looked uncomfortable. "I think I could fall in love with you."

"What?" She couldn't have heard that right. No. This was where he said he had been wrong and ran as fast as possible.

"I think I could fall in love with you and I'm going about it all wrong. I'm pushing you into bed with me before you're ready and that could ruin this for the long term."

Her eyes widened. "What long term?"

He shrugged. "Our long term. Falling in love is a long-term thing. If you do it right, it's a lifetime thing." He opened the door and stepped out. "So, I'll see if my clothes are dry and we'll figure out what's what when I get back from Seattle. Good night, Harlie."

Harlie stared at the empty doorway. What was he talking about? She was ready to have sex with him. She might have been a slow starter but she was more than ready now. If there was a sexual-readiness meter, she'd blow the needle right off it. She'd allowed him to remove her clothes and touch her, hadn't she? She let him lick and nibble her skin. She'd even provided the condom. What else could a woman do to express willingness?

An embarrassed flush warmed her skin. Oh dear. Maybe calling attention to her physical flaws wasn't his idea of pillow talk. Maybe mentioning his perfect ex-wife exposed her insecurities and screamed "I'm not ready for this." Telling him she thought this was a one-night stand might have damaged the mood a bit. Maybe a lot.

But Clay thought he could fall in love with her. She doubted it but thought it was a nice idea to hold close as she fell asleep. She crawled from the bed, grabbed her robe from the chair, and ran out the door, hoping to catch him before he went home. In the living room, he sat on the sofa, the blankets wrapped around him, reading her latest issue of *Modern Baking* magazine. Before he could say a word, she blurted, "What time do we leave for Seattle tomorrow? I need to pack."

She'd never watched a man fall in love before, and if it happened, she wanted a front row seat.

16

Harlie crawled from bed at sunrise and found Clay sleeping on her sofa. She smiled at the sight but didn't have time to linger. If she traveled with him tonight, she had a busy day ahead. She needed to talk with Sam about taking care of the bakery in her absence. Annie would be there in the afternoon and Lisa could cover the morning hours. Maybe Buck would watch the boys and drop in to feed Spud. The Center volunteers were next on the list. Someone needed to take Harlie's place and ensure things went smoothly. When she talked to Buck, she'd also discuss details with Emily. If everyone did what was needed, she could go to Seattle without worrying. Not much, anyway. Her cell phone rang. This early, it was probably Sam. No one else in Angel Beach rose before the sun.

"Well, well," said a now familiar male voice. "Did I reach the elusive Charlotte Carson?"

Harlie froze.

"Hello? I know you're there. Charlotte?"

Harlie gripped the phone and tried to control her anger. She should hang up but couldn't do it. This thing with Skippy the Bloodhound needed to end. "I keep telling you my name is Harlie and you have a wrong number." She leaned against the counter, bracing herself for the fight.

He chuckled. "I didn't buy it the first two times you said it. I know who you are. I have some questions. Give me answers and I'll be on my merry way."

She pinched the bridge of her nose and considered telling him off. Instead, she tried appealing to his human side, if he had one. "Okay, fine. You know who I am. But I can't help you. Please, try to understand. I cannot help you. The divorce was final two years ago. I don't want anything to do with him or your article. Please respect my wishes and leave me alone."

"That's a funny thing, Harlie. Your divorce, I mean."

"Why is it funny? Marriages break up every day."

"Yeah, they do. Mine did. But the funny thing about your divorce is there is no public record of it. Nada."

"Of course there is. We signed the papers years ago."

"Did you see Glen Carson sign the papers?"

"No. They were delivered to him by courier." And immediately after, Harlie had left Seattle. If her attorney tried to inform her of a failed attempt, she'd already disconnected her phone.

"Did you see the returned papers? Did you see his signature on them?"

Harlie's heart pounded like a rock-band drummer playing a solo. "No, I didn't see them. But I know he signed them. I know the divorce is final." She was free of him. She had to be.

"There is no public record, Harlie. I hate to tell you this, but you are not Glen Carson's EX-wife. You're still married to him."

Harlie pressed her hand to her forehead and ran her fingers through her hair, grabbing a handful in her fist. "I don't believe a word of this. Stop bothering me or I'll call the police!" She disconnected the call and tossed the phone on the counter. She took a breath, but her lungs wouldn't expand. She slid down the counter until her butt hit the floor and she hung her head to her knees, counting.

"One...two...three..." Breathe in, breathe out. An imaginary prison sprang up around her; rigid bars pressed against her skin keeping her inside, unable to escape. "Four...five...six..." Breathe, breathe. A cold sweat covered her face and her hands shook. "Seven...eight...nine..." Breathe. "Ten." She gasped and filled her lungs with precious air, rolled to the floor, curled in a ball, and waited for the nausea to pass. She heard footsteps but couldn't raise her head for fear of throwing up. A welcome draft cooled her skin where her bathrobe fell open.

"Harlie!" Clay dropped to his knees and lifted her hair. "What's wrong? Are you sick?" He pressed his hand to her neck and face. "You're clammy. What's wrong?"

"I'm okay," she whispered and pulled her robe closed. "Just give me a minute." She opened her eyes and saw Clay's concerned face inches from hers. Her heart rate slowed to normal at the sight of him. She wasn't alone and, for now, she was safe. "I was dizzy for a sec, that's all." And if she kept looking at the naked man kneeling next to her, she'd be dizzier still. "Your clothes are in the dryer—through there." She pointed to the small laundry room off the kitchen. Clay left her long enough to retrieve his boxers and T-shirt and returned wearing them.

"Come on. I'll help you back to bed," he said, holding out his hand.

She shifted to sitting and allowed him to pull her to her feet. He half carried her to the bedroom. The bed was still warm and she relished the security it offered. Clay followed her beneath the covers and wrapped her in his arms. For a brief moment she pondered the ease with which he crawled into her bed, but the heat from his body comforted her and she drifted to sleep cocooned in Clay's tenderness.

Hours later, she woke refreshed and alone. A glance at the clock, 8:00 a.m. She had to get moving to sort a million details so she could fly to Seattle with Clay tonight.

Seattle.

Glen.

How could she go? What if Glen found her? He'd grab her and have her back in that horrible house in a flash, and this time, she might not get away from him. She needed to call her attorney in Seattle and find out if Skip's story was true.

But she suspected it was.

Glen didn't want the divorce and had threatened to hold it up. His parting words were so cliché she'd almost laughed. "If I can't have you, no one will," he'd said with such melodrama she'd thought he was kidding...until he started stalking her. Maybe he didn't want her dead as she'd speculated at the time, but not signing the papers meant she couldn't marry again. Not that she planned to remarry, but she didn't want the legal connection with Glen either.

"How are you feeling?" Clay stood in the door holding a steaming cup of tea. While she slept, he'd gone home and dressed in jeans and a fresh T-shirt. "I made this for you." He set the tea on her nightstand, touched her forehead, and laid his lips to her skin. "Not clammy now. What happened?"

Harlie sat up and reached for the tea. "It's nothing, really. I stood up too fast and got dizzy. It's a blood sugar thing." She shrugged. "I'm okay now. Thanks for the tea." She sipped and tried for nonchalance. He didn't appear to buy it.

"Maybe we should call that doctor friend of yours," he said, nearly choking on the words.

Harlie grinned. "And tell him what? Gee, Wayne, after you dropped me off last night, I had a hot make-out session with Clay and got a little lightheaded." She giggled. "I didn't eat much dinner and didn't get enough sleep. I think we can leave Wayne out of it."

"Will you feel like going tonight?"

He offered her the perfect opportunity to stay home and she debated using it. If a snapshot of Lisa and her boys hadn't flashed into her head, she would have said no. But too many people depended on her. Selfishness needed to take a back seat to necessity.

"I'm fine. What time do we leave?"

17

Over the years, Clay had received many propositions on airplanes. Back in his commercial flight days, it was usually a businesswoman in the first-class cabin looking for a thrill. In later years, when he switched to private charters, a young flight attendant might offer to help pass the time. He wasn't a member of the mile-high club yet and never considered joining that exclusive membership.

Until now.

They were en route to Seattle, overlooking Mount St. Helens, and he swore he'd drag Harlie into the back of the plane and finish what they'd started the night before if she whispered in his ear one more time. Her earlier reserve hadn't vanished completely, but there was a renewed zing in her kiss and confidence in her smile. Something had happened that morning. Something had caused the panic attack and he suspected this change in attitude was a byproduct of that something. As the landing gear touched down at Boeing Field, Harlie kissed him again and he decided to let her tell him about it in her own time. Asking might spoil her mood.

Sunset and a small army greeted their arrival. Mount Rainier stood majestic in the distance, its snowy cap illuminated by the sunset and resembling a pink craggy ice cream cone. Clay's bodyguard, Stuart, boarded the plane first and guided them down the stairs where a limo waited. Phil stood at his post by the limo door, opening it when Harlie and Clay approached. Introductions made, Phil motioned them into the car. Clay watched Harlie for signs of anxiety but Seattle had lost its boogeyman quality for her.

At the hotel, they took an elevator to the top floor and the presidential suite. A bellman followed, hauling an amazing array of suitcases. Clay didn't know what Harlie needed with all those bags—four large and one small—but she was adamant the driver bring them all. After saying their good nights to Phil and Stu and tipping the bellman, Clay closed the door and pulled Harlie into his arms. The city lights shimmered through the windows, filling the room with shadows. His kiss was a continuation of what she began on the plane. Long, hot, and full of promises. If Harlie's nomadic hands were an indication, she was ready now and wanted him as much as he wanted her. She pulled up his shirt and had her hands on his skin, her nails scraping, driving him wild. His fingers were on her top blouse button, in the process of unnecessary-clothing removal.

"Do you think we should let him know we're here?" said a deep, male voice.

Harlie gasped and dug her nails into Clay's back. He gritted his teeth and sucked in his breath.

A second male voice, with a southern accent, chimed in. "You know, that might not be a bad idea.

If things keep going like this, it could get a little embarrassing for all of us."

"Ah shit," Clay said. The lights flashed on, revealing two smiling men on the sofa. Harlie hid behind Clay.

"Who are they?" she asked.

"Tweedle Dee and Tweedle Dum," he said with a sigh. The posse had caught up with him and was their timing bad.

"Which is which?"

"Take your pick."

"Harv, why don't you try that fancy remote on Clay? I think he needs to be turned off," Tom Black said with a laugh. Harv pointed the remote and Clay rolled his eyes.

"What are you two doing here? This is my suite, isn't it?"

Harlie attempted nonchalance and looked anywhere but at the two men who crashed the party. The suite was large and luxurious with a living room, full bar, and dining room. Clay made the introductions. Tweedle Dee, or Tom Black as he was more often called, was Clay's best friend from Montana and head of his Nashville security. Black hair, dressed in Wranglers, chambray shirt, and cowboy boots, he looked like a western-wear catalog model, and at the moment, was enjoying himself too much at Clay and Harlie's expense.

Next to him, Tweedle Dum, or Harv Stockton: auburn-haired and dressed in slacks and dress shirt. A jacket was thrown over the sofa back. Clay's manager and friend.

Clay walked into the room with Harlie's hand clasped in his, pulling her along. "What are you two doing here?" he asked again.

"Well, Bonehead, you didn't check in like you were supposed to, forcing Harv to fly out here and make sure you got his messages about the concert. If, for some reason, you chose not to respond to his polite summons..." he said and looked at Harv. "You were polite, weren't you?"

"Infinitely," Harv responded, pokerfaced.

"Glad to hear it. So, if you chose to ignore your obligations, I was to accompany Harv to Oregon and drag you to Seattle. Hog-tied, if necessary."

Clay laughed. "You'd try."

Tom smiled. "I'd succeed and you know it. You aren't much different from wrestling a bull. Just about as stubborn, anyway."

"Okay. I'm here. You can go away now."

"Not so fast," Harv said, leaning forward, elbows on knees, scrutinizing Clay. "How are you?"

"I'm fine."

"You weren't fine when you sneaked out of Nashville the way you did."

"What?" Clay laughed. "I'm not fine because I didn't say goodbye? Did you need a hug or something?"

"A phone call would have done it for me." Harv blew out a breath. "This isn't like you, Clay. Or it didn't used to be. You never blow stuff off like this. What am I supposed to think?" Before Clay could respond, Harv looked at Harlie. "Can I ask you if he's telling me the truth?"

Clay rolled his eyes and laughed.

"Is he all right?" Harv said.

Harlie appeared surprised by the question. "I haven't seen any suicidal tendency, if that's what you mean. He seems fine to me, but I just met him." Harlie shrugged and looked at Clay. "If you don't mind, I think I'll find my room." She squeezed Clay's hand and raised her eyebrow at him. To Harv and Tom, she said, "It was interesting meeting you both."

Clay dropped into a chair, kicked his boots up to a coffee table, and watched Harlie leave the room.

Tom chuckled. "The local scenery?"

"Yeah," Clay said, distracted until Harlie closed the door behind her.

Tom smiled. "So, you must have taken care of the apology you were talking about?"

"Yeah, got it done," Clay said, still staring longingly at her door. "And it was worth every inch of crawling she made me do to accomplish it."

Harv and Tom both laughed. Clay didn't mind. As soon as he got rid of these bozos, he'd wander into the bedroom and see what that raised eyebrow was all about. Maybe she'd packed something interesting in those bags. Everything about Harlie interested him. Clay turned his attention to his unwanted company. "You didn't have to embarrass her that way."

Tom shrugged. "We didn't plan it. Harv fell asleep on the sofa and I was in the bar getting ice for my pop. When I came out here, you and Harlie were steaming up the entryway. I thought we handled the whole thing tactfully."

Clay snorted. "Tactfully? You startled her so bad she dug her nails into me." He reached back and grimaced when he hit a sore spot.

Tom laughed. "How was I supposed to know you were breaking your vow of celibacy now?"

Clay glowered at his friend. "I never took any vow of celibacy."

"Could have fooled me. You've hardly looked at a woman for ages."

"I looked. I didn't like what I saw." He smiled. "Until now."

Harv stood and stretched. "I need to hit the sack. You two can finish this intellectual discussion of Clay's revitalized sex life without me." He yawned wide. "Seeing as how you did get here and appear ready to work tomorrow, I'll take off. A car will come by around nine. Jana has some interviews planned, so be ready." Harv grabbed his jacket and was out the door before Clay could comment.

"What's eating him?"

"You didn't call and he's been worried you'd be a no-show," Tom said. "He threatened to quit at least ten times on the way out here. He said if you were going to run off halfcocked like this, you could find new management. You know Harv. He doesn't mean half of it."

Clay smiled. "Yeah, I know. Worrywart is what he is." His eyes again drifted to Harlie's closed door.

"So are you and the lovely lady—"

"I don't kiss and tell."

"You don't need to. It's stamped on your face, pal." Tom leaned back, looking like he didn't plan to leave anytime soon. "What do you know about her?"

"Enough," Clay said. "Ex-husband. Bad family life. A couple of real bad situations from what she says. She'll tell me more eventually."

"I could do some checking and see what I come up with."

Clay laughed. "You mean investigate her? That's a good way to kill the romance."

"It wouldn't be any different than the security checks I run on new employees."

"Do you want her to fill out an application and provide a resume, too? I don't need a human resources department to handle my love life, Tommy."

Tom looked skeptical. "With your track record, it wouldn't hurt."

"Look who's talking."

"Touché," he said, unperturbed. "I don't take chances, Clay. You know that. Your security is my priority."

"I know and I appreciate it. But I doubt you'd turn up anything about her."

"There is something you should think about though," Tom said. "Could she be connected with the notes? She turns up about the same time—"

"You think she's working with my old man?" Clay scowled. "I think you're grasping there. I moved in next door to her. I made the effort to get to know her. Not the other way around." But when the connection was made between them, Harlie jumped in with both feet to get him to contribute to her cause. But blackmail? He couldn't see it. She had the most generous heart he'd ever encountered. But she needed money for her shelter... No. He wouldn't even entertain the thought. He could imagine Crystal dipping into that sewer but not Harlie.

"This may change your thinking a little." Tom extracted an envelope from his shirt pocket and handed it to Clay.

He turned it over in his fingers. "Another one?"

"It came this morning." Tom leaned forward. "Look at the postmark."

Clay blew out a breath. "Angel Beach." Hand canceled. Someone wanted to make sure Clay knew exactly where the card was mailed.

"See what I mean? Harlie lives in Angel Beach. Maybe she's connected somehow."

Clay shook his head. "I can't see it. She probably has a secret or two, but I don't think she's connected to this." He opened the envelope and read its contents out loud. "At the end of the world, angels pray." Clay tapped his hand on his thigh, replaying the message in his mind. "I think you're right about this not being blackmail, Tom. It's like a roadmap and somebody is pointing me to Angel Beach. 'At the end of the world' could mean where the land meets the ocean, like back when people thought the world was flat. 'Angels pray' could be a reference to the angel there at Angel Beach. There's a rock formation that's supposed to look like a praying angel. It's a big tourist draw." He checked the postmark date. "Shit." His heart was pounding. "He's there now and I'm stuck here for two days."

"That's probably a good thing. This gives you a few days to think it over and consider talking to the police."

"I'm not talking to the police. They'll think I'm nuts. I need concrete evidence and I can't get it from here."

"Maybe we'll hear from Ed soon. Last time I talked with him his investigator was part way through the list. He'll give me the report as soon as he's checked all the cities. You concentrate on your show and leave it to them for now." Tom stood. "It's late and I don't think you need a babysitter tonight. No matter what Harv thinks." He picked up a glass from the coffee table and downed the contents in a gulp. "Is she going with you tomorrow?" He tipped his head toward Harlie's door.

"I want her to, but it'll be a long day with the stuff I need to do."

"I'll take care of her for you," Tom said. "Jana says she'll come by to talk with her in the afternoon. After that, I'll get her to the show in the evening and hang out with her backstage."

Clay smiled. "Thanks, bro. I appreciate it."

Tom made his way to the door, favoring his right knee. Tom's tangles with bulls hadn't always ended successfully.

"Night, Tom. Get some sleep."

Tom turned back and smiled "Maybe. Maybe not."

Clay cocked an eyebrow, questioning.

"A good-lookin' redhead said she'd be in the hotel sauna right about now and I'm thinking steam might do my knee some good." He winked and sauntered out the door.

Clay shook his head and chuckled. Tom's bad knee had its uses. Some guys walked dogs in the park to get female attention. Tom Black limped into a room and women swarmed him.

And Tom wasn't the only one with possibilities tonight.

After a quick strip to his boxers in his room, Clay made his way to Harlie's room. It was close to eleven and she was probably asleep. He looked in and nearly swallowed his tongue. Gone were the jeans and blouse she'd worn on the plane. In their place: pink panties exposing a scrumptious amount of leg and hip and a matching camisole. He wanted her desperately but stood in the doorway and watched her sleep, wondering if he should be selfish and wake her. Quietly, he stepped into the room, pulled a blanket over her and was at the door thinking it would be a lonely night in the second bedroom. One morning snuggle didn't give him an automatic invitation to share her bed again.

"Clay?"

He looked back to her. As she sat up, her curly brown hair fell to her shoulders and the blanket slid away. Hallway light spilled over her, illuminating her face and enticing body. Her eyes invited him to take what he wanted.

Before he could RSVP her invitation, she reached to the nightstand and tossed something his way. "Catch," she said. He smiled as he read the label: condoms. The woman was certainly organized, and judging from the size of the box, planned on having one hell of a good time. Her pre-planning would save him from digging through his suitcase. He wasn't a slacker in the preparation department either.

Clay crossed the room and sat on the edge of the bed, turning the box in his fingers and staring at it thoughtfully. He glanced at Harlie and back at the box. Apparently, she'd decided her single vending machine purchase wouldn't do.

"So?" she said, lifting the short word into a question. "You...want to...um...?" She blushed. Um. Boink. Make love. She could call it anything she wanted and he was all over it.

He set the box on the nightstand and leaned until his face was whisper close to hers. He cupped her cheek in his hand. "The question is, are you ready? Last night—"

"Shhh."

"But—"

"We talked enough last night." She brushed her fingertips across his mouth. "Just kiss me."

He closed the gap between them, kissing her, light at first. His lips barely pressed against hers. She responded, taking his mouth with hers, increasing the pressure and heat. He laid her back, stretching his long body over hers, touching wherever he could. While he had talked with his friends, she'd showered and now a light shampoo scent filled the air around her. They kissed—a lingering, heated union. Her lips welcoming, her tongue daring. She tried to take the kiss deeper, but he resisted. Speed wasn't his goal.

He shifted, easing away to better touch and kiss. The slightest stroke of his fingers sent her sailing, wanting more. He wore only black silk boxers, sexy to touch, sexier to slide from his lean hips, sexier still in a pile on the floor.

With a tug, her camisole joined the boxers. Cool air grazed her skin; heated hands warmed it. His talented fingers teased like butterfly kisses. She shivered. His mouth was hot against her mouth and skin, demanding responses she was thrilled to provide. Sighs and groans filled the air, his and hers, in whispered chorus. He murmured in her ear, her hair, against her skin, softly begging for more and more from a woman only too happy to give.

The pink panties she'd carefully selected that morning now slid from her hips to land on the floor. Skin on skin, sweaty, hot, and electrifying. Their racing pulses joined in the same beat, like a wild metronome. She needed him now. He was above her, his breathing heavy, his passionate eyes searching hers. She shifted, welcomed him, and held him tight. He moved. Blissful friction, the world's oldest dance, and both participants instinctively knew the steps.

In sync, they climbed, ozone-bound. Harlie had never felt so unrestrained, so right. With Clay, she knew she was wanted, knew she pleased and delighted her partner, and knew he wouldn't hurt her. This was real and beautiful. She tightened her grip on him, urged him on until she lost coherent thought. As she flew over an undefined edge, his body jerked; he called her name and joined her, falling head first into her waiting heart. He relaxed, his weight pressing her to the bed, his breathing slowing to normal. She caressed his back and broad shoulders, grazed her nails along his lean hips. He kissed her, sweet and long, before rolling with her snuggled in his arms, her head resting against his shoulder. Harlie smiled to herself, pleased and satisfied.

She didn't care what anyone said, love was tangible and tonight, she held it firmly in her arms.

18

Harlie woke up sluggish. Noon, the bedside clock said. Clay was already gone. He'd be busy all day with sound checks, equipment tests, interviews, loads of pre-show bullshit, as he put it. He suggested she sleep in, relax, and join him later. Jana would be here around three. She stretched and yawned, treating herself to a large morning-after sigh. Toss in a steaming bath and it was a viable plan.

She shifted and hugged a pillow. Her legs and hips had a pleasant, well-used achiness. No wonder. A blush rose up her neck when she thought of how they'd made love multiple times throughout the night and again in the morning before Clay left. She couldn't get enough of him.

The TV in the living room drew her attention. Tom Black: her escort for the day. After their embarrassing encounter the previous evening, she wasn't sure about spending the day with him. But her stomach growled, confirming she couldn't hide forever. A quick call to room service and breakfast would arrive soon. She climbed from bed and found presentable clothing—black sweats and a T-shirt.

In the living room, Tom stretched out in a recliner with a 7UP can in his limp hand. Dark bristles covered his cheeks. Harlie removed the can and woke him. He blinked and yawned, looked confused, then smiled.

"Mornin' Harlie," he said, rubbing his whiskered chin.

"More like afternoon. I ordered breakfast if you're hungry." She sat on the sofa and glanced at the TV. GAC. One of Clay's videos was playing.

Tom struggled to wake, finally succeeding after several more yawns. "I'm always hungry, especially when Clay is footing the bill." He squinted at the TV screen. "Gad, he's here even when he isn't here."

Harlie moved to change the channel. He waved a hand. "Don't change it unless you want to. I like listening to him. This isn't one of my favorites but it'll do."

Her attention shifted to the video, a ballad sung with strong emotion. The woman to whom he sang this love song must have touched his heart deeply. A twinge of jealousy jabbed her.

"I'll be waiting when you come home..." Clay sang.

"Can I ask you something, Tom?" she ventured, not sure she wanted the answer to her question.

"Shoot," he said.

"The lyrics. They come from things happening in his life, like a diary of sorts, right?" She thought of the angel song Clay was working on which came straight from their relationship, written in real time.

"Right. He lays himself out there."

"Well...Did he write this for Crystal or was there someone else?" Without realizing it, she'd clenched her fist.

Tom smiled and shook his head. "Most people interpret it as a love song and Clay lets them think it. The way it's written, it could be and I suppose in a way, it is." He looked thoughtful. "But he wrote it for his dad."

"His dad?" She glanced at the video again. Clay sat on the porch of a farmhouse, boots kicked up to the railing, guitar in hand.

"Yeah. When Clay was about thirteen." Tom waved at the screen. "That's his house in Montana...the house he should have grown up in."

Harlie furrowed her brow and looked at the screen again. Tom continued. "Clay's dad wasn't around much when he was a kid."

"But Clay told me they played music together. He never said—"

"He wouldn't. Clay blocks out a lot of his childhood. When he talks about his dad, he only mentions the good stuff and there isn't much of it." Tom's voice was hard. "Hunt abandoned his son after his wife died." He finished his pop, crunched the can in his fist, and tossed the wreckage to the coffee table.

"Abandoned? I thought he was around until Clay was eighteen or so...until the wreck."

"He told you about his mom?" She nodded and waited for more. Tom paused, came to a decision, and continued. "Hunt fell apart after she died. My folks offered to take Clay after the funeral so Hunt could grieve and get himself together. Clay and I were two.

Hunt didn't come back until we were almost four. Nobody knows for sure where he went or what he did. Story he told was he'd joined a country band and they were touring around, playing the bars. It's what he said, anyway. There was a rumor he'd landed in jail." He frowned. "Child protective services got wind of it and tried to put Clay in a foster home. My parents fought it and won custody." Tom's brow knit tight. "When Hunt finally came back, he brought Clay a little acoustic guitar and taught him to play. He stayed home for a few months, long enough to screw Clay up, then dropped him back at our house and disappeared again. This went on for years. Clay spent more of his childhood with us than with his father."

Harlie felt a stab in her heart. "But he eventually came back? Clay told me some stories about him."

Tom nodded. "Yeah, he came back but only because Clay looked useful to him. When Clay was seven, he got the idea that if he played the guitar good enough his dad would come back to hear him. He practiced and practiced on that thing. It was a little cheapie, but he made some great music on it. My parents bought him a better acoustic. Clay saved his money and bought a used Strat with an amp." Tom smiled. "He about blew us out of the house so Mom banished him to the barn." He laughed. "But, damn he was good, even back then." He glanced to the TV. "And now, he's phenomenal. The people who know about this stuff say he's a genius."

"And his dad finally came back?"

"Yeah. Hunt stopped in for a visit when Clay was sixteen, heard him in the barn and decided they should put a band together. Not long after, they were playing locally, doing the fairs and rodeos. Clay finally moved into his dad's house." Tom frowned. "He was disappointed though. By that time, he and his dad were practically strangers. Clay was nothing but Hunt's ticket to Nashville and Clay knew it."

"He told me about performing on stage with him," Harlie said, hoping to hear something more positive.

"It's about the only place they ever connected. When Hunt died in Wyoming, Clay came home to us again and stayed until he took off for Nashville. That was eighteen years ago."

"I didn't realize..."

"That he'd had it rough?"

"Not that rough. He told me about his mom's death but he never said he grew up with you. He also said his dad had a lot of problems with drinking and women."

Tom nodded. "He did."

"It makes his search for his father that much more amazing to me. Even with all the difficulty, he still loves his father enough to search for him." She frowned. "My mother is here in Seattle and I wouldn't waste two minutes looking her up. Clay is an amazing man to forgive his father this way."

Tom narrowed his eyes. "He told you that? That he's forgiven him?"

"Not in those words but he must have, right?"

Tom shrugged. "I suppose anything is possible. He says it's unhealthy to dwell on it so he doesn't talk about it. The divorce was tough on him, too. He's a real romantic and wants the lifetime love. Kids and all that. He missed it though." He looked at Harlie. "He's hung up on you, you know."

"Is he?"

"I saw the way he looked at you."

"And that worries you?"

He gave her a level stare. "Should it?"

Harlie watched the subtle shift from storyteller to alert sentinel: eyes narrowed, shoulders tensed, mental wheels turning. A knock at the door delayed the interrogation. Breakfast. Waffles with hot syrup, fruit, and strong coffee. Tom let the waiter in, tipped him, and sent him on his way.

Over their meal, Tom eyed her once more. She hadn't avoided his inquiry, only postponed it. She jumped in. "About your earlier question...are you asking as Tom Black, head of security, or Tom Black, best friend?"

"Does it matter?"

Harlie shrugged. "It might."

He smiled and relaxed. "I'm asking as Tom Black, brother. That's what he is to me."

"You call him Bonehead," she said with a smile. "Is that a brotherly endearment?"

"I suppose so." He shrugged and smiled. "Honestly? Clay can hook up with anyone he wants. But I do worry about motives where he's concerned. In his position, everybody wants something from him and it isn't always innocent."

"He said Crystal wanted his money."

"And exposure. She's always craved attention. He was well into the superstar stage of his career about the time she came around. She wanted the spotlight, the A-list parties, and to be seen on the red carpet at award shows. Marrying Clay gave her that. But she ditched him for another guy...or two." His smile was tight. "We lost count after a while. It cost him a lot of money but the divorce was the best thing that ever happened to him."

Crystal had wanted the image, the handsome man on her arm in public. Harlie and Clay had one more thing in common. Glen had wanted the same from her, the ornament on his arm. She'd given it to him and lost herself in the process.

"So, you want to know what I want from him," she said with bravado she didn't feel. How could she explain it to him? Did she tell Tom, a stranger, of the attraction and need, not only for the physical connection, but the emotional ties growing between her and Clay? Could she tell him of the protection Clay provided without even knowing it? Her involvement with him was a knife slash separating her from her former life. Their intimacy would damage her in the eyes of

Glen Carson. Could she tell Tom this and expect him to also believe she was falling in love and not using Clay?

"Do you blame me for wondering what you want from him?" Tom said. "Look at his history. Even his dad was only interested when Clay proved useful to him."

"And now you make sure he isn't hurt again?" she asked, unable to hide the irritation in her voice. This was like a job interview and if she didn't pass muster, she'd be ushered out the door with a "thank you for your time." Before he could open his mouth with a retort, she continued, choosing her words carefully. "I don't know what I want from him. I don't know if I want anything. I didn't chase him. He came after me. Ask him. But," she sighed and offered a simplified explanation of her feelings, "dang it, there is something about him." She paused. Tom waited for her to finish. "He makes me laugh, okay? He makes me feel good. Is that such a bad thing to want?" She frowned. "If that doesn't satisfy your need for drama, too bad. That's all there is to it right now." When she finished her speech, Tom was smiling at her.

"I think I see what Clay likes about you, well, other than the obvious. I'll bet you keep him tied in all sorts of knots."

"We're doing that to each other right now."

Tom lifted an eyebrow and his smile broadened.

Harlie rolled her eyes. Men and their one-track minds. "We seem to find a lot of reasons to argue."

"That doesn't surprise me. He likes a good scuffle now and then. He says you've got other things on your mind, too," Tom said, staring at her. "A secret or two, he said."

Harlie tensed. "What would that be?"

He shrugged. "I wouldn't know, would I?" He smiled reassuringly. "I'm not trying to upset you, Harlie. I want you to feel comfortable with us. And if something is bothering you, I can't think of a better guy than Clay to confide in. He'll bust his ass to help someone he cares about." He pushed his chair from the table and stood. "I get the impression he cares a lot about you." He stretched and ran his fingers through his black hair. "Now, if you'll be all right on your own a short time, there's some business I need to take care of a few floors down. Jana will be here around three and I'll be back around six to take you to the show."

With that, he left the suite.

Interview concluded.

Harlie pushed her plate away and sighed. For all his offers of help and friendship, Tom Black was suspicious of her and her intentions regarding Clay. He was the nosy type, and she wondered how long until he put his curiosity to work and discovered Harlie Cates possibly wasn't her legal name.

Tom Black, brother, might not care, but she was sure Tom Black, head of Clay Masterson security, cared plenty. She was convinced filling her in on Clay's background wasn't idle conversation. It was a warning: If you have less than honorable intentions, don't mess with Clay. Do it and you tangle with Tom Black, too.

And beneath that charming exterior, Tom looked like he might be itching for a fight. She didn't plan to give him one. By the time they returned to Angel Beach, Clay would know more about Harlie Cates than he might want to know.

19

Clay was working when Harlie and Tom arrived backstage. Clay and a reporter were deep in conversation until he noticed Harlie. He looked over the man's balding head and gave Harlie a wink and a smile. As soon as he could manage it, Clay escaped the reporter and made his way to her and grabbed her hand.

"We'll be right back," he said to Tom and whisked Harlie to his dressing room before she could protest. She wore the sexy shoes he liked—strappy around the ankles, tall heels—and the speed he moved her along nearly turned an ankle. "I only have a minute before a meet and greet with some contest winners." He slammed the door behind them and his mouth was on hers, hot and demanding. "If I didn't have to work, I'd have you up against a wall so fast..." Again his mouth covered hers and she couldn't have told anyone her name if asked. She certainly couldn't come up with the real one.

"I've missed you so much today," he said.

"I know," she said, breathless. "Me, too."

A knock on the door made Clay groan.

"Clay, you have a visitor," said a male voice.

"Who is it?"

"Says his name is Payton Shaw."

"Yeah. All right. Be right there."

"You've got the meet and greet first. He'll be waiting when you're done," the voice said.

"I'm on my way." He leaned his forehead to Harlie's. "Tom will show you where to sit for the show. I need to get to work." One last kiss and he was out the door, leaving Harlie alone in the dressing room. Dazed. When her brain could function properly, she found the bathroom and checked her reflection. Stunned eyes and abused lips. She smiled. She'd never had anyone want her so bad he considered a wall an appropriate surface to complete the deed.

She located Tom Black leaning against an equipment crate, watching Clay ward off a group of eager fans, amused at the sight. The meet and greet. It was a new concept to Harlie. A large assembly of female fans jockeyed for his attention and he took it all in stride. A typical day at the office for a superstar, she supposed. Each person carried something to sign: a book, a CD, a magazine with his photo, and DVDs of his videos. One woman requested he sign her belly. It was a nice, flat one, but he refused and offered to sign anything except a body part. He fended off overly sociable hands, suggestive glances, and inappropriate propositions. Harlie tamped down a spike of jealousy but smiled after she thought about it. She was the one he kissed in the dressing room and she was the one he would sleep with tonight. She glanced at Tom, who still wore an amused smile as he watched Clay.

"You don't have to help with that?" she said, remembering what it took to free Clay from his fans at the bakery: heavy-duty baking sheets, a locked door, a police cruiser at the back door, and an officer at the front breaking up the crowd.

Tom shook his head. "Nope. Not my turf. I run the ranch. This stuff is Stu and Phil's problem. I'm here for the show."

Harlie turned her attention to Clay and his adoring public. Music blared from the PA system, warming the crowd for the upcoming show. Harlie leaned against the wall, trying to pretend she hadn't seen a pretty blonde grab Clay's butt.

⊙≈⊙

The photographer pointed to the spot Clay should stand and a tall, attractive blonde stepped forward for an autograph and to have her picture taken with him. Clay opened her autograph book and mentally cringed when she snuggled against him, forcing him to drape his arm around her shoulder for the photo. She appeared blissfully unaware of his discomfort. "What's your name, darlin'?" he said with resignation.

"Melody." She stared into his face with unconcealed adoration. "You have the most beautiful eyes."

"Thanks." Clay chuckled when he thought of how often he heard that. They always commented on his blue eyes, his blond hair, his butt, how his jeans fit, his low, smooth voice, and on and on. And at the moment his well-formed butt had a wayward hand on it, squeezing with unwelcome familiarity. Clay raised his eyebrow and gave Melody a scathing look.

"Do you mind? That isn't part of your prize, darlin'. An autograph and picture. That's it."

She smiled at him and removed her offending hand, giggling as she was led away clutching the book Clay hastily signed. He turned his attention to the next woman.

Half an hour later the last of the group came forward for her picture and autograph. Harv moved in and ended the session, earning the expected groans.

"Sorry ladies, but he needs to prepare for the show. Thanks for coming tonight," Harv said as he extricated Clay from the grasp of a particularly fervent young woman. "This gentleman," Harv pointed to a stagehand, "will direct you to your seats."

"I enjoyed meeting all of you," Clay said as he smiled and turned away, looking for Harlie, but she was gone. He returned his attention to Harv.

"Somebody said Payton was here. Have you seen him?"

Harv nodded. "Yeah. He saw you were busy and said he'd catch up with you later. He mainly wanted to let you know he brought Glen Carson with him. He's in the front row. Security has been alerted."

"Glen Carson? Why is he here?"

"Payton says he's a big fan and wants to meet you. Not now though. You have five minutes to show time. Get moving."

⊂∾⊃

Show time: three minutes. Tom led Harlie to chairs inside the stage entrance. He took the one next to her. Harlie looked to the stage, impressed by the amplifier stacks which accompanied a mammoth rack of electric and acoustic guitars. The lights dimmed and a single spotlight appeared. No sign of Clay yet, but a loud guitar riff pierced the air. The audience stirred, recognizing the beginning of a favorite song. Clay slowly appeared, an elevator pushing him up. A butterscotch blond Telecaster in hand, eyes closed, his fingers flying across the strings and frets. After a moment, Clay paused. On that cue, a blast of light and sound exploded. Thousands of fans jumped to their feet, screaming, stomping, and adding to the sound torrent. It was the most breathtaking sight Harlie had ever witnessed.

Was this the down-to-earth cowboy she knew in Angel Beach? The talent, Harlie expected. She'd heard him play enough to know what he was capable of but the stage presence had her reeling. The ease with which he worked the crowd into frenzy amazed her. Was this the same man who'd held her through the night? The black T-shirt, jeans, boots, and hat she recognized. The voice: smooth and low. That, too, she knew well. She'd listened to him as he whispered endearments throughout the night, telling her she was beautiful and how much he wanted her. But this presence, this man who commanded the stage with such

SHARLEEN SCOTT

authority, was a stranger and she was as awed as any fan in the audience.

Seated next to her, Tom leaned forward, elbows on knees, his appreciative smile wide across his face. Harlie saw no envy in his green eyes, just pride in his adopted brother's talent and success. He glanced to Harlie, mouthed, "Isn't he something?" and turned back to the show, not waiting for her response. He didn't need it. Tom already knew Clay Masterson was phenomenal.

As Clay sang, the crowd cheered. Tom joined in with an ear-piercing, two-fingered whistle. The building nearly shook from the crowd's enthusiastic response to the spectacle on the stage. Clay entertained with fine-tuned skill, singing and playing an array of guitars, accompanied by another guitarist, a bass player, fiddle, banjo, steel guitar, and drums. He swerved smoothly between country, blues, and rock. Harlie was entranced by the interaction between Clay, the band, and the audience. The crowd spurred him on, increasing his energy level, fueling him. He encouraged the screaming mass, united them in the single purpose of enjoying the music he created.

There were thousands of them, wearing tank-tops, low-cut jeans, and shorts. Young girls and women alike exposed flower tattoos and bellybutton rings as they clapped overhead with the grinding beat of the band. With his lyrics ranging from tender love to suggestive, Clay reached out vocally to touch their hearts and stir their emotions. A quick flash to the left drew his attention. Clay stood straight and found himself the target of an excited teenage girl in hip-hugging shorts. Without interrupting his song, he spun the excited stage-jumper into a dance, touching only her fingers, until security pulled her away. Clay handed his guitar to a stagehand and worked the crowd, singing without missing a beat. He bent to touch outstretched hands, shook some, and brushed others.

After a few rowdy songs, the stage lights dimmed and the tempo slowed. Two stools were set on the stage and Clay moved to one. "I need to sit down so I can catch my breath," he said. He took a drink from a water bottle and wiped his face and neck with a towel. The water finished, he screwed the cap on and threw it into the audience. A group of women jumped for it. The winner waved it in the air, showing off where Clay had signed the bottle prior to the show. He tugged his shirt neck while the band played the introduction to a love ballad—a slow, sexy tune. "I think this song would be more convincing if I had someone to sing it to. Sexy lyrics need a sexy woman. Right?" The women in the audience cheered and several jumped from their seats to volunteer. "I'd like to introduce a special friend of mine." He turned to the stage entrance and said, "Come on out, Harlie."

She froze when the spotlight turned to her. Tom nudged her, tried to get her to stand, but she grabbed onto the chair.

Tom smiled. "Come on, Harlie. You're part of the show tonight."

She shook her head. "No. I can't."

Clay watched her from the stage. "She seems reluctant," he said playfully. "Let's give her some encouragement." The crowd cheered. "My friend Harlie is an incredible person. She runs a food bank and organizes lunches for the low-income folks in her area. Thanks to you, my audience tonight, the Masterson Foundation will partner with Harlie's community group to purchase a motel to use as a homeless shelter. Come on, darlin'!" He looked her way and grinned.

Harlie shook her head again, fighting the panic. She couldn't panic. She would hang on tight...

Tom gave her hands a tug and pulled her from her chair. "Everybody's watching, Harlie. Come on. It's okay. I'll walk out with you." He clamped onto her elbow and before she knew it, Harlie was center stage, teetering on unstable legs. The lights temporarily blinded her, but she found the stool next to Clay. Sweat trickled between her shoulder blades. Tom disappeared, leaving her alone with Clay and a mass of staring eyes. The band moved into the song. When her eyes adjusted to the bright lights, she saw Glen Carson in the front row.

Her heart raced at the thought of Glen recognizing her and what he might do. She turned slightly, hoping Clay would think she wanted to move closer to him. She'd hide behind him if she could but knew that wouldn't work. She turned her head, tilting slightly to allow her hair to fall forward. Clay winked mischievously. He took Harlie's hand in his and sang a sexy love song to her.

Clay finished the ballad as the lights dimmed, brought Harlie's hand to his lips, and kissed her palm. Tom appeared and escorted her from the stage while the band pumped up to play a rowdy song with grinding guitars and a pounding bass line.

Free of the stage, Harlie broke away from Tom and ran to the nearest bathroom, her chest heaving. Luckily, it was a single bathroom with a lock. She turned it and leaned against the door and tried to relax and not let the panic attack sweep over her.

Tom pounded on the door. "Harlie! Are you okay? Harlie!" He pounded again.

She tried to relax and catch her breath. Maybe Glen hadn't recognized her. She was heavier now, her hair longer. Glen had insisted she stay rail thin and wear her hair short and chic. Maybe, just maybe, he didn't connect the dots between the size-twelve woman on the stage and the size-six wife he'd known.

Her breath came easier now and she could speak. "I'm fine, Tom. I have a stomach problem. I'll be out soon."

Tom stopped pounding on the door, apparently satisfied with her response. Somehow, she needed to get past Tom and out the door. She'd hail a taxi and get out of here before Glen got to her. As quickly as the idea came, she realized the futility of it. Out there alone, she was an easy target. Her panic swelled again.

"When you're ready," Tom said through the door, "I'll take you over to Clay's dressing room. He has a sofa you can lay on if you need it."

Harlie leaned her head against the cool wall and sighed. "As soon as my stomach calms down," she said, buying a few minutes for self-composure. She took a deep breath. Tom was right, of course. Clay's dressing room was the best plan. Once there, she would have the protection of Clay and his bodyguard, safe until the plane lifted off from Boeing field in the morning. Glen Carson wouldn't have a chance.

20

Last encore.

Clay tilted his head to remove the panties dangling from his hat brim. They'd flown through the air like a black lace heat-seeking missile, landing between his eyes. He scanned the crowd for the donor of the charming item, tempted to pull her on stage and offer congratulations on the direct hit, but she was lost in the sea of upturned faces.

The grand finale. Large video screens gave close-up views to those in the back and ear-splitting volume pierced the air. It was his third encore and they yelled for more. "Thank you!" he yelled to the mass of cheering fans as his band ground down to the concluding beat: drums, guitars, keyboard, and fiddle together in the climax. He felt, as well as heard, the roar of thousands of voices together as one, nearly deafening as they encouraged him to sing on and on. He soaked it in, reveling in the high attained during a performance.

Sweat dripped from his brow. His throat was dry and his muscles weary but he felt alive. "Thank you, Seattle! You've been wonderful! I love you all. Thank you! Good night!" Clay removed his black cowboy hat and threw it into the screaming throng. He waved again and sauntered off, tugging the neck of his sweat-soaked T-shirt in an unsuccessful effort to cool himself.

The audience continued to yell, clap, and pound their feet.

"One more song! One more song!"

Adrenaline pumped through his system as he made his way backstage. Harv and Stu flanked his steps. Phil brought up the rear.

"Good show, buddy," Harv said as he handed Clay a water bottle he downed in a few gulps. "We'll run you straight to the dressing room and get you out of here."

"Thanks," Clay said, taking the wet towel Harv handed him. He wiped his face and neck and ran his fingers through his hair again to relieve the hat indentation. He removed the guitar from his shoulder and handed it to Stu. Tom wandered up.

"Where's Harlie?" Clay asked, glancing around.

"Bathroom," Tom said. "Throwing up, I think."

"She's sick?" Clay made a move to find her but sniffed his shirt and changed his mind. If he did find her, the sweat stench would make her sicker.

Tom smiled and shrugged. "Stage fright, in my opinion. After you sang to her, she ran into the nearest bathroom and hasn't come out yet. I've been watching the door. No sign of her."

"Stage fright?" He blew out his breath. "Tom, if you'll keep an eye on her, I'll run in and shower. If she comes out, tell her I need a few minutes."

Tom agreed and ambled off to keep his bathroom vigil.

Clay wandered to the dressing room, closed the door, and leaned against it. He looked around: the typical sofa, table, chairs, and prints of local scenery on the walls, a small refrigerator stocked with drinks, and a plate of chocolate chip cookies. The only thing missing? Harlie backed up against the wall, breathing heavily. He liked the idea. A quick shower and he'd see what the problem was. Since he'd found her lying on the floor that morning he knew something was bothering her and possibly scaring her.

He pulled his sweaty T-shirt over his head on the way to the bathroom, tossed it in the direction of the couch, and unhooked his belt. The reflection in the bathroom mirror caught his attention and he laughed. Dark circles hung heavy under his eyes—a result of his long night with Harlie—and he'd been unsuccessful at removing the hat hair. A sweaty ring circled his head. The sexiest man. Clay chuckled with amusement.

After a quick shower, he wandered barefoot and shirtless from the bathroom, immersed in thoughts of the show, and failed to notice he wasn't alone until he ran into her.

It wasn't Harlie.

His uninvited guest wore tight, low-cut jeans, a midriff-baring shirt exposing her pierced bellybutton, and a knowledgeable look in her young eyes—a look that said she wasn't after another autograph. "How did you get in here? Melody, right?"

The butt grabber.

The attractive blonde smiled. "You remembered me." The knowing eyes flicked over his state of undress and rested on his unfastened jeans.

"Yeah, well, you need to leave." He noticed her interest and zipped his fly.

"Not yet. I thought you and I could, you know, spend some time together." She licked her lips in anticipation, her resonating, hot sexuality bouncing off him like a sonar ping.

"That isn't going to happen. You need to leave. Now." He moved toward the door but she blocked his path.

"Ah, come on, Clay. We made a connection out there. I felt it and I know you did, too. You called me darlin'." She stepped closer. He stepped back.

"That was a grope, not a connection. And I call everybody darlin'. Don't read something into it that isn't there."

Obviously undaunted by his refusal of her attentions, Melody continued her efforts. "I feel like I've known you for years, Clay. We could have something here."

"No, we couldn't. You don't know me and I definitely don't know you."

Melody stepped closer and giggled; her hips swayed in her form-fitting jeans. For each forward step of hers, he took one step back. He could end it right there with a call for Stuart and Phil, but if he did, the guys would never let him live it down that he couldn't handle a skinny thing like her. No, his ego wouldn't let him yell for help. He'd get her to the door and have Stu escort her from the building.

"Yes, I do know you," she said and forced him back another step. "I know your favorite color is blue, your border collies are named Cookie and Clyde, and you love chocolate chip cookies." She moved again. He took another step back. "You grew up in Montana on a cattle ranch, you're divorced, and you don't have a girlfriend." She lowered her voice. "I know you make me shiver when you sing in that sexy, gravelly way, and it feels like you are singing to me. I love the way you get emotional, the way you dance and play your guitar. Come on, Clay, I do know you."

He continued to retreat, caught his foot on a chair, and fell against the wall with a thud and a muttered curse. She placed her hand on his bare chest, leaned in and took a deep breath, inhaling his soapy scent. She looked like she wanted to nibble him from head to toe as if he were a steak kabob on a late-night buffet. "You don't know me." He pushed her hand away. "If you did, you would already be aware that oversexed women or in your case, little girls, barging into my dressing room don't interest me. I don't get involved with strangers and honey, that's exactly what you are to me. Nothing is happening here."

She didn't move, just looked at him with amusement.

He sighed in exasperation. "I'm not interested," he said. "And for your information, I do have a girlfriend and I introduced her on stage tonight. Sorry I haven't had time to alert the media. Now, leave." He looked her over, estimated she couldn't weigh more than one hundred and ten pounds and could be thrown over his shoulder and tossed out the door. While he contemplated the most efficient method of Melody removal, she pulled her T-shirt over her head, establishing she wore no bra. Clay was shocked. He'd never had a fan do this before. Melody then proved herself an effective multitasker by grabbing the front of his jeans, flicking them open, and covering his mouth with hers. He heard a gasp.

"This is why you needed a few minutes? You damned lying bastard!"

"Oh god. Harlie!" He tried to disentangle himself from Melody. "Get out of my way!" He pushed Melody away and made a hasty retreat over the chair he'd tripped on moments before. "Harlie!" He moved fast but when he reached the door, she was gone. He brushed past Tom, who lingered in the hallway. Barefoot, Clay took off after her. "Harlie!" He was at the outside door, ready to push his way through when large hands grabbed and stopped him. He fought, swinging wildly. "Let go! I gotta get her!"

"Clay!" Stu had him in a headlock. Tom ducked fists and kicking feet. "Clay! You can't go out there! You aren't dressed!" Stu tightened his hold, nearly choking him. "Your pants aren't even zipped! Calm down, damn it!"

"I gotta get her, man! It's not what she thinks. I need—"

Tom moved toward the door. "I'll find her." He was out the door and immediately swarmed by a group of waiting fans. They screamed when they saw Clay, half-dressed and wild eyed. It finally sunk into Clay's distorted psyche what Stu was saying. If he ran after Harlie, he'd be lucky if he kept his pants.

Clay gripped Stu's muscular arm but couldn't budge it from his throat. "You can let go now," he said through clenched teeth. Stu released him. Clay rubbed his neck. "You didn't have to strangle me."

"Yeah, I did. You were going crazy." Stu looked like a large, buff cougar ready to strike again if Clay made a move. Phil crossed his arms and blocked Clay's path to the door.

Clay let out a frustrated breath. "Yeah, well," he flung his hand toward the door, "she thinks she saw..." He grimaced when he saw his jeans were open and hanging loosely from his hips. "Aw shit. I'm screwed." He knew what Harlie saw. Melody: no shirt, her breasts staring at him like beacons. Clay: half-naked, Melody's hand practically in his pants and her tongue in his mouth. How was he going to explain it to Harlie? The woman surprised him, that's all there was to it. Melody grabbed onto him before he could react. Oh yeah, Harlie would go for that all right. He scrubbed his hands over his face, growled under his breath, and stomped back to the dressing room, stopping briefly for a necessary clothing adjustment.

Melody stood there, eyes wide, clothes on.

Clay scowled at her. "What are you still doing here? Haven't you caused enough trouble for one night? Stu! Phil!" He looked around for his bodyguards and found they had joined the group assembled around the dressing room. "Get her out of here and make sure this doesn't happen again or I'll can both your asses. Watching this door is your job!" Melody glared and stomped out. "Escort her ALL the way outside." Clay retreated to his dressing room, closed the door, and leaned on it. A moment later he heard a light knock. He opened the door to find Payton Shaw trying to control a smile.

Clay backed away from the door and leaned his head against the wall. "Hey, Payton. Come in and witness the annihilation of my love life." He rubbed his hands over his face and muttered, "Shit."

Payton chuckled. "Well, son, as usual, you do live an exciting life. I wanted to let you know Glen Carson loved the show and had wanted to meet you. Unfortunately, an emergency call interrupted his plans and he'll have to make it another time."

"Glad he enjoyed the show. Did you get my message about the motel property?" Clay thought he saw a brief grimace cross Payton's face.

"Yes. I've taken care of it."

Clay nodded. "Thanks. Harlie needs that property for her homeless shelter and I wasn't ready to do anything on the club idea anyway."

"So I gathered. I'd best catch up with Glen," Payton said. "I'll be in Angel Beach in a few days. I'll call you."

"Great." Payton closed the door and Clay grabbed a shirt from a rack and dropped to the sofa. He pushed speed dial on his cell.

"Did you find her?"

"Yeah," Tom said. "Can't talk right now. I'll call back." Tom disconnected without giving the damage assessment. From Clay's vantage point, it looked like a relationship massacre.

21

Harlie ran, cursing her impractical heels with every shaky step. She didn't cry. She was too angry for tears. All the warning signs were there and she'd ignored them. Sucked in. The too-smooth lines, the talented hands, all led to this. The pre-game show. The warm-up band before the superstar attraction.

She made it through the backstage area, dodging curious onlookers while stumbling on her heels, only to be caught in a clog of Clay's fans at the back door. They cleared a path when they realized she wasn't anyone important. Halfway down the block, a taxi driver awaited a fare. Harlie took off at a trot, twisting one spike heel on the curb. She threw open the door, climbed in, and slammed the door, safe for the moment from Clay's betrayal and Glen's threatening presence. Address given, the driver accelerated but slammed to a stop at the shriek of a two-fingered whistle and a yelled, "Whoa!"

"What are you doing?" she shrieked at the driver as she looked out the windows in panic. "Go! Go!"

Before the driver could respond, the curbside passenger door swung open and a man jumped in the back seat. Harlie grabbed her shoe and clenched it in her fist, spike heel pointed at her intruder. Her heart pounded in her chest until she recognized his face.

"It's taken," Harlie said through clenched teeth. "Find your own." She relaxed her hand but didn't drop the shoe.

"We're heading the same way," Tom Black said as he snapped his seatbelt, unruffled by her threat. "This is the only available cab." The driver looked in the rearview mirror, uncertain until Harlie nodded her head.

"Go ahead," she said.

The night was cool but a sheen of sweat collected on Harlie's brow. The driver's open window gushed air into the back seat; rock music played at a modest volume on the stereo. The air wasn't refreshing. The music grated on her nerves. She wanted to get away from them all, to protect herself from Glen and her heart from Clay, but here she was, stuck in a cab with Clay's watchdog, making her escape impossible.

"It's not what you think," Tom said, staring straight ahead.

"You wouldn't say that if you'd seen—"

"I saw. I was standing right behind you."

"Then how can you say—"

Tom turned to her. "Because I know him. It can't be what you're thinking because Clay would never do that."

Harlie clenched her teeth but remained silent. Tom and Clay were like brothers, watching each other's backs since toddlerhood. Of course he would defend Clay.

"I'm sure he has a good explanation for what you saw," Tom said with confidence.

Harlie laughed. "You have got to be kidding. He was kissing a half-naked woman in his dressing room. She had her hand in his pants. How can he have a viable explanation for that?"

The lights of the city sped by, a streaked blur. Tom took a deep breath. "Weird stuff happens to him."

"You can say that again. But you know what? I think he likes it, maybe even invites it." She gripped the shoe in her hand, wishing she could stab it into something. Like Clay Masterson's heart. "Here's the way I see it, Tom. He has his little flirt session before the show; if he's lucky, there will be a pretty one in the crowd and if he's luckier still, she'll give him a sign she's interested."

Tom shook his head and scowled.

"I watched the whole thing, the whole mating dance. She snuggled up. He put his arm around her. She grabbed his butt. Invitation, connection, and completion in the dressing room after the show. Or it would have ended that way if I hadn't opened the door. I can't figure out where I fit into this. Why bring me along? Does he like getting caught?"

Tom narrowed his eyes. "That's absolute bullshit. That's not what you saw tonight. I'll agree you saw a fan putting the moves on Clay but you didn't see him respond to it. Not like you're saying anyway. He told her to knock it off."

"Did he?"

"He did."

"Would that be before or after she stuck her hand in his pants? Must have been before. I'm pretty sure she had her tongue in his mouth when I saw them. It's difficult to have a serious morality discussion that way." She gave Tom a level stare. "Don't even try to defend him." She turned to the window, tried to focus on anything beyond her own distressed reflection. Why? She kept asking herself, why?

"Women constantly come on to him but he never takes them up on it," Tom said. "Never. Even when Crystal was whoring around and he had a valid excuse to retaliate with other women, he didn't. He stayed true to his vows."

Harlie swallowed. The effort stung her throat. "How do you know that?"

"Like I said, I know him. He isn't like that. Clay isn't into one-nighters. Hell, he's hardly dated since the divorce." He paused. "I also saw the look on his face when he saw you standing there and I watched him chase after you like a madman. If Stu hadn't caught him, he'd be in this cab with you, barefoot and half-dressed, begging you to understand. He was crazed trying to catch you. Give him a chance, would you? Don't push him off without letting him explain. Try trusting someone for a change."

"I give my trust to people who deserve it."

"No matter how it looks right now, he deserves it. You won't find a better guy than Clay," Tom said.

"Is this part of your job as head of Clay Masterson security? Do you always smooth Clay's way for him?"

"No. Honestly, I don't see a lot of him. I run the ranch and he spends most of his time on the road. I'm his brother first, so my interest in this situation isn't strictly security related." He gave her a level stare. "But I am wondering something. Who are you hiding from, Harlie?"

"Hiding?" Harlie tensed. "What makes you say that?"

"I watched you on stage. The way you turned from the audience and let your hair fall across your face tells me you might be hiding from someone. What are you afraid of?"

She shook her head. "Nothing. You've got it all wrong, Tom. I don't like being in front of people that way. I've always hated large crowds."

He shrugged. "Suit yourself. I don't expect an honest explanation from you. You've got a secret and I suppose you'll spill it when you're ready. What I'm hoping is you'll talk to Clay about it. He's the guy who needs to know these things. I covered for you. For now. I told Clay I thought you had a case of stage fright." He smiled. "He was feeling real bad that he'd done that to you. Does that sound like a man who was planning a rendezvous with a girl half his age? He was sweaty after the show and wanted to clean up before he saw you." He gave her a pointed look. "You were the woman on his mind tonight, not that girl in his dressing room. I think she snuck up on him and surprised him. That's all."

Harlie twisted the shoe in her hand. "I suppose it's possible but—"

"But you aren't ready to believe it yet."

"No."

At the hotel entrance, Tom paid the driver and fell into step with Harlie. They drew stares from the few guests in the lobby: the barefoot woman and the limping cowboy.

"You aren't coming in, are you?" Harlie asked when they reached her room. She hoped the guard dog service would end now.

"No. I wanted to see you to the door. Clay wouldn't like it if something happened to you on my watch."

"You make me sound like a prisoner." She slid the key card in and opened the door.

"Welcome to Clay's life, Harlie. He lives with security twenty-four seven because people are always trying to get to him for one reason or another. If you can't take it, maybe this incident tonight is the excuse you need."

"For what?"

"To dump him."

"I don't know if..." She stepped in the door. "I don't know anything right now."

"I agree with you on that. The problem is you don't understand him yet. He's kind of complicated."

Harlie frowned. "What's there to get about him? He's a man with a libido problem and he gets pissed off when he's caught."

Tom laughed and shook his head. "That right there proves it. You don't understand him."

"And you do?"

Tom's smile showed his amusement with her. "I'm a couple of months older than him. When you know a guy since birth, you get a good idea of what makes him tick."

Harlie crossed her arms. "And what makes Clay tick?"

"Hunt Masterson."

She frowned. "His father? From what you've said, he was never part of his life. Why would he matter?"

"Just because he wasn't around doesn't mean he didn't have an effect on his kid. Clay has spent his life trying to prove that Hunt's dysfunctional behavior isn't a Masterson genetic defect. He's always taken the honorable path because his father never would. That's what you need to understand about Clay. He wouldn't cheat on you because it's something his father would have done. He will follow through on every commitment he makes because that's something his father never did. Clay deserves a chance to explain what happened tonight." Tom stepped away but turned back. "I'll warn you about something though."

"What?"

"Right now Clay is probably kicking himself for letting this happen. He's blaming himself."

"As he should," Harlie said.

"But by the time he gets here, he's gonna be mad. You might want to stay clear and let him get it out of his system."

"Why should he be angry?"

"Because you don't trust him. Clay places a lot of importance on trust. He's looking for someone who deserves his too." He moved to the elevator and pushed the button. "Since he brought you with him to Seattle, I'm assuming he thought it was you."

⁂

An hour had passed when Harlie heard Clay return to the suite. The slamming of the first door alerted her to his arrival. The second slam confirmed Tom was right. Clay was angry. After encountering Glen in the front row and witnessing Clay's tongue dance with the bimbo, she wasn't in such a great mood herself. As of tonight, men no longer existed in her world. She didn't care what Tom said about Clay. All men did was use a woman and toss her aside. And Clay had the nerve to ask her to trust him. She'd fly back to Oregon with him, but after that, they were done.

Now that she'd severed her relationship with the male of the specie, she relaxed and propped against a pillow pile and tried to concentrate on the book resting against her knees. The romance novel had appealed to her earlier in the day when she was gushy from the previous night's love fest, but now that Clay resembled a slug, she couldn't get into it. She laid the book aside and grabbed the steaming tea from her nightstand. Room service had been prompt with the tea and scrambled eggs she'd ordered. Just because her sex life was over didn't mean she'd starve herself. Eating not only took the gnawing pain from her stomach but also kept her from surrendering to the crying jag threatening to overtake her resolve. She sipped her tea and returned to her book.

Two pages into the new chapter, she heard a knock. She didn't respond. He knocked again. Before she could call out, he stepped in and leaned against the door. Her stomach did a flip-flop and her heart beat like demented hummingbird wings. He was wearing nothing but silk boxers and was mind-boggling sexy. He frowned but didn't appear angry.

"Is there something I can do for you?" she asked with detachment.

His frown deepened at her businesslike tone. "Tom said you were sick. I wanted to check and make sure you were okay."

"I'm fine. Thank you for asking." She returned to the book.

He stood at the door. If he waited for an invitation from her, he'd be gray-haired before he got one.

"It's not what you think."

She gave him a tight-lipped smile. "I have eyes, Clay. It didn't take a lot of thinking to figure it out. It's okay though. We have less than a week invested in this little affair, so if you want to move on, now is the time. Neither of us will get hurt this way." She yawned. "I'm tired. Maybe this could wait until tomorrow?" This was easier than she thought. Other than the initial urge to drag him to bed and tear off those boxers, breaking things off with him was almost painless—as long as she didn't make eye contact or look at the broad, sexy chest she'd spread kisses across last night.

He took a few steps but stopped when Harlie gave him an icy glare. "Damn it, Harlie. We need to talk about this."

"I don't, but if it will make you feel better, have at it." She shrugged. "Just to satisfy my curiosity though...I would like to know how you could do that after the night we spent together." She kept her voice flat, almost bored.

He raised an eyebrow "What was I doing?"

"You should know better than anyone. If you need a recap of your activities, I'll give it to you. You and Blondie the large breasted, possibly underage bimbo were both half-naked. She had her hand in your jeans and you were kissing her. If I hadn't interrupted, I'm sure you would have taken things to the next level. "

"Try again."

"That's what I saw."

"It's what you think you saw."

"I saw two people getting awfully close to having sex. I've been involved in the activity often enough to recognize it when I see it. You were leaning against the wall. She had her hand in your pants and her tongue in your mouth. Defend yourself if you can, Clay."

He laughed and shook his head. "Think about this. Isn't it unusual for a willing guy to be backed up against a wall that way?"

"How should I know? Maybe you like it that way. You'd said earlier you wanted me against the wall. You seem to have a thing for it." She tried to keep her voice flat but had difficulty. He'd made her feel desirable and she'd thought about it all evening.

"Right. I wanted YOU against a wall. You. Not some girl I don't even know."

"You were kissing her."

He paced across the room. "No, I wasn't. SHE was kissing me. SHE had her hands on my zipper. My hands were not on her. Other than knocking her hand away from my chest, not once during that entire encounter did my hands touch her."

Harlie struggled to control her anger. "I saw you kissing her. I don't care who started it. Her mouth was all over yours and you weren't fighting her off."

Clay ran his hands through his hair and took a breath. "Do you want to know the truth or not?"

She shrugged.

"This girl snuck into my dressing room while I took a shower. She propositioned me. I told her to leave. She didn't want to go. I thought I could talk her out the door without calling for Stu. I tried to keep a reasonable distance between us. I've never touched a fan and didn't plan to start tonight. Every time she stepped toward me, I stepped back until she had me against the wall. She took off her shirt and while I was trying to figure out what to do about that problem, she grabbed me. Then you walked in." He clenched and unclenched his fist. "I could have avoided the whole situation if I had called for Stu but I didn't. It was my mistake."

"If you're innocent, why are you so angry with me? You should be apologizing, not ripping my head off."

He narrowed his eyes. "I'm angry because you have such a low opinion of me. I'm angry because you're telling me being with you didn't mean anything to me, that I could have the most amazing night of my life and turn around and screw some girl I've never seen before. That's why I'm angry."

"I...wait a minute..." she said, frowning.

"Your actions screamed it to everyone in the area. When you ran out like that, it said you don't trust me. You think I'm capable of cheating on you. What was it you called me, a lying bastard? Sounds like you have an incredibly low opinion of me and now everyone within shouting distance knows it." He walked into the bathroom and got a glass of water from the sink. He drank it in one gulp and slammed the glass on the counter. "For your information, I would never do that. Never. I've been cheated on and know how it feels. I wouldn't do that to you. Period."

"And you have no intention of apologizing?"

"For what? I didn't do anything." He appeared to fight for calm. "Okay. You want an apology, I'll give you one."

Harlie picked up her book and pretended to read. "And it will be dripping with sincerity from the sound of it." She looked up at him. "Forget it. Close the door on your way out." She buried her nose in her book and considered this fiasco over.

Clay turned to leave but stopped and slammed his palms onto the doorframe. He couldn't leave it like this. If he did, their budding relationship was over. Since he was an unwilling participant in the dressing room incident, what happened with Melody was not something he should apologize for. But he'd have to apologize for something or she'd think he was a goober again. "I'm sorry."

"For what? You said you didn't do anything."

He smiled, but with his back turned, she wouldn't see. "I'm sorry I dragged you on stage without warning you." He turned around, his face a mask of seriousness. "Tom said you were in the bathroom throwing up afterward. I shouldn't have done it but Jana thought it was good PR for the Foundation."

"It was a stomach bug. No big deal."

"I'm sorry I didn't handle the situation in the dressing room better. If I'd called for Stu, he'd have had her out of there in a heartbeat. It's what I pay him to do and I should let him do his job, but I thought I could get rid of her without a scene. I'm sorry you had to see it. I let my ego control the situation and didn't consider how it might upset you."

Harlie blinked at him. "Thank you. Now you can close the door on your way out." She resumed reading.

"I can't do it."

She gave him a tight smile. "Sure you can. One foot in front of the other. Hand on door knob. Pull door closed from other side. Simple. Good night."

Clay waited a moment before moving across the room to the bed. He started at the end, crawling until his eyes met hers over the book. She pushed the book into his chin and glared.

"I can't do it, Harlie. I can't leave."

"Clay—"

"See, the problem is that you've ruined me for other women. When she was rubbing against me, I didn't feel a thing. I mean nothing. She could have rubbed until I developed a rash and nothing would have happened. I was getting a little concerned there was something wrong with me." He leaned closer. "But the problem was the woman, not the equipment." He pressed against her. "I don't want another woman, Harlie. I want you."

"So, you didn't enjoy it?"

He shook his head. "Nope."

Harlie frowned. "Nude breasts presented at close range and you didn't want to touch them?"

He smiled. "No. I didn't, Harlie, because they weren't yours."

"You only want to touch—"

"Yours. Right.

"Seriously?"

He pulled the book away from his throat and tossed it aside. "Baby, I'm falling for you so hard, I'm gonna break bones if I ever hit the ground."

Harlie laughed, cursing him for his ability to get around her anger so easily. "My gosh, you talk in song lyrics."

"It isn't."

"It could be."

"Maybe, but it's true. I'm completely hooked on you." His lips were a breath from hers. "You make me laugh and feel things I've never experienced before. You surpass every fantasy I've ever had. It's your voice I hear in my dreams."

"Ohhhhh...there you go again with that dreamy song lyric stuff," she said. "Did you really mean what you said?"

"About what?"

"That you thought last night was the most amazing night of your life?"

"Yeah. The absolute best night ever."

Harlie slid her arms around his neck and sighed, "Me, too."

22

It was two in the morning and Harlie couldn't sleep. She was exhausted but her mind churned like a blender. She slipped from beneath the blankets and tiptoed to the bathroom for a drink. When she returned, Clay wrapped her in his arms and snuggled his chin against her hair. In less than a week, she'd become accustomed to him. Even in the dark, she recognized the pattern of his breath, the scent of his skin, and reveled in the comfort of having his body next to hers.

"You okay?" he said, his voice heavy with sleep.

"My stomach is fine now."

"Your stomach was fine all along." He shifted and kissed her temple. "How long have you had panic attacks?"

She stiffened. "I don't have panic attacks."

"It's not a big deal, Harlie. I've had it happen a few times. Like the first time I had to face a stadium crowd." He chuckled. It was a deep sound that vibrated his chest.

"What happened?"

"Well, it was kinda embarrassing. When they called for me to head to the stage, I was stupid enough to ask how big the crowd was. Fifty thousand, they said. Next thing I know, I think I'm either having a heart attack or somebody released a boa constrictor in my dressing room." His chest shook with laughter again.

"When I didn't show up, Harv came looking for me and found me curled up in a ball on the floor, hyperventilating. I was about twenty and still a real greenhorn from Montana."

"Did they cancel the show?"

"No. I got it together. One of the old-timers backstage gave me a tip. He said pick out one person in the crowd and sing to her. Just that one person."

"Did it work?"

"Sure. I picked out the hottest babe in the tightest T-shirt I'd ever seen and you can bet I forget about the rest of them. You've had a couple of attacks in the last few days. Last night I understand. I shocked you and stress can bring one on. But what got you going at five in the morning?"

"Stress, like you said. When we leave, can we make a quick detour on the way to the airport?"

"Where do you want to go?"

"A house on Lake Washington. I need to deliver those suitcases." She stretched across his chest, relaxed now that the decision was made. When she'd packed the suitcases, she really didn't know what the outcome would be.

Now she had a plan.

⚬❦⚬

"So, where are we going? Clay asked Harlie for the tenth time while the limo cruised through plush residential streets. The day was clear and boats sped across the calm water of Lake Washington.

"You'll see."

The limo driver stopped at the gates of an Italian-style mansion sitting amidst impeccably landscaped grounds fronting the lake. A driveway snaked toward the house, where a fountain and reflecting pool added to the opulence. Clay had visited similar homes in the past and wasn't shocked by the lavishness. Some people got into that. Clay didn't. Though he could afford such a lifestyle, he lived modestly in a 1920's farmhouse outside Nashville. He had to admit his four-hundred surrounding acres were well-maintained and picturesque but no one would expect to see a reflecting pool or fountain on his ranch. Tom would probably turn the cattle into it for a drink. He had a trout pond with a boat, though. He and Tom raised cattle and bulls for competition. Mix in a few horses, which they did, and the place was bucolic and homey. Not quite Montana but close enough to keep two rancher's boys from getting homesick. He'd renovated the house extensively over the years and magazine editors occasionally requested to photograph his home, but it wasn't in the league of this behemoth. A guy would need a floor plan to find the bathroom.

He didn't get the chance to ask why Harlie wanted to come here. As soon as the limo's wheels stopped, she was out of the car and pushing the call button at the gate, her body nearly vibrating with tension. When a voice squawked from the speaker, Clay got a surprise.

"I'm sorry Miss, but Mr. Carson is not at home."

"Are you sure of that? Tell him Charlotte is here."

A long silence followed. "Mrs. Carson? Is that you?"

Clay choked. This was Glen Carson's home. That much he could accept, but Harlie was Carson's wife? He was sleeping with Glen Carson's wife? Why didn't the guy scale the stage and punch him last night? Clay climbed from the limo in order to hear the conversation. But the woman speaking into the intercom no longer sounded like his Harlie. Gone were her adorable, oddball words. Now, her speech was clipped and sophisticated, her demeanor stiff and unnatural. It was like watching a chameleon change colors before his eyes.

"That should be ex-wife. Is Glen home? I need to speak with him about that problem."

"No, ma'am. Mr. Carson is participating in a charity golf tournament today. Would you like to leave a message for him?"

"A message? No. I have some things for him. If you'll open the gate, Frank, I'll set them inside."

Another long silence followed. "Mrs. Carson, I can't open the gate for you. Mr. Carson removed you from the security list and I'm to notify him immediately if you come home."

"And you've already done that, correct?" She laughed when Frank didn't respond. "I'd be disappointed in you if you didn't. You were always Glen's most loyal toady. By the way, this isn't my home and it never was. Now, I have some things for Glen. Will you open the gate so I can set them inside?" He didn't respond. "Suit yourself." She turned from the call box. "Louie!" she called to the limo driver. "Could you bring those cases over here, please?"

Louie wasn't a young man. He wasn't big either. Clay doubted he could lift the largest of the cases without damaging his back and offered to lend a hand. When the cases were set where Harlie indicated, she opened one, removed a silver cocktail dress, and flung it over the gate. Next, a black jacket flew like a crow to join the silver dress.

The voice on the speaker squawked again. "Mrs. Carson! What are you doing? I'll call the police if you continue this vandalism!"

Harlie grabbed a pair of silk slacks and tossed them in the air. The light-weight fabric caught on the wrought iron spikes. "Well, Frank," Harlie said as she continued to fling clothes over the fence, "my EX-husband is calling me a thief so I'm returning every-thing to him. Call the authorities if you like. I'm not afraid of them." She tossed a sequined vest over the gate. "You tell that goober I EARNED every dime he gave me but if he wants his clothes back, he can have them. They're too small for me anyway. Tell him I eat food now. Lots of it, and I have a guy here with me who thinks I look pretty damned good!" She turned to Clay. "Right?"

He nodded and smiled when it appeared Harlie was breaking free of the rigid Charlotte Carson exterior. To hear her use the word goober warmed his heart. "Right. You're gorgeous, darlin'." Clay noticed a security camera was now trained on him and he waved and smiled. Harlie opened the next suitcase and pitched lingerie. The pieces were small and lightweight and many caught on the gate and surrounding bushes. It looked like a panties bomb had gone off. When one fell to the ground near Harlie's foot, Clay retrieved it. "You missed one. May I?" She nodded and he shot the panties over the fence. "You aren't tossing that red dress you wore, are you?"

"No," she said. "I bought that myself."

He smiled. "Good. I like that one on you." He went back to lean against the limo with Louie and let Harlie do her thing.

She unlocked the next case and tossed more dresses and a coat. The more agitated Frank sounded on the intercom, the more concerned Clay was about the police threat. "What do you think, Louie? Should we get her back in the car and leave before the police come?"

Louie shook his head. "It appears your lady friend has some unresolved issues with her ex-husband. This display of anger is quite healthy for her and she needs to see it through. It's cathartic."

Clay looked at Louie with raised brows. "What? Are you a shrink or something?"

Louie smiled. "Online psychology classes. You'd be amazed at the number of nuts I get in my limo."

Clay thought he and Harlie probably fit the description. Harlie was working on the last large suitcase. More pants, blouses, and a swimming suit cruised over the fence. When she opened the small case, she turned to the camera with a ring box in her hand. "This," she said, "should have been a symbol of everlasting love. Instead, it was a jailer's key and Glen can have it back!" She wound up like a major league pitcher and lobbed the ring box over the fence. It broke open on contact and a diamond ring bounced out. She grabbed a small wooden box from the suitcase. "This is what's left from the allowance he gave me." She flung the box over the fence and it shattered into pieces. Paper money and change scattered into the grass.

She was winded now and Clay worried she'd have a panic attack, but she put her hands on her hips and stood tall. "Glen Carson! You don't own me anymore! Sign the divorce papers and set me free! I'll never come back to you. Never! Charlotte Carson doesn't exist anymore. She never really did!" She took a deep breath. "If you don't sign those papers, I'll tell everything I know about you. Every nasty little secret will be public knowledge."

Harlie turned and marched to the limo, stopping to look at Clay and Louie. "What are you two staring at? Let's go." She climbed into the limo. Clay shrugged at Louie and slid in next to her.

"Feel better?"

"Much." She nodded. "Thanks for letting me stop."

"Sure. Anytime."

As the limousine pulled away from Glen Carson's home, Clay and Harlie fell into silence. There were a million questions eating at him, but he waited to see what information she'd volunteer. He wrapped his arm around her shoulders and Harlie snuggled into his side, her head leaning against him. A few minutes later she was asleep.

Clay stared out the window as they covered the miles to Boeing Field, not sure what to think of Glen Carson. He'd always heard good things about the guy. Payton had been with the Carson Trust for several years now and he thought the world of Glen Carson. But the details Clay collected from Harlie painted an ugly picture. She thought of her wedding ring as a jailer's key. And that comment about food. Did the guy starve her? The clothes she tossed away were tiny and he couldn't imagine Harlie wearing them. He rested his chin on her head and held her. She was a wonderful woman and should be cherished.

What was wrong with Glen Carson?

⊙≫⊙

He watched from the guestroom window as the limo pulled away, his pulse oddly normal. Seeing Charlotte should have his heart racing but the only racing going on was in his mind. There were phone calls to make and orders to give. Charlotte wasn't as clever as she thought and he would enjoy proving it to her. All that hiding at the concert was foolishness. Of course he recognized her, but it wasn't to his advantage to let her know. The emergency forcing him to leave without meeting Clay Masterson was contrived during the final encores. He doubted he could speak civilly to the man who sullied his wife. For Payton's sake, he didn't try.

Glen wondered if she'd figured it out yet. She was still his and always would be. When he got her back she'd see for herself. He'd give Frank instructions to collect her belongings from the gate and have them cleaned and ready for her return. Since Charlotte had so obviously let herself go, they had a lot of work in front of them.

"Are you coming back to bed, Glen?" a sultry voice said.

The limo taillights rounded the corner and were gone. Glen turned from the window and stared at the woman, momentarily unable to remember how she got there or why on earth she was in the bed. This was Charlotte's room. He shook his head to clear the cobwebs and stepped toward the door.

She frowned. "Glen, darling? You aren't leaving are you?" She shoved the sheet aside, displaying her flawless body. Not an ounce of fat on her. Not a blemish. Her expensive lingerie fit to perfection. She'd even donated a large sum to the Carson Family Charitable Trust—enough to earn Premier status and a private evening with Glen Carson himself.

She was everything he cherished in a woman.

"Glen!" she said, her tone demanding. "Are you coming back to bed or not?"

Well, physically, she was stirring, but she had flaws he doubted even he could correct. Her disrespectful mouth was a problem. Charlotte had never spoken to him that way. Charlotte knew her place and acted accordingly, knowing he'd toss her back in the gutter she came from if he chose to do so.

But this one came from wealth and was enamored with herself. She would never be Charlotte.

Glen smiled. Charlotte would return soon and until she did, he would enjoy this one. She was feisty and liked things a little rough, which suited his mood at the moment. He moved to the bed and slapped her on the rump, making her laugh. "Sorry, Crystal dear, I was distracted for a moment." He climbed onto the bed and straddled her, leaning down to bite her shoulder. If he concentrated, maybe he could pretend she was a brunette.

⤜∞⤛

As the plane lifted off, Harlie hugged her knees and stared straight ahead. Clay was in the seat next to her, probably waiting for an explanation of her peculiar behavior. She'd awakened in his arms when the limo stopped on the tarmac and the wonderful man offered to carry her onto the plane—all five feet ten inches of her. The guy had a great build and she didn't doubt he could do it, but she'd declined, needing a minute to collect her thoughts and plan the next phase of her confession. After her performance at Glen's gate, Clay deserved to know.

She let out the breath she'd held and shifted in her seat. "His office was across the street from the bakery I worked in." She looked at Clay. "Glen's office, I mean." She turned and looked out the window, biting her lip. "He'd come in for morning coffee and talk to me. I didn't know who he was at first, so I talked to him like I would anyone else. If I'd known he was one of the richest guys in the state, I wouldn't have had the nerve. People like that are intimidating. But at first, he was just Glen, the nice man from across the street."

Clay remained silent, waiting for her to continue.

"After a few months, he started coming in during my break and we'd sit in a booth. He was so much older I never thought he was interested in me. I was just a kid he liked to talk to. He said I was refreshing." She took a deep breath. "Not long after, I found out who he was. His assistant couldn't reach him on his cell and came looking for him. I couldn't believe my coffee buddy was Glen Carson."

"On my eighteenth birthday, he asked me to move into his house. Not as his girlfriend or anything, as a sort of ward. For a kid like me who grew up with an addict mother, no father, and felt I had no future, the idea appealed to me and I moved in. He talked me into finishing high school and getting my diploma and everything was so wonderful. I felt so secure there. Over the next three years, Glen hired people to help me fit into his world. Hairdressers, trainers, and so on. Call me Eliza Doolittle, but I was a poor street kid who'd landed in heaven. I didn't care what his motives were."

"But something changed?" Clay asked.

"Yeah, when I turned twenty-one. Glen asked me to marry him. I knew he didn't love me, but at that point, I'd have done anything to avoid returning to my old life."

"He didn't marry you for love?" Clay asked, incredulous.

"Love?" She shook her head and laughed ruefully. "Until I moved to Angel Beach, I'd never experienced love of any sort. I was a burden to everyone, nothing more. The accident that shouldn't have happened is what my mother called me. Buck and Emily are the closest to a loving family I've ever had. Sam is like my sister. And no, Glen never mentioned love," Harlie said. "But, considering my background, I thought his proposal was a great offer. As Glen Carson's wife, I would live like a princess. I was thinking Cinderella. He turned me into Rapunzel. His perfect Rapunzel." She stretched her legs and crossed her arms across her stomach, hugging tight. "Not right away though. I had a lot of freedom for several years. I had some friends I hung out with and I did volunteer work. It was when I asked if I could have a job at the Trust that he started getting strange on me."

"Strange? How?" Clay asked.

"He took away my car and hired a driver to run me around. I thought it was nuts but I couldn't change his mind. I found out later he was having several office affairs and didn't want me showing up there unexpectedly," she said with a shrug. "For all his peculiarities, Glen was generous and gave me an allowance each month. A big one. But he would only allow me to spend it on clothes and other frivolous stuff, like manicures. So, I shopped like a maniac because it was the only way out of the house. He also limited my calorie intake each day to keep me thin and had the staff watch me to make sure I didn't sneak food. I tried one night. Glen caught me with a ham sandwich and you'd think I'd stolen the crown jewels. To punish me, he ate it in front of me, knowing my stomach was growling from the salad I'd been allowed at dinner."

Clay looked at her with shock. "A salad? That was it?"

"Yes. Considering we had a Trust dinner to attend and I couldn't zip my silver evening dress, it was perfectly understandable. At least it was to Glen and my trainer. Charlotte Carson had to be perfect in every way." She swallowed. "And if I didn't do as they said, I'd be punished by spending time in the back bedroom." She shivered at the thought. "It was a small bedroom with a bed in it. If I misbehaved, I spent time there. It's when the panic attacks started."

Clay's eyes were narrowed and his fists clenched. "It's probably a good thing you didn't tell me this on the ground. I'd have—"

"You'd have gone macho cowboy on me and beat the crap out of him. I appreciate the thought but—"

He took a deep breath and released it. "Why did he marry you?"

"Control. He's obsessed with perfection and will do anything to have it." Harlie placed her hand over his clenched fist and he relaxed. "And I'm not the first one. There was another before me. He didn't marry her though."

"What happened to her?

Harlie shook her head slowly, and whispered. "I don't know. I only know she existed because of things the staff said about her. All I know is her name is or was Cassandra. Glen is psychotic, Clay. He preys on helpless young women who have nowhere to go. When he tires of them, he gets rid of them."

"How did you get away?"

"When things started deteriorating I began plotting my escape. Each month, I managed to save a large portion of the allowance by shopping at thrift stores. You'd be amazed at the stuff women either donate or sell in consignment shops. I could buy gorgeous design-er clothes at a fraction of the original cost. Then, I pocketed the extra money. When I had enough, I talked my driver into taking me to a friend's house and

I called an attorney to start the divorce process. Glen found out where I was and began stalking me."

"You called the police?"

She laughed. "Right. A street rat was being stalked by one of Seattle's leading citizens. Who would believe me? No. I was on my own, like always. I stayed in Seattle as long as I could, afraid he'd get hold of me and I'd spend the rest of my life in that small room. I imagined him slowly starving me to death in there." She shuddered. "When my attorney sent the papers for Glen to sign, I left town. I've been in Angel Beach since." She squeezed Clay's hand. "Just so you know, I didn't know until two days ago there is a possibility I'm not divorced. I signed the papers and assumed he had, too." She felt guilty now for sleeping with Clay, knowing there was a chance she was still married.

"The panic attacks..."

Harlie nodded. "Followed the news. There's a reporter doing an exposé on Glen. He's nominated for the American Humanitarian Award and the reporter isn't happy with Glen's standard bio. I don't blame him. It's full of lies and half-truths. My friend Alicia gave him my cell number and he's been trying to convince me to talk to him. He's the one who told me about my divorce possibly not being final. There is no public record of it."

"Will you talk to the reporter?"

"I told him no, but if Glen doesn't sign the papers, I may change my mind. Maybe this reporter could find

Cassandra and..." She shrugged and blew out a breath. "At this point, I may be a married woman. I'll understand if you don't want to see me anymore. If word gets out, the tabloids will make something of it. I'm sorry I exposed you that way."

He shrugged. "I'm not concerned about it. But it could be a problem later on when this thing between us gets more serious."

"Serious? How can this get serious, Clay? When you find your dad, you'll leave. I've had no illusions."

His eyes narrowed. "So, you think you're a pit stop for me? That I could hop on a plane and leave without looking back?" He let out an irritated breath and said quietly, "I'm not like him."

"Who?" she asked, though she had a good idea he meant Hunt Masterson.

He looked away, frowning, and she had the impression he hadn't intended to say it out loud.

"Your ex. I'm not like him. If all I wanted was a bounce between the sheets, I had opportunities and I turned them down. What do I have to do to convince you that what we have is much more than sex? That I'm looking for something more and I think I've found it with you?"

"Really?"

He turned and cupped her face in his hand, stroking her cheek with his thumb. He leaned in for a kiss, but didn't connect. His breath warmed her lips. "You're it, darlin'. The one and only. I haven't even been out on a casual date in ages. I was waiting for you, the most beautiful, sexy, funny, intelligent, socially conscious woman I've ever met and I'm not leaving you behind if I find my dad." He laid his lips to hers and kissed her long and sweet. "I'm sticking. If I find my dad, we'll deal with it. If I don't find him, we'll deal with it. If this thing between us has to be long distance some-times, we'll deal with it."

"Really?"

He nodded. "Really. And when we get back, I'm calling Nashville and telling Harv to release that shark tank I keep on retainer. I'm getting you divorced. I'd like to kill the son of a bitch, but I'll settle for a di-vorce."

"Clay, I can't let you do that. You've already helped my shelter. I can't ask you to pay for my di-vorce, too."

"You didn't ask. I'm volunteering." He pulled her hand to his lips and kissed the palm. "From what you've said, the divorce can't come quick enough. And it needs to get done because I'm planning to marry you someday."

Harlie sat up straight. "You're what?"

"You heard me."

"You've only known me a week. You can't talk like that after a week."

"You didn't think I could sleep with you after a few days and I managed that," he said with a laugh. "I knew Crystal most of my life and look how well that turned out. I never felt this way for her, Harlie. Never."

"It's too soon to think about things like that."

He leaned back and stretched. "I'm just giving you advance notice of where I'm heading with this. We'll work on getting you divorced and this thing with Glen will be over."

Harlie wasn't so sure. Her performance at Glen's gate probably wasn't her smartest move. Therapeutic and satisfying, sure. Wise? Not by a long shot. Glen would see the security tape, and if he hadn't already recognized her at the concert, he was sure to make the connection now. Especially since Clay joined her at the gate. One conversation with Payton Shaw and Glen would have all the information he needed to come after her.

No, this situation with Glen wasn't ending. It was beginning.

23

Voicemail: "This is Harlie. I can't take your call right now, but leave a message…"

"It's Noah. It's time to happy dance, Harlie. Payton Shaw backed off of his motel bid and our offer has been accepted. We're in business now. I called Emily already. Call me later and I'll give you the details."

When Harlie arrived, the Angel Beach Center teemed with lunchtime activity and it was too hectic to share the good news about the motel. She grabbed an apron and claimed a station in the serving line doling out pineapple cake topped with cream cheese frosting. School was out and the building burst with children's voices as well as those of the regulars. Buck was nowhere to be found. On most Wednesdays he entertained the Center diners with his unplugged versions of old country hits and his absence was noted by his low-income fan club. When Emily walked by, Harlie snagged her by a fistful of sweatshirt, stopping her in her tracks.

"Where's Buck?"

"Home with an ice pack on his hand. I thought he was fine yesterday, but today he's back to moaning and groaning. Men are such whiners. How was Seattle?" She adjusted her sweatshirt, pressing down the scrunch caused by Harlie's hand.

"Eventful. I'll tell you later." Emily moved around the counter to clear tables and Harlie turned to find a cop staring at her with purpose in his eyes. It was a different cop this time, older with a smattering of gray in his brown hair. He wore a suit rather than a uniform, and he was more serious than the young guy who had dropped bad news on her like a low-flying seagull. But even in a suit, she recognized a cop. Foreboding enveloped her and she began to sweat. In her experience, cops never brought good news and they usually left Harlie's life in shambles. Her childhood memories were filled with visits from the Seattle PD, which usually landed her in foster care. Some were an improvement over her home life, some were not. She'd go home when her mother was released, but only because the caseworker initiated the move. Her mother never came looking for Harlie and was disappointed when the caseworker dropped her off.

As the cop's presence was noted, the room quieted. Not wanting to upset her diners, Harlie motioned him to the kitchen. The Center lunch should be a reprieve from their stressful lives.

Once inside the kitchen door, Harlie turned to the cop. "I know why you're here and it was just one of those things, you know, a temper tantrum. I didn't cause any damage, just a mess." Her hands were sweating from the vinyl gloves she'd worn for serving but she resisted the urge to wipe them on her apron.

She hadn't expected Glen to call the cops. Kidnapping was more in line with her expectations.

The cop was staring at her now with a perplexed frown bordering on complete confusion. "I sure hope what I'm investigating wasn't the result of your temper tantrum."

She lifted an eyebrow. "You mean my ex-husband didn't call you?"

He shook his head. "No, but I wouldn't mind hearing about this tantrum when we're done."

"Okay," she said with relief. Glen hadn't called but— "What are you investigating?"

"Maybe we could have a seat? I have a few questions." He pointed toward a table and chairs in a corner of the kitchen.

Harlie complied, sitting with her hands clasped tightly in her lap until the cop held out his hand. She reluctantly shook it.

"Detective Ferrell, ma'am." He flashed a badge.

They'd never asked her to sit before and handshaking was a new thing, too. Her apprehension returned. "What are you investigating, Detective?"

He retrieved a notepad from his pocket, studied it and then Harlie. "A body was found yesterday morning."

"Not another one." A weight bore down on Harlie's chest. "It's like an epidemic or something. Do you know the identity of this one?"

"We know." The cop gave her a long look. "This death was not due to natural causes, Miss Cates. I'm investigating the murder of Myrna Snow."

"Myrna?" Harlie gasped. "Murder? Myrna's been murdered?" Harlie was stunned speechless. When she regained her voice, the questions flowed. "Who would want to murder Myrna? And why? I mean, she had issues but was a decent person."

"That's what I'm hoping to find out." He glanced at his notes. "Where were you Saturday night around ten?"

Heat rose in her face. "You think I had something to do with this? That's nuts. I was her advocate. I helped her get the treatment she needed for her anger issues. I drove her to the clinic every month. How could you think—?"

"Miss Cates—"

"I mean, really. She was one of my people here at the Center. I took care of her—"

"Miss Cates, this is only procedure. I'll be talking with everyone who knew her, and the fact that you acted as her advocate means you're the best person to start with."

"Right. Okay." Harlie inhaled and tried to calm her temper. "I was home. I took a long bath and went to bed early." She knew how this worked. He would keep her on the list until he could cross her off and she didn't have an alibi unless Spud learned to talk. He'd slept on the toilet tank while she took her bath but that didn't help much. Damn. She should have spent the night with Clay after all.

Detective Ferrell gave her a long look. "When was the last time you saw Miss Snow?"

"Last Wednesday. She comes...came in for our weekly lunch. I would have taken her to her clinic appointment next week."

He nodded. "What are these issues you mentioned? Anger, you said."

"Right. Myrna would lash out at the least provocation. Dr. Tipton referred her to a mental-health clinic and she was improving with medication and therapy."

He nodded and scribbled Wayne's name in his notepad. "That would be Dr. Tipton at the Angel Beach Clinic?"

"Right. Wayne Tipton. Can I ask what happened to Myrna? How was she...?" She gulped and grimaced, unable to finish.

He gave her another of those long, thoughtful stares. "She was strangled in her home Saturday night. No sign of forced entry, so she may have known her killer. The meter reader noticed her newspapers piled on the step Tuesday morning so he looked in the windows. She was on the floor." He tapped his pen on the notebook. "Neighbors saw men walking in the area that night. Transients, one woman said, talking on the street near the estimated time of death. Do you know all the people who come here for your lunch?"

"They are mostly local people. We get a few transients..." she trailed off and her eyes went wide. "You think there is a murderer here?"

"I didn't see anyone fitting the neighbor's description. But it was dark and her vision may have been impaired." He flipped through his notepad. "She thought one was approximately thirty-five, medium height with short hair. He was seen walking on the street near Miss Snow's house. The other was much older and taller, had a ponytail and carried a cowboy hat. He was seen leaving Myrna's house moments before meeting the younger man on the street. One witness says Myrna was talking with the older man in her open doorway prior to his departure. The other witness didn't see him leave the house but saw him on the street. It's possible he returned later."

Harlie was afraid to say anything since the description fit Buck. What was he doing at Myrna's late at night? She swallowed and tried to appear unconcerned. "So, you don't know who these guys are?"

He shook his head. "No, ma'am. I was hoping you might."

She furrowed her brow. "Well, I'll have to give it some thought. The descriptions are fairly vague."

"I agree. In the limited light, the witness couldn't see the younger man's hair color, so we don't have much to go on there. The other man having a ponytail and cowboy hat gives us a little more to work with. One person I spoke with mentioned an older man who plays his guitar in front of your bakery. The ponytail, cowboy hat, and height fits."

"Um...yes, there is a man who occasionally drops by to play, but he hasn't been around lately. I don't know his name. He's joked about it but tells me something different every time I ask." That much was true. She'd always suspected Buck was an alias and he'd given her at least six different last names—mostly celebrities or character names from books and movies. He hadn't been around for a while either, not since hurting his hand. "If he comes back, I'll let you know."

The detective nodded and tucked his notepad in his shirt pocket. "Thank you for your time." He stood to leave, handing her a card. "Call me if you think of anything that could help the investigation or if the guitar player returns." At the door, he paused. "I'm sorry about your friend. I'll do my best to find her killer."

Harlie nodded. "Thanks. I'll let you know if I think of anything helpful." After he left, Harlie laid her head on the table and groaned. She'd lied to a cop to protect a man who wouldn't tell her his name.

Buck had better have a good explanation for this.

24

Shelves filled with rare antiques lined the walls of the elegant office located high above Seattle's Puget Sound. Each item created the appropriate impression and stirred the viewer with the owner's subtle style and taste. In the distance, a Washington state ferry wended its way from Bremerton to dock at the pier below. Payton Shaw stood in the panoramic windows facing the Olympic Mountains, at peace.

He'd done what was necessary in Angel Beach. Staying longer would compromise his plans and possibly expose him. He couldn't have that. Clay mustn't know he'd been there. Not ever. It wouldn't do him any good to know and Payton didn't want to explain his clandestine detective work. With any luck, Clay would never know his father was still alive. It would only upset him to know that Hunt had purposefully stayed away all these years. Hunt already did what was best for his son when he left him in Sheldon Black's care. On his own, Hunt would have turned Clay into a drunken womanizer. Like father, like son. Living with the Blacks had given Clay a solid base, a firm concept of family, and Hunt didn't need to reappear and destroy it.

Hunt's sudden reappearance would destroy everything for Payton, too, and he wouldn't allow it. A strong bond had formed between Payton and Clay over the years, a fatherly sort of bond that was far too profitable for Payton to allow it to crumble. He'd nurtured the bond by helping with Clay's search and offering sympathy when Hunt failed to turn up again. This time, the rumor wasn't false. Hunt Masterson was masquerading as a street musician named Buck and it wouldn't be long until Payton flushed him out and ended this thing.

He'd wait a few days, let Clay spin his wheels, and then arrive to convince him the search was futile. He'd done it before in other locations. Clay would get frustrated and have doubts his father was alive and Payton would agree, reluctantly, of course. Stopping was best. After Clay returned to Nashville, Payton would revisit Angel Beach and finish his business with Hunt.

The door opened. "Mr. Shaw?" his assistant said. "Mr. Carson is on line one."

"Thank you, Leann." He stepped to the oversized cherry desk and took the call.

"Yes, Glen," he said as he settled into his chair, staring at the future location of the angel painting he still planned to purchase. It would be his souvenir of this latest search. He'd collected something from each one.

"Payton, I need you to do something for me."

"Certainly."

"It's rather delicate," Glen said. "That reporter is making a nuisance of himself and I need to know I can count on you to keep this situation confidential."

CAUGHT IN CROSS SEAS

This piqued Payton's interest. He knew Skip Hyatt was sniffing around and wondered what all the intrigue was about. "Of course, you can count on me. What can I do for you?"

"I'm in need of a...service."

"Oh? Whatever you require, Glen."

"I need you to take a short trip and take care of something for me," Glen said.

"What would that be?"

"My wife, Charlotte," he said. "I know where she is."

⟨≈⟩

The Angel Beach Center lunch crowd dispersed, the dishes were done, and the food bank shelves were depleted. Harlie managed to dodge Emily on her way out the door. What could she tell her? She needed to talk to Buck and find out what he was doing at Myrna's house and warn him about the cops. She'd leave it to him to tell Emily and contact the detective. She wouldn't rat out a friend.

It was anyone's guess where he might hang out today. He wasn't home and she knew he wouldn't play in front of the bakery with his injured hand, so that left the Angel Viewpoint. The late afternoon weather was fair; light clouds drifted across the blue sky. She parked and headed to the trailhead landing. He wasn't on the beach. She blew out her breath and turned to leave when something familiar pricked her ears: music drifting on the breeze. She cocked her head to listen, trying to figure out where the guitar player might be sitting. He wasn't in the viewpoint parking lot. She'd have seen him by now. She made a circle around the area, covering the parking lot, picnic area, and information kiosks. The music began again and she figured it out. The Angel View Motel. Chain link and a wide chasm separated the two properties. She'd need to drive or walk around.

Minutes later, she parked her Smart Car in the overgrown parking lot of the motel and took a moment to admire her acquisition. Well, admire was too strong a word. The old motel needed repairs and paint, but it suited her purpose. There were several single-story buildings in a horseshoe shape with walkways between them. Cabins with small carports filled the area to the north. She stepped gingerly through the overgrown grass.

The guitarist began again, a complicated song requiring talent and dexterity. Buck had the talent, but at the moment, he shouldn't have the dexterity. She made her way through the brushy overgrowth at the south side of the complex. As she neared the corner, she heard something that made her suck in her breath. She peeked around the corner and saw Buck sitting on a rickety deck overlooking the ocean. His cowboy boot clad foot rested against a large rock, and his duffle lay on the deck next to him. He played a familiar tune. When she stepped into view, he stopped and smiled.

"Hey, Angel. I heard the deal was going through on the motel so I came to break it in for you. Emily was thrilled with the news."

Harlie nodded. "Me, too."

"We've got a lot of work to do around here though." He waved his hand toward the cliff. "That split-rail fence will have to go. It's rotten and won't do a thing to keep someone from falling off the cliff onto those rocks down there."

Harlie frowned at his hand, noticing how he held the guitar pick without difficulty. "Your hand is okay?"

He flexed it and wiggled his fingers. "It was kinda sore this morning but seems good now. Good enough for old country songs, anyway." To prove it, he launched into the same song he'd played moments before.

Harlie listened, her stomach churning with the thoughts barreling through her mind. A gust blew loose strands of dark hair into her face and she wiped them away. "What's that you're playing, Buck?"

He stopped. "Oh, just a little thing I made up years ago."

Harlie clenched her fist, digging her nails into the palm of her hand. "What's it called?"

"It doesn't have an official title. I've always called it my protest song."

Harlie swallowed hard. "What are you protesting?"

"Whatever comes to mind. War, the government, artificial sweeteners," he said with a chuckle. "That stuff tastes like crap and I always thought someone should protest it."

"It's a mood thing, right?"

"Guess so." He narrowed his eyes and studied her. "What's the problem, Angel? You're looking a little peaked."

It felt as if the cliff fell from under her feet and she was tumbling onto the rocks. "You're him," she whispered.

Buck frowned. "What are you talking about?"

"You're him!"

"Who?"

She slapped her palm to her forehead. "I can't believe I didn't figure it out before. He has your eyes. He even walks the way you do. Why didn't I see it?" Because subconsciously, she didn't want to see it. She didn't want anything to change and if Clay found his father, everything would change.

Buck narrowed his eyes. "What are you babbling about, Angel?"

"I'm not babbling. You're HIM! You're Hunt Masterson. You're Clay's father."

Buck laughed and shook his head. "Good lord. A road-rough bum like me is the father of a country music superstar?"

"Sure," she said with a nod. "I can see it now. The eyes, the walk, the sense of humor. He says he doesn't look like you but he's wrong."

"Clay Masterson is my son? Really?" Buck scowled. "If I have a son like him, what am I doing living in a tool shed?" He harrumphed. "You've got an overactive imagination, girl. Way too overactive."

She stepped closer, her anger climbing. "Don't lie to me! I know who you are now."

He remained cool. "What makes you think so? My extravagant lifestyle? My sports cars and mansion in Malibu? I know. It's the Armani suit and custom boots." He laughed. "Not much proof of me having a wealthy son, is there?"

"It's the song, Buck. I've heard that song before."

"Where? I wrote it. I'm the only one who knows it," he said with defiance.

"Not true." She shook her head. "Clay knows it. He played it for me."

"There's no way he could—"

"He did. He said his father wrote it and called it his protest song. He sang it to me."

Buck laid his guitar aside and stared out to sea, his lips in a stubborn line.

"You didn't hurt your hand, did you? When you saw Clay on the road that day you cooked up this garbage so he wouldn't see you at the bakery." She paced away. "I can't believe I bought all that nonsense. I'm such an idiot. Clay's dad has been under my nose all this time...lying to me."

He looked tense now, not the normal laid back guy she knew. He clenched his jaw and looked like he might jump up and run. "What if I am?"

"Clay needs to know," she said. "He's spent years searching for you and deserves to know you're alive. He loves you."

Buck looked up at her. "Love? That boy isn't looking for me out of love, Angel. He's after revenge. Some I deserve and some I don't."

"What do you mean, revenge? He hasn't said anything about that to me."

Buck let out a tired breath. "And he won't. He's probably figured out you won't help him if you know his reasons."

She dropped to her knees next to him. "What reasons? All he said is that he wants to know if you're alive. Come home with me. Your son deserves to know you're here."

Buck shook his head. "No. Clay needs to think I'm dead. He's better off that way."

"Why, Buck? What can be so bad that your son should think you're dead? Is it because you abandoned him?"

He looked at her with pain-filled eyes and seemed to shrink. "Clay told you about that?"

"No. Tom Black did. He says Clay won't talk about it and he's right. Why'd you do it?"

Buck swallowed hard and looked down at the beach below. "A lot of things happened a long time ago."

"Your wife died."

He nodded. "Abigail died and I found out how weak I am. I couldn't do it without her and figured Clay was better off without me. It looks bad, I know, but leaving him with the Blacks was the best I could do for him."

"But you went back."

"I did. But things happened. Accusations were made. But no matter what Clay thinks, I didn't do what they say I did."

"What happened?"

He shook his head. "I'm not going to talk about it. I won't be responsible for you getting hurt if you know."

Harlie stood. "Fine. I'll ask Clay. Maybe he'll trust me enough to tell me."

Buck narrowed his eyes. "Let it be, Angel. Nothing good will come of you knowing about my troubles. People have been hurt because they knew too much about it."

Harlie backed up a step. "Like Myrna? Are you saying Myrna knew too much?"

"Myrna?" he said with a scowl. "Myrna doesn't know anything about anything. Why are you bringing her into this?"

"Because Myrna is dead."

Buck looked like he'd been punched between the eyes. "Myrna? Good lord, I saw her Saturday night and she was fine."

"You were at her house, right?"

"I stopped in to talk to her for a few minutes before heading out to meet some friends. How did you know that?"

Harlie sat next to him and sighed. Buck was her dearest friend and she wouldn't jump to conclusions. He cared about people the way she did, offering to help whenever possible. She took his hand in hers. It was warm and familiar, gentle. Not the hand of a killer. "A detective told me Myrna was murdered Saturday night. A witness saw you at her house. She didn't know your name, just called you a transient. But she described you, Buck, and the cop knows you play your guitar in front of my bakery. He's looking for you."

"Did you tell him where to find me?"

"No. I told him I hadn't seen you recently and I didn't know your name. Until now, I didn't. Not really."

Buck inhaled and let the breath out slowly. "I don't want you lying for me. If they ask a question, answer it. I'll deal with the fallout."

"I'm not going to rat on you—."

"You aren't ratting on me, darlin', you just tell them what they want to know. Lying to the cops will get you into trouble and I don't want that on my conscience. There's enough crap parked there already."

Tears pricked her eyes and she wiped them away. The similarities between father and son astounded her. How had she missed it before?

Buck pulled a handkerchief from his pocket. "Egad. You aren't going to do that, are you? I'm not worth crying over, Angel. You ought to know that by now."

"Yes, you are." Harlie sniffed and accepted the hanky to wipe her eyes. "It's just...when you call me darlin', you sound like Clay. You really are his dad."

"I thought we established that. You want DNA testing, too?" He brushed a wayward strand of hair from Harlie's brow. "Stop that sniffling and tell me, how was Myrna killed?"

"Strangled."

He was still a moment. "With what? What was she strangled with?"

Harlie shrugged. "I don't know. The detective didn't say."

Buck closed his eyes tight and shivered. "Damn it."

"You know, don't you?"

He shook his head. "No. I don't. I don't know anything about it. I stopped by her house the other night to check in with her. I'd told her there was somebody looking for me and that she shouldn't talk to him. You know Myrna, she can't...couldn't control her mouth, so I asked her to stay away from anyone who might ask about me. But she was fine when I left. You gotta believe me, Angel. I had nothing to do with it. I talked with her a few minutes, drank a beer, and left. I ran into Jack on the street out front of her house and we headed to the beach together to find Joe Campbell."

"The detective's description of the other man does fit Jack. Mid-thirties, short hair, average size."

He nodded. "We talked for a few minutes, mostly about some noises we heard."

"What kind of noises?"

He shrugged. "Somebody walking around. A cat yowling. Night sounds."

"Or not. Maybe you heard Myrna's killer. You need to talk to the detective and tell him about this."

"I suppose I should." Buck pulled a pack of cigarettes from his pocket, tapped one out. "You and my boy are...um..." He blushed. "You're getting to know each other pretty well, aren't you? Em told me you went to Seattle, that he's the one helping with the shelter." His hands shook as he pulled a lighter from his pocket and lit the cigarette hanging from his lips.

"Yeah. The Masterson Foundation is helping," she said. "That ought to make you feel good. Your name is on a charitable foundation."

He shook his head. "Not my name anymore. I stopped deserving it years ago. Clay's the one that made it something to be proud of again after I dirtied it up." He took a long drag. "What's he like now? Does he treat you good?"

"I've only known him a week but I like him a lot. It's too bad it has to end."

"Why's that?"

"Unless you plan to tell him you're here, I can't see him anymore. I can't live with that kind of lie. You and Emily are the only real family I've ever had and I can't give that up for a big maybe. He talks like he wants to stay around here because of me but I can't let him. I'll have to break it off with him."

"Because of me."

"Because of everything. He has a real romantic nature, Buck, and thinks this thing with me is what he wants. I know better. Who I am and where I come from will bother him someday. The media will get a hold of it and make life miserable for him. I know how this stuff works."

Buck laughed. "Where he comes from isn't so grand either." He took her hand and squeezed. "Don't do anything because of me. I'll do what needs to be done."

Harlie leaned her head against his shoulder. "What were you accused of?"

"Nothing you need to know about. Just believe me when I say I didn't do it. That's enough for me."

"Do you know who did whatever it is?"

"I know. You knowing will get you in trouble. Possibly dead. He's somebody I knew a long time ago and he'll do anything to protect his current high-society life. He framed me tight to keep the cops from looking his way. That's why I left when I had the chance." He patted her head. "Don't stir this thing up. I'll do what I need to do. You stay out of it. If you insist on knowing what's what, ask Clay. Get him to tell you why he's chasing after me." He took a drag of the cigarette.

"But I'll guarantee you he won't be talking about love. I destroyed that a long time ago."

⟨❧⟩

Clay sat at his dining room table, his back to the wide expanse of windows, his father's face staring at him from the laptop screen. The table was littered with files, photos, newspaper clippings, and printed Internet pages. The afternoon sun shone through the glass, warming his back. His heart was cold. "Where the hell are you?" he muttered to his father's picture. No answer came and he laughed at himself for expecting one.

A knock on the door told him Harlie had arrived. Sunlight flashed in the entryway, and he heard her footsteps. They had that comfort level already and he loved it.

"Clay?"

"In here! On the computer!"

She came around the corner, her cheeks flushed from the ocean breeze. He smiled. She'd released her hair from the braid because he liked it that way and she was glorious, the kind of woman he could look at every day for the rest of his life. She didn't believe him but it was true. He felt something when he looked at her. His smile broadened but she didn't return it. Her eyes were haunted. She leaned against the wall, arms crossed. Clay held out his hand to her but she shook her head.

"I can't stay. I need to go home...for a nap. I'm wiped out," she said with a frown. "The trip...seeing Glen...all that. I'm tired." She took a breath. Something was wrong. Her hands were clenched in fists and her breathing wasn't smooth.

He waited for a panic attack to begin. "What's wrong? You didn't hear from Glen, did you?" He stood, walked to her, and cupped her face in his hands. Her eyes were bloodshot.

"No...just a really bad day. The thing with Glen was bad enough, but I found out a friend died. Murdered. I had to talk to the cops about her." She sniffed. "I thought he'd come to arrest me for messing up Glen's yard."

"Murdered?" Clay tensed. "That's horrible. What happened?"

"Somebody strangled her Saturday night and her..." She grimaced. "Her body was found yesterday. It's so awful, Clay. Myrna didn't deserve that." She wrapped her arms around his middle and snuggled her face into his neck.

"I'm sorry," he said, but his mind was racing around the idea of a murder in Angel Beach. Could Tom be right? Could his father be a serial killer? He hadn't wanted to believe it but death by strangulation wasn't common. "Any idea what she was strangled with?"

She shook her head. "No." She held him close a few moments longer before she pulled away and turned toward the computer and the picture of his father. "Do you really think he's alive?"

"Some days, yes. Some days, no."

"So, you'll stop looking soon?"

He shook his head. "No."

"What drives you, Clay? If you think he's dead, why keep going?"

What should he tell her? All of it? None of it? His indecision amused him. He considered a lifelong connection with this woman but he didn't trust her to know the truth about his father? It made his pleas for her trust hypocritical if he wouldn't trust her, too. He was surprised to realize he was afraid to tell her. If Harlie knew what kind of monster his father was, would she turn her back on the monster's son?

Her dark eyes were inquisitive and sharp. "But won't it hurt to know for sure?" She stared at the screen as if she'd never seen the picture before, her brow furrowed and her lips tight.

He nodded. "It hurt the first time. I was only a kid when the state police told me he was dead. It tore me to pieces when they handed me the urn." He stood next to her, staring at the picture of his father. "And it nearly destroyed me when they said he'd been fleeing a murder charge when that truck flattened him on a Wyoming highway."

She turned to him, her eyes wide with shock. "Murder? Your father was accused of murder?"

He nodded. "Her name was Lynette Dalton. From what I understand, she and Dad were involved. Witnesses saw him leave her house the day she was murdered. His fingerprints were found at the scene."

Harlie stared at him, blinking.

"Say something, Harlie."

She blinked again. "Why didn't you tell me this before?"

He shrugged. "Because I don't talk about it. A handful of people know and I want to keep it that way."

"Do you think he did it?"

"I know he did. The evidence pointed right at him. I'll show you." He led her around the table and pointed out the files. "According to the police, Dad visited Lynette at her home, drank a beer, and was seen leaving. Later that night, her body was found. She'd been strangled to death." He swallowed hard, wondering if Harlie would make the same leap he did between her murdered friend and Lynette. If she did, she didn't comment. "Lynette fought him. She was covered with bruises and bloody scratches. He punched her multiple times around the face. Then he strangled her. He was seen driving out of town with a friend soon after."

"Why did he kill her?"

Clay shrugged. "Speculation was that she was messing around with another man and he found out. Another man was seen coming and going from her house the weeks leading to her murder. No one could identify him."

Harlie's eyes brightened. "Maybe your father didn't murder her. Maybe the other man did."

"The police never thought so. Now, I have a new problem." He picked up the copies of the notes he'd printed. "Somebody knows and wants me to know he knows. I thought it was a blackmail attempt at first." He picked up the first one. Low E plays death's song. "This one refers to the murder weapon. Lynette was strangled with an E string. My father's Telecaster was missing the E string." He wished Harlie knew how her friend had been strangled. He needed to call and see if he could find out.

"Wait a minute," Harlie said. "Why would he use a string off his own guitar? Seems pretty stupid."

"I agree. But it happened."

Harlie frowned. "Maybe he was framed. Maybe this other guy took the string knowing it would incriminate your father."

"The police kicked the theory around but couldn't prove it. The evidence stands. The string came off his guitar." He pointed to the next one. Beer cans don't lie. "This one refers to a beer can found in Lynette's house. My father's fingerprint was on it. There was a second, partial one but they never figured out where it came from. The police speculated it could belong to a store employee who handled the beer."

"Or the other man who was seen at Lynette's."

He shrugged. "Maybe. But they never came up with another suspect." He showed her the next one. At the end of the world, Angels pray.

"This brought you here?"

He shook his head. "I was already here because of somebody seeing him. This note came while we were in Seattle and it's what convinced me this isn't a blackmail attempt. It's a roadmap. It was postmarked at the Angel Beach post office. It proves to me he's here somewhere."

"Or someone wants you to believe he's here."

"I've thought of that." He picked up the last one. Follow the blood. He was there. "Tom and I haven't figured this one out yet. He's working on it and will let me know what he finds out."

How Harlie's friend was killed might confirm it, too. Serial killer.

Harlie wrapped her arms around her middle and frowned. "I can see why you might think he did it but that second fingerprint casts some major doubt for me. Just about all this could be a frame up."

"The police didn't agree. At this point though, they believe he's dead and the case is closed. I tried to tell them about the sightings but they don't believe it's him. So I keep looking."

"What will you do if you find him?"

"Return him to Montana and let the police do their thing."

Harlie's face looked pale to him. Probably all this talk of murder was making her sick. It didn't do much for him either.

"You'll send your own father to prison?"

"He's sending himself to prison."

"Can I ask you something? If your father hadn't left, would you do this? Would you feel the need to see him punished?"

He smiled. "The dumped kid must have a big chip on his shoulder, right? It's there but not as big as it used to be. Here's the way I see it. If my father was a better person, he wouldn't have done the things he did. I'm not after vengeance, Harlie. I want justice for the woman he killed, and I seem to be the only person who cares enough to try." He wrapped his arms around her and pulled her warm body to him. "I would like to know how he could do it though."

"The murder?"

He shook his head. "How he could run like he did. How he could be such a coward. He's spent his whole life running away. From the police and me." Harlie relaxed against him.

"Will that end it for you?"

"I don't know," he said. "I haven't thought that far ahead."

Harlie yawned. "I need to go home and take a nap."

"Stay." He held her close, inhaling her sweet scent. He'd stay this way forever if he could. "You can sleep in my bed. I won't bother you. I might need to go out for a while to run a few errands anyway and the house will be quiet." He kissed her temple. "I'd feel better knowing you're here with me tonight, just in case."

She looked up and frowned. "In case of what? You think your father—"

"I was thinking about Glen. You were worried he'd come after you. Stay with me tonight. We'll both sleep better."

⤬

Harlie kicked off her shoes and sat on Clay's bed. When he leaned and gave her a disappointing perfunctory good-bye kiss, she could feel the tension radiating from him. With a quick tug, she pulled his T-shirt up and over his head and tossed it to the floor. When she tried to return to the kiss and deepen it, he pulled away.

"Maybe later, okay?"

If Buck talked to Clay, Harlie knew there wouldn't be a later for them. When Clay found out she knew his father, he'd end their relationship. She sighed and lay on the bed, her back turned to him. "Fine. Later then." She grabbed a fist of pillow and listened as he walked away. A moment later, she heard his footsteps on the hardwood, felt his weight on the edge of the bed, and recognized the clunk of two cowboy boots hitting the floor. His weight left the bed and she heard a zipper and then his jeans sliding to the floor.

Everything was right again as he snuggled against her back and wrapped his arms around her. His warm breath tickled her skin.

"Changed your mind?"

He pressed his lips to her neck and slid his hand under her shirt, cupping her breast. "I don't think my mind had a lot to do with it."

She pressed tighter against him. "It bothers you to talk about him, doesn't it?"

He inhaled and let the breath out slowly. His hand stopped its teasing journey across her skin. "I worry about what you think. I'm the son of a murderer, Harlie. It taints me."

"I'm the daughter of a drug addict. Am I tainted by that?" she asked. "I don't let what she did affect me anymore."

"Yes, you do."

Harlie stiffened. "How? I don't live the way she does. I'm not as self-absorbed as she is and—"

"And you won't drink alcohol. You don't like caffeine. You eat organic foods. You have a fluoridation hang up—"

"So?"

"So, she affects you. She put crap in her body, so you won't. I'm not sure what the car is about though. Not sure why anyone would voluntarily drive a puny car."

Like father like son where her car was concerned. "The car," she said, "is a perfectly valid personal choice."

"You keep telling yourself that. Considering everything else you do is a form of rebellion against your old life, I'd bet money the car is, too."

"Fine. Think what you want." It wasn't rebellion in the sense he suggested. The little car enabled her escape. She remembered the sense of freedom when she drove from the used car lot with nothing but a pile of clothes and a small wooden box full of secrets, knowing a Smart Car was the last thing Glen Carson would look for. It was the first step toward her new life where she could be Harlie Cates again, no longer Charlotte Carson, the marionette caught in a puppeteer's strings.

Harlie tried to roll away, but Clay held her close. It looked like their last moments together would end in argument. So be it. She could dish it and hold her own. "What about your dad? He wasn't convicted, was he? Since he didn't go to trial, how do you know for sure he's guilty?"

"I know." He pulled his hand from beneath her shirt, rolled her to her back, and stretched out on top of her, staring into her eyes. His anger was palpable. Not angry with her, she knew, but his father. "I wish I didn't know. I wish he'd died in that accident. I wish— Oh, hell. I don't want to think about him, fluoridated water, or puny cars. I don't want to argue. I want you.

I just want to think about you. Everything is right when I'm with you."

His kiss was slow and gentle, turning quickly to hot. She savored the feel of his weight on her, the taste of his kiss, and the thrill of his wandering tongue. But she wondered if she'd ever hold him again. By not telling him about Buck, she was lying to him and she knew it was a deal breaker for Clay. Tom was right. She hadn't understood then, but she did now. Clay had spent his life erecting a barrier between himself and Hunt Masterson. Clay was an honorable man and liars weren't welcome in his world. "You'll stay with me for a while?"

"I'm here," he said.

For now, she thought, and then thought scattered like startled birds. His mouth was on hers; his hands were everywhere. He dragged her shirt over her head and yanked her bra down. His mouth was on her breasts, hot, angry. Good. She felt it, too. Anger at Buck for keeping secrets and forcing her to lie to Clay and anger at Myrna's killer. Clay sat back and pulled her jeans off. He stripped her panties from her hips and was inside her. Harlie groaned at the quick intrusion but was ready and more than willing. She joined his rhythm, encouraging him, taking what she wanted as he took from her. He filled her, over and over, his sweat-slicked body glistening in the late afternoon light streaming in the windows. When an orgasm ripped through her body, she cried out and rode the wave.

Clay closed his eyes and ground into her, harder and faster, until he flew over his own edge, gasping her name, until he collapsed on her. Harlie wrapped her arms around him and held him close as his trembling muscles calmed.

When he rolled, he pulled her into his arms and kissed her. She looked into his eyes and the anguish returned. With it, her tears flowed. Gasping sobs wracked her body and she couldn't fight or stop it. Not only did she cry for Myrna Snow and her brutal end, but also for Buck and Clay, and finally, for the life she and Clay couldn't have together. She would lose him soon and there wasn't a thing she could do about it. Clay held her but remained silent until she'd cried herself out.

"They'll get her killer, Harlie. I know they will. They'll stop him."

"I hope so," she said, sniffling into his shoulder. "Stay for a little while, okay?"

He nodded and tightened his hold on her. She'd never been in love before and wanted to cling to him forever.

Unfortunately, Harlie's forever with Clay now had an expiration date.

Clay sat on the edge of the bed with his head in his hands. Harlie slept on her stomach with her hair running amok across her shoulders. She was everything to him and he'd been a damned animal with her. His lack of control sickened him. She deserved tenderness and he gave a quick screw like she didn't matter to him, like she was just another woman. He scrubbed his hands over his face and tried to control the feeling he was about to blow apart. This thing with his father was messing him up and Harlie was paying for it.

The desire to climb back into bed with her was strong. She was his anchor in the sea of anger and anguish that trapped him and he needed her but instead of giving in, he kissed her bare shoulder and pulled a blanket over her. She smiled in her sleep. He picked up his jeans and boots from the floor and left the room, fighting the pull to return to her.

After grabbing a shirt from the laundry room, Clay checked his e-mail for word from Tom on the follow-the-blood note. There wasn't one. He called Tom's cell and paced the floor waiting for the call back, grabbing his phone on the first ring.

"Well?"

"Ed isn't done with the list yet."

"What does he know so far? Are there more?"

When Tom spoke, his voice was a whispered croak. "Yeah. He's checked four locations and there is a similar unsolved murder in every one of them."

The room pitched. Clay closed his eyes and tried to regain his equilibrium. He'd hoped Tom was wrong. He wanted him to be wrong.

"Clay? Are you all right?"

"Are you kidding? I never thought of the old man as an ambitious person but he found his calling. Six murders is a lot to take in at once."

"You mean five."

"I mean six. A woman's body was discovered here in Angel Beach yesterday. A friend of Harlie's, so I think you can put away your suspicions of her having something to do with this." He'd never bought into Tom's idea that Harlie was working with his dad. If Harlie knew anything about his father, he trusted her to tell him.

"I'm only suggesting possibilities based on existing facts. How was the woman killed?"

"Strangled, but I don't know what was used."

"Maybe you should get out of there, Clay," Tom said. "This thing is getting—"

"No. I can't. I have to follow through before he kills again. I gotta go. Thanks, Tommy." He hung up and turned off the phone. Tom would continue to insist he leave Angel Beach and Clay knew he couldn't. Since he'd been unsuccessful in finding his father all these years, the victims' blood was on his hands, too.

With his files and the new information from Tom piled in the passenger seat, Clay drove through Angel Beach, circling to postpone the inevitable. He found himself parked at the Angel View Motel and Cabins, unsure of why he landed there. He locked the Jeep and walked around the buildings and cabins. Something good would happen here. Maybe that potential goodness lured him. With the help of his Foundation, Harlie would turn this old rattletrap motel into a haven. He wandered aimlessly around the buildings, imagining the place populated with those in need, hoping to remove the hopelessness filling him. It wouldn't budge.

On the ocean side of the property, he found a dilapidated deck. The cigarette butts scattered in the weeds indicated a recent visitor. He was alone now, wrestling the weight of his responsibility. Once it was done, nothing would be the same. Most of all, Clay himself would never be the same. This thing was ripping his guts out.

Maybe he should have taken the easy way and ignored the sightings. But he couldn't do it. Dodging responsibility was Hunt Masterson's path, not his son's. Clay wouldn't have made it to the top of the music business taking the easy way and he wouldn't do it here either. He and Payton decided long ago to pursue any lead and they were obligated to see it through.

Back in his vehicle, he drove. The town was small and he found his destination with ease: the Angel Beach Police Department. He walked through the door with the collection of files and was greeted by a young, fresh-faced officer.

"How can I help you, sir?"

"I need to know how Myrna Snow was murdered."

The officer frowned. "I can't tell you—"

Clay leaned across the counter. "She was strangled. I know that much. I need to know what she was strangled with."

The young officer looked like he wanted to retreat but held his ground. "Sir, that's classified."

"It was a guitar string, wasn't it? She was strangled with an E string. Right?"

The officer swallowed hard. "Maybe I should get the detective handling the case. Who should I say wants to see him?"

"The man who knows who did it."

25

The house was quiet when Harlie woke from her nap. No music or television noise came up the stairs, just the ever-present crash of waves on the shore below. Clay said he had an errand to run and she assumed he was still at it. Dusk settled and grayness permeated the house. The living room was dark as she wandered through.

As she turned on the kitchen light, she had the sensation she wasn't alone. A man's cough confirmed it.

She turned around, afraid of who might lurk in the shadows behind her. He slumped in the recliner, a whiskey bottle in one hand, a large glass in the other.

"Want a drink?" Clay said, holding the glass out to her. "It's good scotch. Your buddy who runs errands for me bought a good one. It ought to have me shit-faced in record time."

"I don't drink."

He shrugged. "Looks like I do. Got a problem with it?"

He looked peculiar, like his compass was off-kilter. "What's wrong?" She stepped closer, wanting to touch him and reassure herself he was okay. She knelt near his chair and reached for his hand. He waved her away.

"Nothing I want to talk about."

Belligerence wasn't a tone she'd heard from him before. She stood and backed up. "Did you have a visitor or something? Get some bad news, maybe?" Had Buck come by? If so, why was Clay getting drunk and where was Buck?

He shook his head slowly, his movements dulled by the alcohol. "Visitors? No. Payton says he'll come tomorrow but I don't think it'll help. Nothing will help now. Everything has gone to shit, Harlie." He looked at her with bloodshot eyes. "You know what it feels like when everything turns to shit in your life?"

"What happened?"

"There's no going back now. It's done. Out of my hands for good."

"So, no one came by?"

He leaned forward. "No. I've been sitting here alone and I'd like to keep doing it." He held up the bottle and swished the remaining contents. "Another couple of glasses and this'll be gone. Go home, would you? I can't stand to look at you right now. I can't stand that hoity-toity 'I don't drink or put impure stuff in my body' look you're giving me. Don't pass judgment on me when you don't know what I'm going though."

Harlie frowned. "I don't care if you drink. I don't for my own reasons. Maybe it would help to talk about it. Tell me what you're going through so I can understand—"

"No. I'm not talking to you or anybody else. Get out of here, Harlie." He waved the bottle. "You're interrupting a Masterson tradition. We drown ourselves in booze so we don't have to see ourselves in the mirror. That way, we don't have to see what monsters we are." He narrowed his eyes. "I said get out."

She was afraid to leave him this way but was more afraid to stay. She'd felt his anger earlier, but it hadn't been aimed at her. This was different. She backed away and was out the door before Clay could show her what kind of monster he was. She didn't want to know.

⁜

The ringing phone jolted Harlie awake. A glance at her bedside clock made her groan: 3:00 a.m. She'd been asleep an hour and had to get up in two. She grabbed the phone.

"Hello?" She could hear breathing, but nothing else. "If this is a prank call, I don't think you're funny—"

"Harlie, it's me."

Clay. "So?"

"Can I come over and talk to you?"

"You're drunk."

"Not so much now. Can I?"

Harlie could feel herself giving in. He didn't sound as drunk as he did earlier and her empathetic nature was kicking in. She heard a cry for help in his voice and was compelled to help. Why didn't her compassion have an off switch? "I don't know. You were kinda scary earlier. Maybe we should do this on the phone."

"Please, baby. Let me come over. I need to talk to someone."

"Then go find someone. I'm going back to bed." She almost disconnected the call.

"I need you, Harlie. I need to talk to you." He paused and whispered, "I killed him."

She was alert now, sitting straight up. "What are you talking about?"

When he spoke, his voice was filled with anguish. "I killed him. I killed my dad."

Buck. Harlie froze. Not Buck.

"Can I...can I come over...I need you. I need to see you."

She gulped for air and tried to hold off the panic. Not Buck. Oh god, not Buck.

"Harlie?"

She swallowed hard and tried to breathe. "I'll unlock the door."

She watched through the window panes as Clay staggered down the driveway. No matter what he said, he was still drunk. As he neared, she opened the door. "What did you do, Clay? Where is he?"

He weaved to a stop and grabbed the doorframe to prevent his fall. "Can I come in?"

Harlie wrapped her arms around her middle and walked in the door, leaving it open for him. Once inside, she swung around. "What did you do? Please tell me you didn't kill him! It's the booze talking, right?"

He staggered to the middle of the room and ran his hands through his hair. "I had to do it, Harlie. I had to. People were dying and I had to stop him."

"What do you mean, people were dying?"

"Lynette was the first."

The pain in his eyes tore through her but she didn't go to him.

"My dad is a serial killer. A goddamned serial killer. Tom says there are similar unsolved murders everywhere he's been. Four of them so far and they aren't done looking." He paced across the room. "Your friend Myrna was the sixth one. I talked to the detective handling the case. She was strangled with a guitar string, like Lynette. An E string! I had to do it. I had to stop him."

He dropped into an overstuffed chair, his long legs stretched across the floor. He leaned his head back and looked as if he'd been to hell and back. "Now I know how they felt. I always wondered how they could do it to one of their own. Now I know. If you know, you gotta stop it or the blood is on your hands, too." He looked at his hands as if he expected to see crimson there.

"Who?"

"The Kaczynski family. They're the ones who figured out the Unabomber was one of them, one of their own family, and they turned him in. They sent their brother to death row. Now I've done it, too. I might as well stick the needle in his arm or send the electricity through him. I've killed my father, Harlie."

Harlie pressed her fingers to her temples and frowned. "So, you didn't kill him? I thought you shot him or something."

He shook his head. "No. But what I did will have the same result. He'll be dead."

Harlie felt like collapsing on the floor when the tension left her body. She walked to Clay on unsteady legs and sat on the arm of his chair. "Tell me what you did."

"I gave the police my files and told them about the other murders. I gave them copies of the notes. They're running it through a crime database to see if what I told them is true. The Feds will probably come to Angel Beach now."

She blew out her breath. Not good for Buck, but not as bad as a bullet delivered by his own son. "It's good the cops know about the other murders. Maybe they'll figure out who the killer is."

"You know what's funny? They told me not to leave town because I have to be ruled out as a suspect. I know too much about Myrna Snow's murder." He laughed. "Me? A suspect? I told them who the murderer is. Now they need to find him before he can do it again. But it sure as hell isn't me."

Harlie sighed and stretched her back. "The detective made me feel the same way but he said it was procedure. Nothing to worry about."

He pulled her from the chair arm and held her close, his breath warm against her neck. Harlie wrapped her arms around him and brushed her hand across his hair.

"I never wanted him dead," he said. "You have to believe me. I was angry when I said that."

Harlie tightened her hold on him. "I never thought that, Clay. You did what you felt was right, what your conscience required you to do."

"I didn't think you'd understand." He took a deep, shaky breath and released it slowly. "I love you, Harlie."

"You think you do."

He looked up and gave her a lopsided smile. "I do." He pulled her into a whiskey-flavored kiss, his usual finesse a victim of the alcohol in his system. He left his hand on her shoulder, rubbing his finger against her neck. "Here's the way I see it. You and me got a great thing going here."

"I suppose..."

He shook his head. "No supposing about it. It's good. Really good. I've had the world's worst marriage so I should know when something's good. I want us to get married—"

She laid her hand on his and squeezed. "Clay, it's too soon for that. I may not be divorced and—"

He placed a finger on her lips. "Hear me out. This is good. Me and you." He blinked and fought to focus his eyes. "Right. We're gonna get married. I know it's quick and all, but when something's good, you don't let it get cold. We can have whatever kinda wedding you want. I like small ones...no reporters...but we'll do what you want."

Harlie smiled. "Sam will be disappointed but small is good."

He nodded. "And we'll have some kids. I have a really good house for kids. Big yard. Fishing pond. Me and Tom can build a big swing set."

"Kids?"

"Right. Kids. Children. I've never had a family and I want one with you."

"I don't want kids." Harlie frowned. "I've never wanted kids."

He blew out his breath. "Oh, come on. Everybody wants kids, darlin'."

"I'm serious, Clay." She shook her head. "I don't want kids."

He scowled. "Why not?"

"I can't believe you have to ask after what I've told you about my childhood."

Clay held up his hands. "Whoa. Wait a minute. I may be drunk right now but I don't do this all the time. This was an emergency."

She took his hand, lacing her fingers with his. "I didn't mean you. I decided a long time ago I didn't want children. Life is too uncertain. The world is too cruel."

"But our kids would have everything I could give them. Not just stuff but love, too. Lots of love. I'd always be there for them, too...not like..." He blinked slowly. "We'll talk about it when...I can...keep my eyes open...better." His head lolled and he sighed.

"How about if I get you to bed before you pass out?"

"Good plan," he muttered.

She stood, still holding his hand. He staggered to his feet and allowed her to lead him to her bedroom and remove his boots, jeans, and shirt before she helped him into bed. As Harlie slid between the sheets, he pulled her to him and rested his cheek against her shoulder.

"I can't remember if I told you," he said.

"What?"

"He left me behind. When my mom died, he left and didn't come back for two years."

She couldn't see him in the dark but heard the pain in his voice. "Tom told me in Seattle. He didn't think you'd care if I knew. You were lucky his family was there for you."

Clay smiled against her skin. "It's okay. Tommy is the best brother a guy could have. Always there." He sighed. "When my dad came back, I didn't even know who he was. I was only two when he left." Clay brushed his hand across her arm. "Do you know how it feels to be dumped like that? To know you aren't important enough to hold someone?"

She knew first-hand how it tore a child's heart to yearn for a parent's love and know it wouldn't come.

But Buck was such a warm and generous man; she had difficulty reconciling the irresponsible father Clay described with the man she knew now. "Maybe he was grieving for your mother."

"That's what they said. He couldn't get over losing her. Maybe if my brother had lived, maybe the two of us could have held him. I couldn't do it alone."

Harlie frowned. "I didn't know you had a brother." But Buck had mentioned having two sons, past tense.

"He died in the accident. He wasn't even born yet but his name was Ryan. Maybe Ryan and I would have been enough for him. I always wanted to ask Dad if the two of us could...just to see what he'd say..." His voice drifted and his body went slack.

Harlie held him and listened to his steady breathing. The scotch had finally done its job and he could sleep. She didn't agree with his opinion that Buck was a murderer but she didn't wish him bad dreams. He tortured himself enough.

They both were, father and son. Harlie wished she could tell Clay his father wasn't a beast. It broke her heart to hear two wounded souls screaming and be unable to help. She held the key to reuniting them, but was forced to keep them apart. Weak, Buck had said. He'd been weak where Clay was concerned, wallowing in his grief at his son's expense. But saving Clay from his current grief would send Buck to prison for crimes he didn't commit. She couldn't do it to him, not after the friendship he'd given her. Not when she loved him as a daughter loves a father.

Clay shifted and mumbled in his sleep. Harlie kissed his lips and rested her palm against his rough cheek. When she was sure she wouldn't wake him, she slid from beneath his arm, kissed his forehead, and whispered, "I love you." She dressed and tiptoed out the door, her apprehension cruising in high gear.

⚬⚬⚬

Buck's place was dark and her knock on his door echoed through the night. "Buck!" she whispered. "Wake up! I need to talk to you." A screen door slammed behind her and she heard footsteps approach.

"That's Jack you're waking up. He's been hanging out here the last few days."

Harlie turned to see Emily standing on the back porch, wearing a pink robe. Harlie climbed the dark porch steps. "Where's Buck? I need to talk to him about...something."

Emily shook her head. "He's gone."

"Will he be back soon? I can wait."

Emily's lip trembled. "He's gone for good, Harlie. He packed his stuff last night and said he won't be back."

Harlie's heart beat faster. "Did he say why he was leaving or where he was going? I really need to see him. It's important."

"He said he was getting too close and it was time to go again."

"Who was getting close?"

"His son. He said it wouldn't be long and the police would find him. He had to move on again."

"The police?" Harlie feigned shock. "What do the police have to do with Buck?"

"Sweetie," Emily said through her tears. "You are one horrible actress. Come in and we'll have some tea. You look like you need it worse than me."

A short time later, chamomile tea steeped in mugs on the table. Harlie paced the kitchen floor.

"So?" Harlie shrugged and looked at her friend as she sat at the table. Emily's eyes were bloodshot and her blonde hair was rumpled. "What did Buck tell you?"

Emily leaned back and gave Harlie a level stare. "Everything. When things got serious between us, he said he wanted me to know all of it. I also know what he told you, so stop pussyfooting around. I know he was accused of murdering that woman in Montana and I also know he's innocent."

"How do you know?"

"He told me and I believe him. Buck wouldn't lie to me or you either. He may have kept some facts from us for a while but I don't think he ever lied."

"A thin line, wouldn't you say?" Harlie moved to the table and removed her tea bag from the steaming water.

"He did what was necessary to stay alive. There's a man who wants him dead."

"Clay doesn't want him dead."

Emily shook her head. "Not Clay. Another man. The one who did the killing. Buck can testify against him and the man wants him dead."

"Who is it?"

Emily shrugged. "He wouldn't tell me. He said my life would be in danger if I knew."

Harlie frowned. "He told me that, too."

"Okay. Buck has us on the same page." She leaned forward. "So, what got you so fired up at three in the morning?"

Harlie sat at the table and explained her night with Clay, his revelations, his guilt and remorse over going to the police. "Clay still thinks his dad did it. He just feels like crap for having to turn him in. If Buck is convicted, he'll get the death penalty, Em. Serial killers almost always do. There are six victims in six different states. The feds will probably come in now."

Emily frowned. "Six? I wonder if Buck knows. He said there was no way he could defend himself in Montana and he wasn't dying for another man's crime. There's no way he'd get out from under six accusations."

"Which way did he go? Did he tell you? I can look for him and tell him what's going on," Harlie said.

"Looks like it's too late for that, sweetie." Emily walked to the kitchen counter and increased the volume on a small TV. Clay's photo of Buck was on CNN. "It looks like the story is out already. Buck will know sooner or later there is a massive manhunt going on. I just hope he finds a hole to hide in."

Harlie hoped the hole wasn't six feet deep.

26

Buck hadn't walked far before getting his first ride. A thumb in the air wasn't necessary at 2:00 a.m. Some truckers were sympathetic to an old cowboy with his guitar slung over his shoulder if he added a tired limp to his gait. If they wanted somebody to keep them awake in the wee hours of the morning, Buck looked harmless enough.

He'd done his share of trucking years ago and knew the ropes. Back then, Clay was just a tike and was safe with the neighbors, leaving Buck to ramble wherever the roads led him. After Abigail died, he couldn't sit in one place anymore. He'd planned to take the kid with him when he got bigger, at least in the summer when Clay was out of school. It could have been a grand adventure for the two of them, riding the highways in an eighteen-wheeler.

If he hadn't had too much to drink in Colorado, it might have worked out. He remembered how the evening started with a beer and ended with a barroom brawl and jail time for assault. One assault turned into more as his drinking escalated. After a while, it was easier to not go home and face the condemning eyes of Sheldon Black and the hopeful eyes of his son. He didn't want Clay to know his father was a mess so he stayed away. Clay was a better man than Buck could ever be and Sheldon was the reason.

The first trucker who stopped asked Buck to play a few favorite songs. It was a good way to pay for the ride, so he played for an hour. The next driver was a beefy guy, a talker, and Buck had to fight to stay awake. When the conversation turned to news of a serial killer in the area, Buck perked up.

"A serial killer? I hadn't heard about it."

"Heard the story on the radio. A bad one from the sounds of it." The driver laughed. "Not that any of that sort are good, but this guy kills women. Six of them so far. The last one was in Angel Beach—out on the coast, you know. It's a nice little beach town. I took the wife there for our thirtieth anniversary. It's not the sort of place you'd expect to find a serial killer."

Myrna. Buck took a deep breath. "So, how do they know it's a serial killer? Just one person so far."

"Six of them in six states. The first one was in Montana. He beat her up and strangled her. They say there's a bunch more. Everywhere the jerk goes, he kills a woman."

Buck tensed. "How did they find out about this? Six states is a lot of territory to cover."

"I dunno. Somebody turned him in, I guess. There's some connection to that country music singer Clay Masterson, but I missed the first part of the story." The truck slowed. "I gotta turn at this next exit. You're welcome to ride with me to Lake Oswego. If not, stay on the interstate and it'll take you east through the Columbia River Gorge. It's a beautiful trip."

East meant Montana. Nothing said he had to go that far. "Drop me off. I'd like to see the Gorge."

From the shoulder of I-84, Buck waved thanks to the driver and continued on foot. Six murders? What was going on? A copycat, maybe. Someone found out about the Montana murder and wanted to cash in. Or Tony was more of a monster than he'd thought. Six...

It was 4:00 a.m. and traffic was picking up. He wanted to get further from Portland and the heavier concentration of police. With his thumb in the air, he walked backward, hoping a trucker would take pity on a gray-bearded old geezer. As the sunrise peeked over the horizon, a Peterbilt pulled to a stop ahead of him. He limped as fast as he could and climbed up to the cab, opened the door, and looked in.

"Thanks for stopping, buddy," Buck said with a grin. "My feet were starting to protest." The limp he'd faked earlier had become painfully real during the last miles.

The driver was a young man, late twenties maybe, wearing a blue Naches Valley High School Football cap and a friendly smile. "Where you heading, Grandpa?"

"Wherever the road takes me. Which way you going?"

"Yakima Valley," he said. "Interested?"

Buck clambered into the passenger seat, slammed his door, and settled in. "Never been there but it sounds like a place to go." He never planned ahead. Wherever the road took him was his only rule. He'd landed in Angel Beach that way when a truck he rode in blew a tire. Rather than wait around, he'd headed into town, bought a cup of coffee at the bakery, and met the sweetest, most argumentative young woman on the planet. He already missed that girl. Em, too, but he didn't dare think about her yet.

The driver shifted into gear and rolled onto I-84. "Toss your gear in the sleeper if you like. There's pop in the cooler if you need something."

The sun rose, slow and steady. The hum and grind of the Peterbilt made him sleepy and he fought to stay awake. Pop wasn't usually his beverage of choice but he needed the caffeine. He dug in the cooler and grabbed a couple of Pepsis for himself and the driver.

"So, where you from, Grandpa?" the trucker said as he popped the can's top.

Buck shrugged. "Everywhere and anywhere. There are so many places, I can't remember anymore." The past eighteen years were a blur of places and people. He'd never allowed a connection with either and had been happy that way. Or at least, he'd tried to convince himself of it.

The driver shook his head slowly. "I've been in the same place all my life. Like my parents and my grandparents. I have roots so deep, I'll never move." He grinned. "My wife and I bought a place last year with some apples and pears on it. When the trees start producing, I'm hoping to cut back on the trucking so I can take care of my orchards. My wife doesn't like it when I'm gone. We have three kids and I can't wait to get home to them."

Buck smiled. There had been a time when he felt that way, when he couldn't wait to get home to his family. There at the last, Abigail would meet him at the door with her belly swelled with their second son. Ryan his name would have been. Clay was a little pipsqueak—a happy kid who was adored by his father. But a drunk driver ruined it all, took his wife and unborn son. Clay became a victim of his father's weakness. The irony of it all, Buck turned to alcohol to ease his pain. Funny how that turned out.

He tipped his hat brim to shade his eyes from the sunrise. He wasn't a big fan of morning. It came too early in the day to suit him, but this sunrise was a beauty with its blister-red streaks scorching across the sky like flames licking the placid Columbia River. The driver turned on the stereo, his iPod hung from the faceplate, bouncing with the rough highway. The music selection: Toby Keith and George Strait to start. When the next song began, the kid turned up the volume.

"I love this guy's music. You a Clay Masterson fan?"

Buck nodded. "I've listened to him a time or two. He has a nice way with a guitar."

"I hear you on that. This song is one of my favorites. I mean, he really nails the whole meaning of home and family. Guys like him really got it made, you know?"

Moisture collected in Buck's eyes. He knew the song and knew what it meant when he saw the video. Seeing Clay sitting on his own porch in Montana singing, "I'll be waiting when you come home," was like a kick in the gut. He knew who Clay was singing to but he couldn't figure out why the kid wrote the song about a useless old dog like him.

"I'm listening to this song and keep thinking about you," the kid said. "Having a home is so important to me. How do you wander the way you do? Do you have any family?" He frowned. "Maybe you don't. Sorry. I shouldn't have said that."

Buck was silent a moment, and then said, "I had a family. I have people who are important to me." Emily, Harlie, even all those folks at the Center who needed his help from time to time. He had people who cared about him now, people who expected him to do the right thing, not run away like a coward. He'd told Harlie he'd do the right thing. He knew what she expected him to do—talk to Clay and the police. But he took his usual route and saved his own hide without worrying about whom he hurt.

Well, that was going to end now.

"Hey, kid? Could you pull over and let me out? I've had a change in plans."

It was harder to hitch during the day. People were occupied with their lives and didn't pay attention to old men wandering down the road, no matter how much he emphasized the limp. He'd managed to snag a ride back through Portland and was thankful for that. City traffic was a nightmare for a guy on foot. His last ride dropped him outside McMinnville and he'd been hoofing it since. His stomach growled and he decided to find some chow when he got into town. A big burger with fries would do the trick. With each step, he added another food item: a milkshake, maybe a cookie. His guitar was heavy on his shoulder so he stopped and shifted it, looking around for a place to rest.

He'd seen signs for the Evergreen Aviation and Space Museum. Across a field to the north, he saw the glass-fronted hangar, the Spruce Goose fully visible, and thought it was time for a detour. The place might have a snack bar. It would certainly have a bathroom and bench to sit on. Considering he was probably heading to prison for the rest of his life, he'd better make the sightseeing trip while he had the chance. He doubted prison guards allowed field trips to museums. He hadn't killed anyone but the evidence would put a noose around his neck anyway.

Tony would make sure of it.

As he contemplated his best route to the museum, a black car slowed and stopped ahead of him. The passenger door swung open. Buck debated a moment.

Flight intrigued him and he'd really like to see that plane. Howard Hughes was one crazy bugger to build such a thing, but who knew when the next ride would come along. He sauntered to the car and leaned in the door.

"I'm heading out to Angel Beach? Any chance you're going that way?"

"Well, isn't this your lucky day?" The driver turned to Buck and smiled.

"Oh, shit," Buck said when he saw the handgun pointed at his chest.

"Get in the car, Hunt, and you might see the end of the day," Payton Shaw said, his voice calm.

Buck hesitated as he debated the chances of getting away minus a bullet in his back. Unless things had changed, Tony couldn't hit the broad side of a movie theater. But at this short range, the guy might get lucky.

"Get in the car now and your son's girlfriend might see tomorrow, too."

"What are you talking about?"

Payton looked thoughtful. "Harlie, I think her name is these days. I have my instructions concerning her. Behave yourself and I may not carry them out. It's entirely up to you whether she sees another Angel Beach sunset."

He doubted Payton would shoot him now and risk getting brain tissue on his leather upholstery. But he wouldn't risk Harlie's safety. Buck opened the back door and slid his guitar in the seat. When he looked up, the gun barrel was in his face.

"Don't even think about trying anything. I've known you too long and know all your tricks."

Buck laughed. "If you did, you'd have caught up with me before now, Tony. It's taken you eighteen years to find me. You never were much of a hunter. An elk could walk right under your nose and you'd miss it." He slammed the back door, chuckling, and slid into the passenger seat of the sleek Mercedes, stuffing his duffle bag between his feet. He crossed his arms and let out a tired breath as Payton accelerated onto the highway. "So, here we are. Two boyhood friends reunited. If I cared, I'd ask how you been doing. Judging from the car, I'd say crime does pay." He paused. "I have a couple of concerns with this situation though," he said. "First is that you have no intention of turning me over to the cops and I'll probably be buried in a shallow grave alongside the road." He looked at Payton.

Payton smirked. "It's a valid assumption."

"Thought so. Next, I'm worried that you have somehow undone all Sheldon Black's positive influence and have turned my son into a homicidal lunatic like yourself. Does he know what you're doing today?"

Payton laid the handgun in his lap. "Finding you here was luck. Setting your lunatic comment aside, Clay hasn't confirmed your presence in Angel Beach yet. The information he received was vague and he's been spinning in circles. I did my own research. I talked with a bunch of your so-called friends and some business owners and discovered you were calling yourself Buck, play your guitar in front of the bakery, and had grown a hideous gray ponytail that makes you resemble the horse's ass that you are. I felt he'd be happier not knowing I found you. He seems torn between wanting to find you to see if you are alive and wanting to kick your sorry butt back to Montana so he can see you locked up for good. I'm partial to your shallow grave idea, myself. Less fuss that way."

Buck harrumphed. "That's not surprising." He glanced at the handgun lying in Payton's lap. "I hope you put the safety on that thing. As much as I'd like to see you shoot your balls off, I don't want to get caught in the crossfire. If you're gonna shoot me, at least try to get a clean shot."

"Shut up, Hunt."

"Clever comeback." He crossed his arms and frowned. "So, what kind of instructions do you have about Harlie? She doesn't know anything about this mess of yours."

Payton laughed. "It isn't my mess, Hunt. You've got yourself tied every which way and you'll never get free."

"I heard you've done your share of lying about me to make sure they didn't look at the real killer."

"No need to lie. The evidence did its job. Your guitar string killed her. Your fingerprint was on the beer

can. You were seen leaving her house that evening.
You can sputter all you want but you are going down
for Lynette's murder." He smiled. "Well, unless I decide to clear this muddle myself."

Buck didn't let Tony rile him and did his best to
appear unconcerned. He knew who killed Lynette and
it sure as heck wasn't Hunt Masterson. He had a lot of
faults but killing women wasn't one of them. He re-
clined the seat and settled in. As annoyingly fastidious
as his old friend was, it was a safe bet he wouldn't
shoot him in the car and he could catch up on the
sleep he'd missed last night. "Let me know when we
get there." He pulled his hat over his eyes.

Hours later, Buck awoke to a sound that made his
teeth hurt. "Mozart? You gonna torture me before you
kill me, Tony?" he said from under his hat.

"Will you stop using that stupid nickname? I left it
in Montana."

Buck chuckled. "Let me tell you something. You
can try to outrun your past but it will always catch up
to you, Tony Baloney." He tipped his hat back and
gave him a grin. "Maybe you like that better? I think
we were eight when I gave you that one."

Buck knew he zinged him that time. Tony gripped
the steering wheel until his knuckles were white. Tony
would try to kill him before they got to Angel Beach
but there was no way Buck was going down without a
fight. Even if it was only verbal. He knew how to irri-
tate Tony Shaw. It was an art form he began perfect-

ing when they were five years old and he knew all the guy's sore spots. Years ago, the teasing was good-natured. Not now. Not after Tony turned on him in the worst way.

"No, siree," Buck said. "I've tried to outrun my past for eighteen years and look where that got me. Staring at your prissy face. City life has softened you up. Not that you had far to go. Egad, look at that wimpy suit you're wearing. Your father would have a fit seeing you this way. Connor Shaw was a real man's man. I always wondered if he felt shortchanged in the son department. The man had that beautiful office filled with hunting trophies like he was Hemingway or something and you couldn't find your way out of a dark closet." Buck sat up. "I mean, listen to that bullshit you're listening to. That classical crap will numb your brain." He reached to the radio and found a gun in his face.

A nervous tick in Payton's jaw bounced like a rubber ball. "Leave it."

Buck pulled his hand back and sighed. "Suit yourself. I'll entertain myself over here." He sang an old country song, mustering as much twang as he could. The more annoyed Tony appeared, the louder he sang.

"You aren't doing yourself any favors, Hunt. There are a number of secluded areas between here and Angel Beach where I could stash your dead carcass. Don't push me."

Buck shrugged. "Have at it, buddy. From what I hear, you've already pinned five murders on me."

"Six."

"Well, how about that? I don't even know how many murders I've committed." He leaned close to Payton and whispered, "But the guy who did it sure does. Six, you say? How do you sleep at night?"

"I sleep fine knowing you will be convicted and get a well-deserved death cocktail in your veins."

"Yeah, I'll bet that gives you a warm fuzzy. Is that what you think about when you kiss Nadine good night? How safe your upscale marriage is since you pinned your lover's murder on me?" He laughed. "Wouldn't she love to know the truth?"

The tick in Payton's jaw bounced faster. "Shut up. It's your fault Lynette died. Yours! If you'd stayed away from her—"

"What? You wouldn't have killed her? Did you think I was messing around with her? I wasn't. And what business was it of yours anyway? You're married. She was single. End of story in decent society."

"She was mine," Payton said. "Mine!"

"Maybe you should have married her instead of Nadine." Buck slapped his palm to his forehead. "Oh, silly me. Nadine had those nice social connections that were supposed to impress your daddy." He glanced over at Payton. "He wanted you to be a cattleman and a skilled hunter, like him. I wonder what he'd think of your hunting skills now. Six kills is pretty impressive. Too bad they were women and not deer."

A few minutes later he spotted a sign, ANGEL BEACH NEXT EXIT, and wondered what Tony planned to do with him. His answer came when the Mercedes pulled to a stop in the Angel View Motel and Cabins parking lot. As he suspected, they wouldn't be visiting the Angel Beach cop shop.

"Get out of the car," Payton said. "Don't try anything."

Buck did as he was told, grabbing the duffle from between his feet. When he moved to open the back door, Payton stopped him.

"I'll get the rest of it."

Buck shrugged. "Okay."

Payton pointed the handgun at him. "Get over there. Room twelve."

Buck walked toward twelve, weaving through the tall grass in the parking lot, smashing some down. He reached the door and turned.

"Open the door. It's unlocked."

Buck turned the knob. The door stuck and he had to push hard to open it. The room was pretty much what he expected: a small studio unit with a sofa bed, chair, dinette, and a small kitchenette.

"Go in," Payton said.

Buck stepped into the room and turned around. "Tony, if you're gonna shoot me, why don't you do it and get it over with?"

"Okay." Payton smiled and pulled the trigger.

27

Harlie searched every possible location, drove up and down Highway 101, made exhausting circles, and couldn't find Buck. What made her think she could find a man who'd successfully hidden from the world for eighteen years? Even though Harlie had done her share of hiding, Buck probably had tricks that wouldn't occur to her or he really was gone.

Sam called at 6:00 a.m. One of Lisa's kids was sick and she wouldn't make it to work. Sam couldn't work alone, so Harlie abandoned her search until after closing.

At two, she was finishing some bookwork in the small back office when a light knock on the door interrupted her. She spun her chair around to find Clay leaning on the doorframe, his cheeks covered with two days of beard, his eyes red rimmed and bleary.

"You survived the night," she said.

Clay grimaced. "If you call this surviving." He rubbed his hands over his face and sighed. "Can I ask you something?" When she nodded he continued with a confused frown. "How did I get in your bed last night? Not that I'm complaining or anything. Waking up in your bed is as good as it gets, but not knowing how I got there is bothering me."

Harlie cocked her brow. "You don't remember calling me in the middle of the night?"

He shook his head and grimaced. "I don't remember leaving my house. I found the almost empty bottle of scotch by the recliner, which explains this skull-splitting headache. I don't usually drink like that." He frowned. "Did we talk or anything?"

"A little," she said. "You told me to get out of your house and then called me later wanting to talk. I wasn't excited about the idea but you got around me, as usual." She hated how he could do that so easily. The thought of those beautiful blue eyes coupled with the cry for help in his voice and she was toast.

"Ah." He winced again, but not from the hangover. "That explains why you look angry. Whatever I said, I probably didn't mean it. I was out of it."

Harlie shrugged and gave him a level stare. "Don't worry about it. I didn't think you meant it at the time."

"I was incredibly drunk, Harlie, and I doubt I said anything worth repeating. If I said anything to upset you—"

"I said don't worry about it and I meant it."

"I know I was a little rough before—"

"I said—"

"I'm sorry about that and anything else I did or said. This thing with my dad is getting...difficult."

Harlie bit her lip, but remained silent. He was doing it again, that getting around her easily thing he did so well.

Clay sighed. "I guess I'd better go. Payton is here with me. We stopped in for lunch before checking in with the police."

Her fingers tightened on the chair's arms. "Payton Shaw? Your friend who works for Glen?"

"Yeah. He wants to meet you."

"Why? So he can drag me back to Seattle?" She shook her head. "No."

He frowned. "I know his connection with Glen worries you but he hasn't said anything and I'll be honest with you, strong-arm tactics really aren't Payton's style. He's..." Clay shrugged. "Well, he's too classy for that. If Glen plans to come after you, I doubt Payton would be part of it."

"And you think Payton would tell you if he had something planned? I know Glen and I know how he operates. His employees will do anything he tells them to do."

Clay frowned. "When you meet Payton I think you'll see he isn't the hired-muscle type."

Harlie wasn't so sure but she didn't argue the point. She'd meet him and watch closely to see what she could figure out about the guy. "Any news on your dad? You did tell me about that last night."

"I thought I might have. I haven't heard anything yet so I don't know if I'm on or off the suspect list today. It should help for Payton to talk with the police. He's been with me every step of the way and might be able to add something. I'd better get going." He leaned and gave her a quick kiss. It was more of a brush than an actual kiss and considering his retraction of everything he said last night, she wasn't surprised.

"I'll get your lunch order in a minute." She twirled her chair around to the desk and shuffled papers.

"Harlie?"

"What?"

He spun her chair around and leaned with his hands on the desk, surrounding her. His mouth was a whisper from hers. His breath was warm against her lips. "Did I happen to mention anything last night, like maybe I'm in love with you and want to marry you? I have a foggy memory of something like that."

"Yeah. Something like that." She tried not to meet his eyes.

"Okay. I meant that part. The rest of it? I don't have a clue. Maybe you can fill me in later."

Coupled with his declaration, his second kiss was unbelievable.

"Can I see you tonight? I haven't been at my best the past few days and I want to make it up to you." He smiled.

"How?" she whispered.

"Real slow," he said. "I want to make your toes curl."

"They already are."

Clay grinned. "Payton is staying in a hotel so we don't have to worry about entertaining him. He plans to turn in early."

"Maybe he can run a few miles on the beach to be sure?"

"I'll suggest it."

"I don't know what time I'll be home though. I have some errands to run."

"Keep me posted, okay? Payton isn't a concern, but it's possible Glen knows where you are now. I want you close to me tonight. Very close." He nipped her lips one last time and backed out of the office.

Harlie followed a moment later, rubbing her fingertips across her lips. When she reached the front counter, she saw Clay and Payton seated at the corner table. Afternoon sun streamed through the large windows. She filled two water glasses and joined them. Clay wrapped his arm around her waist and pulled her close, his fingers hooked in her jeans. She set the glasses on the table and got a good look at Payton Shaw. He was familiar but she didn't know why. In his expensive gray suit, he belonged in a boardroom, not a beachside bakery. His shoes probably cost more than her monthly rent and he had a fastidious manner, like he and dirt hadn't been properly introduced. Not at all what she expected of Clay's good friend and former father-in-law, but she could see why Clay doubted he would act as Glen's muscle. Clay was incredibly masculine in his jeans and cowboy boots. In her imagination, she could see him on the back of a horse driving cattle across a Montana ranch or camping under the stars. Payton was city from his professionally styled hair to his buffed shoes. And he was supposedly Buck's friend, too. That was an even bigger stretch. Buck and Clay had cornered the market on masculinity. Payton didn't fit the picture.

Clay made the introductions and Harlie watched Payton for any sign of recognition. Nothing. He held out his hand and Harlie shook it.

"It's nice to meet you, Mr. Shaw."

He waved the formality away. "Call me Payton. I'm sorry to have missed you in Seattle. Clay told me he was bringing a friend along and I'd hoped to meet you." He gave Clay a knowing look. "He hasn't dated much since the divorce and I wanted to meet the lovely lady who caught his eye. But duty called me away."

There was something about his voice that stabbed Harlie's memory. She was sure she'd talked with him before. But where? He didn't start working at the Carson Family Trust until after she left Seattle. She hadn't seen him at the concert.

"She caught more than my eye," Clay said as he gave her a squeeze. "We probably should get lunch taken care of so we can get moving."

Harlie shook free of her thoughts. "Right. What can I get for you?" Clay ordered a turkey sandwich and chowder. Payton, a turkey sandwich on Ciabatta bread, with chowder. She left to prepare their meals, wondering how she knew Payton Shaw.

While she filled their orders, it hit her. Payton had been in the bakery before. Twice. And he sat at that same table. Why hadn't he mentioned it? The men were deep in conversation when she returned to the table with their food. As she turned to leave, Payton called to her.

"Harlie, I believe this may be another patron's meal. I ordered the turkey on Ciabatta bread and chowder."

She stepped back to the table and, sure enough, she'd brought him chicken noodle soup. Embarrassed heat rose up her neck and face. "I'm so sorry. This is what you ordered the last time you were here."

Clay looked from her to Payton, his brow knit tight. "When were you here?"

"Never." Payton shook his head. "She's mistaken."

"Sure you were," Harlie said. "A couple of weeks ago. You wore a fishing hat and looked like you'd been out on a charter. You ordered the chicken noodle soup."

Clay frowned and looked at Payton. "Fishing? You said you were on a business trip."

"Like I said, Harlie is mistaken." He glared at Harlie and their eyes locked. A tremor ran through her. This was Buck's friend from Montana. This was the friend with the hoity-toity lifestyle he couldn't tell her about because her life would be endangered. This man killed Myrna Snow.

"I've never been to Angel Beach before," Payton said. "If I had, I'd certainly remember it."

He'd been here all right, bearded and dressed in old clothes. He'd been fishing, but not for salmon or tuna.

He asked about Buck. Twice. Harlie swallowed hard. Payton looked at her with narrowed eyes.

"You're right," she said with an uncomfortable laugh. "I'm thinking of someone else. You know what they say, everyone has a twin somewhere."

Payton's smile was tight. "So I've heard."

She backed away. "I'll get your correct order now."

A few minutes later, she returned with Payton's chowder and removed the chicken noodle soup. As she set the bowl in front of him, she could feel his eyes burning into her as she retreated to the kitchen.

⁘

Clay leaned back and crossed his arms as he watched Payton sip chowder. His own bowl steamed in invitation but he'd lost his appetite. Clay narrowed his eyes and studied Payton.

Payton looked up from his bowl. "Aren't you eating?"

Clay shook his head. "What was that about?"

Payton wiped his mouth with a napkin and frowned. "What?

"The way you treated Harlie. It was a bowl of soup, for Pete's sake."

Payton pursed his lips. "Good service is imperative if she hopes to make a success of her business."

"Good service," Clay muttered. "Harlie is important to me, Payton, and you treated her like garbage."

"You're serious about this relationship?"

"Very serious."

"You want to marry that woman?" He frowned.

Clay leaned his elbows on the table. "Yes. That woman."

"Have you thought this through? I mean, she is absurdly inappropriate for you."

Clay laughed. "Excuse me if I don't take your opinion to heart. You thought Crystal was appropriate and we both know how that turned out."

Payton tossed his napkin on the table. "Crystal is of good family and if you two had figured out how to get along, it would have been a perfect marriage."

Clay snorted. "There's more to marriage than pedigree—"

"That woman," Payton said as he pointed toward the kitchen door, "is highly unsuitable. You have your public image to consider."

"Harlie is a wonderful woman with the biggest heart I've ever seen. She sacrifices daily to help the homeless people in this area."

Payton nodded. "And that is the crux of it. It's acceptable to help them, not befriend them."

Clay wasn't sure but he thought he saw a shiver of revulsion run through Payton. "Right. She's a decent person and doesn't look down on them because they're having a tough time. I find that quality admirable."

"Don't you see how that will reflect negatively on you? You help those people from a distance. You don't take them home to dinner." He picked up his sandwich and was poised for a bite when a blonde woman walked in the bakery and approached their table. Clay prepared for an autograph request but she walked straight to Payton.

"Mr. Smith! It is so good to see you again." She turned to Clay and held out her hand. "Gwen Banks from the Ocean Mist Gallery."

Clay shook the offered hand, looking between the new arrival and Payton. "Clay Masterson. Nice to meet you."

"The country music singer?" She smiled when Clay nodded. "I see you survived your ordeal with your fans. I didn't realize you and Mr. Smith were acquainted when he was in the gallery. It was the day you were accosted here and I was telling him about you."

"I've known Mr. Smith all my life and I'm fine. Thanks."

She looked to Payton. "So, have you returned for the angel painting?" She gave him a conspiratorial look. "I've had a great deal of interest since you were in. She won't last long."

Clay was staring at Payton, waiting for an explanation.

"Madam," Payton said, irritated. "My name is Shaw, not Smith, and I don't know what you're talking about."

She frowned. "I'm sorry to remember your name wrong, but I never forget a face. You were here a few weeks ago admiring Lisa Corolla's Angel. You planned to bring your wife Nadine for a look, you said."

Clay leaned on his elbows and raised his brow. "Is Nadine into angels?"

Payton's face was flushed and a nerve in his cheek bounced. "Oh. That painting. I'd forgotten which gallery you represent. I've changed my mind so if you'll excuse us..."

Gwen's smile was strained. "Yes, of course. I'm sorry to bother you." She turned and walked to the counter, her back straight.

Clay gave Payton a narrow-eyed glare. "So, you've never been here before? Two people recognize you, Payton. The woman even knows your wife's name. What I don't get is why you'd lie about it."

Payton blew out his breath. "Fine. I was here."

"And?"

"And what? I don't have to account to you for every moment of my time."

Clay resumed his crossed arm stance and stared at Payton. "You said you'd be here two weeks ago. If you don't want to help, say so," Clay said, his voice rising.

Payton leaned across the table. "Keep your voice down. If you must know, I was here. I did stop in the gallery to view a painting and I asked a few questions about your father."

"Okay. I'm still waiting for the reason you needed to lie."

Payton took a deep breath and let it out. "To protect you. I know how much these searches upset you so I came on my own to look around."

"Upset me? What am I, a hothouse orchid now?" Clay laughed. "I think I can handle it. What did you find?"

Payton looked at him with sympathy. "What we always find. What we will always find. Nothing. Hunt really is dead and it's time to let go. It isn't healthy for you to go on with this fantasy that your father is still alive. There is no way he survived the accident and to keep holding on to the idea is, well, ludicrous."

Clay put up his hand. "Whoa. Hold on a sec. If you think Dad is dead, who killed all those women? Who is sending the notes?"

Payton shrugged. "I don't know. Honestly, I don't. Maybe it's a copycat. Maybe it's coincidence."

"Coincidence? There were six women killed in the same way, in places my father has been seen." He frowned. "There is no way it's a coincidence. I'm convinced there is one killer."

"And that certainty is why the police have you on the suspect list, Clay. You handed them the evidence against you on a silver platter."

"Against me? I'm sending myself silly notes?"

"In a sad attempt to keep him alive." Payton reached across the table and grabbed Clay's wrist. "Don't you see what you're doing? No one can prove your father was in those cities where the murders occurred, but they can prove you were there. You need to let this go. The police will do their job and find the killer. Stop making it look like it's you."

Clay pulled his hand away. "That's crazy, Payton."

He shrugged. "Maybe so but it's how it looks. That's why I came here on my own. I needed to satisfy my own doubts, but I'm done now. I won't help you with this fool's errand again. Your father is dead. Accept it." He pushed back his chair. "This is the end for us, too. Continuing this friendship after your divorce was ill-advised and uncomfortable for my family. Crystal is in a serious relationship with Glen Carson now, and considering your association with Harlie, I'd say a friendship between us has become impossible."

"So you do know who Harlie is. Did Carson send you here to take her back to Seattle?"

Payton scowled. "Of course not. He and Crystal are making marriage plans. What would he want with her?" He tilted his head toward the kitchen.

So that was Crystal's project. Landing Glen Carson. Clay smiled. "Marriage plans, huh? Tell Christy I'm happy for her. If she gets her hooks into the Carson fortune, maybe she'll stop bugging me for money." This was the best news Clay had heard in a long time. Too bad it couldn't happen. "But you might want to tell her to hold off on booking the church for a while."

"Why is that?"

Clay leaned on his elbows. "Because Carson hasn't signed his divorce papers yet. He told Harlie he never would. It looks like you need to have a talk with your future son-in-law. And do it soon, would you? He's holding up my wedding plans, too."

Payton stood and pushed his chair to the table. "I don't believe a word of this. You can't handle the fact that Crystal has moved on any more than you can accept your father's death. I refuse to participate in this farce any longer. This is goodbye, Clay. Do not try to contact me again. Your call won't be welcome." He was out the door before Clay could say a word.

Clay sat for a while, mulling over Payton's loopy ideas. When he couldn't come to any logical conclusions, he went to the counter and rang the bell. Sam came out wiping her hands on a towel. He pulled his wallet from his pocket and grabbed some bills.

"Are you paying for both lunches?" She glanced to the empty table.

He smiled. "It appears that way. Is Harlie still around?"

She shook her head. "She wasn't feeling well and decided to take off. The stress of all this is really getting to her. I suggested she find Buck and watch some seagulls or something." She handed him his change.

"Watch seagulls?"

Sam smiled. "Yeah. It's something she and Buck like to do. They sit on the rocks down by the Angel and watch the seagulls. She says it's relaxing. She had some errands to run, too, so I don't know for sure where she went."

"She mentioned the errands. If she comes back, tell her I went home. She's supposed to call me when she's done."

As Clay walked to his vehicle, he saw Payton further up the street putting a large package in his car's
trunk. He shook his head. Even after their argument,
Payton took the time to shop for a painting. As
though feeling Clay's stare, Payton turned to him and
glared before climbing in his Mercedes. When Payton
drove by, Clay waited for the remorse over the lost
friendship to arrive. It didn't. He tried to feel something about his ex-wife finding another man. He
couldn't. The feeling he'd been had by a couple of con
artists crept in and stuck. He often wondered why
Payton had pursued his friendship after the divorce
and now he knew. Payton had harbored the idea Clay
and Crystal would get back together, but Payton
didn't need him anymore. Crystal had found their next
mark: Glen Carson.

"Good riddance," he muttered. The only downside
of this rift was the police. Payton was supposed to give
his statement regarding the search but Clay doubted
he could count on him now. Since Payton seemed to
have his own fantasy life perking along in full force, his
statement probably wouldn't help the situation. Clay
found his Jeep and drove the short distance to the
beach house. Harlie's car wasn't in the driveway. He
settled in front of his computer and had his e-mail
open when he heard a buzz from the security system.
On the screen: a middle-aged man with graying hair
and wearing a dark suit. "I'll open the gate, Detective.

Drive up to the larger house," Clay said over the intercom and wandered to the door to greet his visitor.

"Thanks for seeing me, Mr. Masterson," he said as he held out his hand.

Clay grasped the offered hand and stepped aside as the detective entered the house. "Any news yet?"

"Can we sit down?"

Clay led him to the living room where the detective took a seat in the recliner. Clay sat on the sofa. "Has someone seen him?"

Detective Ferrell shook his head and took out a pad and pen. Clay waited as the detective perused his notes. "Where were you the night of Myrna Snow's death? Around 10:00 p.m."

Clay frowned. "We already went over this at the station."

Detective Ferrell gave him a long look. "And we'll go over it again until I'm satisfied."

Clay leaned forward. "Satisfied about what?"

"That you didn't have anything to do with the murder of Myrna Snow."

"I didn't even know Myrna Snow," Clay said, irritated. "Why would I...this has got to be a joke. The only reason I know about her is through my girlfriend, Harlie Cates. She was friends with Myrna and told me about her death."

The detective scribbled in his pad. "No joke. Where were you the night she was murdered?"

Clay blew out his breath. "Right here. All night long."

"Alone?"

"For a while. I talked with Harlie on the beach in the late afternoon. I came home and had some dinner. I cleared some e-mail and worked on a song I'm writing."

"And that would take all evening?" Detective Ferrell said with doubt.

"The e-mail? I had over five thousand in my fan club account. It takes a while to answer them. Writing a song can take minutes, hours, or days. It depends on the song."

"And you did answer the e-mails? Not just delete?"

"Right."

"I may need to see your computer to verify that."

Clay tensed. "Do I need a lawyer?"

"That's up to you. You aren't charged with anything yet, Mr. Masterson. I'm only placing all the players."

Clay scowled. "The only reason I'm a player is because my father killed those women. I'm just the messenger."

"Maybe. Maybe not," Detective Ferrell said. "You said you weren't alone all evening."

"I wasn't. My ex-wife arrived around nine thirty. I already told you that."

Ferrell raised his brow. "Can you prove she was here?"

"She stayed the night on the sofa. Harlie talked to her in the morning. Ask Crystal. She'll tell you."

The detective sighed. "That's where we run into a problem. Your ex-wife denies your version of the evening."

"What's to deny? She was here."

"She isn't saying she wasn't here. She says she didn't arrive until after eleven. Myrna Snow was murdered around ten. If your ex-wife didn't arrive until eleven..."

Clay shook his head and laughed wryly. "Detective, my ex-wife is a habitual liar. She came here looking for money and when I wouldn't give it to her, she threatened to make my life miserable. I consider this her follow-through on the threat."

Ferrell looked skeptical. "We still have a problem with your whereabouts at ten."

"Not as far as I'm concerned. I was right here and my e-mails will prove it. Don't let Crystal's personal agenda cloud the truth."

"Do you use a laptop or desktop?"

"Laptop," Clay said and then realized why Ferrell asked. A laptop was portable and wasn't such a great alibi after all.

Ferrell gave him a long look, glanced at his notes, and moved to a new subject. "We've received the case files from the locations you mentioned and are comparing them."

Clay shrugged. "Okay. So you know each victim was murdered in an identical way. You know one person is responsible, right?"

"On the surface, it appears that way. As you said, all the victims were murdered with the same weapon, a guitar string. Other than that, the only common factor is you."

"I told you why I was in those cities. I received tips that my father was seen there." Clay leaned back and folded his arms across his chest. "I wasn't the only person there. Payton Shaw has assisted me in every search, including here in Angel Beach."

Ferrell nodded. "So you said. But we can't prove it." He looked at his notes again.

"He was there and here. Harlie can confirm it. So can Gwen Banks at the Ocean Mist Gallery. Both women saw him here several times within the last two weeks." Clay looked out the window and watched a seagull fly by. His head was beginning to pound and he doubted it was his hangover. "You do realize I was only eighteen when Lynette Dalton was murdered."

"I don't disagree that your father is the best suspect in her murder. But I don't believe the same person killed the others."

Clay snapped his attention back from the window. "But everything is the same."

"Someone wants us to believe it, but Lynette Dalton's murder is unique. She was violently assaulted prior to death. There were obvious signs of the fight and there were fingerprints found at the scene." The detective leaned forward. "Not so with the others. None of them were assaulted prior to strangulation and the crime scene was clean of evidence. The others appear well planned. The murderer probably wore gloves and went to a great deal of effort to not leave evidence. Lynette Dalton was a crime of passion. The others are facsimiles."

"And what reason have you come up with for me to do this?"

"Oh, just an idea I'm kicking around," Ferrell said. "Any chance you've seen the Hitchcock movie, *Psycho*?"

28

Harlie needed to tell Buck to get out of town if he hadn't already left. Her intuition wouldn't let her believe he was gone.

After leaving the bakery, she checked his usual haunts and couldn't find him. As she drove, she noticed an unusual number of police vehicles on the highway. It looked like a full-scale manhunt was on.

"He's innocent," she said, wishing she could tell the cops, but the best she could do was to warn Buck about Payton Shaw.

An hour later, Harlie parked at the Angel View Motel and Cabins. She stood in the weed-covered gravel and sighed. It wasn't the same without Buck. He'd planned to help her with the restoration and maintenance. He was an integral part of the project and now he was gone. With her shoulders slumped, she walked across the parking lot kicking at weeds. For the heck of it, she tried a few doors, hoping Buck had found a safe haven here. Unit one was locked up tight. She moved on to unit two, jiggled the handle and moved on. Three, four, five...all were locked. Six, seven...no luck.

Frustrated, she headed through the gap between the buildings, hoping to find Buck with a cigarette in his hand and his duffle between his feet.

She rounded the corner and saw the old deck was unoccupied. Everything was wrong now and she doubted it would be right again. Buck was gone for good and when Clay found out she knew Buck was his father, he would leave, too. She sat on the deck, leaned against the building, and stared out to sea, listening to the waves crashing incessantly below. Her world was crashing in much the same way. She leaned her chin against her knees and sighed. Maybe if she sat here long enough Buck would materialize and solve her problems.

A seagull landed on the deck and stared at her. She laughed and waved it away. "You aren't what I need right now." When her cell phone rang, she debated answering it but caller ID said Masterson. She had to answer it.

"Hey, Clay."

"Have you ever seen the movie, *Psycho*?"

"A long time ago. Why?" Another seagull swooped in and landed near Harlie's open purse. She shooed it away. Right now, her thoughts leaned toward Hitchcock and his birds.

"You know how the story goes, right? Norman Bates' mother dies and he goes crazy and pretends to be her."

"Right. What does this have to do with anything, Clay?" Maybe he was drunk again. He certainly sounded agitated.

He laughed. "Well, that detective, who is supposed to be looking for my dad, told me he thinks I'm the killer."

Harlie tensed and sat straight. "What? That's crazy."

"That's what I said. He says it's plausible since there's no proof my father is alive. None. All the evidence indicates he died eighteen years ago. So this detective thinks I flipped out and manufactured this whole thing. He says I'm impersonating my father so I don't have to admit he's dead. Can you believe that bullshit? He thinks I'm like Norman Bates."

Harlie rubbed her hand on her neck and frowned. "Oh man. Where did this idea come from?"

Clay laughed. "I have a real good idea. Ferrell says he got an anonymous tip and the guy spelled it out how I'm suffering from some sort of psychosis."

"Who would do something like that?"

"Payton gave me the same song and dance at lunch."

"Payton? I thought you were friends."

"So did I. It's a long story. I'll tell you when you get home. Where are you now?"

"Um...I just left the pharmacy and have another stop to make. I'll be there real soon." She cringed at the lie.

"I called Tom and he's bringing my attorneys out here...just in case."

"Clay, you won't need them," she said. "You're innocent."

"Thanks for the support, darlin'. You and I seem to be the only people in town who think so. My loving ex-wife is lying to the cops about the night she was here and Ferrell sounds like he believes her."

"Why is Crystal lying?"

"She and her father are working on a bit of character assassination together." He blew out a breath. "I need to go out and look around some more. I have to prove Dad was here before Ferrell locks me up."

"I'll be home soon. Wait for me, okay?"

"I can't sit here, Harlie. I need to move on this thing. That detective is serious about locking me up. Chances are good my attorneys can get me out, but I have to use the time I have."

"Clay! Please wait for me. We have to talk first," she said.

"About what?"

"I'll be right there. Wait for me."

He was silent, probably considering her request. "Okay. I'll wait. But I might go for a walk or something. I can't sit still. If I'm not at the house, I'll be on the beach. Call my cell."

He disconnected the call before Harlie could suggest Payton was the killer. First Payton tried to pin it on Buck and now, Clay. What was she supposed to do? She needed to tell Clay his father was alive but promised Buck she wouldn't tell.

She pounded her fist on the deck. "Damn you, Buck! Why didn't you do what you were supposed to?" There was only one thing she could do now. She had to tell Clay his father was alive and it wasn't something she wanted to tackle over the phone. She'd go home, tell Clay the truth, and they could look for Buck together. If they found him, she'd make Buck talk to Clay. The two of them could sort this mess out. She was tired of occupying the middle of the Masterson's dysfunctional family sandwich.

She got to her feet and headed back around the building, trying more doors. Near number twelve, the weeds were beat down and she wandered over for a look. Sure enough, the grass was matted as if someone had walked through. It was possible the cops had searched already. An unoccupied motel should be high on their list.

The units had solid wood doors. The windows were covered with heavy curtains. She couldn't peek in, so she pressed her ear to the door, listening and holding her breath. If Buck's boots had trampled the grass, she had nothing to worry about. He was innocent and wouldn't hurt her. But, there was Payton Shaw to think about. He'd made an offer on the motel. He knew it existed and knew it was unoccupied. Would he come here looking for Buck?

She clasped the doorknob and tried to turn it. Nothing happened. She tried again, rattling the old knob, pushing against the door with her shoulder. She blew out her breath and knocked into it again, grunting at a sharp pain. Still, nothing happened. She stepped back and inspected the flattened grass and the footprints in the gravel. Someone had been here, but who and when? And how did they get in without a key? The door must be unlocked.

She clasped the doorknob again, leaned against the door and shoved. With a loud creak, the door swung open, surprising her.

Late afternoon light illuminated the kitchenette unit but left eerie shadows in the corners. She stepped inside, glancing from side to side. Pressure against her tailbone startled her and sent her flying across the room. She couldn't stop her forward momentum and fell hard on the floor, her head slamming against a table. Sunlight streamed in, creating a silhouette of a man standing in the doorway. Blood trickled down her face and her head swam. She couldn't focus well enough to see his face. I'm dead, she thought, and everything went black.

29

Harlie's nose itched. It started with a twinge and progressed to an annoying tickle needing serious scratching. She wiggled it, which did nothing to alleviate the tingling. She turned her head and rubbed her nose against the pillow, stirring a musty smell. How long had it been since she'd changed her sheets? Too long, apparently.

The itch persisted and so did the stale odor. She tried to scratch her nose but couldn't move her arm. She could waggle her fingers and twist her hands at the wrist but couldn't move her arms. The right one was prickled with pins and needles. No wonder, since she was laying on it. She tried to move it and couldn't. She rolled to her stomach to take the pressure from her arm and realized both hands were restrained behind her back. She tried to kick her feet but couldn't separate them. She rolled again and tried to sit up but couldn't. There was something around her neck. Whatever it was gave her enough slack to roll over but not much more. She was leashed like a dog.

She swallowed hard and tried to fight the cascade of panic. She wasn't at home in her bed.

She remembered the man in the door, the one she couldn't see. The one who pushed her. Was it Glen?

She couldn't see and the pressure around her head felt like a blindfold. Glen hadn't done that before, but she supposed there was a first time for everything. Had he taken her back to Seattle? Was this the small, locked room at the back of his house? Is this what happened to the mysterious Cassandra? The panic wave increased.

She tried to take a deep breath. "One...two...three..." She fought the nausea swimming in her stomach. If she threw up, she'd have to lay in it. "Four...five...six..." The mildew smell was bad enough. She didn't want to make it worse. "Seven...eight...nine..." But she couldn't remember Glen's small room smelling of mildew. It was dry and clean. "Ten." She took a deep breath. Her face was bathed in sweat but the urge to throw up subsided. Her body shook with residual panic-attack tremors but she fought them, not wanting to surrender to the potentially debilitating assault. She could control this. She took a calming breath and tried to think of something pleasant. She imagined Buck's hearty laugh without the gravelly cough. But thinking of Buck made her angry. Buck took the easy way out and left her to deal with this problem alone. She thought of Clay and his beautiful smile and easy humor. But thinking of Clay made her heart heavy. She knew how he valued honesty and integrity. In that area, he was as rigid as a post and she'd lied to him about Buck.

Now Clay was under suspicion for the murders. If she'd told Clay about his father, she could have saved Clay from this ordeal. But saving Clay sacrificed Buck. "Oh, god," she muttered. Buck was gone. Clay could go to prison if his shark tank of lawyers couldn't get him off, and Harlie would spend her life locked in a small room. "I think I screwed myself more than anyone," she said. She tried to find a comfortable position, shifting from one place to another on the old mattress, and was close to frustrated tears when she heard a scrape.

And then, a groan.

Harlie froze and the hair on the back of her neck stood up.

"Who's there?" Her body was so tense, her muscles hurt. "I'll do whatever you want. Just tell me what it is."

The room remained quiet and Harlie wondered if she imagined the noises. Then she heard it again, a scrape and a moan.

"Who are you?" Her breath was coming in small gasps now. "What do you want?" She tried to swallow but her mouth was dry. "Whoever you are, please don't hurt me."

After a long silence, a gravelly male voice said, "I'm not gonna hurt you."

"You aren't? Why not?"

The man's laugh ended in a raspy, tired cough. "You sound disappointed, Angel Girl."

"Buck?"

"I don't know of anybody else who calls you Angel. You can relax, honey. I'm not gonna do anything to you."

"So why did you tie me up like this?" She wiggled again to see if the ropes would loosen. "It looks like you have some sort of plan."

"Nope. No plans," he said, his voice slurring. "I'm plumb out of plans."

Harlie frowned. "Are you drunk?"

"That sounds like a fine idea, but no. I'm not drunk." He wheezed and coughed.

"Well, you sound weird. Kind of puny."

He laughed. "You're always telling me I got emphysema. I'm starting to think you're right. I haven't been able to breathe right for a while now."

"So you didn't leave? Em told me you left town and weren't coming back."

"A man's conscience is a funny thing, Angel. You can try to fool it but the thing is smarter than you give it credit for." He took a loud, rickety breath. "I took the coward's way and left. Got out toward the Columbia Gorge and had an attack of conscience."

"What happened?"

"A kid from Yakima gave me a lesson in family responsibility. I decided I'd run long enough and came back to talk to the cops."

Harlie frowned. "But you didn't. You're hiding in here."

"Hadn't planned to."

"You aren't making any sense. If you don't have any nefarious plans, could you untie me so we can get out of here?"

He wheezed. "Can't."

"Why not?"

Buck laughed and coughed. "Cause I'm trussed up tighter than a hay bale. If I could move, I'd have found a more comfortable spot. This linoleum floor is cold and hard and my old bones are aching. The bastard even has me tied to the stove handle like a rabid dog. I'm not going anywhere."

Harlie gulped. "Who tied us up, Buck? Or should I call you Hunt?" She sighed. "I don't even know what to call you anymore."

"Buck is a better man than Hunt could ever be. Call me Buck."

"Okay. Buck. Who did this? I thought it was Glen, but he wouldn't have a reason to do anything to you."

"Who is Glen? I don't believe we've been introduced."

Harlie laughed. Even tied like a rolled roast, Buck could still make jokes. "Glen Carson. My ex-husband."

He whistled. "The dude with all the money? You were married to him?"

"Right. When I left he told me he'd never let me go. I thought he'd followed through on the threat."

"I don't know about that." He heaved a heavy sigh. "Tony is the only guy I've seen so far."

"Tony?" Harlie wiggled her hands. "We need to get out of here, but I can't get my hands free." She bucked and struggled against her bindings until breathing became hard.

"Keep trying, Angel. Tony never could tie a decent knot." He inhaled. "I'm kinda tired but I got a few things to tell you. I want somebody to know."

"We'll get out of here and you can tell the cops—"

"Just in case. I want you to know. I want you to tell Clay so he'll understand. I didn't mean to leave him. Not when he was two and not when he was eighteen. It's just how it turned out."

She stopped struggling and rested her head on the stale pillow. "That's not how he sees it. He had too much to drink the other night and he told me how much it hurt to know he wasn't enough to hold you. He thought if Ryan had lived, the two of them would have been important enough for you to stay. By himself, Clay wasn't enough."

Buck was silent a moment. When he spoke, his voice was weaker and she thought she heard him sniff. "Dumb kid has got it all wrong. It wasn't that he wasn't enough for me. Good lord, I knew I could never be enough for him. I couldn't give him what he'd need to grow into a good man. I wanted more for him."

"But you did go back," Harlie said. "When he was older. Tom says it was because he finally looked useful to you. His talent was obvious by then and you planned to ride his coattails to Nashville."

Buck blew out a breath. "I suppose it looked that way to some." He paused. "He was showing such incredible talent I couldn't help feeling proud of him and wanting a part of it. I thought I could help him get where he was heading. I'd been around Nashville a few times and had an idea of how things worked. I wanted to help him and try to make up for all those years I wasn't there."

"But Lynette died."

"Lynette was murdered and I was framed." He launched into a coughing fit. "Egad," he said with a groan. "She wanted my help. She called and asked if I'd come see her. When I got there she begged me to take her to Wyoming."

"Why would she do that?"

"Tony was going crazy. He had some idea that Lynette was going to tell his wife they'd been messing around. If Nadine knew about the affair, she'd toss Tony out and he'd be ruined." He took a breath. "Somehow, he found out I talked to her and dreamed up some story about me and her, and he convinced himself it was true. He says I tried to take her from him and he couldn't stand it. So, he stole the string off my guitar and killed her. When I heard all the evidence against me, I knew I couldn't fight it, so I left. When I heard they'd declared me dead, I decided it was best to go with it. Even if I was found innocent, all those accusations would follow Clay to Nashville and ruin his chances at success."

Harlie wiggled and rubbed her head against the mattress, chaffing her cheek, but the blindfold wouldn't budge. "Well, if she was having an affair with him, she must have liked the guy. Why would he think she'd cheat with you?"

"Tony has always been insecure. I tried to be his friend. Nobody else wanted to do it, so I took on the job when we were kids. But something went wrong. When he locked me in here yesterday I asked him when he'd started hating me."

"What did he say?"

Buck laughed. "He said he'd hated me from the day we met. I was everything he could never be. I was the kind of son his father wanted and Tony always hated me for it." He snorted derisively. "Wish I'd known that earlier—I wouldn't have wasted all that time on him." He groaned. "How you doing on those knots? Did you loosen them yet?"

Harlie shifted her shoulders and tried to pull her hands apart. "No. They're still tight."

"Keep trying. I'm tired, Angel, and there's more you should know. Don't let the cops take my duffle. There's nothing in there to concern them."

"Buck, you're innocent. We'll get out of here and Clay will help get you out of this mess. His lawyers are already on the way."

"Why's that?"

"Because Payton Shaw told the cops you're dead and Clay killed all those women. They've turned the investigation onto Clay."

"Good lord. The little bastard has gone crazy. First he frames me and now my kid. You should have stayed away from here, Angel. Now he's got you in the middle. When Tony unties you run as fast as you can and get away from here. He's already killed six women that I know of. He won't have a problem doing it again."

"Buck? Is Tony Payton Shaw?"

"Yeah."

"Then it wouldn't matter. I can place him here when Myrna was killed and he'd probably come after me anyway. He works for Glen Carson. I'm screwed either way." She tossed around on the mattress again, careful to avoid strangling herself. She kicked her feet, trying to pull the ropes. "What's the deal on your duffle?"

"Give it to Clay so he'll understand."

"Understand what?"

"Everything. Promise me you'll get it to him."

Harlie pulled her hands apart with a brisk yank, elated when the rope slackened. "Okay. I promise—" She heard a rattling and the doorknob turned. She froze. "Buck?"

"Shhh, Angel," Buck said. "When he unties you, do as I said and run."

Harlie knew the door had opened by the shift of shadow. She heard footsteps across the carpet and on the linoleum. He stopped and she heard a muffled thump.

Buck groaned and muttered, "You bastard. Kick me again and I'll break your leg."

"So, you're still alive. I didn't expect you to last so long," Payton Shaw said, sounding disappointed. "I even blindfolded her so she wouldn't have to look at you."

Buck groaned. "Leave her alone. She doesn't know anything."

"She knows enough."

Harlie heard footsteps across the floor and sensed Payton's presence next to the bed.

"What are you going to do with her, Tony?"

"We're going for a little ride but that's none of your concern, Hunt. You should be dead shortly anyway. And if you can't manage it on your own, I'll give you some help when I get back." He leaned against the mattress.

His soft hands were on her neck. She braced for his attack but he only scraped her skin as he removed the rope. She laid still, her hands held behind her back as if restrained. The longer she fooled Payton into believing her hands were firmly tied, the better her chance for escape. He moved to her feet and removed that restraint as well. Harlie held her breath waiting for him to do something. He yanked the blindfold from her eyes. She blinked and squeezed her eyes shut against the sudden burst of light. When she was able to focus, she saw Buck lying on the linoleum floor, his shirt soaked in blood and his face ashen. She tried to push past Payton. "Buck!"

Payton grabbed her by her shirt collar and said, "You can't help him now. Get up and get moving. Maybe you can save yourself."

The last thing she saw as Payton pulled her toward the door was Buck closing his eyes as his head lolled to the side.

30

It was two miles from his house to the Angel. Clay hadn't planned to walk that far but time got away from him while he waited for Harlie's call. She hadn't phoned yet. Now he stood with his hands on his hips, staring at the Angel monolith and wondering why they called that misshapen rock an angel. He'd heard some story that the position of the sun played a big part in it. Apparently, the sun wasn't in the right spot or he wasn't in the mood to see angels in rocks.

He considered turning back to see if Harlie was home, but he decided to climb the rock mound jutting from the sand near the Angel and find a place to sit. If Harlie found comfort in watching seagulls here, he'd give it a try. The muscles in his neck and shoulders were tense and he couldn't sit still. Maybe seagull surveillance would do something for him.

He grabbed a rock handhold, pulled himself to the top, and settled onto a smooth spot. A wave crashed, nearly wetting his feet before the tide slithered back out. As he got comfortable, his cell phone rang. Caller ID: Detective Ferrell. So much for tension relief.

"Detective Ferrell. It's a little late in the day, isn't it?"

"I wanted to ask you about your art collection."

Clay frowned. "What art collection?" Ferrell was running down a different rabbit hole now.

"What paintings do you own?"

"What does this have to do with anything?"

"Maybe something, Maybe nothing. Tell me about your paintings."

"I can't see where this is any of your business but if it's meaningful to you, I have two paintings in my house in Nashville. Both are painted by an artist who lives near Flathead Lake. One is a mountain scene I received as a gift from a friend. I liked the guy's work, so I hired him to paint a scene from my ranch in Montana. Other than that, I have a few gold and platinum records on the walls, some photos. But no art collection. I put my money into my charitable Foundation. Not art."

"What do you keep in your storeroom?"

"My storeroom?" he said with irritation. "Brooms and cleaning stuff for my housekeeper. My closets are full of clothes. What else would be in there?"

"Look, Mr. Masterson. You can cooperate and tell me what I need to know or I'll get a warrant and have your home searched."

The muscles in his neck tensed again. "I will say it again. I own two paintings of Montana scenery. Period. Whoever told you different is lying. Payton Shaw is an art collector. Talk to him. I have no use for the stuff."

Detective Ferrell was silent a moment. "Paintings were stolen from four of the murder victims."

"And you think I have them?"

"Nothing was stolen from Lynette Dalton's home, which again makes her the anomaly. There is no proof Myrna Snow had any art to steal. The closest thing we found was a gas company calendar with Norman Rockwell prints."

"And you think I did it? If I want art, I'll buy the stuff."

"Clay..."

"Are you on a first name basis with the other suspects?"

"There are no other suspects."

"Then call me Mr. Masterson. I don't see you and me becoming pals anytime soon."

"Mr. Masterson. I'm talking with you because you are the only person who can be placed in all locations. No other reason." He paused. "Most serial killers have set patterns. They do things exactly the same way each time. So far, Lynette Dalton is an anomaly in nearly every way except the murder weapon. With the next four victims, details are the same. Then, there is Myrna Snow. Identical except for the painting. You...or he," he hurried to add, "broke the pattern and I'm trying to figure out why."

"Not me," Clay said again. "Look, as much as I love talking with you, Detective, I need to get going." He glanced to the horizon; judging from the sun's descent he'd been sitting too long. When his gaze caught on the Angel, a thought occurred to him. Payton was an avid art collector. In fact, he said he visited galleries at each search location, just to relax, and usually had something shipped home. Maybe Payton wasn't buying paintings in those locations. Maybe he was stealing them. "But no painting was stolen from Myrna," he said.

"That's what I said and I can't figure out—"

"And not having a painting would break the killer's pattern. If he's as psychotic as you think, he'd have to have a painting, right? Like a souvenir of his victim? It would drive him crazy not to have one," Clay said with dread. "If he couldn't steal one, he'd have to buy one to satisfy his obsession and complete the pattern." Clay stood and jumped from the rock. He needed to get moving. Fast.

"What's your point?"

"A few hours ago, Myrna Snow's killer bought an angel painting at the Ocean Mist Gallery. I watched him carry it from the gallery and put it in his car." Clay was running now, heading to the Angel View-point trail.

"Who?"

"Payton Shaw. Talk to Gwen Banks at the gallery about the angel painting and she'll confirm it. The guy who bought that painting is your killer. I gotta go." Clay disconnected the call and tried to speed dial Harlie's cell. No answer. He ran up the trail as fast as he could. He had to find Harlie before Payton did. It all made sense now. Payton's rudeness at the bakery had nothing to do with her inappropriateness as a potential wife or the soup. Harlie could place Payton in Angel Beach. Harlie had made the connection and Payton knew it.

Harlie was also in the way of Crystal's marriage to Glen Carson.

It all made sense now. Payton hadn't befriended him in hopes of reuniting Clay with Crystal. He'd framed Hunt Masterson for Lynette's murder and wanted to continue tightening the noose around his neck. Each time Clay received a call about his father, Payton had dropped everything to aid the search. Payton was probably sending the notes to further implicate Clay's father. But why cut his ties to Clay now? They hadn't found Hunt yet.

At the top of the cliff, Clay stopped to catch his breath and think. He couldn't get Harlie on the phone, which could mean something or nothing. He wasn't taking a chance. Not after the way Payton looked at her. The evening sun was dropping on the horizon and the viewpoint area was empty. Clay made his way to the parking lot wondering where he should go from there. Angel Beach didn't have a taxi service so he'd need to hitchhike home and get his vehicle. He was passing the Angel information kiosk when he thought he heard a scream. He stopped and listened, waiting to hear it again.

"Damned seagulls," he muttered. He heard it again and swung around, looking for the source.

"No!"

A woman's voice.

He ran, looking around the parking lot and adjacent picnic area as he moved. Then he saw them, a gray-haired man and a dark-haired woman at the Angel View Motel. Payton and Harlie. Clay ran across the parking lot but was stopped by chain-link fence running from the cliff's edge to the highway. Even if he wanted to climb over, it wouldn't help. The Angel Viewpoint sat on a sharp pinnacle, jutting toward the ocean. A chasm at least a hundred feet wide separated the viewpoint from the motel. The only reason he heard Harlie's scream was the wind. From here, all he could do was watch as Payton dragged Harlie to his car.

Clay ran along the fence until he reached the highway, searching for a break when it joined the solid land. He continued along the viewpoint driveway as it meandered through the trees. Once on the highway, he ran. Cars honked and swerved to the center line.

When he reached the Angel View Motel entryway, Harlie was gone.

31

Harlie played along, clasping her hands behind her back as Payton dragged her across the weed-strewn gravel to his car. After dark, she had a sneaking suspicion she'd be dead, her body dumped in the woods. Buck said to get away as soon as possible, and for once, she didn't plan to argue. The thought of Buck, and her last glimpse of him, made her stomach lurch. He'd been gut shot and was bleeding. The wound soaked his shirt bright crimson. She wanted to question Payton but didn't. His current agitation level guaranteed a quick bullet if she angered him.

She held the rope draped across her wrists, creating the illusion of confinement. Payton was stronger than he looked, so Harlie bided her time and allowed him to tug her along. As they neared the car, highway traffic distracted him but only momentarily. Payton stopped near the Mercedes and looked her in the eyes. She didn't like what she saw.

"Don't move," he said.

Harlie remained still as he dug the keys from his pocket and unlocked the passenger door.

"Get in."

"Where are we going?"

He laughed without humor. "You'll see."

Harlie leaned into the low sedan, sucking in her breath when she saw an open guitar case in the back seat. In it lay Buck's acoustic guitar, its E string removed. Harlie had a feeling the string was close by and intended for her. She turned and sat on the seat, wiggling her hands to free them.

"Hurry up," he said looking around.

"Let's tie your hands behind your back and see how fast you can do this," she said as she lifted her feet into the car. Before Payton could slam the door, she freed her hands and swung her feet out, kicking Payton in the knees. He lost his balance and fell to the gravel with a thud. Harlie was on her feet and running toward the highway. If she could reach the road, she could flag down a car and get help. She thought she had a good lead on Payton and was unprepared when he did an end run and blocked the exit. He was panting and sweating, his pants bloody where his knee had contacted with the gravel.

"Get back in the car, Harlie." He pulled the handgun from his waistband and pointed it at her.

Harlie gulped and assessed her choices. She could get in the car, make her lunatic captor happy, and wait for guitar-string strangulation. She didn't know how long it took to die that way and she didn't want to find out. She could surprise Payton and run at him, tackling him in the gravel. Chances were good he'd shoot her. Or, she could turn and run. He'd probably shoot her in the back.

"Get in the car, Harlie," he said again. "You saw Hunt, right?" His face lit up. "I don't have a problem doing the same to you. Get in the car."

"No!" Harlie turned and ran. Getting shot in the back seemed preferable to strangulation. At least she wouldn't see it coming. From the look on Payton's face, he'd enjoy it too much and she wasn't going to play along. She heard him swear but he didn't shoot. He was behind her, running. She didn't turn to look for fear of tripping. The gravel was punctuated by grass clumps and she needed to keep her eyes sharp or she'd land on her face. She picked up speed and zigzagged, thankful for her plaid Converse All Stars. If she could get around the building, she might have a chance to hide. Some of the old carports were filled with junk: old carpet cleaners, brooms, mops, and trash cans. She could hide or possibly find a weapon. A broom wasn't much of a defense against a gun, but she'd take what she could get. As she rounded the corner, she glanced back. Payton wasn't there. When she saw the ocean-side deck, she knew why. He was waiting for her. He lunged. She dodged and ran toward the cliff, stopping at the dilapidated split-rail fence. She had nowhere to run except back to the building. Before she could make her move, Payton rushed her and grabbed her arm, twisting it behind her back. He pressed her against the rotting fence. The cliff edge loomed less than two feet away.

"Running was a bad move, Harlie." He twisted her arm and pressed her tighter to the fence.

Harlie closed her eyes and withheld her scream. One shove and she and the fence would be on the jagged rocks below. "It seemed like my only viable option at the time."

"You have no viable options. Now, we are turning around and walking to my car. If you run, I will shoot you this time. " With a rough yank, he pulled her from the fence, nearly knocking her to the ground in his anger.

"Let her go, Payton!"

Payton swung Harlie around. Clay leaned against the corner of the building. Sweat ran down his face and he panted heavily.

"Run, Clay! He has a gun!" Harlie yelled. Payton wrapped his arm around her, holding her tight to his chest. The gun rested on her ear and she felt the tension coursing through his body. He backed up a step, pulling Harlie with him.

"Do as she says, Clay, and leave while you can. This has nothing to do with you."

"When you have a gun stuck in my fiancé's ear, I'd say it has something to do with me." Clay took a step away from the building. "Harlie doesn't know anything about this mess, Payton."

"She's in the way!" Payton said.

"Of what?" Clay lifted his eyebrows. "Oh. Carson must have confirmed his divorce status." When Harlie looked at him with a questioning frown, he said, "Crystal wants to marry Glen Carson but he won't sign the divorce papers."

"She can have him," Harlie said with an eager nod. "Really."

Clay stepped forward. Payton shifted, shoving the gun tighter to Harlie's ear. She flinched when the cold steel bit her skin.

"Look," Clay continued, "I've been thinking about that problem and I have a solution for you. There's a reporter who has been hounding Harlie for a story on Carson. If he doesn't sign, we turn Skip Hyatt loose on him. Most likely he'd sign and Crystal can have the guy."

Payton shook his head. "No, he won't sign. He said Charlotte is the only woman for him and as long as she's alive, she'll be his wife. So, you see, I have no choice. She has to die so Crystal can marry Glen." He took a step, pulling Harlie along. "But not here."

Clay nodded. "Yeah, I get that. Killing her here breaks the pattern. Can't have that."

"What pattern?" Payton asked.

"You know," Clay said with a smile. "The pattern you've established with the victims. They all have to be strangled with a guitar string and only one per town. I see why you need to get Harlie out of here. Two bodies spoil the symmetry. If you kill two women in Angel Beach, you'd have to go back and kill another woman in each city. That would be kinda messy."

Payton tensed. "I don't know what you're talking about."

Clay nodded. "Sure you do but you can't kill everyone who knows. That would mean taking out Harlie, me, the Angel Beach PD, and probably the FBI. How much ammo you got with you? I'm thinking you'll need a hefty arsenal for that."

Harlie appreciated Clay's effort to distract Payton, but she really wondered about his methods. Was it wise to patronize a lunatic? "Clay, I don't know if this is helping," Harlie said through her clenched teeth.

"For once," Payton said, "I agree with her. I don't know what you're implying—"

Clay shrugged. "I'm not implying anything. You're a serial killer and the police are on to you. It was the paintings that gave you away. I feel like such a sucker. All those paintings you said you bought and all this time you were stealing them from your victims."

Payton started to argue, "That's not—"

"It sure is. Each victim's family reported a stolen painting. And you know what pulled it all together and pointed the finger at you? The Angel." Clay glanced over to the Angel rock formation. "If you'd been patient and waited for me to leave town, I wouldn't have seen you put the angel painting in your trunk."

Harlie gasped. "You bought Lisa's Angel?"

"He sure did. Right before I got here I had a nice little chat with Detective Ferrell and filled him in on it. He should be talking with the gallery owner right now." Clay smiled and shrugged. "So, give it up, dude. You can't get away. They know you killed all those women. I've seen the paintings in your office. You're toast."

Payton made a gurgling sound and loosened his grip on Harlie. She took advantage and twisted, elbowing him in the stomach. The gun fell to the ground. Before Payton could retrieve his weapon, she swung at him. He grabbed her arm and they tumbled over the crumbling fence. The last thing she saw was the horror on Clay's face as she and Payton fell over the cliff's edge.

∽

"Harlie!" Clay called as he ran to the edge. "Harlie!" His heart pounded as he looked to the jagged rocks below. He saw a body, sprawled on the rocks, bloody, battered, legs bent in odd angles.

"Harlie!" he cried out again. He couldn't see her. Had she fallen between the rocks? Was she in the water?

"Harlie!"

"Clay!"

"Harlie? Where—" He looked frantically. All he saw were rocks and ocean.

"Help me!"

Then he saw her in a scattering of obstinate shore pines growing from the rocks, their foothold on the rock face tenuous at best. Harlie hung from one, her leg swinging as she tried to get a better hold.

"Oh shit," Clay muttered. "Oh shit." His heart thumped hard. "Hang on, Harlie! I'll get you!" He surveyed the cliff and figured he could shimmy partway down and get hold of her somehow. Luckily, it wasn't a sharp drop, but a slope for twenty feet or so. Then, it dropped off right where Harlie clung to the tree. He'd need something to drop to her. A rope, but he didn't know if the motel had anything. Neither would Payton's Mercedes. He was on his own with nothing but his hands.

"Hang on, darlin'!" he called to her as he hung his feet over the side. Once on the rocky slant, he realized it was steeper than it looked, but he had no choice. He had to get her. An inch at a time, he worked his way down, careful to not kick rocks on her. Harlie was hanging on but a falling rock could knock her down. He was close enough to hear her frantic breathing.

Her hand slipped and she screamed.

"Hang on, Harlie! I'm almost there. Don't look down! Look at me!"

She did as he said and stared up at him. "Help me, Clay! I don't want to die!"

"You aren't going to die!" He inched down, making a foothold in the rocks for his boot heel. One foot at a time, inching along on his butt, keeping his eyes locked on her. "You're going to live a long, healthy life! We're getting married. We're having those babies we talked about. Four or so. I can't do that without you."

"You said you didn't remember!"

He laughed. "After the hangover settled, I remembered and I meant it." He moved a few inches more, sent a rock flying near her head. She cried out.

"You all right?"

"Yeah. It missed me. Hurry, Clay. I can't hold on much longer. Hurry!"

"I am! Hang on!" He reached the base of the slope, stopping on a rock above the sheer drop off. Harlie was below. He laid flat on the rock and stretched his hand to her. Even if she stretched as far as she could, he would miss her by about a foot. "I'm right here, darlin'. Don't panic. I'll get you."

She was clinging to the tree trunk. He could see blood on her hands, scrapes on her arms and forehead, and a bloody gash across her leg looked deep. Her face was pale and he hoped she hadn't lost much blood. If she went into shock, he'd have a heck of time getting her up the cliff.

"Reach up! See if you can reach me!" He stretched his hand and leaned as far as he could. He couldn't look down, not beyond Harlie. Seeing Payton's broken body drove home the spot they were in. She tried to reach up but nearly lost her balance.

"I can't do it! I'm going to fall if I let go!"

Clay let out the breath he held. He couldn't reach but his belt might be long enough. He unhooked it, slipped it off, and ran the leather though the buckle, making a loop. He wrapped the other end around his hand and suspended it to her, hoping he didn't drop it. The belt reached.

"Put your hand in the loop and grip the belt. I'll pull you up."

She let go of the tree with one hand, reached tentatively but didn't grab it.

"Come on, Harlie. Put your hand in the loop. It's the only way. I'll pull you up." He waited while she steeled her nerve. The belt dangled in front of her. She let go of the tree only to grab it again. She closed her eyes.

"I can't let go."

"You have to. Grab the belt. I'll pull you," he said again.

"What if you drop me? What if you—"

"Grab the belt."

She opened her eyes and looked at him, locking her gaze with his. Slowly, she released her grip on the tree with one hand and slipped it into the belt. Clay watched, holding his breath, hoping she didn't lose her balance. She tugged the belt.

"Okay. I'm going to pull you up. Let go of the tree."

She didn't.

"You have to trust me, Harlie. Just this once. Trust me."

Harlie took a breath and let go of the tree. Clay pulled. She pushed as much as she could with her feet, but the brunt of the work fell to him. He was sweating, muscles straining as he pulled, inching her up the cliff. The terror on Harlie's face mirrored his feelings. One slip and they were both over the side. Harlie found a handhold, steadied herself, found a place to dig her toe into the rocks for leverage. When her foot slipped, she gasped, "Oh no! My shoe! I lost my shoe!"

"It's just a shoe, Harlie."

She looked up at him. "It's not just a shoe! It's my plaid Converse All Stars! I love those shoes!"

"Focus on the problem, Harlie." He groaned as he pulled her up further. "Shoes can be replaced. You can't. I'll buy you some new shoes. Lots of them." Finally, when Clay thought his muscles would explode and his hand would break, she popped over the edge. He pulled her onto his rock perch, holding her tight in his arms. His breath came in gasps.

"I got you." He panted. "So far, so good." He gave a sigh of relief but it was too early to celebrate. Now, they had to work their way up the twenty-foot incline. Harlie's face was ashy and she was gasping. He kissed her. "No panic attacks, okay? I need all the help I can get now. Be strong and keep your hand in the belt. I'll hold the other end." He instructed her to hold onto him as he inched his way back up the slope. Her eyes were wide, her breathing uneven. A light sheen of sweat covered her face. He grabbed the waistband of her jeans and pulled her with him. "Stay with me. I've never known a more amazing woman than you. I know you can do this." Another couple of inches. Rocks scraped his hands. "I have some ideas for names."

"Names?"

"For the kids," he said, his breathing labored as he climbed, pulling Harlie along. He talked to keep her from thinking about what they were doing, to keep her from looking down and seeing Payton.

"I don't want any kids."

"Humor me. If we have a girl, I'm thinking Abigail after my mom."

Harlie nodded and moved up a few more inches, sliding her butt over a rock, wincing. "I suppose we could adopt," she said.

"Now you're thinking. For the boys, I'm thinking Ryan, after my brother. What names do you like?"

"Buck."

Clay frowned. "Okay. We'll work Buck in somewhere, too."

"Okay," she said with a nod. "Abigail. Ryan. Buck. Got it."

Clay grunted as he pulled her up more, scraping his hand again. He ignored it. "You doing all right?" he asked. She nodded. "We're almost there. You're doing great. Hang on." They were near the top. Clay stopped talking and concentrated on getting Harlie to the edge. Reaching it, he rolled, taking her with him, landing on his back. He held her tight.

"We made it," he said panting. "We did it."

Harlie shook in his arms. Her breath escaped in sharp gasps but she didn't give in to an attack. "I was so scared, Clay. I thought...I thought I was going to die." She clung to him and he to her. "I didn't push him. The cops will think I did."

"I know you didn't. He knew he was screwed and he jumped with a smile on his face." He kissed her forehead, squeezed her tight. "It's okay. It's over now. It's all over."

"No, it isn't," she said. "We have to go. Right now." She rolled from his arms to her hands and knees. When she stood, she swayed unsteadily. "Come on, Clay. We have to find him."

Clay was on his feet, ready to catch her if she fell. "Find who?" She swayed and he caught her. "Sit down, darlin'. I'll call the medics and get you taken care of." The gash in her leg was gruesome and needed tending.

"No, Clay. We have to go now." She took a step and faltered. "Go! You have to find him!"

"Who? Where?"

"Buck! He's in unit twelve. Go find him now."

"What's he doing there?"

"He's been shot and he's going to die if we don't hurry!" Harlie grabbed his shirt to steady herself. "Hurry!"

They limped along with Clay nearly carrying her. He wondered how Buck managed to get himself shot. Payton was the only guy with a gun. Why would he shoot the old man? Wrong place at the wrong time, maybe. As they neared number twelve, Harlie broke away and ran inside. When Clay reached the doorway, it took a moment for his eyes to adjust. When they did, he saw Harlie huddled over a gray-haired man whose flannel shirt was crusted with blood.

A flood of tears ran down Harlie's face. "Buck. Are you okay? Please don't be dead. Please."

The old man's eye lids fluttered open. "I'm not...yet. Too stubborn to die..."

Clay heard Buck's voice and froze.

Harlie looked up and yelled, "Call 9-1-1, Clay! He needs help."

Clay clenched his fists but didn't move.

"Clay! Call now! He's going to die!" She looked at him with exasperation but Clay didn't move. "Damn it! If you don't call right now your father will die!"

His gaze met hers. How long had she known Buck was Hunt Masterson? Quite a while from the look of it.

"You said you didn't want your father dead! Prove it! Don't let Buck die, Clay! Please." She held Buck's head in her lap. Tears streamed down her face. "Please, Clay. He's like the father I never had. Don't let him die. Please!"

"Lucky you," Clay said as he reached for his phone. "He is the father I never had."

32

"I'm fine, Wayne. Really, I am," Harlie said as Wayne Tipton examined the emergency room physician's handiwork on her leg. The unsightly gash was nicely stitched and Wayne nodded his approval. "Will you stop poking at it? I want to put my clothes back on and get rid of this horrible gown."

Wayne stepped back. "You need to go home. I'm finished with my rounds so I can drive you."

Harlie sat up, adjusting the hospital's idea of clothing. "I can't. I need to see Clay and find out how Buck is. Any chance you can find out for me?"

A slight frown marred his face but he didn't comment on her relationship with Clay. "I already checked," he said. "He's still in surgery but doing fine so far."

"I'm so glad. I thought he was dead." She let out a sigh of relief and gave Wayne an indignant stare. "Go. I need to get dressed."

He smiled. "I'm a doctor. I doubt you have anything I haven't seen before."

"But you aren't seeing it on me. Go away."

"You're sure?"

Harlie nodded, making her curly hair bounce. "Yes. I'm fine." She reached for him and gave him a hug. "Thanks for being here, Wayne. You're a good friend. Now, go away."

He smiled and headed for the door. "Call me if you need anything."

After she dressed, Harlie made her way to the surgical waiting room with Buck's duffle in hand. The lights were low, reflecting dimly off the pale green walls. Clay sat in the corner, legs stretched out, arms across his chest, head back, and he looked like he'd been through a battle. Now that she had a good look at him, she saw how their climb had mangled him. His jeans were torn at the knee and his right arm had a cut coated in dried blood. His right hand had a red abrasion from the belt. At some point he'd probably run his hands through his hair, which now stood up in odd patches. Dirt smeared his bearded cheek and his boots were more scuffed than usual. She wanted to hug him, to run her fingers through that messy hair and straighten it.

She wanted him to hold her and tell her it was going to be okay, that they would be okay. She wanted to hear again how they would be married and have a bunch of kids together. She wanted to hear him say "I love you" one more time. But he wouldn't. Not now. She knew their relationship was doomed the moment she didn't confess her knowledge of Hunt Masterson's return from the dead.

It was late, nearly ten, but she doubted he was asleep. She knew him well enough to recognize the change sleep brought to his breathing, the relaxed rise and fall of his chest. She didn't see that now. He was tense and feigning sleep. She sat in the chair next to him and tucked Buck's duffle between her feet like she'd seen her friend do so many times. Clay opened one eye and closed it.

"I know you're awake." Harlie waited for him to say something. If he yelled and screamed at her it would be better than this painful silence.

"When did you know?" he said.

"What?"

"The million-dollar question. When did you know Buck was my dad? Did you know all along? Maybe this was a little joke the two of you were playing on me? Let's see how long we can string the sucker along."

"No, that's not the way it was, Clay."

"Looks like it. I just can't figure out why."

She twisted her fingers together. How could she make him believe her now? "I didn't know until we got back from Seattle."

"And he told you?"

"No. He was at the motel, playing a song on his guitar I recognized. "'The Protest Song,' you called it." She turned to Clay, hoping he would look at her.

He opened his eyes and she saw fire, not forgiveness. "Two days ago. You knew for two days and didn't tell me. You let Ferrell accuse me of the murders knowing my dad was alive," he said with undisguised anger. "You let him put me through the ringer to save his lying carcass. Why, Harlie?" He looked at her now, his eyes filled with fury and hurt. "I thought I meant something to you."

"You do, but so does he."

"Right. The father you never had. Well, join the club, darlin'. I never had one either."

Harlie sighed. She knew this would be hard. "He feels bad about that. But he loves you. That's why he stayed away."

Clay stared straight ahead. "Yeah. Neglect is a sure sign of parental love."

"He does, Clay. He loves you a lot." She reached her hand toward him but stopped, knowing he wouldn't welcome her traitorous touch. "So do I."

Clay clenched his jaw but remained silent. Knowing he wouldn't bend, she grabbed Buck's bag and stood. "I need to go. I told Detective Ferrell I'd give him my statement before I left. He's waiting in the cafeteria."

He looked at her. "You should have been honest with me. None of this would have happened if you'd told me sooner."

"Maybe," she said. "Or maybe Buck would go to prison for something he didn't do and Payton would go free."

"Why would you lie for him? You could be considered an accessory if he's convicted."

"Maybe it worked out the way it was supposed to. They know Payton is responsible."

Clay shrugged. "We aren't clear yet. The detective wants proof of Payton's guilt. Right now it's our word on it."

"The paintings should prove it."

Clay nodded. "They should prove he killed the others but not Lynette and Myrna. Dad's prints were found at both places. He drank a beer in each house. Payton didn't steal anything from Lynette, and Ferrell says connecting the angel painting to Myrna's death is speculation."

"What about the second fingerprint on the beer can at Lynette's? Did they check it against Payton's fingerprints?"

"I don't know."

"So you'll help Buck?" she said.

"He's my father. I suppose I have to help him."

"But you don't want to."

He gave her an exasperated look. "I don't even know him. We share DNA and some disjointed history. That's about it."

"He's your father—"

"Biologically speaking, yes. I'll do what I can for him, which is more than he ever did for me."

"He knows you're bitter—"

"Bitter is putting it mildly."

Harlie gritted her teeth. She knew Clay was hurting and needed time to reconcile himself to his father's return. "I have to go. Will you call me when he's out of surgery?"

He nodded.

Harlie stood a moment, debating. She wanted to wrap her arms around him and tell him how much she loved him, but he was closed off. Knowing she deserved his animosity didn't make it easier. She'd known how he would react to her lies and she couldn't condemn him for being predictable. Harlie turned to leave but stopped when the weight in her hand reminded her of a promise. She stepped back and handed the duffle to Clay.

He frowned at the dingy, worn-out bag. "What this?"

"It's Buck's. When we were in the motel room, he told me he didn't want the cops to have it. He said to make sure you got it so you would understand."

Clay dropped it on the chair next to him, dismissively.

"You'll open it, won't you?"

"Later."

Harlie resisted the tears pricking her eyelids. The rift between Clay and Buck might be too huge to mend and the fissure between her and Clay was growing by the minute. "Soon, okay? It's important to him, Clay. Really important."

He glanced at the bag. "Why? What's in it?"

"I don't know. But whatever it is means everything to him. I've never seen Buck when he didn't have that duffle in his hand. When he sat down, he always placed it between his feet. He never let it out of his sight. The way he guarded it, I always wondered if it held gold or some sort of treasure. Whatever it contains is especially dear to him." She glanced at her watch. "I have to find Detective Ferrell. I'll check back when I'm done."

An hour later, she'd told Detective Ferrell everything she knew and returned to the surgery waiting room to check on Buck's progress and Clay's mood. She hoped he'd had time to think this through and could see Buck wasn't a monster. When she stepped in the waiting room door she saw Clay wasn't alone. Five chairs were drawn into a circle around Clay's corner. In them sat Harv Stockton, Tom Black, and three men in suits who looked like lawyers. Clay's army was amassing to save him. She wished she could help, but try as she might, she couldn't summon the strength tonight.

The men were huddled together, deep in conversation. Harlie waited, hoping Clay would see and invite her in. She imagined him looking up and holding his hand to her, welcoming her into his inner circle. After a minute, he did look up and his eyes locked with hers. She wasn't sure what she saw there but it was fleeting. He looked away and said something to Tom, tilting his head toward Harlie. Tom nodded and stood. Clay went back to his conversation without another glance her way. Harlie's heart dropped to her knees when Tom Black walked toward her and not Clay.

"Hi, Tom. Any word on Buck?" she said with false cheerfulness when inside she was dying.

He glanced over his shoulder at the men and indicated he and Harlie should step to the hall. Confused, she followed. "He's out of surgery and doing well. The detective posted a guard at his room and said only Clay can see him."

"A guard? But he's innocent."

"They don't know that for sure. And from what I've heard, when the manhunt started, the news that Hunt is a serial killer was broadcast across the country. The guard is also for his protection. There are some people who will take the law in their own hands."

"And I can't see him either?"

Tom shook his head. Harlie bit her lip to hide her disappointment. Though she thought of Buck as a father, she wasn't family. "So, are those guys the shark tank?"

Tom laughed. "Yeah. As soon as Clay called, I chartered a flight and got everyone together. They're here for both Clay and Hunt, so don't worry. He'll have the best representation Clay can afford. They're grilling Clay for info right now and he probably won't be done soon."

There it was: the brush-off. Tom was on duty as Clay's head of security and she was being ushered out of the building. "I'm tired and need to go home anyway. Tell Clay to give me a call later. Okay?"

Tom nodded but wouldn't meet her eyes. "Sure. I'll tell him." He turned and went back in the room, taking his seat near Clay.

Harlie waited in the doorway, hoping Clay would look up. He didn't. It was then she knew what Clay had said to Tom before sending him out. Get rid of her.

33

It was midnight. Harv and the attorneys were on their way to a hotel and Clay wished Tom had gone with them. He was tired of talking and didn't want to answer any questions. Tom seemed to get this and concentrated on a magazine. When Clay noticed the cover, he laughed.

"Into *Cosmo*, are you, bro?"

Tom looked up at him, wide eyed. "Have you ever read one of these things?" he said with awe. "There is info in here most men only dream of knowing. I think I need a subscription to this."

"Like you need help with women," Clay said with a laugh that turned into a sigh. Tom wasn't the one who needed help with women. It was Clay who chose the most inappropriate, dishonest women in the world. And the funny thing was, he could have his pick of women. So how had he ended up with Crystal and Harlie? At the thought of Harlie, he felt a tug in his chest. He knew how he ended up with Harlie and given the chance, he'd probably repeat the mistake again. For now, he'd keep his distance. If she lied to him about his dad, there was no telling what lies she'd tell next.

He needed to take a tip from Tom's love-life manual. He was a champ at short-term relationships. No woman got close to Tom's heart and he planned to keep it that way. Tom held the magazine for Clay to see.

"Take a look at this." He turned the magazine to different angles. "There's stuff in here I never thought of before." He turned it again. "Is that even physically possible?"

Clay smiled and waved the magazine away when Tom tried to hand it his way. "Spare me the details. Right now, I'm contemplating life in a monastery."

"Mr. Masterson?" A young nurse in flowered scrubs stood in the waiting room doorway. "Your father is in his room if you'd like to see him."

Clay stood, picking up the green duffle. "Is he awake?" He stretched his back as he walked to her.

She shook her head. "No. But you're welcome to sit with him if you like."

Clay nodded. "All right. Tom," he said but stopped when he saw his foster brother's wide eyes. Apparently, *Cosmo* was full of wonders. He looked at the nurse. "Could you tell him where I went?"

She smiled. "Sure. Follow me."

Clay stood in his father's doorway, frozen in the same manner as he'd been at the motel. The sight of his father stunned him. Hunt had been considered dead for so long it was a little freaky to see him alive and breathing. Clay unwound from his shock and sat in the chair next to the bed.

The beard and mustache were gone and he looked more like the Hunt Masterson Clay remembered. If he'd seen him clean-shaven he might have recognized him earlier. The long hair pulled back in a ponytail had been surprise. Last time he'd seen his father, he'd had short blond hair, no beard, and no wrinkles. Now, his face was lined, his eyes accented by crow's feet, and his hands were roughened from the weather. Calluses on his fingers proved he still played a guitar.

The sight of him made Clay angry. For years, he'd tried to tell himself he didn't care anymore. It didn't matter that his father had abandoned him and faked his own death. All Clay knew was this man didn't want his son around. No matter how much Harlie tried to convince him otherwise, Clay knew Hunt didn't care about him. It was probably another of her lies.

Hunt moaned and licked his lips but didn't wake up. Clay wasn't sure why he was waiting around. He didn't want to talk to him. Sure, he'd pay his legal bills and do what he could to get him freed—if he was innocent—but he didn't want to spend any quality father-son time with the guy. Clay leaned back in the chair and tried to relax. The evidence still pointed at him in Lynette's murder even though the police now knew Payton killed the others. He knew Lynette had been Payton's high school sweetheart but the romance soured and he married Nadine. There were two possibilities. First, there was Payton's version. Hunt was involved in a relationship gone bad and he killed her. The other direction pointed straight to Payton. There were rumors Payton married Nadine for her family's money and connections. Considering everything he'd learned about Payton today, the theory was possible. There had been a man visiting Lynette for several weeks prior to her murder. Was it Payton? The other beer-can fingerprint might answer that. If Payton moved the can from the trash to further incriminate Hunt, his print could be on it, too. Clay was tired of thinking about it and considered going home.

But home meant Harlie and he didn't want to see a woman he couldn't trust.

He yawned and stretched, sending the duffle to the floor. With a tired sigh he bent and picked it up. The bag was a grubby, worn out old thing and he couldn't figure out what was so special about it. The handle was frayed and the color faded. He scrunched it with his hands, trying to figure out what was in it. He couldn't tell so he unzipped it and peered inside, frowning at the jumbled pile. It looked like his father's CD collection and junk mail. Why would that be precious to him? Clay shifted his chair closer to the dim bedside light and pulled out a CD. Then another and another. He piled them up and dug out the rest. When he had them all, he laid them on the table in chronological order and stared in disbelief at the complete Clay Masterson music collection. Eighteen years worth. Even the Christmas album he'd put out a few years ago.

He stacked them back up and took more items from the bag. A lump formed in his throat when he saw copies of country music magazine articles featuring himself, printed website pages, copies of his tour schedules, and a black T-shirt from one of those tours. There were newspaper stories, top-forty listings with Clay Masterson in the number-one spot, a promotional guitar pick with Clay's name on it, and the pictures of his house from some women's magazine spread. Next he found a photo of himself, framed and autographed. He swallowed hard and removed the last of his father's treasure: e-mails to and from Clay. His hands shook when he saw the screen name: Countryman.

"Ah, shit," Clay muttered as he flipped through the pages of printed e-mails. Most were commentary on his performances. Some contained guitar advice from a man who talked like he knew Clay's style intimately. Of course he did. He taught Clay to play. Now that he knew the author, some of the comments took on more meaning. Hunt Masterson was giving fatherly advice to his son and Clay had missed it. Or had he? Hadn't he watched for correspondence from Countryman? Hadn't he worried when months went by and Countryman was silent? Hadn't he smiled when an e-mail finally arrived? He read the familiar e-mails, catching nuances he'd missed before, recognizing his father in every word. When he reached the last one, his eyes filled with tears at what Countryman said: "I'd be proud to have a son like you but I'm content being your biggest fan. Countryman."

In the e-mails he thought he saw the man Harlie knew. He remembered how her face lit up when she talked about her good friend, Buck. He was her buddy, her helper, the man who filled a void in her life. Through the e-mails, Hunt had tried to do the same for his son. With shaking hands, Clay returned the items to the bag and zipped it. He sat for a moment holding it in his lap and thought about Harlie's comment: Whatever the bag contains is especially dear to him. Buck always had the bag with him. He always kept it between his feet, guarding it as if it held treasure. Clay picked up the bag and slid it between his feet. He agreed with her assessment. The bag did hold treasure.

It held the father he never knew.

He drifted into sleep, startled awake when his father coughed. Clay fought to focus, his mind heavily clouded. Hunt was staring at him with a quizzical look in his eyes.

"Lordy. Is that you, Clay, or am I dreaming?" His smile was weak but sincere.

"It's me." Clay shook his head and tried to clear the cobwebs.

"Got anything to drink?" He stuck out his tongue and tried to lick his lips. The gesture made him appear older than his sixty-two years.

"Water," Clay said as he reached for a cup and straw.

"That's the stuff."

Clay leaned across the bed and held the straw to Hunt's mouth. When he finished a sip, Hunt leaned his head on the pillow and tried to focus on Clay. "What happened? You look like crap."

"I could say the same about you."

Hunt groaned and shifted. "At least I'm not dead."

"No." Clay thought about the duffle bag and its contents. "You aren't dead anymore."

34

Harlie had to give Tom Black credit. He was proficient at following orders. If Clay wanted her out of his life, Tom made sure she was out. If she called Clay, Tom answered. If she went to the hospital, Tom met her at the door.

The bad part was that Harlie knew she deserved it. She knew it would come to this and accepted the blame for the whole mess. But she hadn't anticipated this level of heartache. She hadn't expected Clay to shut her out before she could apologize. That weight around her heart was tearing her to pieces. If she could explain it to Clay, tell him she was keeping a promise to Buck, maybe everything would be okay.

But maybe Clay knew her better than she thought. He had probably figured out she'd do what she could to protect Buck or any other friend in need. Since it wasn't her only transgression, Clay had good reason to grow leery of her. There was that whole red-dress and sexy-kiss debacle.

But that was one heck of a good kiss and she'd do that again, too, if she had the chance.

She sighed as she parked her Smart Car near her cottage. There were a lot of things she'd do if she had the chance. She'd tell Clay she loved him, for one. Not that he'd listen now.

She grabbed a grocery bag from the passenger seat and climbed from the car. As she slammed the door, she glanced down the driveway and noticed an open door at Clay's house. His Jeep was parked by the garage. Her heart fluttered and her mind whirled with possibilities. She unlocked her cottage and set the grocery bag and her purse on the kitchen counter. A quick look in the bathroom mirror had her pulling the rubber band from her hair and unleashing the curls.

"Whatever it takes," she said. Her T-shirt was spotted with frosting. She grabbed a blouse from the closet and put it on. Her jeans were acceptable. Her shoes were not Converse but would have to do. She may deserve Clay's cold shoulder but she wasn't accepting permanent banishment from his life without a fight. She'd corner him and make him listen to her. She at least deserved a face-to-face breakup.

The door to Clay's house was still open when she arrived. A knock would alert him to her presence, so she snuck in and checked the kitchen, the living room, and the downstairs bathroom. When she didn't find him, she ran up the stairs, considering it lucky she might find him in the bedroom. She'd give him a big kiss, drag him to bed, and let their pheromones take over.

The light was on in Clay's room. She stopped in the hall and took a big breath before stepping in and saying, "Clay..." Her voice trailed off when the man who turned toward her had black hair, not sandy-blond. He was a couple of inches shorter and had a limp when he walked, too.

Definitely not Clay.

"Tom," she said with a forced smile. "Is Clay with you?"

He shook his head. "No. He's at the hospital."

Harlie watched him fold Clay's shirt and put it in the open suitcase on the bed. Her heart dropped to her knees. "He isn't coming back, is he? If you're packing his stuff..."

Tom shrugged. "He needed clothes and I offered to come out."

"So, you aren't taking everything? He'll be back?"

Tom hesitated. "He asked me to get everything. Just to make things easier..."

Harlie pasted a smile on her face. "I imagine with everything going on, it is easier for him. I've said it before, he's lucky to have you, Tom." She swallowed hard. "How is Buck? Do they still think he did it?"

Tom smiled. "Hunt...or Buck—I'm not used to that yet—is pretty much the way I remembered him. Kind of crusty and opinionated."

Harlie fought the tears that welled in her eyes. It had only been a week but she missed Buck so much. "Yeah. That's Buck. He has an opinion on just about every subject and he likes to share it with anyone who will listen."

"I've noticed." Tom grabbed Clay's spare boots and dropped them in a paper sack. "He says he's innocent and Clay is inclined to believe him. He says Payton framed him and he ran because he didn't figure he could get out of it. He didn't even know about the other deaths until a trucker told him about a news story. The attorneys are working the Payton angle pretty heavy. The police have the paintings from Payton's office and they match the reports. They ran the fingerprint on the beer can in Montana and it is Payton's. Between your statement and other witnesses, Payton can be placed in Angel Beach at the time of Myrna Snow's death. It's all coming together." He folded another shirt and set it in the suitcase before locking it. "That's it. I already have the rest in the Jeep."

He looked at Harlie and she could see sympathy in his eyes. Maybe Tom wasn't the cold-hearted villain she thought him. He was Clay's loyal brother and best friend.

"Clay is preoccupied right now with the police and his dad and everything. I'm sure he'll call you as soon as he has a chance."

Harlie shook her head. "No, he won't."

"He will—"

"It's okay, Tom. I knew it wouldn't last. I knew all his talk of marriage and a future together would never happen and it's okay. It's probably better this way for both of us. We can get on with the lives we were intended to live and not hang on to a fairy tale."

Tom gave her a long look and Harlie worried her tough façade would break. If her lip quivered, she was a goner. Quivering lips and tears were always a package deal.

"He'll get over this and call you. You'll see."

Harlie shrugged. "I lied to him and now I have to live with the fallout." She picked up the paper sack and handed it to Tom. "Have a safe trip. And tell Clay—"

"You love him?"

She nodded. "And I'm sorry."

"I'll tell him."

He set the suitcase and sack near his feet and surprised Harlie by wrapping her in a brotherly hug. His arms were strong, warm, and comforting. Tom stepped back and gave her a cheerless smile. "I wish it had turned out different for you two. I think you're the best thing that ever happened to him. Right now, he's too pigheaded to see it." Tom picked up the suitcase and sack and headed out before Harlie could respond. At the slam of the Jeep's doors, she walked to the window and watched as her last connection to Clay drove out. She looked around at the empty space, much too quiet and lonely now, and decided to leave before she became sappy with grief. With Clay gone, it was as if a vacuum had occurred in the house. Even her shoes didn't make a sound on the hardwood floor.

As she neared the door, she stopped for one last look at the bed they'd shared and noticed something underneath. She kneeled on the area rug and grabbed one of Clay's black T-shirts from its hiding place under the bed. It was too late to catch Tom, and she figured Clay could buy a million other T-shirts. She'd keep this one as a souvenir.

She stared at the shirt and remembered the last time he'd worn it, how his arms strained the sleeve, how yummy he looked when she peeled it from him. Not a bad memory to tuck away for those long winter nights. She tossed the shirt over her shoulder, stood, and straightened her spine before walking through Clay's house for the last time.

She locked the door behind her and wandered home. The late afternoon air was brisk but not unpleasant. On the porch at home, Spud rolled to his back, writhing in invitation for her to scratch his belly. Harlie bent and accommodated the large white cat with a smile.

He was the best man in her life now. Not the only one, but the best. She still had Glen and his unwillingness to sign the divorce papers to contend with, and she was sure Skippy the Bloodhound was just taking a break from his quest for a story.

Harlie finished Spud's belly massage and went into the cottage. There wasn't much she could do today about either Glen or Skip, so she'd forget both for now. Late afternoon sun streamed through the window panes, highlighting her favorite chair. She slid a CD in the player and plopped into the chair. She grabbed Clay's T-shirt from her shoulder and breathed deep while his beautiful voice filled the room.

Glen and Skip could wait. Right now, she needed to spend some quality time with a great smelling T-shirt and a few well-deserved tears.

35

"And that wraps it up." Skip Hyatt turned off his recorder and closed his notebook. "I can't tell you how much I appreciate this, Harlie. I knew Glen Carson's golden-boy persona was an act and this info, along with Cassandra Hale's corroboration, is what I needed to prove it."

After Harlie told Skip about the mysterious Cassandra, he'd found her, alive and well in Idaho. Her story was simple: After Glen discovered Harlie, he'd tossed Cassandra out on the street. Harlie said quietly, "This has been difficult, but it had to be done. Maybe I can save someone else from going through what she and I did." Harlie nearly laughed at the irony of the situation. If anyone deserved to be locked in a small room, it was Crystal Masterson. But Harlie wasn't the vindictive kind. She helped whomever she could, and sometimes, people like Crystal inadvertently benefited.

Skip leaned forward and gave her an earnest smile. "What you told me validates my existing research. And after this story runs, Glen Carson is through toying with people." He took her hand and squeezed. "So, the divorce is final?"

She nodded. "Last week. It took some high-powered lawyers, but he finally signed." They were the best cutthroat divorce lawyers Seattle had to offer and Clay's money could buy. He was true to his word and did get her divorced. Too bad she couldn't thank him for it. Her only contact with him in the last three months was watching him perform on the Grand Ol' Opry. It wasn't just Clay, but Buck, too, harmonizing a new song, "Angel Girl," that quickly climbed the charts. When introducing the song, Clay explained how his father wrote it and deserved all the credit, not him, and her hope bubble burst. This wasn't the angel song Clay wrote about them. If she hadn't seen the camaraderie between father and son on stage, she might have cried. But her loss was Buck's gain. And her own, too. Seeing the love in Buck's eyes when he looked at his son made Harlie think she'd underestimated the whole parental bonding thing, and that reestablished father-son bond prompted Harlie to make a phone call.

"Mama? It's me, Harlie," was how it began. Tears prickled her eyes when she thought of it and the reunion that followed. Like Clay and Buck, Harlie and her mom where making the effort to heal.

She returned from her reverie and noticed Skip's hand was still on hers. He was a bear of a man and had large hands to match.

"Can I take you out to dinner tonight? We'll celebrate the completion of our interviews and maybe," he said with a smile, "see where things go."

Harlie returned the smile but shook her head. "That sounds nice but I can't." She pulled her hand from his. "I'm on the rebound right now and you know what they say about rebound dates." She shrugged. "It wouldn't be fair to you."

Skip sighed but his smile remained. "You can't blame me for trying. When you get over him, give me a call." He collected his things from the table and stood to leave. "I'll let you know when the articles run. Thanks again, Harlie. I enjoyed getting to know you."

After he walked out the door, Harlie blew out her breath. It was done. The chains were removed. When Skip's articles went to press, Glen Carson's monstrous behavior would be exposed and her freedom restored. Maybe it was time for the Smart Car to go, too. With her confession to Skip, her quiet rebellion against Glen was over. Her little escape pod had done its job. She considered volunteering with the foster parent program and a larger vehicle would be more practical. Harlie stared into space and was startled when Lisa sat in the chair vacated by Skip.

"All done?" Harlie nodded and Lisa said, "Then why don't you go home. It's almost closing time and I know how to close."

"I guess I could if you are sure you'll be okay." Harlie let out a tired breath. Lethargy was her constant companion these days. "Be sure to lock the back door when you go."

Lisa smiled. "Yes, boss. Now, get out of here."

Harlie did as she was told and grabbed her jacket from the office closet. Lisa was in the kitchen washing counters as Harlie headed toward the door. "When is the gallery show?"

"Gwen said it would open in two weeks. Can you believe it? I'm having my own show." Lisa giggled with excitement.

"I've always believed it would happen. You're extremely talented."

Lisa stopped scrubbing. "All the national coverage of the stolen artwork really boosted interest in my work. Gwen said she's had a lot of callers wanting to know what else I've done." She frowned. "It's creepy that a serial killer liked my painting though. Does this mean I tap into the criminally psychotic mind?"

"No, and don't think that way. Nadine Shaw paid for the painting, not Payton, and she said she was donating it to one of the local hospitals for its annual fundraising auction. Good things will come from it." She pushed the door open. "See you later." Harlie wandered through the back room wondering how long Lisa would work for her. Once her art career took off, she wouldn't need this job anymore. She was destined for greater things. "And that's as it should be," Harlie muttered to herself. It was the reason she was compelled to help those in need. The gratification she received when a life turned around was immense. It was the same with Clay and Buck. It pleased her to know father and son were reunited. Unfortunately, Harlie was a casualty of the reunion, but she'd do it all again to see that gleam in Buck's eyes when he looked at his son on the Grand Ol' Opry stage. By now, Clay must know what she said was true. Buck had made a lot of mistakes but he loved his son.

She climbed in her Smart Car and headed home. Her empty, lonely home. Solitude was Harlie's companion now and she was learning to live with it. Clay was gone and she was so over him, she could hardly remember what he looked like.

She punched in the gate code and made her way along the driveway, dodging potholes. Maybe the new property owner would fix the driveway before her tiny car fell into a hole and she couldn't get out. The rental agency didn't know the details on the sale, just that her rental agreement would be honored. She was up to her neck in motel renovations and was relieved house hunting wasn't on her to-do list.

As she parked her car near the cottage, the hair on the back of her neck stood up. Someone was here. She could feel it. From the safety of her car, Harlie saw a pickup parked near the larger house. Either the new owner had arrived or Glen was using an earthier hit man these days. Payton Shaw had driven a Mercedes.

Then she saw him standing on the cliff edge and reassessed the notion she'd forgotten what he looked like. His sandy-blond hair, broad shoulders, and intense blue eyes were permanently seared on her brain. Harlie leaned her head on the steering wheel and groaned. "No. Not again. I'm over you. I'm over you. I'm over you." When she sat up straight, the feeling remained. "I. Am. Over. You. Go away."

Her stomach fluttered when he turned her way. She grabbed her purse and walked into the cottage only to realize she'd forgotten her groceries in the car. With a deep breath, she went back and was hurrying to the cottage door when she discovered Clay was nearly to her car.

"Harlie! Wait up."

Harlie took a deep breath and turned around. He was a few feet from her, holding a shopping bag and looking tense. Good. Lowlife goobers who dumped her without a word should look tense.

He gave her an uncomfortable smile and said, "Hey."

She didn't say anything.

"I brought you something for..." He shrugged and seemed at a loss for words. "Well, because I saw these and thought of you." He held the bag out to her.

She hesitated but took it, glancing inside to read the shoebox lid. Converse. Harlie resisted the urge to throw herself at the man and kiss him. Search and Rescue couldn't retrieve her lost shoe and a new pair wasn't in her budget. She wanted to take them from the bag, slide them on her feet, and dance. But anger appeasement by gift wasn't going to happen. Not even fabulous, well thought-out gifts from the man who still held her heart in a death grip. She held the bag out to him. "As much as I appreciate the gesture, I can't accept this." She set her jaw and hoped she looked defiant and tough.

"Yes, you can. I said I'd replace your shoes and I'm replacing your shoes."

He also set his jaw, and she had to admit he looked more defiant and tough than she did. "It's not your fault I lost them." She again held the bag out to him.

"I said I'd buy you the shoes. They are custom ordered and I can't return them." He shrugged. "But I suppose I could find a Goodwill to donate them to if you really don't want them."

Harlie blinked several times and looked at the bag. Custom-ordered Converse All Stars. Only in her dreams could she buy these. She clutched the bag to her chest and again resisted the urge to kiss him. "I'll find a use for them. Thank you." She swallowed hard and stared at him, wondering what she was supposed to do now. He stared at her, obviously expecting her to say something.

"So, you won't forgive me?" he said.

"For buying me shoes? I thanked you. I thought that was appropriate."

"Not about the shoes. For leaving the way I did. For not calling."

Harlie shrugged. "It's okay. It made the whole end of the relationship thing much easier. No arguments. No tears. You made it possible to walk away and pretend it didn't happen."

"But it did," he said with firmness.

"Right. I had a wild fling with a country music legend who bought me shoes and the whole episode will be a crazy story to tell my grandchildren some day. Thanks for the shoes and the memories." She turned, balancing the grocery and shoe bags while she tried to turn the doorknob. As far as dramatic exits went, this one was kind of clunky.

"So, that's it? You can walk away without giving me another chance?"

She glanced over her shoulder and saw an incredulous look on his face and her temper climbed. "You did. Looks like it's my turn. Have a nice life, Clay. It was fun, but I don't think we need to continue this." Her hand clutched the doorknob and her thumping heart threatened to beat her to a pulp.

"Harlie—" He reached for her shoulder. She shrugged off his hand and turned back.

"Did you think you could leave for three months and walk back into my life with a 'hey' and smile and we'd pick up where we left off? Did you?" She swung around and again tried the dramatic exit, her heart pounding jackhammer hard.

"You're angry. I get that. Talk to me and you may feel differently."

She turned back. Frowning at the apology she heard in his voice. "Aren't you?"

"I was, but I got over it after Dad explained a few things about the situation."

"But I lied to you. That should have ended it right there. The rigid Clay Masterson I knew couldn't just get over it. Everything is black and white where you come from. There are no gray areas for you."

He winced. Apparently, she'd hit a nerve. "I know you lied," he said. "Let's get over it. Let's get past it and move on."

Harlie leaned against the door. "Get over it? That's all you have to say? I'm hurt that you could leave like that. I'm angry that you didn't let me apologize about Buck. I've felt like garbage over it all and you say get over it? You broke my heart, Clay." She blinked hard to restrain impending tears and fought to control her trembling lip. "You smashed it to pieces."

Clay grimaced and looked away. "Yeah. Mine, too."

When he looked at her again, she saw the pain in his eyes and the defeat in his shoulders. Okay, the heartache was mutual. Now what? Her problem-solving skills abandoned her and she was lost.

"Can we talk about it? Maybe we could..." He shrugged. "Try to fix this?"

She debated running inside and locking the door, but she set the bags aside and wrapped her arms around herself to stop the shaking. "Just so you know up front, I think you are a huge goober right now. The hugest goober ever. But talk if you want to. Start with why you didn't call. That was...heartless."

Clay took a deep breath and let it out. "I didn't call because my life had been flipped upside down and I was screwed up. Everything I'd ever thought was true turned out to be wrong and I was pissed off. I couldn't deal with you in the middle of it." He paced a few steps. "You know that chip on my shoulder you said I carried around? Well, you hit that one on the head. When I saw my dad, all the anger I tried to say I didn't have jumped me. When I saw him in that motel room, I was mad I didn't get to beat the crap out of him and put him in the hospital myself."

Harlie was sure her mouth hung open. "You wanted to beat up your dying father?"

He nodded. "I said I was screwed up. That kind of proves it, don't you think?"

"I'd say so. Is that why you wouldn't let me see him? Or why you wouldn't answer your phone? Tom's a nice guy, but I got real tired of him running interference for you."

"Tom is a real perceptive guy and the best friend I could have. He knew I wasn't operating on all cylinders and he took my phone away from me. He knew I'd really blow it if I got you on the phone." He looked at her with a frown. "And I had nothing to do with you not seeing Dad. That was the police. The security around him was so tight they only let me see him at first. By the time he explained the situation with you to me, a phone call seemed all wrong. What I wanted to say needed to be said face-to-face and I had to wait until I could get back here."

"Three months later?"

"We had a lot going on with the police. He wasn't cleared until after they got him back to Montana. Once that was cleaned up, I had to get to know my father. I really didn't know him at all, Harlie. I needed time alone with him to find out who he is and see if we could have a relationship. I still don't know him well but we're working on it."

Harlie's heart melted for him all over again. He was willing to give Buck a chance. "I could have helped you. I know what a great guy Buck is and I could have helped you see it."

He shook his head. "No, you couldn't. I know you want to save everyone—and I love that about you—but this was something Dad and I had to do on our own. I hated the man he used to be and I needed to see who he is now. I needed time to..." He paused. "Remember when we talked about that song I was writing...the angel song?"

Harlie nodded. "The angel who needed mending."

"Right. But it wasn't you who needed mending, Harlie. It was me. I was close to breaking apart and you were holding me together." He laughed derisively. "I spent my life consumed with anger and hatred for my father and I tried to say it wasn't true. Any other emotion I allowed myself went into my music. Then I met you and I finally felt something real." He frowned.

"And I ruined it. When you didn't tell me about Buck being my dad, you didn't fit into my unbending moral code that separated me from my father."

"So why did you come back?"

"Because..." His eyes were intense but his voice was soft. "Every woman with brown curly hair made my pulse race. Every pair of plaid shoes I saw made me wish you were there with me. I couldn't stop thinking about you." He kicked at a rock and watched it roll. "And also because of something Dad said. He told me it was wrong to leave you the way I did. " He half-smiled. "He said it was the sort of cowardly thing he would do and he expected better of me. So do I."

Harlie waited, not sure what to say.

"So I came back to apologize and see if we could work things out, to see if we could mend together. And maybe finish writing that song about the broken angel. I hate the ending I have now and I can't write a better one alone." He stuffed his hands in his pockets and hunched his shoulders. "I'll be around if you think I'm worth a second chance. If not..." He frowned and shrugged. "Have a good life, Harlie. You deserve it."

She watched him turn and walk away, fighting the tears welling in her eyes. "Clay?"

He stopped but didn't turn around. His shoulders remained rigid as he waited.

She steeled her nerves and jumped into situation recovery mode. "Would you like to stay for supper? It's nothing fancy, just organic spaghetti sauce from a jar and whole grain noodles. I have some low-fat Tilla-mook ice cream if you'd like some dessert. I understand their cows are almost local and live long meaningful lives."

Clay turned back. "I've heard that, too."

Harlie swallowed hard. "It won't take long to fix...if you are in hurry to get somewhere."

He shook his head. "There's nowhere else I'd rather be."

⚬≈⚬

The spaghetti noodles boiled in the pot and beef simmered in the skillet. Late afternoon sun streamed through the paned window. Clay had pulled a chair from the table and sat with his elbows on knees, watching her. If she'd been a pat of butter, she'd melt from the intensity of his gaze. He'd already laid his heart wide open to her, admitted his faults, and offered her a chance for a future with him if she was willing to forgive. So why hadn't she? Fear. When he'd talked marriage before, she hadn't believed him. Now, she could see he was serious. He was back and his heart was open for business.

Harlie opened a jar of sauce and poured it into the skillet, stalling. "How's Buck?"

"Opinionated as hell," he said with a laugh.

Harlie grinned. "That's Buck. He's okay though?"

Clay nodded. "They figured out that he was telling the truth. Payton killed Lynette and the others, so Dad is free from all the charges."

"How—"

"The partial fingerprint. You were right. The second print was Payton's. He'd never been a suspect, so his prints weren't checked," Clay said. "Payton also sent the notes to try and frame Dad, and then me. When he confirmed that Dad was in Angel Beach, he murdered Myrna and sent the angel note, trying to place the blame on Dad. Dad told me what happened and how it was his fault you didn't tell me."

"I tried."

"I know. He said you wanted to drag him to my house the minute you found out he was my father and he wouldn't go."

"Buck said he'd do the right thing," she said. "I expected him to talk to you and the cops, and I promised him I wouldn't tell you because I thought he'd do it himself."

"And he ran instead. I know. He said he was on his way back to talk to the police when Payton got a hold of him."

Harlie shuddered when she thought of Buck lying in a puddle of blood. She was certain he would die. "Did he come back with you?"

Clay nodded. "I dropped him off at Emily's on my way here. She's another reason it took so long for us to get here. He's proposing to her and wanted to be clean when he did it."

"Clean?"

"Yeah. He joined AA and hasn't had a drink in months. Tom sponsored him."

"Tom?" Harlie said with disbelief. Sponsors had to be in the program and she couldn't imagine solid, upright Tom with a drinking problem.

"He lost someone he loved and it sent him over the edge. But he hasn't taken a drink in ten years. He offered to help Dad and it's working." Clay smiled. "Dad has a patch, too. He quit the cigs cold turkey. It's making him grouchy but he isn't coughing so much."

The stove timer rang. Harlie grabbed a strainer and drained the noodles over the sink, the steam circling her head. They grew silent, both apparently unsure of the next step. Clay finally broke the uncomfortable quiet.

"Dad and I are working on an album together, so I'll be around." He paused as though waiting for a reaction.

Harlie raised her brow but remained silent.

"He wrote a ton of songs about his life. His closet bones he calls them, and I thought we should record them. My label is interested." He paused. "I bought this place and will put a studio in a spare room so we can work here."

Her brow rose again. "You bought it?" Egad. He was serious about staying.

"Yeah."

"Are you raising my rent?"

Clay frowned. "Do you want to pay more?"

"Of course not."

"Then I don't think so. I hadn't even planned to collect rent from you." A seagull flew past the window and he watched until it was out of sight. "It doesn't seem right to charge my..." he looked at her "...fiancé rent."

"Fiancé?" Harlie swallowed hard. "I'm not your fiancé."

He smiled but not with his usual confidence. "Not yet, but that's one of those things I'm kinda rigid about. I love you and want to marry you. If it's too soon," he said, "we can wait and you can think about it. We'll take it slow, talk things over—"

Harlie shook her head. "There isn't any point in talking it over."

"Oh," Clay said, dejected. "So this is just a meal? Not the beginning of anything?" He blew out a breath. "I thought—"

"I didn't say that." Harlie removed the skillet from the burner, turned off the heat, and walked to him. "There's something we need to settle first. I can't think about marriage and the future until we do."

"What needs to be settled? I love you. I apologized. What—?"

She climbed onto his lap, straddling him, and stared into his stunned blue eyes. He didn't reach out to touch her and remained tense. She brushed her hand across his cheek, cupped his face, and kissed him. When she pulled away, he appeared bewildered.

"That settles it," she said with a smile.

"Settles what?"

"It still means something."

"What does it mean?"

"That I love you," she said.

Clay reached around her neck and loosened the ponytail holder from her tight braid and set her curls free. He wrapped his arms around her and pulled her against him, his face buried in her hair. He let out a relieved sigh. "I'm sorry," he whispered against her skin. "About everything."

"Me, too."

"You'll give me another chance?"

"I already am."

"And you'll think about marrying me?"

"I already did. Is tomorrow too soon?" she asked.

He chuckled softly. "Not for me. Want to know something else Dad told me?"

"What?" she whispered.

"He said Angel Beach made him the man he always wanted to be." He kissed her neck. "I'm hoping it will work on me, too."

Harlie sighed with contentment. He was already one of the best men she knew and if she had her way, she'd snuggle against him forever. With the love they shared and her expert problem-solving skills, they could spend a lifetime writing one heck of a good ending to the broken angel song.

SHARLEEN SCOTT

Coming soon from
Out West Press

Caught in the Spin
By Sharleen Scott

When bull rider Tom Black earned his business and psychology degrees, his goal was to manage his championship winnings and entertain his friends with intellectual psychobabble. Years after a near fatal bull riding wreck ends his career, a spooky nocturnal visit from a former love has Tom wishing he'd paid more attention in psych class.

An attorney confirms his ex-fiancé's death and drops the news Tom is the father of a resentful eleven-year-old stranger. Tom isn't sure he's up to the task and thinks his recent acquaintance with sexy single mom Tallie Peters is his best hope for parental success.

Tallie Peters is up to her eyebrows in troubles of her own. She survived her ex-husband's attempt on her life and has kept her son safe. But budget cuts and phony good behavior put her ex back on the streets early, and he's vowed to finish the job that put him in prison. Tom offers Tallie and her son refuge behind the gates of the Masterson-Black ranch, but soon finds the best security measures are no match for a determined ex-con with nothing to lose.

Sharleen Scott lives in the foothills of the Cascade Mountains in the beautiful Pacific Northwest with her husband, Brett, two kids, and two spoiled cats. You can visit her at www.sharleenscott.com. If you enjoyed this book, please leave a review at Amazon.com.